PRAISE FOR
FENCE JUMPER

"*Fence Jumper* is everything you want in a novel—compelling characters, timely wit, and fast-paced action woven throughout. As a US Secret Service special agent, Mark Brandenburg brings rare authenticity, drawing from real-life insights into the machinations of Washington, DC's, power structure. A riveting and entertaining political thriller that will keep you on the edge of your seat."

—Evy Poumpouras, Former US Secret Service Special Agent, Author of the Bestseller *Becoming Bulletproof*

"*Fence Jumper* is a page-turning thriller written by veteran US Secret Service special agent Mark Brandenburg, who brings wry humor and a Washington insider's knowledge and experience to every page. Fence Jumper will hook you from the very first moment."

—Gary Edgington, SAS/CT-Task Force Commander CA DOJ (ret.), Author of *Outside the Wire*

"In *Fence Jumper*, Mark Brandenburg draws his readers into an entertaining, page-turning political thriller about James Ford, a suspended Secret Service agent battling his own demons and insurmountable odds against the power brokers of Washington, DC. Filled with compelling characters, detail, and action, this unique story is a must-read. Few stories capture modern Washington, DC, with such clarity and wit."

—Jonathan Wackrow, CNN Law Enforcement Analyst, Former US Secret Service Agent

Fence Jumper

by Mark J. Brandenburg

© Copyright 2023 Mark J. Brandenburg

ISBN 978-1-64663-894-9

This is a work of fiction.
All the characters in this book are fictitious,
and any resemblance to actual persons, living or dead,
is purely coincidental. The names, incidents, dialogue,
and opinions expressed are products
of the author's imagination and
are not to be construed as real.

Published by

3705 Shore Drive
Virginia Beach, VA 23455

800-435-4811

FENCE JUMPER

MARK J. BRANDENBURG

VIRGINIA BEACH
CAPE CHARLES

Dedicated to my father and mother,
Fred and Patricia Brandenburg.
Also dedicated in loving memory to
my wife's father and mother,
William and Louann Maley,
my sister, Brenda Brandenburg,
and my brother-in-law,
Lawrence "Ted" Pearson.

Preface

I created James Ford when I was in second grade. That might sound made up, but it's true. James Ford was a cowboy I'd scribble little stories about. He was a good guy, damn near perfect.

I've always loved stories, and my imagination was exceptionally active, even by grade-school-boy standards. I'd write words like *BANG* and *POW* to describe the action as my idealized cowboy protected the weak and made the bad guys pay. James is my middle name. Ford is the last name of my favorite actor, Harrison Ford. Harrison Ford played both Indiana Jones, an archetype of the American cowboy, and Han Solo, a cocky, imperfect, well-meaning rogue. Both characters made an indelible impression on me, and I grew to love the imperfect hero. Frankly, I find human imperfection the most interesting aspect of what it is to be human. We are all trying to figure things out, and our own imperfections are our biggest enemy. James Ford is no exception; he is defined by his flaws.

For over twenty years, I have served as a United States Secret Service agent—the most apolitical job in a town whose primary industry is politics. I'm a paid observer. Washington, DC, is an interesting place. A menagerie of type-A personalities populate this drained marsh along the Potomac. The mix of trust-fund staffers, career military officers, remora-like lobbyists, self-important journalists, and opportunistic politicians makes for a unique ecosystem. I find much of it rather amusing. To be clear, none of the events or characters I portray in this work of fiction are real or based off reality. No politician or leader I have had the honor to protect is depicted in this story.

I am a big fan of Carl Hiaasen. He writes wonderfully humorous mystery/thrillers set in Florida, and Florida is almost a character in his novels. I set out to write a political thriller in the same vein: DC is my Florida. If my writing has landed anywhere close to my desired goal, I consider it a success.

In America, the current political climate is polarized and toxic. I find it all an imbecilic waste of energy. Though this book is not political, many political and cultural upheavals were taking place as I wrote and revised it, and I didn't pretend these things weren't happening. You'll find satirical references to our current political atmosphere—identity politics, media, and the overall state of affairs as it pertains to Washington—sprinkled throughout the story. What I didn't do was offer an opinion on these matters. Truth be told, my experience has revealed that most folks at the Executive Mansion or on Capitol Hill are very decent. But as I stated above, I enjoy the flaws, so those decent people are given little representation in this book. My goal was to offer the reader a fun story where, upon closing the cover for the final time, they remain ignorant of my political leanings.

Over the past twenty-five years, I have worked with amazing people. I feel blessed. The Secret Service, FBI, cops, firefighters, political staffers, military personnel, politicians, and journalists I've met filled my mind with memories that I, the interested observer, mix up, twist, and manipulate to conjure a tale aimed to enthrall, amuse, and paint a snapshot of modern Washington. I have a little fun with some of them along the way but hope the varying denizens of this crazy town take it in the light with which it was intended.

And I hope you, the reader, enjoy the story.

Mark J. Brandenburg, Bristow, Virginia
June 1, 2022

CHAPTER 1

Tuesday, March 1

THE CAR STOPPED. From the trunk, Kat heard the fat one hurling a litany of Southern-twanged insults at his partner. She inhaled the metallic odor of the duct-tape across her mouth as she wriggled her bound wrists and ankles in the darkness. They must have shut the lid on her hair; her scalp ached from the strands yanked out when she rolled onto her side.

"Goddammit, Cornhole, you was supposed to had gassed this sumbitch up. Jesus, Joseph, and Mary, we ain't barely out the District." One kidnapper, a short, stocky, bearded character with a distended belly, had been wearing a red "Bring Back My America" ball cap when they grabbed her. His counterpart, going by Cornhole, was a lanky fellow with long hair who grimaced as he walked.

Having never been inside the trunk of a midsize sedan, Kat discovered the dimensions unaccommodating for a five-foot-eight former dancer. The muffled conversation continued in the front seats. The fat one, JC, did most of the talking. From what she could make out, the fuel gauge was inoperable, and Cornhole had failed to perform his assigned task of gassing up. Once the beratement concluded, she heard someone rummaging through the rear seat, followed by JC ordering Cornhole to stay awake and saying he'd be right back—then, silence.

Kat had known her husband was a duplicitous schemer with

libidinous impulses but never suspected he'd devolve to kidnapping. After graduating from UCLA, unable to gain traction as an actress, she was introduced to him at a climate change fundraiser. Gene was married and considerably older, but a correspondence began regardless. He possessed a gravitas she was drawn to—a welcome respite from the vacuity of LA. He ditched his second wife and married Kat, who quickly adapted to her new role as spouse to one of Washington's leading legislators. Though unsavory perverts in Washington society were uglier, LA had prepared her for the pomposity needed to navigate the ritualized soirées of elite society. But now she was in a car trunk. She'd watched enough prime-time, real-life crime shows to know this was a murder plot.

Earlier, the two nitwits had aggravated her tennis elbow as they wrestled her arms behind her back. After some performative whining on her part, they acquiesced and bound them in front. A fan of *Dateline*, *48 Hours*, and *20/20*, Kat recalled a *20/20* segment highlighting various ways to escape sinking cars, elevators, burning houses, and—coincidentally—car trunks. John Quinones had performed a drawn-out demonstration of how to free oneself from such a predicament. Feeling along the interior, she groped for a release. Some law had made them mandatory, but the old beater likely predated the legislation. Hoping to remain undetected, she pawed around the tight space.

Holy shit, he was right, she thought as her hand grabbed a taut, rubber-lined cable running along the edge. She gave it an abrupt tug, popping the trunk open.

With a few awkward jerks, she swung her bound legs over the trunk rim. The car bounced as she struggled to her feet and scanned her surroundings: a very large, cold parking lot, sometime past midnight. Peering around the back of the car, she spotted the fully reclined passenger seat containing the snoring, sleeping, skeletal figure of Cornhole. She pulled the duct tape off her mouth and took an orgasmic gasp of air, then bent over and attempted to loosen the tape and nylon rope around her ankles.

Her abductors might be dim, but they tied strong knots. Worried JC might soon return, she straightened and whipped her head around, searching for a means of escape. About two hundred yards distant in the dim lot were a few parked cars. Evidenced by the swooshing of speeding vehicles beyond the tree line, a freeway passed nearby. She examined her kidnappers' car: an unpainted Dodge Saturn with West Virginia vanity plates: TBIRD. Good to know.

Turning, determined, Katherine Sterling made a deliberate hop forward. She kept her balance—no easy feat with bound ankles and wrists. She made a second hop and swayed side to side but again remained upright. Thank God for years of dance training. With a few more hops, she got into a rhythm and bounded toward safety.

⊙ ⊙ ⊙

James Ford knew the third rum and Coke was a mistake but didn't much care. He found himself staring up at CNN on a mounted television at Champs Sports Bar, located in a shopping mall off I-66 in Fairfax, Virginia. It was his sole distraction from leering at the only other two patrons: an overly affectionate couple across the square bar. Twice now, the buxom brunette had caught him glancing over while her friend nibbled her ear. The two clearly weren't married, at least not to each other; a shopping mall sports bar on a Tuesday seemed a wise choice for a clandestine rendezvous.

On his drive east toward Georgetown, returning from his old house, the reality setting in that his stable life was a thing of the past, James had decided a drink, or three, was in order. The neighbors once thought he and Audrey were the pinnacle of suburban serenity, but James had compartmentalized a side of himself that ran counter to the image of domestic perfection. Poor Audrey deserved better. She had clearly moved beyond her grief to a white-hot anger that he, in fourteen years, had never witnessed. Instead of crying like so many previous episodes, she was coldly stoic. Little Emma and Jimmy were as adorable as ever, despite their unspoken confusion about Daddy's absence. Things simply could not get worse.

Sipping his drink, James's glance was arrested a third time by the adulteress. He flicked his gaze back up at the television. A chyron in large font jumped from the bottom of the screen: AGENT IDENTIFIED IN SECRET SERVICE SEX SCANDAL. Things just got worse.

> *"The identity of the Secret Service agent at the heart of the Brazilian sex scandal has been revealed,"* stated the smarmy anchor. *"Special Agent James Ford has been identified as the agent who procured a prostitute in Sao Paulo, Brazil, prior to the visit of President Frum. Viewers, be advised the following story contains information that is sexual in nature and may not be suitable for younger audience members."*

A pre-taped segment displayed a familiar hotel as the on-site correspondent reported, *"Agent Ford allegedly solicited a prostitute at a popular night club the night of January 16 while on assignment for a pending visit of President Ronald Frum. Ford, a twelve-year veteran of the Secret Service, was implicated when a verbal disturbance near Ford's room alarmed Renaissance Hotel security. Rafaela Pero, whom Ford met at the night club A Vida e Grande, claimed she accompanied Special Agent Ford to the hotel that evening. According to Pero, she and Ford went to his room where they continued drinking and agreed to have sex for which she would be compensated one hundred American dollars. After intercourse, Ms. Pero contends Agent Ford seemed to have forgotten the agreement and refused payment. Their argument continued, prompting hotel guests to contact security."*

James's official Secret Service photo appeared on the screen as he self-consciously shielded his face.

"Hotel security responded to find Ms. Pero in the hallway, yelling and striking Agent Ford's locked door. Hotel security claims that Ford was heavily intoxicated when he disputed Ms. Pero's assertions, stating Ms. Pero's teeth had injured him during oral sex, rendering any agreement null and void. At this point, according to hotel security, Ford exposed himself in order to provide evidence of his allegations.

"During the subsequent investigation, three other members of the Secret Service and two members of the White House Military Office were placed on paid leave as documents from the front desk register indicated they too brought likely prostitutes to their rooms. Agent Ford, a member of the Secret Service's elite Presidential Protective Division, resides in Chantilly, Virginia. CNN has attempted contacting Ford's residence to no avail. To date, Ford has not spoken publicly about the incident and is on paid leave pending further investigation."

So, there it was. His identity had remained anonymous since the story broke nearly two months ago, but this revelation had just been a matter of time as the Fourth Estate scrambled to uncover more salacious details of the incident. No wonder Audrey was so cold. She was undoubtedly on the receiving end of countless press inquiries.

Gulping his beverage, James glanced across the bar to find the alert philanderer staring at him with renewed interest while her friend, Handsy McNibbler, continued his public foreplay. Raising his glass, James toasted her with a smirk, which she acknowledged with a knowing grin before returning to her infidelity. *Did I just join some secret slut guild?* James wondered before ordering— against his better judgment—another drink.

Dynamic graphics flashed across the television once again: BREAKING NEWS. The anchor, in an ominous tone, stated Metro Police were investigating an ongoing situation in the Spring Valley Neighborhood of northwest Washington, DC, and jumped to a local affiliate.

"Thank you, Carol. We are here on Hillbrook Lane Northwest near the residence of Senator Gene Sterling where there are preliminary reports of a home invasion. Senator Sterling and his wife, Katherine Sterling, returned earlier this evening from a primary campaign event in Indiana. The police have been on scene for an hour or so, but one officer I spoke with advised Mrs. Sterling, seen here, is missing and believed to be the victim of a kidnapping."

A photo of Katherine Sterling filled the screen. James couldn't help thinking the mid-forties stunner constituted the one person in Washington having a worse night than himself.

"Senator Sterling, of California, we are told, is alive, but we do not yet know of his condition. An ambulance was on the scene for some time, and we believe Senator Sterling was transported to George Washington Medical Center for

evaluation. No information has been released regarding any suspects, nor is it clear, at this time, when the incident occurred."

Big news night. James assumed come sunup *Morning Joe* and *Fox & Friends* would lead with the missing senator's wife, but no doubt his mug would be displayed for ridicule after a short commercial break. James was lost, and he knew it. He'd taken all his good fortune for granted: the happy marriage, the beautiful children, and his dream job of protecting the president of the United States. He tossed it away for a toothy blowjob and blackout sex. He had to make things right for Emma and Jimmy. Audrey might never come back to him, but he would not abandon his kids. One way or other, he had to get his life right.

Paying his tab, James stumbled off his bar stool and tried to play it off as the trollop across the bar repressed her laughter. He stepped into the brisk March air and hit his key fob to unlock his Ford F-150. He would sleep off his stupor.

Though his eyes were still adjusting to the night, he swore he saw a figure hopping toward him in the manner of a grammar-school sack race.

That fourth rum and Coke was a mistake.

"Please help me," the figure faintly implored. "Please, please help me." The woman bounded into focus: yoga pants, a Washington Commanders pullover, bound at the wrists and ankles, her dirty-blond hair a mess above a face full of fear. Rubbing his eyes, James realized this wasn't a Bacardi-induced hallucination.

"Jesus, are you alright?" She began to lose her balance, but James caught her. "Are you okay? We got to call the cops."

"We don't have time," she breathed in a pleading tone. "Please just get me out of here. I'm Katherine Sterling, and I was kidnapped tonight. My husband is Senator Gene Sterling." She panned the horizon in frightened desperation. Adrenaline unclouded James's brain, somewhat.

"I know who you are. I just saw you on the news."

"It's already made the news?"

"Yeah, is somebody after you? Are they nearby?" asked James. For a moment, he thought of retrieving his Walther 9mm semiautomatic pistol from the glove box—before concluding such action inadvisable considering his current blood alcohol content.

"They are. That's why I really want to get out of here."

"Alright, Mrs. Sterling, you're coming with me," he declared and carried her to the passenger seat. Diving into the driver seat, he started the truck and looked over at his bound, disheveled passenger before shifting into drive.

"I'm Kat," she stated, still panting from exertion. "I hope you're a good guy."

"James. Some of my friends call me Jim. As far as a good guy? Presently speaking, it depends on who you ask."

"Please tell me you're a good guy."

"I'm a good guy. I won't hurt you."

"Have you been drinking?"

"Yeah, can you tell?"

"You reek."

"I was planning to sleep it off." He widened his eyes as if to enhance his alertness. "I'm having a really bad day." She responded with a blank stare. "Okay, you're having a worse day, but I'm a close second." It dawned on James that he was driving drunk with a kidnapped senator's wife. This could end poorly. "We should get you to a police station. According to the news, your husband should be alright. He was transported to GW." Sullen, Kat stared at the dash. "I'm sure he's okay."

"No, John, it's not that."

"James. My name's James."

"Sorry, James, um . . . I don't know how to explain this."

"Explain what?"

"My husband planned my kidnapping."

"They found him tied up in your home."

"He had help. Where are you taking me?"

"Fairfax Police."

"Can we stop? I need a minute to think." Passing the interstate entrance ramp, James pulled into the parking lot of another strip mall and put his truck in park. He pulled a Smith & Wesson folding knife from his pocket and cut her wrists free.

She rolled down her window, sighed, and stared into the darkness as James rubbed his face, hoping to sober up.

"Kat? I know you've had a trying day, and I want to be respectful here, but what the hell is going on?"

Turning, she took in his visage for the first time: a manly, chisel-jawed, rough-shaven forty-something with a bloodshot, nonplussed expression.

"We can't go to the cops," she stated flatly.

"Yeah, you said that. Look, as a former police officer, I typically recommend that all kidnap victims file a police report. Call me hypervigilant."

"You were a cop?"

"Yeah, but we'll leave it at that. It's a long story. What's going on?"

"My husband had me kidnapped. I'm certain he wanted me killed. I was in the trunk of a car belonging to two dumb rednecks when they ran out of gas. One of them left, I got out and hopped my way to you. I need to go somewhere. I've got to think on this. I assume you're married; is there somewhere you can take me for the night? There are things I need to sort out."

James nodded with about a million questions crowding his brain.

"I am married," he confided as he restarted the truck, "but

that's another story altogether. I got a place where you can crash for the night. You can stay with me."

"Don't get any ideas, James. You've been drinking, a lot." She appeared uneasy.

He looked her in the eyes with sincerity. "Kat, you've got nothing to worry about with me. I've recently learned some difficult life lessons. I'm the safest stranger you'll ever meet." Pulling out of the lot, he steered toward 66 East.

CHAPTER 2

Wednesday, March 2

Our thoughts and prayers go out to Senator Sterling and his family. We pray for his wife's safe return. No matter how foolish and ineffective one's political policies, nobody should endure such tragedy. As we remember the Sterling family do not forget that unemployment is down to 3.4% as we are bringing back the middle class. #BBMA @PresidentFrum

SENT AT 4:43 AM, the presidential tweet elicited predictable disgust from MSNBC and CNN, while *Fox & Friends* highlighted the president's concern for his political rival and the veracity of his unemployment boast. The president's chief of staff, Gary Boxterman, popped a Tums and rubbed his temples as he hovered near the secretary's desk just outside the Oval Office, taking in the morning news accounts of Senator Sterling's ordeal.

"This is just awful," he observed with unmasked sincerity. President Frum stepped out the Oval Office, brow furrowed.

"Maybe I should call *Fox & Friends*," the president suggested. "You know, give my take on the breaking news." Gary masked his revulsion. "Did you see my tweet? Pretty good. Over 64,000 likes so far, and its's only eight in the morning." The chief of staff gave a lukewarm nod. "This will help his numbers," continued President Frum. "A grieving widower will be hard to vote against. If they find her dead, I could see, at minimum, an eight-point bounce."

"That is, if he doesn't pull out of the race altogether," noted Gary.

"Gene? Leave a race? His whole damn family could be held ransom and the bastard wouldn't drop out."

Gary conceded the point. Gene Sterling was more outwardly envious of the seat behind the Resolute desk than your average senator, which was no small statement.

"Hell, the only reason he hasn't already locked up the nomination is his bland, poll-driven talking points. This kidnapping is the only thing remotely interesting about him. Besides, he isn't giving all the money he's raised to Cassandra."

"If the Democrats were to go all in on her with his political purse, we'd have our hands full next year," Gary said.

President Frum looked down at his miniscule staff chief. "You haven't lost faith in me already, have you now? No matter who they put up, we've got the middle of the country; and great numbers—I mean, unbelievable numbers—on our side."

"Mr. President, we can take down whomever they put forward. But truth be told, I like our chances against Sterling best. We'd be foolish to underestimate Congresswoman Lightner. The media love her; she checks a lot of progressive boxes and has a story to tell."

Cassandra Lightner, a forty-nine-year-old lesbian, African American Air Force veteran and the first person of color elected to Congress by Vermont voters, had an ease at the podium that made old, tired White men seem old, tired, and White. So far, GOP research into the budding star turned up little more than a few questionable gifts she'd received during her short time in Congress. With plenty of free media coverage, she made Senator Sterling appear the weathered Beltway operative he was. Gary recognized a political talent when he saw it—he'd recognized Frum's instincts sooner than most—and Congresswoman Lightner was still considered new to the Beltway and thus an outsider in the minds of voters. If she survived the Democratic primary, she would prove formidable come fall.

"What states are up this weekend?" asked the president.

"Saturday there are caucuses in Kansas, Maine, and Nebraska, with a primary vote in Louisiana," said Gary. The president nodded while examining the news coverage.

"And Tuesday?"

"Primaries in Michigan and Mississippi, Mr. President."

"If he stays in, he'll win. She'll be forced to pull back her attacks on his insider corruption and shady associates. Any attack on him would seem cruel given what happened to his wife. Believe me, if he stays in, he's got this." In the past, Gary had questioned Frum's reflexive political analysis, but as each prediction proved prescient, he now refrained from doubting his boss on this front.

"We should make a statement today regarding the kidnapping," Gary said as he perused the president's schedule. "You have executive time from one to three. Maybe we could do a shot from the Roosevelt Room during the two o'clock hour."

"Suppose that makes sense. Have Stan put something together. Include something about the FBI and putting all our resources on this—you know, bringing the full weight of the federal government and all that; you get the point. Just don't have him put any nonsense about Gene being some patriot. I won't read it. Get to the point and cut out the flowery bipartisan 'We are all Americans' horseshit."

"I'll have you something by noon," Gary assured him as President Frum retired to the Oval Office. The chief of staff turned to Emily, the president's secretary. "This is going to be one hell of a day." She nodded. Every day was an adventure in the Frum administration.

⊙ ⊙ ⊙

The president's phone rang. His secretary informed him that Senator Joe Bratton of West Virginia had arrived. After the previous night's incident, President Frum's staff had reached out to Joe's. Joe was a man's man, and Frum liked him. The West Virginia Republican had many friends in Washington and possessed political instincts rivaled by few. Joe declared he would not run for reelection when his term ended at year's end. What he hadn't declared was President Frum's pledge to fire his current energy secretary and nominate Joe as his replacement.

"Good morning, Mr. President," greeted the short, portly Senator Bratton. They sat on the sofa as a steward poured coffee. "I spoke to Gene, and he remains in good spirits, all things considered. He was badly bruised but expects to be released from the hospital today. May have suffered a mild concussion."

"That's good to hear," replied Frum, void of sincerity.

"I spoke to him briefly this morning and told him I was paying you a visit. He wanted to thank you for the tweet you sent out requesting thoughts and prayers for his family," Joe lied.

Frum feigned concern. "Are you okay, Joe? I know you've known each other a long time."

"Thank you for asking. It is hard. Eileen is shaken up, as you can imagine. She didn't know Katherine well, but something like this is so unexpected; it shocks the senses."

"I spoke to McMann. Doesn't sound like they have much to go on," the president shared, referring to the FBI director. Joe disguised his relief with a concerned nod. "Do you think she's alive?"

"The odds are against it," Joe murmured.

"She was a piece of ass," the president noted.

"Yes, she was."

"The media are going to blame me for this. MSNBC is calling this the 'new normal' under my administration, and CNN was speculating whether I could be charged as an accessory."

"You haven't lost Fox News, have you?"

"No, I had *Fox & Friends* on earlier. They blamed Democrats and the media for vilifying my supporters. I love that show." Frum sipped his coffee. "So, how does this affect me?"

"What do you mean?"

"The suspects were described as White guys wearing 'Bring

Back My America' hats. Those are my people. This can't be good."

"Well, Mr. President you're not up for election right now; the Democrats are. Politically speaking, if Gene stays in the race, this could give him a bounce."

"That's what I was telling Gary. He'll need it if he plans to hold off that young, brown chick."

"Cassandra Lightner," Joe reminded him.

"Yeah, Cassandra. Looked like she was gaining momentum. People like her a lot."

"She connects very well. She does well on the East Coast, and her polling has improved out West. Affluent White liberals think she's the second coming. She's impressive. What are you thinking, Mr. President?"

"I'm thinking if this incident gives Gene the momentum to take the Democratic nomination, I'm going to kick his ass next year."

Which was exactly what Joe had in mind.

◉ ◉ ◉

Senator Eugene Sterling applied the bronzer lightly to ensure the bruising around his right eye remained visible. Looking in the mirror, he teased his coifed, silver mane. From the windows of his room at George Washington University Hospital, he beheld throngs of reporters and well-wishers gathered on all corners of Twenty-Third and I Streets.

He had a splitting headache. The mysterious fixer to whom he had been introduced just days prior, Oscar, had explained the necessity of beating the hell out of him. Gene had never been punched in his life, but with his deep accent Oscar explained he was well trained and would bruise the senator without causing extensive injury. Then the foreigner laid into him. It happened with such rapidity that Gene was too stunned to realize when the ass-whipping was over.

Interviewed by the FBI and Metropolitan Police till the wee hours of the morning, the senator told the officers he and his wife had just returned home from a Super Tuesday campaign stop in Indiana. From his kitchen, he heard Kat's screams upstairs and ran to her aid, only to witness two men assaulting her in their bedroom—one a short, pot-bellied man wearing a red "Bring Back My America" cap, jeans, and a brown canvas jacket, the other a lanky fellow in woodland-camo coveralls.

The lanky one struck Kat hard enough to render her unconscious. After gallantly intervening in an attempt to save his wife, Senator Sterling stated, the men turned their ire on him, taunting him as an "N-word-loving commie Lib" and other epithets disparaging his left-wing political stances. Both intruders attacked the senator. Before delivering a particularly forceful blow, the lanky one exclaimed, "This is for President Frum!" The next thing the senator remembered was awakening bound on his bedroom floor, not knowing how long he'd been unconscious. He managed to free himself and dial 911 when he realized Kat was missing.

One of the Metro cops, a fifty-something African American named Derek, appeared skeptical of the senator's recounting and pried his story for inconsistencies. The interview went on for hours while the crime scene investigators combed his home for what seemed an eternity.

Senator Sterling provided accurate, detailed descriptions of the kidnappers just as Oscar had coached. It seemed counterintuitive. Why provide the police an accurate description of his accomplices? But Gene did as he was told, even recalling the short one smelling like stale beer. Oscar assured him everything would be taken care of. The voting public would now see Gene as the victim of targeted political violence. In America, victimhood was political currency. Gene envied his colleagues who were able to parry any political attack with claims of racism, sexism, homophobia, or whatever ism was currently in fashion. He was an old White guy and—no matter how progressive—had to account for his old Whiteness. But having his wife kidnapped by Frum supporters allowed him to climb upon the cherished mantle of victimhood.

It was his turn to have a shot at the White House. He hadn't planned on Cassandra Lightner. Through his political channels, Gene was aware of a contingent within the DNC pushing her through the ranks in hopes of taking out President Frum, which explained how she was booking appearances on *Good Morning America*, *The Today Show*, and what seemed like hourly CNN hits a mere year into her first term. The media was on board the Cassandra train with her exuberant campaign slogan, "Cassandra Can!"

Now beginning his third term, Senator Sterling had earned his chance at the ultimate prize. The young, lesbian veteran's opportunity would come soon enough, but she had dues to pay. Last night, she took Vermont, Virginia, Tennessee, and Georgia. Making matters worse, his past bubbled up as voters were reminded of his infidelity during two previous marriages. Weeks prior, his friend Senator Joe Bratton floated an idea on how to flip the script not only on his career but on his entire life. With the primary tightening, desperate measures had to be taken. If successful, not only would he solve his spousal problems, but Cassandra Lightner would be booted off the front page.

"Father?" Gene's youngest daughter, Addie, knocked as she peered into his hospital room. "Are you ready to go?" Addie was twenty-eight and one of four adult children from his first two marriages. She was the only one who visited him, though another daughter, Jennifer, did call. Addie had retrieved a blue button-down, khakis, and sport coat for Gene's departure. Sitting on the edge of his bed, Gene thanked her for bringing a change of clothes.

"I don't know what I'll do without her," Gene lamented before burying his face in both hands as Addie put an arm around him.

"They will find her, Daddy. The FBI is on it. They're the best in the world."

"You think so? That they'll find her? I feel so sick inside. Like I'll never see her again."

"You've got to be strong, Daddy. Kat is a fighter. If anyone can get out of this, it's her. She's not some DC kid. She's street smart."

Gene sobbed in quiet thought. No tears streamed from his eyes.

◉ ◉ ◉

"You've got to be fucking kidding me," scoffed Kat as she leaned toward her husband's image on the television. His daughter pushing him in a wheelchair, Gene exited the hospital. "Of course you used more bronzer," she noted as throngs of sympathizers erupted in supportive applause. Acknowledging their cheers with a meager wave, Gene wore a canonized expression of humble gratitude. The senator motioned Addie to stop and, grimacing in pain, rose from the chair. Kat wanted to reach through the screen and choke the sexagenarian.

> "Yesterday, my family endured an ordeal no family here, in the richest nation on earth, should go through," began Senator Sterling in a breathy, emotional tone. "Returning home last night, both Katherine and I were attacked by two White men who had somehow managed to gain entry. One wore a 'Bring Back My America' ball cap declaring the wearer a bigot. I fought both with all my might but was overcome and severely beaten. Katherine is missing." His lips began quivering. A chorus of still-camera shudders clicked in unison.

"I think I'm going to be sick," moaned Kat.

Gene continued, "It was clear to me these men's motives

were political and personal. They spoke with vitriol about policies I have dedicated my life to, namely the environment, the need to restore the planet, and social justice. They scapegoated these values as the source of their woes and invoked our president as their redeemer. One of these evildoers stated, and I quote: 'You and your liberal friends won't destroy our country as we bring back America in the name of President Frum.'

"The rhetoric of this president has marshaled in a new era of hatred and bigotry. His reckless, racist ideology inspired these miscreants. Now, even as a White man, I too know what it is to be a minority in this flawed country. To be hated and loathed for your existence. For simply being who you are. My dear wife is now a victim of this president's irresponsible remarks and incitement. Please, look at this photo."

Gene held up a picture from a Key West vacation a few years back. *"This is the love of my life, and she was taken from me. Because of my conviction, my steadfast pursuit of what is right, and my unyielding fight for social justice, my dear Kat is now in peril. She has done nothing to deserve this. She is my one true love, and I need her back. To be clear, I will not be silenced. These deplorable, unhinged bigots will not stop my crusade for a fairer America. If Kat were here with me, she would have one thing to say: 'Fight on.'"*

Lips quivering with repressed agony, he turned away as Addie helped him to a waiting car. The vehicle pulled away, and the CNN anchor, clearly moved, could barely find the words to editorialize the dignity and bravery of the senior senator from California.

"Go to hell, Gene," Kat cursed futilely. Her husband's sociopathic gall was boundless. As usual, he played it to the hilt. The impulsive side of her wanted to Uber to GW, march in front of the cameras, and cry out that the country was being duped by a lying charlatan. The thought faded as quickly as it occurred. Gene had been in Congress for over two decades. If she claimed the kidnapping a hoax, he would parry the charge with political dexterity. Meanwhile, Kat was sitting on an overused couch in a Georgetown rowhouse basement apartment, shacked up with a stranger.

Emerging from his bedroom, James looked like a homeless person in his wrinkled Kenny Chesney T-shirt. He gave Kat a quizzical stare.

"What's that look supposed to mean?" she asked.

"Nothing. When I woke up, I wasn't certain last night actually happened. I gave it fifty-fifty odds you were real. Couch suit you fine?"

"Lovely. Do you have any beer?"

"It's ten in the morning." After a pause he offered, "I've got Sam Adams."

"That'll do."

James opened two bottles and sat next to her.

"You're pretty hungover," she observed and took a sip.

"I feel like ass. So, where do we go from here, princess?"

"Princess?"

"I forgot your name."

"Katherine. Kat."

"Oh yeah. I'm in a bit of a transition period, Kat. Forgive me if I seem less than engaged."

"I take it you're renting this place?" The rowhouse had to be worth two million dollars, and her new acquaintance didn't strike her as making that kind of scratch.

"It belongs to a friend. Well, actually, it belongs to a friend's family. It's a temporary setup; again, transition." He took a gulp from his bottle. "We have a lot to talk about."

"I imagine you're full of questions."

"I see your boy's on TV." James nodded at the television as the newscast displayed stills of the senator's injuries. "They did a number on him. Looks like he went four rounds with Tyson. How is he so tan in March?"

"I didn't expect to see him so beat up. He's rather obsessed with his face. I don't know how many times he bitched about TV hits and the glare on his forehead and shadows on his jowls. Always blamed the lighting."

"Those concerns are by no means an anomaly in this town."

"Why are you looking at me like that?"

"You're very attractive. Especially for a gal with no makeup who spent a good portion of the previous evening in a car trunk."

"Thank you, I suppose."

"I mean, you strike me as one of the spin-class yoga crowd. Mid to late forties, keeping it together for your wealthy husband, paying an assload at the salon. Tight, slender body—"

"Enough," she interrupted. "You're getting creepy. I know men. And I know how horny they get the morning after boozing."

"Sorry, just an observation. I wasn't going for creepy."

Kat was amused by his genuine discomfort at getting busted. Her unlikely rescuer was of the athletic sort, with three days' whisker growth; attractive but not pretty, he was of the T-shirt, blue-jeans crowd with creases on his forehead and crow's feet forming near the eyes.

"I don't think you're creepy, Jim. Thanks for getting me out of there. I can't imagine how alarming it was to see me hopping toward you in the dark. Not everyone would have done what you did."

"Happy to help."

"I mean, it's not enough for me to sleep with you or anything, but I appreciate you helping me."

"I—I wasn't expecting anything," he fumbled.

Finding his blush endearing, she raised her bottle. "I'm only messing with you. Thanks." She smiled as they clinked longnecks.

Retrieving two more beers, James returned to the couch. "I don't really know where to begin. But I guess I could start with why your conniving husband is pleading for your safe return on every major news outlet." Finishing the final swig of her first beer, she pondered how to piece the past twenty-four hours into a coherent narrative. Recent events were too surreal to convey concretely, and the more she thought of them, the more dreamlike the whole episode seemed.

"We'd just returned home from Indiana. I don't know if you follow politics, but Gene is in a primary race, and we were out campaigning. I hate elections, but his campaign manager had me go, thinking the image of a typical heterosexual couple might play well."

"Wait," James interrupted, "why would that play well?"

"What play well?"

"The heterosexual couple thing."

"He's running against a lesbian."

"I thought Democrats loved lesbians."

"We do love lesbians. But Gene's advisors said voters vote for people with whom they're most familiar. There're more straight people than gays, so they wanted to put a straight married couple out there. And don't forget we are talking about Indiana, not Oregon."

James shook his head. He hated politics.

"Like I said, I hate campaigning. I was only doing what my husband thought needed to be done. Anyhow, we came home. I went upstairs and changed. I enter my bedroom and see two hillbillies. One had one of those idiotic "Bring Back My America" hats on, and the other was some skinny guy in camo. I screamed for Gene just as they charged me."

"Jesus, Kat. That's awful."

"Fortunately, a few years back I took a krav maga class—never thought I'd need it, but I was able to push the thin one away and wriggle fatty off me. They kept ordering me to be still. When skinny fell off, he complained about his back. The fat guy, who seemed to be in charge, said something along the lines of 'This little bitch is squirmy as hell.'"

"Lovely."

"Yeah, real charmers. When I ran into the hall, I slammed into Gene. He grabbed my shoulders. I looked up at him and knew. I knew he was in on it. He said, 'Katherine, it's over. This whole thing was never meant to be,' then shoved me to the floor. Sometimes, usually after a political setback, Gene would drink and get kind of physical—you know, pushy. When he was like that, he'd call me a slut and use my past against me. I think he always viewed me as beneath him. Last night his shove jolted me like never before, as if he were throwing me over a cliff. The back of my head hit the floor, and before I knew it, those assholes were tying me up."

"This is crazy." James looked on with concern as Kat took another long swallow. "I'm so sorry, Kat." Though she dammed her emotions with well-practiced suppression, it was clear to James how deeply she'd been affected.

"At that point I kind of gave up. Gene and I hadn't been doing well. You wouldn't guess it from the *Washingtonian* articles, but our marriage had devolved into little more than adults sharing a checking account. I was home alone most of the time. But I never thought it would come to this. When I hit the floor, I just gave in. I didn't care what they did to me. I was so tired of it all."

"Well, you obviously didn't give up completely, or you wouldn't be here."

"In that car trunk I thought of Gene getting away with it. I told myself my story can't end this way. If they planned to kill me, they were going to be in for a fight. I'd come too far for this to be the end."

"You're a tough broad," James observed, eliciting a faint smile. "Did these guys say anything to you? Anything significant come to mind?" His investigative instincts were kicking in.

"Only that fatty went by the name JC and the other he referred to as Cornhole; he was always holding his back as if he had some injury." She thought further. "You know, as they tied me up, I do remember hearing voices in the hall. Their tones were serious. It was Gene and another man with a thick accent."

"What kind of accent?"

"Hard to make out but sounded Eastern European."

"What happened next?"

"They tied me up and carried me downstairs and into the car trunk."

"Did it ever feel like you were outside?" Kat thought about it and shook her head. "Your house has an attached garage?" She nodded. A thoughtful expression crossed James's face, which surprised Kat as nothing thus far had indicated her new friend was remotely contemplative. "You know they were going to kill you, right?"

"When I was devising a way out of that trunk, I knew it was for my life. Jesus, I can't believe this is real." Both went silent in thought as the newscast flickered in front of them.

"What part of DC do you live?" asked James.

"Off Foxhall."

"And they only made it as far as Fairfax?"

"Like I said, they ran out of gas."

"Clearly pros; how the hell did you get out of there?"

"John Quinones."

"Excuse me?"

"Never mind, I'll tell you later. They were driving a Dodge Saturn. It was unpainted with West Virginia plates: TBIRD. I made sure to remember that."

"You're sharp. We're the only two people who have the suspects' vehicle description. Look, why don't we give this to the police, let them run the tag and find these guys? They would need an alibi; who knows, maybe they broke down on the interstate."

Kat appeared skeptical. "I don't know what to do. What I do know is that Gene would have planned for every eventuality. I don't know why he had these hapless dolts take me. But I can assure you, he thought of every possible outcome and has a counter to it. He's always four steps ahead in politics, and he'll have a plan B. I married a rotten son of a bitch, but he's a smart son of a bitch."

"Kat, just to be clear, I'm currently going through a lot of crazy shit. I'm concerned about losing the rather tenuous hold I have on my life. So, I guess my question is, what exactly is it that you want to do?"

"Like I said, I don't know. But within twenty-four hours I've gone from being a senator's wife to bound, gagged, and thrown in a car trunk, and now I'm drinking beer at ten in the morning with a perfect stranger who has time midweek to drink in a suburban mall and no reason to set his alarm in the morning."

Stung, James set his beer bottle down.

"I'm sorry," she said, rubbing her temple before finishing her beer. The room remained soundless, TV on mute, the hum of passing cars on O Street filling the void. "I could use one more," she admitted. He got up and moved to the kitchenette. Grabbing two more cold ones and returning to the living room, James saw his face on TV above the caption SECRET SERVICE SCANDAL UPDATE: AGENT IDENTIFIED. From the couch, Kat looked at him as if he were a wraith. She unmuted the TV to hear the anchor carry on about salacious details of a night in Brazil involving Special Agent James Ford refusing to pay a prostitute for her services. As he sat next to her, the anchor finished the segment by mentioning Agent Ford was on paid leave pending completion of an internal review. As CNN went to commercial, James re-muted the TV, placed a beer in front of Kat, and took a sip of his own.

"Did I mention I was in a transition phase?" he quipped.

Closing her eyes, Kat shook her head. Six weeks ago, during a much slower news cycle, every third segment on every outlet was covering the debaucherous escapades of the presidential advance team in Sao Paulo. The scandal brought in big ratings for the twenty-four-hour news channels, and Kat was as captivated by the story as the rest of America. Now, the alpha horndog of the Service was sitting next to her.

"We're quite the headline grabbers. Imagine the advertising revenue we're responsible for," James observed in an attempt to break the tension.

"This isn't funny."

"Just trying to remain positive."

"I cannot believe you were a Secret Service agent."

"I still am an agent. On paid leave for now until all this gets hashed out."

"What the hell were you thinking? What kind of person hires a prostitute while working for the president? Jesus."

"I'm a good agent. In fact, a very good one, which is why I was heading up the advance team, Little Miss Judgy. It's a cultural thing down there."

"So, you were just taking in the culture?"

"Sort of. We went out for a few drinks. A couple of United Airlines pilots recommended a night spot. We go, and the place is full of women—Brazilian women, mind you; hot, young Brazilian women. I was overserved and got a little carried away."

"A little carried away? She could have been a spy. I've been following the coverage. You could have put the president in real danger."

"It was a terrible mistake. I was just a drunk, horny guy doing drunk, horny-guy things."

"Are you married?"

Wounded, he answered, "Yeah, with two kids."

"My God, you're an asshole. What is wrong with the male species? Men are complete ass-hats."

"I'm in no position to argue the point. You're really disgusted with me, aren't you?"

"I just can't believe of all the people in DC, I ran into the 'Secret Service sex scandal' guy."

"Washington, DC, is just a big small town. It doesn't surprise me." James's phone dinged an incoming text alert. "Want to make a trip to West Virginia?" She looked at him oddly. "I hit up my friend Freddie, with our uniformed division. He ran that 'TBIRD' tag. Seems your hillbilly captors hail from an address in Harpersburg, West Virginia. At least, that's where the car's registered. Ready for a road trip?"

"You're two and a half beers in, you're already suspended from your job, and you want to drive to West Virginia?"

"I think we've established sound decision-making isn't my forte. Besides, you said you want to stick it to your husband? We have information on the biggest case in the country, information no one else has. We have to make our own breaks. What do you say?"

She huffed a sardonic laugh.

"Tag comes back to a John Connor Donovan. You did say the fat fellow went by JC."

"Holy shit."

"My thoughts exactly. So, are you game?"

"Why the hell not?" She took a drink. "And if we find them, what do we do then?"

"Haven't got there yet. First things first, princess."

"Don't call me that."

"You're no fun." James stood up. "Black or brown?" Again, she looked at him funny. "Your face is all over the media. You can't go out looking like Mrs. Gene Sterling. We need to cut your locks, dye your hair, and find a wardrobe befitting a West Virginia local."

"Wait, this is a bit much." A sense of panic came over her. "I don't want to cut my hair and dye it. You know how much this hair costs?"

"Look, princess, you're already the latest missing White girl in the country. Everyone presumes you're dead. Let's set vanity aside and see what we can uncover. You don't want to go to the cops? Fine. I was a cop long before I was an agent. We can get some answers if you trust me."

"Well, I have every reason to have faith in your trustworthiness, now don't I?"

"Cute."

"I'll go with black. Do you have any scissors?"

"Kitchen, upper right drawer, but no need to go Vidal Sassoon just yet. We can make you over once we get to West Virginia." James entered the bedroom and came out with a tuck-away holster carrying a Walther 9mm he inserted in the rear of his jeans.

"Expecting trouble?"

"The way my luck has been going, I expect damn near anything. I'm off to get the hair dye. I'll be back, princess," James said, heading to the door.

"Don't call me that." Kat shook her head. "What a strange man," she said to herself before finishing her beer.

CHAPTER 3

"HER HUSBAND was a senator?" John Charles Klingerman sat in his cramped trailer with his Rottweiler, Bocephus, drooling by his side. Last night, he'd driven out of Northern Virginia as if escaping some invisible tidal wave, making it home about the time Cornhole was recovering from his Oxy-induced narcolepsy. Now safely on his bourbon-stained couch, he took in the news coverage.

Had he known the lady was the wife of a senator, he'd have balked at the job. According to news accounts, the lady's whereabouts were still unknown. He looked over at Cornhole. The skinny bastard was asleep on the recliner; atop a mattress on the floor, Cornhole's girlfriend, Chrissy, was likewise zonked out, with paraphernalia nearby evidencing her heroin use. JC never understood the opioid thing. All he needed was a cold beer or eight, though he envied their anxiety-free slumber.

Unmuting the television, he heard the news anchor gushing platitudes about the glamour and refinement of Katherine Sterling. Every channel was running wall-to-wall coverage of the two pals' handiwork; this was not what JC signed up for. He was told some rich dude wanted to get rid of his wife. What rich dude didn't? If some millionaire wanted to off his old lady to keep her from taking him to the cleaners, JC wasn't going to pass judgment. He'd killed before and for less reason.

Eleven years ago, armed with a long-handled shovel outside Rufus T's, he'd squared off in the gravel lot against his adversary, Don Mabry, who wielded a six-foot folding ladder he'd retrieved from his pickup. Both assailants were piss drunk when an argument regarding the high school game broke out. Mabry's boy was flagged for pass interference, which JC asserted cost Harpersburg High the game. Don Sr., hearing his son's name so dishonored, demanded JC meet him outside. Years later, no resident of the town could explain why Don chose to arm himself with a ladder, but the decision proved fatal; as he flailed about with the clumsy bludgeon, an off-balance stumble allowed JC to drunkenly fell his foe with a sideswipe of his shovel. He felt bad about killing Don. It hadn't been his intention. Regardless, the jury found him guilty of manslaughter, and the judge sent him to Mount Olive for eight years.

That's where he met Squinty. John Conner "Squinty" Donovan was severely nearsighted, an ailment he never bothered to correct. Squinty had been incarcerated for aggravated burglary for a daytime invasion. Though he swore he was unaware the residence was occupied, only wishing to pilfer some jewelry, he damn near sent an elderly widow into cardiac arrest. Squinty had been hooking up with the woman's caretaker, from whom he'd received the intel about the jewelry. The caretaker was arrested on drug charges and gleefully cooperated to reduce her sentence by ratting on Squinty.

A month ago, JC and Cornhole had been drinking beers and discussing their money woes at Squint's place. Cornhole was on disability for his back, and JC received SSI checks for a supposed heart condition, as did Squinty for a questionable case of glaucoma, but all three agreed the stipends were inadequate. It was then Squinty made the proposal: what would JC and Cornhole do for $20,000? Joking, Cornhole said he'd kill for that kind of money. With a wry smile, Squinty stated that's what he had in mind.

A family friend, he explained, knew of a rich dude looking to off his wife. Cornhole was all in, but JC remained skeptical. Where did Squinty catch wind of a hit job for some rich DC fella? Squinty explained he'd learned from a second cousin that a third party was looking to find the right men for the task: ones with no plausible connection to the victim. The thought of returning to Mount Olive was unconscionable, and JC was aware with his record it could well be a life sentence, but ten grand was a windfall he couldn't pass up. Both he and Cornhole agreed to meet with the third party, which pleased Squinty, who would land a generous finder's fee. A week later, they met with a slick, foreign-sounding gentlemen who went by the name Oscar. Oscar laid out the plan: a staged kidnapping and murder. JC pushed for more money, and Oscar acquiesced, upping the purse to $25,000.

Now JC sat on his couch, staring at Fox News reports of the missing senator's wife, who, hours ago, had been tied up in his car trunk. Cornhole proved to be the liability JC feared him to be. The gas gauge hadn't worked on the piece of shit for over a year. The news folks were still reporting the pretty lady's whereabouts unknown. Oscar had yet to contact JC on the throw-down phone sitting silently on the coffee table. JC didn't quite know what he'd say when the foreigner called, but he needed the money.

"John?" yelled Myrtle from the bedroom at the far end of the trailer. "You home?" Pushing Bocephus away, JC made his way through the wood-paneled rectangle, grabbing a McDonald's sack and drink from the kitchen.

"I'm here, darlin."

"I was so worried. Why didn't you come see me when you got home? Did you get me my breakfast? Where have you been?" Myrtle's pleading, childlike tone made him feel awful. She expected her breakfast by 8 AM, and he knew any deviation from the routine upset her. At over 600 pounds, she enveloped their queen bed, the pale folds of her gelatinous legs spilling from her gown to the edge of the straining mattress. Her torso and head were perpetually propped up by an army of pillows.

"Sorry, my love, it's been a busy mornin'. Here ya go." JC pushed away several previously emptied food containers, then set the sack and jumbo Coke on the end table. Sacks, boxes, and cups littered the bedroom floor, the relics of countless meals. Rummaging through her newest sack, a disturbed look crossed her face. Two egg McMuffins, two sausage biscuits with egg, and two hash browns, but something was missing.

"I always get three hash browns, John." She looked up at him pitifully. "Where's my third hash brown?" Truth was he'd been damned hungry after a long night and hoped she wouldn't notice the missing potato wafer.

"I'm sorry, love, they musta forgotten. I'll make it up to ya at lunch."

"Where have you been?" There being no room on the bed, JC slept on the living room couch, but his tardy breakfast aroused her suspicions.

"I'm lookin' into doin' some work for a fella. Just temporary employment, but it's better than nothin'."

"That's wonderful, but I hope it doesn't take you away from me. I need you, baby."

"It shouldn't take long."

"What kind of work is it, baby?"

"Helping him move a few things. Just a side job. Haulin' some stuff for this fella who got tired of whatever it is he's gettin' rid of."

"Well, don't strain yourself. You know what the doc said about your heart condition."

Anytime JC attempted to gain employment, Myrtle cited his supposed heart problem. The doctor who diagnosed his "condition" was the same one doling out prescriptions of Percocet and OxyContin to every stiff back and bum knee in the county. He kept up the charade for the disability checks it provided. But he was tired of daily fast-food runs, daytime television, and day drinking, which was what made Squinty's referral so appealing. Maybe this payday would break the cycle, get Myrtle her surgery, and right the ship. With President Frum in the White House, anything was possible.

"I'll be careful. He promised me sixty bucks for an afternoon's work. Chrissy will be here." Biscuit crumbs cascading down her chins, Myrtle ceased chewing with a look of displeasure. She was jealous of Chrissy and most anyone who could spend time with JC. "I'm just sayin' she'll be here if ya need anything. I'll bring your dinner home once I'm done. KFC fine?"

"That's fine. Just don't let that little bitch in here. I'm just fine on my own."

JC became acquainted with Myrtle when he received a letter from her while in prison. She had read about his sentence and thought it unjust as it was clear that the Mabry boy's blatant pass interference lost the game. The correspondence continued, and shortly after his release, they were married. She was always a thick girl, which suited JC fine. He worked at the plant while she took care of the trailer bequeathed him after his mom passed from lung cancer. Every night on his way home from work, he'd pick up dinner: McDonald's, Hardee's, Taco Bell. He enjoyed making her happy. Now she could barely get out of bed.

"I wish you'd stay here with me," she admitted, her eyes misting.

"I've got to make some money, love. Now, you enjoy your breakfast. *The View* should be coming on before long. I'll be done as soon as I can, then I'll get home to you." He kissed her forehead. A doleful expression crossed her fat face as she bit into a hash brown.

Grabbing a Natty Light can from the fridge, JC found Cornhole groggily waking.

"Corn, take a look at the TV," JC ordered as he reclaimed his spot next to Bocephus. Rubbing his eyes, Cornhole focused on the screen. Having completed a story about some horny Secret Service agent, Fox's gaudy graphics led into a Fox News Alert about a senator's wife kidnapped from her home. It didn't seem to dawn on Cornhole the import of the story; his gaunt face remained unfazed beneath his long, oily hair.

"That's the gal we done nabbed last night," JC clarified.

"That's our gal?" Cornhole looked confused. "Didn't she get away?"

"Yeah, dumbass, she got away. Thanks to you."

"Who killed her?"

"Nobody done killed her, but they can't find her neither. So far, I ain't seen nothin' about us. I don't get it. Wonder if she took a bad fall down a ravine or somethin'. Maybe she done broke her neck." JC had been mulling theories about her possible demise all morning.

"That older fella was a senator?"

"I suppose so. Them senators must get paid a mighty lot." Both JC and Corn had marveled at the legislator's extravagant abode. "He's some liberal, commie-fag Democrat."

Since the beginning of the presidential campaign, JC had been a Frum guy. He attended a Frum rally in Morgantown, and it was the best night of his life. Finally, somebody gave a shit about him. Someone was going to tell these foreigners to fuck off and build shit back here in the US of A. The media was shocked he was elected. JC wasn't; fact was, everyone he knew voted for Frum.

"Wonder why Oscar never mentioned he was a senator?" JC asked rhetorically. Cornhole stared at the screen with a stupid expression. JC was pretty certain Corn didn't know what a senator was.

"She's hot," Chrissy said as she sat up on the floor, gazing at the TV while lighting a cigarette. "Is that the gal y'all killed?"

"Goddamn it, Chrissy, don't say that shit out loud," scolded JC. He looked up, wondering if the NSA had a satellite focused on his trailer. "We had some complications last night. Just tryin' to figure things out right now."

"The gal got away," Cornhole said. Amid cigarette smoke, Chrissy raised her eyebrows.

"Where the fuck is she?" she asked.

"If we knew that, we'd finish the job." JC was irritated. "Why the hell did you tell her about this, Corn?"

"He tells me everything," Chrissy boasted, leaning on Cornhole seated in the recliner. With a wince, he leaned over and kissed her. "Sorry, hun, your back hurting?" Two years prior, Cornhole injured himself loading a pallet of hardware at the warehouse. Beneath his coveralls, his back wrap was Velcroed tight but did little to ease the pain; only Oxy could do that.

"I want that money," stated JC, ignoring the affectionate couple. He'd been told to expect a call today. His conundrum was that Oscar would expect a picture of the deceased. Being that the dead girl was MIA, he had a dilemma: admit the truth or convince him the girl was dead. Admitting failure was out of the question, both financially and in the interest of self-preservation.

Taking a healthy swig of beer, he turned up the television when he saw the chyron POLICE RELEASE DESCRIPTION OF ABDUCTORS.

The dolled-up anchor recited from her teleprompter, "One suspect is described as approximately five eight, heavyset White male in his late forties with a dark beard and wearing a red 'Bring Back My America' ball cap."

JC self-consciously rubbed his matted beard.

"The second suspect was six two, very lean White male, also in his forties, with long hair, wearing woodland camo."

JC looked over at Cornhole tongue-kissing Chrissy, who was rubbing his crotch along the exterior of his woodland camouflage coveralls. Taking another sip, JC muted the television once again and pondered. The back of Chrissy's head bobbed and turned as the two junkies made out like tenth graders, her thin, dirty-blond hair tossing about with each passionate sway. JC had an idea.

Getting up, he returned to his bedroom and retrieved his

Redskins hoodie from a pile of dirty laundry. When he reentered the living room, Chrissy was gingerly easing Cornhole onto her floor mattress.

"No time for that right now, you two." Tossing the hoodie next to Chrissy, he said, "Put this on. I'm gonna take your picture." She looked confused, as did Cornhole, confused being his default expression. "You're about as tall as that senator's wife. Now put on that hoodie, and let's go out to the backyard."

"Can't you just let us rut first?" pleaded Cornhole. "She was just gonna climb on top a while."

"I don't get it. What you want?" asked Chrissy, extinguishing her cigarette.

"I need you to be our dead senator's wife."

"I ain't as purty as that there senator's wife."

"No, you ain't. But your hair is close enough, and you're both thin. We just need to go out back and have you play dead. Hell, you look dead most times anyhow."

"Fuck you, JC. What's the sweatshirt for?"

"That rich lady was wearing a maroon 'Skins hoodie kind of like this one. Put it on, and I'll meet you out back."

"What if I don't want to?"

"Then I guess you don't want your lover boy there gettin' his share of the twenty-five grand."

Immediately, Chrissy removed her shirt, revealing her small, flabby, braless tits as she grabbed the hoodie.

JC grabbed the drop phone and went out the back door as Bocephus tagged along. The backyard was littered with an old refrigerator, a washer and dryer, a wheelless Dodge Dakota, rusted swing set, and three old televisions. Most of it was dirt, but the property edge consisted of high, wild grasses along the base of a forested hill.

JC had Chrissy lie facedown in the grass. Placing her hair to hide her facial features, he ignored Cornhole's countless suggestions as he took a knee and, with great care, used the camera feature on the drop phone to take the photo. He thought it looked fine. From what JC could recall of his kidnap victim, Chrissy seemed a suitable stand-in.

As he and Cornhole reviewed the pic, Chrissy began to holler as if possessed by the devil.

"You laid me in a goddamn ant bed!" Performing a high-stepping dance routine and yodeling for help, she pulled off her hoodie and swiped the tiny buggers off her arms.

Cornhole, not knowing how to help his lover, kept asking, "Are you okay, hun? You alright? What can I do?" as her arms and tits flailed about.

The phone rang. JC stared at it as it vibrated and chimed in his hand. "Goddammit, Chrissy, Oscar is callin'." She couldn't hear him amid her freak out. He entered the trailer.

"Oscar?"

"Yes. How was your fishing trip?" asked Oscar. His Eastern European accent made fishing sound like "feesheeng."

"Good. Caught a big one."

"Pleased to hear that. I would love to see your prize."

◎ ◎ ◎

"Gene, you need to calm down," Joe suggested in his deep, Southern voice. The last of the FBI and Metro Police had departed the residence, giving the longtime friends a moment to sort things out. Sipping straight bourbon, Joe handed Gene a three-fingers-full tumbler and sat across from him in the California senator's library. The library provided a welcome respite from the gaggle of reporters camped across the street.

Senator Joseph Bratton III and Senator Eugene Sterling were unlikely friends in contemporary Washington politics. Nearly three decades ago, each were freshmen congressmen and, though geographically and ideologically worlds apart, shared traits of uncommon zeal and surplus ambition. Like oxygen to fire, they needed each other to survive.

They had debated immigration, healthcare, taxes, and all manner of foreign policy objectives over the past few decades with little measurable substantive effect, each using the other as a toothless foil to get reelected. Folks in California hated Joe Bratton, thinking him a Hitlerite, misogynist power-monger willing to destroy the planet while capitalizing on his White privilege. Likewise, the citizens of West Virginia viewed Senator Sterling as a vapid, bleeding-heart squish aiming to confiscate most of their paychecks to dole out free shit while kowtowing to foreign powers. But their respective constituencies swore by their guy and dutifully rubber-stamped their tickets back to Washington.

"This'll all work out just fine," Joe reassured his friend. "You oughtn't be so morose. You gave a virtuoso performance this morning. This time next week, you'll be the front-runner. Now that you're a widower, that rambunctious bitch won't be able to prattle on about White-privilege bullshit." Joe couldn't stand Gene's opponent, Cassandra Lightner, and loved the notion of defanging her favorite political move: decrying the treachery and privilege of old, straight, White men.

Gene's bruised, overly bronzed face was tight with stress as he took a sip. "You think the deed is done?" Joe's three chins bobbled affirmatively. "Do you know it was done or just suspect so?" Gene pushed.

"Not confirmed yet. Oscar is supposed to get confirmation from the hired help sometime today. Don't you worry yourself. My guys know what they're doing."

"And what if our 'hired help' is arrested? What then?" Gene asked, a variant of the same query he'd posited innumerable times over the past month.

"What if they do? You saw those two. Let's suppose they're

nabbed for Kat's disappearance—a highly unlikely scenario, mind you, but for argument sake, suppose they are. You have two ardent supporters of President Frum kidnapping the wife of Frum's most effective political nemesis. This on the heels of the president's border security plan being stymied in Congress to the dismay of White, nationalist racists like these two? Heck, it may be preferable to see them boys apprehended."

"I'd like to share your confidence, but frankly, they weren't all that inspiring."

"Rest easy. The short one is a convicted murderer, and the injured fella is a drug addict. Nobody, including the cops, would take them seriously. If they're arrested and implicate your involvement, it would be mocked and dismissed on CNN, MSNBC, and most other outlets. You're a Democrat, after all; the media will carry your water."

Gene smiled. Joe always bitched about Republicans being treated unfairly in the press.

"Fox News," continued Joe, "may run some piece insinuating your involvement, which would be roundly slammed by other outlets as a heartless, cruel smear."

"I could see O'Hanlon doing that."

"That's who I had in mind. But you get my point. The story will be how you bravely soldiered on after the cruel death of your wife. Congresswoman Lightner will be disarmed and unable to go on the offensive. Every channel is now *The Gene Sterling Show*. There won't be any oxygen left for her." Leaning forward with gravitas, Joe continued, "It is your turn, my friend. You know it. This is your moment."

The California senator nodded with equal gravity. It was all falling into place. A showdown with the glandular, divisive oaf in the White House was looming. Nobody saw Frum coming four years ago, but Senator Sterling was primed to put an end to this disruption—to restore honor to the office.

"You have always been a steady friend, Joe."

"And your money situation is good?"

"Oh yes, that was never in question. As you know, the committee has been behind me since last summer. I anticipate the super PACs supporting me will get a boost from this. My foundation is doing well, though the cash flow has flattened in the past few months." The Sterling Foundation had been founded by Gene and Kat a decade ago. Though the foundation was ostensibly a nonprofit organization promoting clean energy, education, and other interests, the influence-seeking celebrity donors primarily funded an elaborate lifestyle for the Sterlings, tax-free.

"Well, I can assure you this: Americans are a sympathetic bunch, and sentimentality opens wallets. I guarantee you'll get a bump in grassroots donations. Your poll numbers will go up, and as you know, when the polls swing in your favor, that's when the real players begin ponying up, hoping to get in the good graces of the future president of the United States."

"So, what's next? I can't very well campaign in next week's elections after my wife was kidnapped."

"The media is already speculating on whether you'll remain in the primaries. Your showing today has them praising your fortitude and resilience. That's a good start. Play your cards right, and there may be no need to hit the trail. At least, not right away."

"There are caucuses this weekend in Kansas, Maine, Louisiana, and Nebraska. Do I simply ignore them?" wondered Gene.

"You don't have a prayer in Maine. The White PhD crowd love Cassandra. More to the point, they feel good voting for a lesbian minority. How do you like your organization in the Midwest?"

"We are strong. The Midwest doesn't concern me. Louisiana, however, will be close. That's a true primary, and the Black vote will go Cassandra's way. It'll depend on turnout. What are you thinking?"

"Friday you hold a presser," Joe responded with an air of

certainty. "You announce you will not be intimidated by the forces of bigotry and greed. You exude courage tinged with sorrow and vow to continue the fight not just for you, but for your missing wife. You hint that the 'Bring Back My America' crowd is a stain on the body politic and the source of this cancer is residing at 1600 Pennsylvania Avenue.

"Americans like things simple. They want a good guy and a bad guy. President Frum will be the bad guy. You'll don the white hat on Friday. It will be replayed on a loop for the next news cycle. You won't need to stump, Gene. Your story will dominate every news segment; it's a ratings bonanza for them. Cassandra won't get a minute of airtime, and when she does, she'll be forced to remain conciliatory."

Pleased, Gene nodded and took a sip. If he could take three of four states without pressing the flesh of flyover yahoos, all the better. Hell, he might even sweep if the Mainers were moved by his performance. For the first time in several days, he was at ease.

⊙ ⊙ ⊙

Though he understood their value, Metropolitan Police Detective Sergeant Derek Roland hated press conferences. The Federal Bureau of Investigation loved press conferences. Square jawed in his pristine suit and white shirt, the special agent in charge of the Washington Field Office stood before the microphone as Derek stood off to the side, wearing a tweed sport coat over a mustard-yellow button-down.

With well-practiced gravity, the SAIC laid out the preliminary findings of the previous evening's incident at 4949 Hillbrook Lane: Senator Sterling and his wife, Katherine, having just returned from campaigning in the Midwest, were attacked in their home by two men who had embedded themselves at the residence prior to their arrival. All the FBI had were the senator's account of the incident and the image of a vehicle, which was the most promising lead thus far. A screen set up adjacent to the SAIC displayed a grainy video capture of a suspicious car.

"The FBI wishes to identify the occupants of this vehicle. It appears to be a gray, possibly unpainted sedan with two occupants," the SAIC informed his audience. "It's difficult to make out, but the driver appears to be wearing a ball cap similar to the one described by Senator Sterling. This vehicle was seen in the Spring Valley neighborhood of Northwest Washington, DC, around 6 PM. As you can see here, close to midnight"—the screen now displayed a nighttime still of a barely visible sedan—"the video reveals what may be the same vehicle leaving the neighborhood. Let me be clear, we do not yet have a suspect in this investigation. We simply wish to speak to the occupants of this vehicle to determine what they may have seen or any information they can provide regarding this incident. With that, I'll be happy to take your questions."

The room of reporters exploded in a torrent of queries the SAIC dodged with a self-satisfied air.

Derek was responsible for the discovery of the grainy video. He'd contacted a retired defense contract executive who lived cattycorner from the Sterlings. Years of milking the Department of Defense and bargaining with various kleptocracies left the septuagenarian not only wealthy but paranoid; an array of cameras and motion detectors sentineled the property. Reviewing footage of four cameras with street views, Derek noticed a gray sedan hooptie pass by several times. Late in the evening, the streetlights provided just enough illumination to silhouette a similar vehicle with two occupants. Other than the Mercedes, Teslas, and BMWs of the residents and the occasional landscaper truck or housekeeper van, there was little traffic in this toney cluster of mansions. The sedan stuck out, and neighbors couldn't recall having seen it before.

The press conference mercifully over, Derek sipped room-temperature coffee in his soulless cubicle. He had dismissed the rest of his team for the time being; he needed a moment to step back a bit. Having been on the force for twenty-six years and nearing his fifty-fourth birthday, he was surprised by nothing. Mothers drowning their children, fourteen-year-old murderers, stabbings born of petty squabbles—Derek had borne witness to mindless, inconsequential lethality for most of his adult life.

The blank computer monitor reflected his image: a bald Black man with gray creeping into his mustache, thrice married and now heading an investigation that was the water-cooler talk of not only the country but the world. Why would right-wing rednecks kidnap the beautiful wife of a left-wing senator when they had said senator in their grasp? The media—and in turn, the public—embraced the real-life drama without questioning the veracity of the senator's account. Detective Roland was no fan of President Frum, but unlike the media, he didn't have the luxury to indulge the presupposition that Frum loyalists were violent, radical reprobates. The senator was a sympathetic figure and seemed credible, but something was not right.

Over the years, Derek had learned that like most aspects of life, evil had patterns. It was as predictable as the nature of man. Granted, he was a cop. And as his children well knew, decades of police work fostered marble-hard levels of skepticism. It could well be the incident was an outlier and the poor woman was kidnapped by politically motivated yahoos. There was very little evidence. Derek hoped Katherine Sterling was alive, but he knew the odds and suspected she was stiffened by rigor mortis in some overgrown field.

The media and the world cared because she was the wife of a senator—attractive, White, and rich. Three Black teens had been shot and killed the previous weekend in Southeast. It didn't even lead the local newscasts.

Derek Roland was about done with it all. But he'd have to see this through. He was hand-selected by the captain due to his proven ability to close out homicide cases. All this would be fine with him, but the thought of playing second fiddle to the feds was nauseating. Most Feebs were law professors playing cop. Nice enough guys, but he preferred his autonomy.

What the feds did have was resources, and in just twenty-four hours, they had combed through Katherine's phone records and texts. Little had come of it other than the revelation that she was flirty with a personal trainer at a Soul Cycle in Georgetown. They interviewed the cardio Casanova and verified he was just a typical DC cougar-chasing ass-hound of no investigative interest. Derek would find the dead White girl. He'd track down her killers. Then he'd be done with it.

There was a time when a high-profile case of this sort would have thrilled him. Adrenaline would course through his veins at the thought of such a challenge. Now it was just tedium. Looking up at the mounted television, he saw her pretty face splashed on the screen for the umpteenth time and whispered to himself, "Where are you, Katherine Sterling?"

CHAPTER 4

Thursday, March 3

WHEN JAMES returned with gas station coffee, he found Kat in the same condition he'd left her: crying in the bathroom. The prior evening, they had driven to the run-down Sunny Uplands motel off Highway 48 outside Harpersburg, West Virginia, where the two most Googled names in America entered room 22 and crashed from exhaustion on adjacent twin beds. This morning their room served as an impromptu barbershop. It didn't go well.

"I look like a member of a boy band," sobbed a despondent Kat as James set her coffee near the sink. "Even worse, I'm the nonthreatening nice one." Her hair was short. James didn't think too short, but his opinion didn't really matter. Her dirty-blond locks were dyed obsidian, which she teased while looking into the mirror with reddened eyes.

"I know it's a big change. You'll get used to it. I think you look cute."

"Don't bullshit me," she sniffed with tear-streaked cheeks.

"I'm not bullshitting you; it's not as bad as you think. You make a good brunette. Remember, this is temporary." James knew women like Kat—strong willed and independent, but not so much that they didn't enjoy feeling attractive. This unwanted infringement, added to the stress of her ordeal, would have broken a lesser woman. But he recognized it was more than that. It was as if losing those locks had exposed the reality of her circumstances. James coaxed her to the edge of the bed as he sat beside her.

"Jesus Christ, how did I get here?" She rubbed her temples. Not knowing how to respond, James sat silent. A few feet away, the newscast continued piling up ratings with updates on the Katherine Sterling case. "My Q rating has never been higher," she sniffed.

"Q rating?"

"Measures your brand recognition. Advertisers and marketers use it. Gene always spoke about it, which was stupid because it doesn't really apply to politics. He talked like that to feel like a part of the entertainment industry. He loved rubbing elbows with celebrities. They'd kiss his ass about all the sacrifices he was making for the environment. Anyhow, my Q rating is probably nearing Bradley Cooper levels."

"I didn't know that was a thing. Makes sense; you are getting free, nonstop face time on every news outlet."

"It's kind of hard to believe. The twenty-five-year-old me would have loved this attention."

"And the current you?"

"I'm more practical now. I mean, I've always enjoyed attention. You don't become an actress to be ignored. When this is all over, I can assure you, I'm going to monetize this." A healthy smile crossed her face. James was happy to see her mind off her hairdo.

"You mentioned your husband. Think he just used climate change to snuggle up to Hollywood types?"

"No, he thinks it's a real problem, but nowhere near to the extent he'd lead you to believe. Celebrity approval is like a drug to him. Once a year we'd hold a fundraiser for the Sterling Foundation at the Beverly Wilshire, and he realized nothing got the stars stoked more than raising his voice against earth-destroying corporations; mind you, those corporations pay the foundation handsomely. President Frum's election was a boon for fundraising. In January, Gene declared a second Frum term would turn this planet into a desolate wasteland. DiCaprio cried during the standing ovation. Gene wouldn't shut up about it for weeks."

"I've seen Bradley Cooper before. Taller than I expected."

Kat looked at him oddly.

"You mentioned him earlier. You know, your Q rating?"

"He's pretty hot," she observed.

"Think he could play me in my biopic?"

"No, he's way hotter than you."

"Just gauging where I stand, you know, on your hotness chart."

Kat smiled and shook her head. "I'm going to ignore that. Anyhow, my point is I could have several million Twitter followers if I come out of this alright. I could promote products on Instagram and do a prime-time sit-down with Oprah, maybe pitch a reality show called *Back to Life* where they document my comeback story after the betrayal."

"Is this the kind of stuff you think about, princess?"

"First, stop calling me princess. Second, it's the world I live in; don't judge. Look, I'm everywhere right now—television, social media. I'm bigger than Dwayne Johnson."

"This feels a bit like a defense mechanism."

"Don't Dr. Phil me right now. Can't you just let me enjoy the thought of worldwide celebrity instead of wallowing in the shitstorm that is my life?"

"Fair. Point taken."

"Something good has to come of this. It would be nice to have some notoriety of my own and not for being married to some douchebag, celebrity suck-up. If Gene goes down for this and I can make money, it would be the sweetest revenge."

"I'll be sure to never cross you." James finished his coffee.

"Thanks for listening. Gene never listened to a thing I said. Dismissed every thought I ever shared to the point where I just stopped talking."

"Things were pretty shitty between you two, huh?"

"Well, he had me kidnapped."

"That's certainly a red flag."

She laughed for the first time in days. Her laugh had an honest girlishness James enjoyed.

"He was cheating on me," she confided. "I didn't even really care that he was, and I don't know who she is, but some other woman was in the mix."

"Not a topic I should comment on, my record on such matters being what it is."

"Why do men cheat?" she asked. Staring at the television, James struggled to answer. "You don't have to answer that."

"Good, because I don't have an adequate one."

"I've told you what I want. What do you want, James?"

"Me? What could I possibly want? Things are going swimmingly."

She looked annoyed at the sarcastic answer to her sincere question.

"Okay, I'll play along. I want my job back. I'm good at it. You want to be famous. I'm not famous, but the Secret Service is. Whether you're deplaning out of the back of Air Force One or looking through a window at the tourists outside the White House, you're on the inside of something big, while everyone else is on the outside looking in. I was given weighty responsibilities and did them well; it was satisfying. And I want to see my kids. I will never get everything back to the way it was, but I want something close to that."

"That was the most forthright thing I've ever heard you say."

"You've known me for thirty-six hours."

"I know. And until just now, I took you for a cynical, boozy man-whore," she admitted, causing him to feign hurt. "Why'd you do it?"

"Do what?"

"You know, go whoring in South America. You said you love

your job. I can tell you do. And that's pretty damn impressive, being a Secret Service agent, so why'd you risk everything?"

It was the first time someone had asked him this obvious question, though he had asked himself innumerable times.

"You wouldn't understand."

"How come?"

"For one, you're not a man. It's hard to explain things like this to a woman."

"That's a cop-out. I know men. You simply didn't plan on getting caught."

"Look, I saved your life. Do we really have to discuss this?" he asked with mild irritation.

"Saved my life? I escaped on my own. You just happened to be leaving a bar. It's your business; I just remember seeing it in the news and thought anybody who would solicit a hooker on an overseas presidential trip would have to be an epically dense dumbass."

Eyes wide and mouth agape, he stared at her.

"Well, that's what I thought," she maintained.

"Well, that dumbass gave you a place to stay and is helping you find your kidnappers. But you're right. I suppose I wasn't thinking at all. Certainly didn't imagine a night out in Sao Paulo would lead to this. I don't know what I was thinking."

"Men don't think."

"I think."

"Men think about solving problems. They don't think, or even realize, when they're creating problems. I knew Gene was digging himself a hole, creating problems he couldn't undo."

"Like?"

"He didn't share things with me, so I can't be certain. But my woman's intuition sensed something way off with him the past month or so. Like I said, he was sleeping with somebody else, but the way he was behaving, there was more to it. I know men. I can't explain them, but I know them, and nothing they do, no matter how inexplicable or destructive, surprises me."

James stared at the dingy floor in thought. Next to him, Kat observed his introspection as his broad shoulders slumped beneath a plaid, flannel shirt. Manly and handsome in the way only American men can be, he also had a boyish way about him. It was a refreshing departure from Gene's domineering, conniving presence.

"Thank you, Jimmy," she said and put her hand on his knee. He looked at her.

"Jimmy?"

"You don't like that?"

"No, I don't. Princess." He smirked. She returned the grin, when an image on the television caught her attention.

"That's the car," she declared. The newscast displayed the video still of a gray coupe followed by clips of an FBI press conference sharing little more than what was already known.

"Well, that doesn't help very much, but at least the FBI got their press conference," observed James.

"Do you think the cops know the license plate?"

"No," said James with certainty. "They wouldn't release that image if there was more to go on. This feels desperate. If they had the tag, they'd either have that car under surveillance or release it to the public and hope for a tip."

Again, James wore his pensive look. Part of him thought he should call in the tag anonymously and let the feds check out this John Connor Donovan character. In all likelihood the tag was stolen, but if it wasn't and the feds took someone into custody, how would he explain holding the kidnap victim for two days? What if the feds couldn't connect Senator Sterling to the suspect? If her story didn't hold up, he could find himself in a precarious position. Conversely, if he could help her identify the kidnappers and take the suspect himself, the cable news networks would get into bidding wars for exclusives. The image-conscious Secret Service would have to reconsider the suspension of the hero agent who saved the senator's wife and took down the culprits.

"What are you thinking?" she asked.

"I'm thinking we stick to the plan. We go to 1122 Schafer's Mill Road and see if you recognize this JC Donovan character."

⊙ ⊙ ⊙

Squinty's home sat on a ten-acre plot that had been in the Donovan family since his grandfather returned from World War II. It was a small, ranch-style brick abode typical of the era. A gravel drive stretched sixty yards from Schafer's Mill Road, from which the home was only visible in the fall. Over the decades, the property became littered with car and truck remnants—some on blocks, but all rusted by weather and time. A large work shed contained a '55 Ford Thunderbird and a '69 Mustang. Both were inoperable but once were the pride of Squinty's father. The Donovans were Ford men, and any mention of Chevy's primacy among American automobiles would unleash a flurry of emphatic disputations.

Granddaddy Donovan started an auto repair shop in town, which was handed down to Squinty's father, who destroyed the establishment's solid reputation. Like his father, Daddy Donovan joined the Army. Unlike his father, he couldn't handle his wartime experience and returned from Vietnam a broken man. The only thing Daddy Donovan passed down to Squinty was his home, mechanical aptitude, and love of booze.

The maternal side of Squinty's family was far less self-destructive. One cousin was a judge, another a successful attorney specializing in grand action suits, and a third worked in the governor's office. It was the latter who surprised Squinty several weeks ago. Knowing the type of company Squinty kept, the cousin mentioned an opportunity to earn five hundred bucks if Squints recruited a couple guys to take out a fella's wife. Understandably, the client wished to keep his distance from the deed. Having drank or smoked most of his SSI money, the prospect of five hundred dollars seemed mana from heaven. Squinty told his cousin he knew a guy who could use a financial windfall—a friend of his who'd done time for manslaughter.

Now fifty-one, Squinty averaged thirty beers a day. Most days incorporated a steady beer buzz from morning till bedtime while he tinkered with his cars or watched online porn. Now and again, however, he liked to hit the hard stuff. The previous evening, he'd spent some of his recruitment earnings at Clive's, a roadside beer joint with a shitty pool table. His thrice-divorced, occasional fuck buddy, Lisa, had her eldest babysitting the youngins, which typically boded well for Squinty.

When he suggested they tab out and head over to his place, Lisa protested that she hadn't finished partying. This didn't please Squinty, but he kept buying her whiskey sours, hoping she'd get randy. Several times, Lisa prevented Squinty from falling off his stool during his persistent, drunken pleadings for a tryst. His doggedness began to grate on her with every passing whiskey sour until she blurted, "Why the rush, Squints? You gots nothin' to do tomorrow anyhow. It ain't like you got a job to go to."

On a beer day, the innocuous taunt would warrant nary a flinch. But in his bourbon-driven state, coupled with Lisa's reluctance to fulfill his needs, the assertion was like a punch to the sternum. He cursed Lisa with frightening vehemence, calling her a "pancake-titted whore" and worse. The other six drunkards initially laughed at the spectacle but grew concerned as he worked himself further and further into a lather. Two highway workers, still donning reflective vests, intervened. Clive was forced to evict Squinty.

A well-practiced drunk driver, Squinty managed to remain on the road long enough to get home, where he turned on the TV, grabbed a beer, and splayed out on the couch. He passed out after two sips.

Several hours later, a rush of cool air woke him. The morning sun silhouetted a figure in the front doorway. Assuming it was the cops, Squinty bolted up to a seated position, trying to recall if he had any outstanding warrants.

"Relax" calmed Oscar's Eastern-Bloc accent as he stepped forward into focus—dark goatee and slicked-back hair coupled with a mock turtleneck and skinny jeans. Squinty hadn't expected to see him again, though he was relieved it wasn't the cops.

"You got another job for me?" he asked. This brought a wry smile to Oscar's face.

"No, John." Oscar never addressed Squinty by his nickname. "You have done enough for me. My client is pleased thus far with the work of your cronies. I'm sure you've caught the news."

"News?"

Oscar was amused by his ignorance. "You not hear of the missing senator's wife?"

"Sure I did," lied Squinty.

"Have you spoken to JC?" Squinty shook his head. "Unlock your phone."

"How come?"

"I'd like to see it." Oscar's cold, businesslike demeanor made Squinty uneasy. Taking his smartphone off the coffee table, Squinty unlocked it before handing it to Oscar, who scrolled through the texts and phone calls.

"You are a man of your word, John." Oscar threw the phone on the couch. It was then Squinty noticed Oscar wearing black leather gloves. It was chilly this time of year but by no means glove weather. Oscar slowly walked toward the kitchen.

"Your friends appear to have taken care of the situation." Oscar peeked into the bedroom. "The entire country is looking for them, wondering who they are and what vile creatures would kidnap such a beautiful, successful woman. Imagine that, John. We know the answer to the one question the whole world wishes to know."

Oscar now loomed over the coffee table. Staring up from his couch, still buzzed, Squinty wondered where Oscar was going with this. "May I have a beer?" asked Oscar. Confused but wishing to be hospitable, Squinty stood.

"Sure," he began as he took a step toward the kitchen. "But why exactly are you here?"

"To thank you and to distance myself."

"Distance yourself?" Squinty felt cold.

"From malcontents, from the type of men that would kidnap a woman and kill her. I am a successful man. Successful men cannot be associated with men of ill repute."

Squinty felt something he hadn't since prison—an undefinable omen that something was off. Like a ghost in the room, unseen but terrifying all the same. He kept an older-model Smith & Wesson .357 revolver in the drawer near his bed. Sensing where this was going, Squinty bolted for his bedroom only to find his dash cut short by the force of a garrote cinched around his neck.

His legs crumbled beneath him and his temple veins protruded while he vainly strained to breathe. It dawned on Squinty that this probably wasn't the first time Oscar had killed a man with a cord. Within a minute, he realized the futility of his struggle. Before his final breath, momentary clarity overcame John Connor Donovan with two disparate thoughts: one, by killing him, Oscar was erasing his one association with whatever JC and Cornhole had done, and two, wherever death took him, he hoped his father was there, fixing a Ford Thunderbird.

◉ ◉ ◉

Wearing a West Virginia Mountaineers hoodie with her short, dark hair, Kat looked cute as hell. It was the Washington Nationals ball cap that pushed it to the next level; James had a penchant for attractive women in ball caps.

Following his phone's directions, he winded his truck through the back roads of the Mountain State. He was contemplating how to identify the suspects without getting himself or his new, attractive friend killed. With ubiquitous media coverage, the kidnappers would be on edge, and James—short haired and broad shouldered—exuded cop. A knock on their door could well be answered by a hail of bullets.

Mulling the scenario for most of the morning, he hoped his pickup truck and decidedly un-law-enforcement-looking partner would be enough to disabuse the suspects of any notion the pair were there to make an arrest. His plan, if one could call it a plan, was to pull up to the house and ask for directions. Kat would be by his side to identify any kidnappers who might answer the door. It was simple, but James couldn't think of a better alternative. If things went sideways, he had his Walther 9mm hidden beneath his untucked flannel shirt.

As they turned onto Schafer's Mill Road, Kat thought West Virginia a place of humble beauty and took in the sylvan scenery, hoping it would calm her. Groundhogs, deer, and a few turkeys appeared as they meandered up the winding mountain pass. The forests were showing the first signs of spring. Nervous energy caused her to fidget with the string of her hoodie. Glancing over several times, she noticed James was as relaxed as a Sunday drive.

"Aren't you worried?" she asked.

"About what?"

"We're going to the house of a would-be murderer. That doesn't concern you?"

James smiled and shrugged as if it never occurred to him to be anxious.

"Have you ever thought, Jimmy, that maybe you live a little too much 'in the moment'?"

"In the moment?"

"Do you ever worry? You know, contemplate the gravity of a

situation? This is a big deal, and you look like you're going to get your oil changed."

"I think about stuff. I just don't overthink it. I take things in, make a decision, put it into action, then live with the consequences."

"No, you'll never get accused of overthinking."

"Well, you don't have to be insulting."

"I can't say I've ever met a man like you."

"Then you obviously haven't hung around many cops, but I'll take the compliment."

"It wasn't a compliment."

He looked down at his phone. "We're about there. Now, remember, I'll do all the talking. They won't recognize you, but they may recall your voice. One thing I noticed about you so far, you can be a bit chatty." She shot him a disapproving stare. "Just an observation. I'm just going to ask for directions on how to get back on I-77. Got it?"

"I'm nervous."

"Don't be; we'll be fine. Done this sort of thing a thousand times."

"Yeah, but you were a cop acting in a professional capacity. We're just private citizens. Hell, we're vigilantes."

"Once again, you're overthinking this, princess."

"I'm a woman. I was put on this earth to overthink for all the men underthinking. And stop calling me princess."

James smiled, conceding the point.

"Almost there, should be to our left—wait, what's that?" A silver BMW 3-Series pulled out of the gravel driveway and passed them. "That's the house," he confirmed. "Don't see a lot of 3-Series Beamers out here." He passed Squinty's driveway and used the next drive to turn his truck around and catch up to the BMW. "Princess, there's a pen in the glovebox. We need to grab this tag. Virginia, A-E-R-7-3-1; got it?" To avoid alarming the driver, James pulled into a gas station and parked. "That was kind of weird, right?"

"Yeah, I didn't get a look at the driver, but I did get the tag," Kat observed and displayed the number scrawled on the underside of her forearm.

"It is odd. Thought about following him for a while, but it's hard to be inconspicuous out here in the boonies. Surveilling is a bitch in a county with, like, six traffic lights," he opined.

"Should we still go by the house?"

"I think we should." James reversed his pickup out of the parking spot. Retracing his route down Schafer's Mill Road, he pulled his F-150 down the long, gravel drive. "Must be a car guy," he observed amid the derelict domestic models littering the property. "Remember, we came out here to meet a dog breeder, but got lost. The cell service sucks, and we blame that for draining our phone batteries. We just need help getting back to the interstate."

"Isn't that a bit involved?"

"If your boys are here, they may test us to ensure we aren't the authorities. Better safe than sorry. If you recognize any of those guys, put your right hand in your pocket so I know."

James spoke with a commanding certainty that belied the buzzed loser she'd first met, his resolute expression a striking contrast to the man-boy for which she had him pegged. "You good?" he asked. She nodded, face tight with anxiety. Grabbing her hand firmly, he looked her in the eye. "We're going to be okay, Kat. Just let me do the talking."

With that assurance, he exited the truck. She pulled her ball cap low over her face and did the same. The old, brick, ranch-style home was in poor shape. The landscaping was nonexistent: what once passed for shrubs adorning the sides of the front stoop were little more than lifeless twigs protruding from the earth.

Meant to avoid sounding like the testosterone-fueled rap of a cop, James's one-knuckled, effete tap was enough to push the door open. He peered inside and saw flickering images on the wall from a running television.

"Hello? Excuse me? Is there anyone home?" James turned his right hip back and pulled up his untucked shirt enough to grip his sidearm. This didn't help Kat's nerves. "Hello?" James continued and pushed the door further open. Kat wanted to run to the truck. She felt her pulse in her ears as she looked down, hiding her eyes beneath the creased brim of her Nationals cap.

"What the fuck?" gasped James.

"What is it, Jimmy?"

"Some dude's on the floor. Sir? Are you alright? We got lost and were hoping you could help us out," he said, trying to stick to the ruse. "Aw, screw it. Stay here, princess."

"To hell with that. I'm not leaving you."

"Anyone home?" Once inside, he instinctively scanned the corners of the room as if clearing it for a warrant service before approaching the body on the floor. It was an older man in jeans and a thermal undershirt, sprawled near the kitchen counter at the edge of the living room. Kneeling, James examined him. The man wasn't breathing. He felt for a pulse before looking up at Kat. "He's DRT."

"What?"

"Dead right there."

Kat covered her mouth in panic. James put a finger over his lips to shush her as he drew his 9mm. He cleared the pantry and both small bedrooms, the panic-stricken former beauty queen at his hip. James returned to the body. Lifting the arm, he dropped it lifelessly to the floor. Observing the dead man's neck, he noticed severe bruising. He pulled down the lower eyelid and noticed tiny black spots on the whites of the eye. Like an autopsied victim he'd witnessed decades ago, this guy had been strangled.

"Don't touch anything, princess."

"Why?"

"We're at a murder scene. And a pretty damn recent one."

"Oh my God. Are you sure? Maybe he had a heart attack."

"No, it ain't a heart attack. Rigor mortis hasn't set in, no vein marbling, and his eyes have petechiae spots."

"What?"

"Never mind." James stood. "Look at him. Is this one of them? JC or Cornhole?"

Breathing heavy, she was nearing hyperventilation.

"I know it's scary. But you have to look at him."

Willing herself through fear, she examined the face of the dead man. It was the first dead body she had seen outside a funeral home.

"I've never seen this guy before. He's not one of them."

"You sure?"

"Positive."

"Let's get the fuck out of here."

"Should we call the cops?"

"Really? Call the cops? I believe it was you who asserted the futility of going to the cops."

"That's before I saw a dead body. Maybe we can explain things," she posited. An ambivalent expression crossed James's face.

"So, where do we start with our little story, princess? When you came hopping away from your kidnappers who were paid minions of your senator husband? Or do we start with us running down the address registered to said kidnappers only to find a freshly murdered corpse lying on the floor? How exactly the fuck do we explain this? I'm all ears."

Between the dead body and James's irritated state, Kat hit emotional overload. She didn't want to show weakness, so she hid her quivering face beneath her hat brim and stormed outside. James followed sheepishly, realizing she was reaching her breaking point—and that he'd allowed stressors to get the best of him. When he entered the truck, she was slouched over, arms folded, staring at the floorboard. He wanted to apologize but figured his newfound companion wasn't amenable to reflexive contrition. Turning the truck, careful to remain on the gravel so as not to leave tire impressions on the lawn, he drove away.

◉ ◉ ◉

Oscar made JC nervous. The lean foreigner was considerably younger than the West Virginian, but something about his impeccable grooming and cold, matter-of-fact manner put him ill at ease.

As arranged, JC parked his beat-up Saturn behind the remains of Bert's Tire and Auto, which, like the rest of the strip mall, had been vacant for years. Cornhole remained at the house with Chrissy, both passed out from snorting Oxy. The clock on the dash indicated it was 2:04 PM; Oscar was late. The uncharacteristic tardiness increased JC's apprehension.

He kept telling himself everything was fine, but a gnawing tension grew in his chest. Looking around for any sign of Oscar's arrival, all he saw were dilapidated, empty businesses backed by the wooded hills.

"Just calm the hell down," he whispered to himself, "get the money, and get home. This will be over. One and done. Goin' on the straight and narrow from here on. Hear me, Lord? I'm gonna live right. You'll see, Jesus. Let me get through this day, and I'll do right by you."

As the dash clock turned to 2:10, he spied a metallic BMW parking in his rearview mirror. JC scanned the area for any possible witnesses, then climbed out of the Saturn and into the Beamer's front passenger seat as instructed. To his relief, nobody was hiding in the back seat.

"Open up your shirt," Oscar ordered.

"Huh?"

"You're not wired, are you? Open your shirt and empty your pockets."

"You got nothing to worry about," JC said, happy to empty the pockets of his overalls and unbuckle the straps to prove he wasn't in with the feds. It appeared to satisfy Oscar.

"So, the trip went well?" asked Oscar calmly.

"Yes sir, we took care of her. No problem at all," JC lied. Oscar looked at him crossly. JC handed over the loaner phone and sat nervously for his reaction. Brow furrowed, Oscar swiped through the photos in silence as the Lord's Prayer played on a loop in JC's head.

"What is this? I can't see her face." The images depicted a thin female lying facedown amid tall, unkept grass. Though built like Katherine Sterling and wearing a maroon hoodie similar to the one she wore the night of the kidnapping, the corpse's identity was impossible to verify.

"What the hell is this? How do I know it's her?" As anticipated, Oscar was pissed.

"What do you mean? That's the girl. Who the hell else would it be?"

"I cannot see her face."

"It creeped me out. She was dead. It's hard to look at the face of a girl you just killed."

"Unacceptable, unprofessional—how do you expect me to pay when I cannot even make out who this is?"

"Whoever said I was a professional? You guys wanted a job done, I did it, and I expect to be paid. By the way, you could've mentioned the gal was a senator's wife. Kind of an important thing to leave out." JC was genuinely irked by the omission.

"Her husband is not important. But this photo proves nothing."

"Who the fuck you think it is? My sister? Listen, that rich gal is buried not ten miles from here. I'd be happy to take you there and dig her up." It was a bold bluff, and JC knew things could go south quickly if called on it. Shaking his head, Oscar reexamined the images, mentally going over the odds of this yahoo pulling a feint. Oscar was concerned with how Oleg would view the pics but, after weighing the risks and rewards, decided against visiting the burial site.

"Very well," Oscar began, "behind my seat are two shopping bags; take them. All the money is there." Unsure, JC peeked back and saw the bags. With a deep breath, he leaned over between the front seats to reach the rear floorboards, his stubby arms and protruding belly wedging him tightly between the seat backs.

"Ow, I think I'm stuck. I don't move too good," said JC painfully. "I'm sorry, can you pull my arm over." After an annoyed sigh, Oscar pulled JC's hand and shoved his shoulder, freeing the portly hitman, who fell back into the passenger seat.

"Just get out, go around, take the money, and go," ordered an exasperated Oscar. "Remember, if you attempt to get clever and go to the authorities, it will end poorly for you. You may run, but we know your sweet Myrtle can't go anywhere. Wouldn't want anything to happen to her."

JC nodded at the implication, stunned Oscar knew of Myrtle. Exiting the BMW, he opened the rear door and retrieved the two shopping bags. He refused to look back as he returned to his Saturn, terrified that Oscar might exit at any moment and shoot him dead. To his relief, the Beamer backed up turned and drove away. JC hoped it was the last time he'd see Oscar.

Throwing the bags on the passenger seat, he sat behind the wheel and peered over at the bundles of cash. It was the most money he had ever seen. Holy shit, he had done it. Cranking the ignition, he put the transmission in drive.

"Thank you, Jesus," he whispered as he pulled away. "You won't regret this, Lord. Straight as an arrow from here on out."

CHAPTER 5

CHET BATEMAN was a passionate young man with a good heart. He was always quick to give of his time and money in support of worthy causes. The one thing he could not stomach were climate deniers burying their heads in the sand to avoid accepting the scientific reality that the earth was warming. By "climate deniers," he meant anyone who did not dogmatically adhere to the belief that not only was the pumping of CO_2 into the air wreaking havoc on the atmosphere, but also a drastic overhaul of the entire global economy and governmental systems must be implemented—rapidly—to avoid a cataclysm.

He did not grow up with this conviction. In fact, he did not grow up as Chet Bateman. Stephen Goldberg was born on Manhattan's Upper East Side to a secular Jewish father and his second wife, Hannah, who was a nonpracticing Methodist. After attending American University, the young Goldberg secured—through his father—a staffer position on the Hill for a New York congressman. The congressman recognized Goldberg's writing talent and appointed him his primary speechwriter.

Being an adept politician, the legislator recognized his cosmopolitan constituency's enthusiasm for environmental causes. The marching orders for young Goldberg were clear: go heavy on the global warming stuff. The young writer scribed countless diatribes with doomful statistics prophesying all manner of disastrous outcomes if powers weren't ceded to the government. Terms like "corporate fat cats" and "billionaires" were sprinkled through the texts as he railed against the elites raping Mother Earth for their own gain. Through his association with the crusading congressman, Goldberg befriended like-minded scientists and celebrities. As he learned the language and studied the theories, he joined the ranks of the climate clergy.

Fortunately for Stephen Goldberg, his passion proved lucrative. Taking on the WASP-y name Chet Bateman, he began a podcast: *Resuscitate Earth.* Celebrities, scientists, and prominent alarmists sat across from him to warn of the damage being done and what measures were needed to save the planet. His listenership grew to well over two million followers, mostly comprised of young college grads on the coasts. Chet acquired representation and a glam team to improve his image. Netflix took the podcast and threw enough money at it to create a ten-part documentary.

Resuscitate Earth, starring Chet Bateman, became a cultural phenomenon. Democratic politicians clamored for his endorsement. Any association with Chet would assure a double-digit bump in the coveted eighteen-to-twenty-five demographic. The final episode featured Al Gore dourly predicting the earth's demise—particularly effective on the young target audience not old enough to have witnessed the former vice president making the same prediction in '94.

Once a nerdy writer tucked away in solitude, Chet was now recognized at trendy New York and LA hot spots. The tabloids even speculated the young "planet saver" was seeing Taylor Swift. Women who wouldn't give him a second glance a year ago were eager to bed the thirty-two-year-old activist. His dark, professionally coiffed hair and cultivated image of intelligence clothed in virtue made him the darling of all right-thinking global citizens.

But he wanted more than mere celebrity. Chet wanted to prove he wasn't just some polished TV personality. Approached to be the face for the exciting new green-energy venture Emerald Solaria, he jumped at the chance. The proposition was headed by European investors expressing a desire to heal the planet while generating heavy profits. It promised a revolution in how the world was powered. Following a slick promotional campaign leaning heavily on Chet's notoriety, additional investors flocked to its mission as left-wing politicians, including Senator Gene Sterling, sang its praises. Chet's celebrity and environmental sainthood made him perhaps the most beloved citizen of the Golden State. His endorsement of Senator Sterling provided the political foundation for Gene's primary bid.

Chet had been interviewed by MSNBC, CNN, Bloomberg, CBS, and most other prominent news outlets. He'd been on *Maddow*, *Morning Joe*, and *Don Lemon*; Don's personal cell was saved in his phone, as were some pics from an epic night in SoHo. The interviews were lovefests. Mika Brzezinski called him the "boy genius" and "the most important mind in America." All appearances had been essentially advertisements for Emerald Solaria and its potential to rid the world of fossil fuels while still meeting the West's energy needs.

Tonight, Chet found himself at the Fox News studios in New York for a segment on *The O'Hanlon Effect*. He had been invited numerous times but always declined, assuming he wouldn't get a fair hearing. Besides, there was no way he could turn the yahoos and octogenarians comprising Fox's audience to his way of thinking unless he convinced them it was in the Bible.

But here he was, as a friend of Gene Sterling's. The media speculation on whether the California senator would remain in the race was eclipsed only by predictions about his wife's demise. Countless segments on every outlet ran chyrons stating some variation of CAN SENATOR STERLING GO ON? or SENATOR

STERLING QUESTIONING HIS BID FOR THE PRESIDENCY AMID TRAGEDY. Gene had confided to Chet he would remain in the democratic primary race and asked the star to make the rounds on the political shows to promote his announcement, scheduled the following evening. Having received assurances from O'Hanlon's people that there would be no questions regarding the validity of climate change, Chet reluctantly acquiesced. The subject matter would remain within the spectrum of Katherine's kidnapping and how the senator was holding up.

The Fox News Channel staff retrieving coffee and copy for the on-air talent noticed Chet as he came off the elevator. Abundant gazes scanned the environmental phenom as he strolled to the main studio where he was slated for the "A" block of Bill O'Hanlon's top-rated opinion show. Before he entered the green room, a young, nervous intern notified Chet that Mr. O'Hanlon wished to greet him in his office. O'Hanlon's office door opened, and a disheveled, twenty-something blonde scurried out while pulling her tight skirt down to mid-thigh; Bill O'Hanlon appeared at the doorframe. The imposing sixty-three-year-old, six-foot-four-inch king of prime-time cable scream-fests looked flushed as an Irishman on St. Patrick's Day.

"Chet." Bill smiled. "Welcome to Fox News." His handshake was unnecessarily firm. "Come into my office. We've got a few minutes. Need anything?"

"Some warm tea maybe?"

"Kelli, get Mr. Bateman some warm tea, and, please, shut the door—we wish to visit."

Chet didn't want a private chat with the conservative windbag but sat on the couch in the large corner office nonetheless. The room was decorated with prominently displayed television awards interspersed with photos of O'Hanlon mugging with famous people. "I was pleased to hear you finally accepted our invite."

"Yes, my pleasure," lied Chet.

"How is the senator? Awful what he's gone through."

"I spoke to him when he got out of the hospital. He seems overwhelmed. His voice was emotionless, like he was shutting down or in a state of shock. This conversation is off the record, right?"

"Yeah. Of course, this is between you and I. It's hard to imagine what it must have been like to see his wife taken like that. When you see him again, please give him my sympathy."

"I will."

"Did you know his wife?"

"I knew Kat very well. She was a very sweet woman. Strong willed, motivated, and easy to talk to. I can barely wrap my mind around this." Chet's eyes watered.

"She was a beautiful woman," Bill intoned. The intern girl entered and bent over to place hot tea on the coffee table, allowing Bill to stare at her cleavage. Chet thanked her as the host patted her butt. "You're the best, Kelli." With an uneasy smile, she left. "Sounds like the cops don't have much," Bill continued.

"Doesn't sound like it. Just the car."

"The percentages aren't on her side. Haven't heard anything about a ransom letter or demand of some kind. I started at a local station in Charlotte. If a kidnapper takes a woman from the crime scene, they don't typically make it. Wonder why they only roughed up Gene, given this was obviously politically motivated."

"Yeah. I don't know. Things have gotten so polarized. With all the heated rhetoric on social media poisoning the discourse, this sort of thing was bound to happen."

"It has gotten bad, hasn't it?"

"You do realize, Bill, that the guys who did this were likely your viewers? Your constant bullshit about conspiracies against the president and villanization of his opponents could easily have driven these morons to do this."

Initially taken aback, Bill's face creased into an amused grin.

"You're young, Chet. You think this is new? This back-and-forth jostling for political narratives? I've been at this for forty years. Started in a midsize market in shit-fuck nowhere. I give my audience my angle, the angle they want. I'm sorry about your friend's wife, but you millennials think the earth began spinning the day you were born. Fact is, this game began a long time before you and will keep being played long after you die."

"This isn't a game. Literally, the fate of the planet is at stake. You promote this hate and don't give two shits about the human cost. You support a racist, homophobe president."

Bill was tickled by the young man's passion.

"Save your energy for your next Netflix special; save it for *your* audience. And save the lazy labeling your side loves to employ to avoid serious debate. I've seen it all." Bill's condescension grated on Chet, who wore his annoyance. "We're more alike than you want to admit. I give my audience what they want, and you give yours what they want. You tell them what they want to hear, just as I do."

"Don't compare me to you. The planet is dying, and you apologize for its murderers."

"You're very dramatic. No wonder those lefties love you. Look, your folks made it clear to mine you want to focus on the plight of your friend and steer clear of politics. We can bring these disagreements on air if you like." Irritated, Chet thought about it before shaking his head in declination. "Very well," continued Bill, trying to lighten things. "Let's focus on tonight's show. We have you leading off."

"Gene's making an announcement tomorrow that he's remaining in the race for the democratic nomination. That's off the record, mind you. I'm here to get the word out that an announcement will be made tomorrow."

"I see. You know I'll press you to reveal what you know, what Gene has said to you."

"I'll deny any knowledge of what he plans to announce tomorrow—only that I'm aware he has made a decision."

"I get it. I'll also ask you about your thoughts on President Frum."

"You know I can't stand him. He's an absolute disgrace. He's a piece-of-shit raci—"

"Racist?" finished Bill. "You guys are so predictable."

"I'd be happy to discuss politics with you," said Chet defensively. "It's just not the right time, under the circumstances."

"Fair enough. Anyhow, we'll begin with your update on the senator's condition and how he's holding up. But at some point I'll ask you about Ronald Frum, and you can lay into him. Some emotion in the 'A' block gets the audience's blood up. Besides, we've been teasing your appearance for the past twenty-four hours."

"Are you going to let me talk or just yell over me when I try to answer your questions? You always talk over folks you disagree with."

"Depends. I know my audience, and if I think we're losing them, I may raise my voice and push back on you. You'll get your message out, but I need ratings."

"I get it."

"So, how is Taylor Swift in the sack?"

Chet chuckled at Bill's bluntness.

"Only met her a couple times; we never dated. Our publicists thought it would benefit us both to insinuate we're seeing one another. She hadn't been in the tabloids for a while, and I'm still expanding my fanbase."

"I wondered if that was the case. She's a pretty girl, but I imagine she's a dead lay."

Chet had no response.

"You're from Manhattan, right?"

"Yes. Upper East Side. I heard you're a Long Island guy? You don't have an accent."

"I grew up in Westchester. Born in East Meadow and lived there till I was two."

"You always make it sound like you grew up there."

"Once again, audience, kid. My viewers are more a blue-collar, Long Island crowd than Westchester types."

"Did you actually write all those American history books?" It always bothered Chet how Bill O'Hanlon pumped out a book a year. It just didn't seem plausible for a busy television host to have time to extensively research and complete a history book annually. His latest, *John Jay: The Forgotten American*, sat atop the *New York Times* best-seller list for three months.

"Of course I wrote them all." A greedy smile crossed Bill's face. "My name is on the cover, isn't it?" Chet knew he was full of shit, and Bill knew he knew he was full of shit. "Well, we got to get to the studio." They both stood. "Nice meeting you, Chet. If it gets a little hot on air, just remember, it's my job."

"No worries. But before we go on set, you might want to take care of that," Chet advised, pointing to Bill's gaping zipper fly.

"Has it been open this whole time?"

Chet nodded and thought of those poor interns. Bill zipped up and grabbed his sport coat before opening the door. Kelli was there, phone in hand. "Chet, get a quick photo with me." Before the environmentalist realized what was happening, Bill leaned over with a grin, and Kelli took the pic. Chet didn't have time to register what transpired, much less smile. "Kelli's got a nice rack, am I right, Chet? See you on set."

☉ ☉ ☉

"Why are you calling me to run tags?" asked Freddie on the other end of the line. "This is the second time in two days."

"Well, I can't very well run database checks myself," James reasoned, sitting on his motel room twin bed.

"No shit. You're suspended, which begs the question: why the hell do you need to be running tags?" James heard radio traffic in the background; his friend—a Secret Service Uniformed Division officer—was on duty in his patrol car. "Wait, these tags aren't related to some dude seeing your wife, are they? I don't want to get involved in your personal mess. Last thing I need is getting called on the carpet after you kick some dude's ass."

"No, it's got nothing to do with Audrey. Hold on, is she seeing someone?" For several seconds, the phone remained silent. James had known Freddie for years and knew he was incapable of deceit. "Trust me, Freddie, this has nothing to do with Audrey. I'm simply putting a few things together. I've got a lot of time on my hands. Is she seeing someone?"

"Tasha told me she met a guy a couple times," sighed Freddie. Freddie's wife was tight with Audrey and remained a supportive friend after the split. "It's nothing serious, Jim. She was just tired of being alone at the house every night."

"Did they meet for drinks?"

"Once for lunch, then drinks."

"Were they out late?"

"Tasha said they just had a couple drinks. Look, I can't do this. She speaks to Audrey in confidence, and I don't want to get involved." When the Brazil incident revealed James's infidelity, Tasha went into a murderous rage. James knew she hated him and suspected she'd encouraged Audrey to move on. "If it makes you feel better, they weren't out late. This whole process is hard on Audrey. I told you how I can hear her crying on the phone when she and Tasha talk."

James's chest contracted with heartache. He wanted to be pissed, to feel betrayed, but knew he could only blame his lustful selfishness.

"What does he do?"

"Dammit, I'm not doing this."

"Come on, Freddie, is he some lawyer?"

"Not doing this, Jim. Don't get all worked up. It's been hard on her."

"I fucked this up so bad, Freddie."

"You really did."

"I'm such an idiot. I've created so many casualties."

"Maybe you should move on. You seeing anyone?"

"Well, there is this one girl, but it's nothing serious." James glanced at Kat. "I'm still hoping Audrey finds it in her heart to forgive me. I'm trying to change my life. I'm in a bit of a transition phase."

"I'd love to chat with you, but I'm at work. You needed a tag run?"

"Yeah."

"And what's this about again?"

"I'm looking into some things. I can tell you more sometime over beers. I've been keeping myself busy. I hope this is the last time I'll need your help."

"Save your false promises. Go with it."

"Virginia, A-E-R-7-3-1."

He heard Freddie typing on his mobile data terminal.

"Looks like a rental. A BMW belonging to Luxury Rent-A-Car time out of Reagan National."

"Thanks, Freddie. Next I see you, I'm buying." James sat up in his bed.

"No problem. Later." They hung up.

"Everything alright?" asked Kat from her bed.

"I suppose. As alright as things have ever been the past few months."

"I take it your wife is testing the waters?" She sipped merlot from a plastic, hotel-room cup.

"That was one of my best buds. He's a UD officer—great guy. His wife is tight with Audrey. She apparently met some dude for lunch and drinks." James's typical swagger had evaporated. Kat poured some wine into another plastic cup and slid it across the nightstand toward him on the adjacent bed. "I got nobody to blame but myself," he admitted.

"I know. It's all your fault. If I were Audrey, I'd have fucked six guys by now."

Eyebrows raised, James gave her a quizzical look.

"You're in no position to judge," she surmised smugly. James sucked down the cupful of wine, then placed it on the nightstand. Dutifully, Kat refilled it.

"I want to be mad at Audrey for going out with some guy, and I want to be mad at you for your candor, but mostly I want to blame someone other than myself."

"I would ask why you did it, but there's no need. Most men are sluts. Sexual pleasure is just a part of it, though. I think it feeds something reptilian in your brains."

"You may be onto something, princess." Kat rolled her eyes. "No, really, I think you've identified something very real about men. When a woman sleeps with you, she accepts you. It's validation, of sorts."

"So you paid a Brazilian hooker out of some deep-seated need for approval? Color me skeptical."

"I wasn't implying feminine validation was the sole motivator, just that there's something to it. I was hammered. I didn't plan on taking some gal back to my room. From what I remember, she was very attractive in the sultry way Latin women have perfected."

"She is hot," Kat seconded.

"How do you know?"

"When you went to get the wine, there was a commercial. TMZ has an exclusive interview with her airing tomorrow—I think her name was Rafaela. She looked really good. Even had a bikini shot of her."

"I'll be sure not to tune in." He shook his head and took a sip. "You know, I was just informed my wife is nearing the fellatio phase of a relationship; you'd think you could have withheld the bit about my jilted hooker's upcoming exclusive."

"Sorry, seemed important. Was the sex any good?"

"Sloppy drunk sex. I wasn't all that with it. I'd say it was just okay."

"You had whiskey dick, didn't you?"

"I didn't have whiskey dick. Everything worked fine. I was just shitfaced."

"Yeah, you had whiskey dick." Her relaxed expression and playful grin indicated the wine was doing its job.

"I'm glad this gives you so much amusement."

"I'm sorry. Today was very stressful. I needed some levity. I do have one question, though, and you don't have to answer this: why didn't you just pay the girl?"

"It's all a bit fuzzy, as you can imagine. But after I—well, you know—hooked up with her, I paid her a hundred bucks in American money. That's what I thought we had agreed to, but she insisted it was twice that amount. Mind you, her English was terrible. Hell, for all I know, she was right, and I was wrong. But as drunk as I was, I thought she was pulling a fast one on me, which pissed me off. When I threw her out, she began yelling and beating on the door. It all spiraled from there. I was stupid. For a hundred more dollars, I could have kept my family and my job."

"I think you're missing the lesson here: don't pay for hookers."

"I learned the only thing worse than paying a hooker is not paying a hooker. I'm such a fool." For several minutes they sat in silence in their respective beds. Turning on the television, he flipped it to Fox News before muting it. The fuzzy video stills of a gray car still dominated the coverage of Kat's kidnapping.

"You're not a fool, Jimmy. I was just thinking of what we saw today, at the house. I was so scared. I tried to hide it, but inside

I was, like, full-fledged freaking out, and you were so calm and under control."

"You sound surprised."

"Well, no offense, but having known you for a couple days now, there was little evidence of you being a guy with things under control."

"Fair enough. It's funny, when it comes to a crisis, everything kind of comes into focus. Always been that way for me. I remember responding to 'shots fired' calls, and I never got amped. Things just slowed down as I processed my environment."

"I was so nervous about seeing my kidnappers. When we arrived at the house, I wanted to run away."

"I noticed. You don't have much of a poker face, princess." James smirked and refilled their cups.

"And instead, I see a dead body. Are you sure he was murdered?"

"One hundred percent."

"At the time I didn't appreciate it—again, I was freaking out—but being with you, the way you kept it together and knew exactly what to do. You make me feel safe. I can see why you're such a good Secret Service agent." With a nod, he looked at her, the lamplight illuminating her appreciative smile. With her cropped, dyed hair and hoodie, she looked cute as a sorority girl. "Why would someone want to kill him?" she wondered.

"Not sure yet, but the tag on your kidnappers' car was registered to that address, and two days later some dude is murdered there. That's no coincidence."

"So, how does any of this help us?"

"Hard to tell, but there's a lot we don't know. We need to find out who these JC and Cornhole characters are. As I see it, without them, it's your word against your husband's. Those bozos are the only folks who can corroborate his involvement. We identify them and go to the authorities."

"And how do we identify them?"

"Working on that."

Kat suddenly leaned forward. "Jim, unmute the TV. That's Gene's good friend Chet. What the hell is he doing on this creep's show?" Looking up, James turned up the volume. A lean young man was being interviewed on *The O'Hanlon Effect*.

"How is Senator Sterling holding up after enduring such a horrific incident?" asked the host.

"As good as can be expected, Bill," answered the well-groomed phenom. *"Gene loves Kat very much and believes she is alive and will be found. As you saw the other day, evidenced by the lumps and bruises on his face, Senator Sterling was assaulted violently while trying to save his wife from these monsters. When I spoke to him, he sounded shocked and expressed disbelief that people could do this to him for apparently political reasons."*

"Did he relay to you anything that the authorities haven't shared regarding the investigation into Katherine's whereabouts? As you know, remarkably little has been revealed to the public, which is thirsting for information," queried Bill.

"He didn't, but he did express his confidence in the FBI investigators. He knows they are the best in the world at what they do."

"Senator Sterling has been a strong supporter of green energy and shares many, if not all, your convictions when it comes to what measures should be taken to meet our energy needs while reducing carbon pollution. As you know, I'm skeptical of such measures, but you have stumped for him,

and Emerald Solaria has forked over loads of cash to the Sterling Foundation and supportive super PACs. How is it that you, an entrepreneur in your thirties, and a sixty-something senator have become so close? Because from the outside, it appears he's most interested in you for your ability to raise funds and court young voters."

Chet smiled tensely, appearing to regret agreeing to be on this shithead's show. *"Our friendship is so much more than politics or what favors we can do for each other. It's about the very survival of our planet. Fact is, when you are teamed up with a fellow green warrior in this struggle, it makes little difference what generation you belong to. Many in his generation would gladly hand the problem of climate change to mine."*

Chet's voice grew indignant.

"Gene was attacked by 'Bring Back My America' conservatives who wish to turn back the clock to a time of racial segregation when coal plants billowed carcinogens into the atmosphere with impunity. Katherine is a victim of the hateful rhetoric of this obnoxious, vengeful president—"

"Now, now, Chet, that's not fair to President Frum, who's got nothing to do with this incident," interrupted Bill.

"Not true at all. Your network has pandered to this president and spewed misinformation, and now Katherine has likely been killed by his followers. He may as well have ordered these goons to do this—"

"This is completely irresponsible, and you're out of line,"

interrupted Bill once again. *"No matter your nutty political views, you have no right to come on my program and impugn the president and throw this garbage out there—"*

James re-muted the television. "I can't take anymore."

"Why does he always interrupt people?" asked Kat. "Look at them. They're just yelling at one another."

"These segments are so short, and they need to lock viewers in. Once that Chet kid called out Frum and his supporters, you knew Bill would jump on it. He just says what his viewership would say if they made thirty million a year and sat in his seat. Same thing on CNN. They all pander."

"He makes thirty mil?"

"Interested? I think he's divorced."

"I'm done with rich sixty-year-olds."

"Well, if you change your mind, I hear he's an ass-hound. I'm sure he'd take a shine to you." She smiled sardonically, her eyes still wine dreamy. "So, you know this Chet kid? And where have I heard that name before?"

"He had a huge Netflix special about climate change. Gene reached out to him when he rose to stardom and saw the numbers Chet's show was pulling. We hit it off immediately. He's such a good person—maybe a bit naive, but I always enjoyed being around him. When you live with Gene, it's refreshing to be around people who actually care about others. And Chet's no lightweight; he knows what he's talking about. He's the spokesman for Emerald Solaria, a green-energy company producing solar panels."

"Emerald Solaria? Weird, that name sounds really familiar, but I can't remember why."

"Chet has helped Gene tremendously with securing donations and bringing aboard young voters."

"Sounds to me he was being used by a senator eyeing a

presidential bid," James opined as he Googled Chet on his phone. "Holy shit, he hooked up with Taylor Swift. I like this kid."

"You are consistent. And that's complete BS. It was a PR stunt."

"According to Wikipedia, Chet pulled in fifteen million last year. Being a climate prophet is a better living than I thought."

"I took a selfie with him at one of the foundation events, and it had something like two hundred thousand likes on Instagram. I never had anything like that many likes."

"Popular guy."

"Gene loves him. And you're right: he said on more than one occasion that Chet's support might be the key to him winning the presidency."

"Judging by his passion, the love is mutual," James observed, looking at the television where the heated, partisan exchange ended with Chet stripping his mic and storming off the set. "Look at Bill. It's all he can do to disguise his glee at this ratings bonanza."

"I've never seen Chet like that. I wish I could tell him the man he is defending is the biggest lying lowlife on the planet."

"We should get some rest," said James, turning off the TV. "Want me to come over there?"

"To my bed?" she asked with incredulity. He nodded in the affirmative. "I've known you two days."

"In fairness, they were two *long* days."

"Yeah, I know. You don't need to remind me. You might recall I was kidnapped and saw my first dead body."

"This feels like a no."

"Jim, it's a hard no. Stop being creepy. I'm going to brush my teeth." Getting out of bed, she went to the bathroom. Even though she was wearing men's gym shorts, he liked how she looked. She emerged with a toothbrush in her gums and murmured through the frothy toothpaste, "What are we going to do tomorrow?"

"Head back to DC. See what we can find out about the driver of that Beamer we saw leaving the dead guy's house." She went back into the bathroom and he heard her rinse and spit.

"And how you going to do that?" she asked, reemerging and plopping on her bed.

"I . . . have . . . a . . . plan," answered James, doing his best Adam West Batman impression.

"I may be wrong about you. You just might be an idiot." Smiling, she lay sideways, propped up on an elbow. "Can I trust you?"

"You're the one who said you felt safe with me. And don't start getting all flirty. I'm horny enough as it is."

"Flirty?"

"You're propped up on your elbow with your mussed hair looking all inviting."

She shook her head and smiled. "You're ridiculous. Let's get to bed. If the past few days are any indication, tomorrow is going to be eventful."

"These are the kinds of things that just seem to happen to me. You get used to it, I promise." He grinned and clicked off the lamp.

"Goodnight, Jimmy."

"Goodnight, princess."

CHAPTER 6

Friday, March 4

"Chicken Little" Chet Bateman embarrassed himself on
Bill O'Hanlon's show last night. He keeps yelling "the sky is
falling" so Shifty Gene and the Dems can take your money.
The sky is not falling but the stock market is rising LIKE
NEVER BEFORE! Bill stood strong and schooled Chicken
Little on reality #BBMA #ReelectFrum - @PresidentFrum

THE PRILOSEC was not enough to quell Gary's indigestion.
The president's chief of staff had cut out greasy foods, especially
Mexican, of which he was particularly fond. But even with a
consistent routine of unseasoned chicken breast and edamame,
early-morning presidential tweets could rouse a tsunami of
stomach acid.

Gary Boxterman's Secret Service detail was accustomed to
the chief departing his Potomac, Maryland, home at 5:30 each
morning so as to arrive at the West Wing by six. As the two-
Suburban motorcade cruised along the Clara Barton Parkway,
Gary would—with apprehension—check his Twitter feed. On a
good morning, there was little more than political bickering and
one-upmanship among the pundits and journalists comprising
the Washington Twitterverse. Then there were mornings like this
when the president of the United States joined the noisy morass by
calling out a guest on his favorite cable news show.

Gary understood the president's motivation. Republicans
loathed Bateman as a naive job killer selling doomsday prophecies
to his millennial audience. What he could not understand was why
his boss labeled a senator as "shifty" when said senator was the

planet's most sympathetic victim of politically motivated violence. Gary rubbed his eyes and felt the burn of acid reflux surge to neck level. He noticed his detail leader—a thirty-something former Marine named Alex—eyeing him through the rearview mirror. Alex always gauged Gary's moods in the morning. He was professional in the disciplined manner of military men, pleasant and sociable but never prying.

"Looks like our commander in chief is posting this morning, Alex," Gary commented.

"Yes, sir, I saw that."

"Going to be another interesting day."

"They always are, sir." Gary enjoyed the way his detail leader said "sir." Alex was from Alabama where the term "sir" was embedded in their DNA and stated without a bit of irony.

"Did you watch *O'Hanlon* last night?"

"I did, sir. My wife likes when Bill goes after the Libs. Myself, I think it's all rather silly."

"I side with you, Al." Gary scrolled through news articles on his iPad. "It didn't sit well with me. I mean, Bateman went on Bill's show to speak about the horrific kidnapping of his friend's wife, but they end up bickering about petty political differences. Just awful."

"Your boss seemed to like it, sir."

"The exchange exuded all the nuance and refined argument cherished by our president. And dutifully, CNN are clutching their pearls over his remarks this morning. I'm old enough to remember when the news wasn't simply media types reacting to the presidential Twitter feed."

"We live in odd times, sir."

"We certainly do." The remainder of the motorcade ride was silent. Gary continued to scan articles, feeling out the day. Besides the faux outrage at the presidential tweet, the news centered around Senator Sterling's upcoming announcement. With the *New York Times*, MSNBC, and CNN opinion-makers predicting the senator would remain in the race, it was clear Senator Sterling's PR team had leaked his intentions to their preferred outlets.

Most days, Gary felt besieged by a media that assumed only ill motives on the part of the president and anyone associated with his administration. The chief of staff and his team circled the wagons on innumerable occasions against well-coordinated TV and Twitter barrages. Younger members complained about the inequitable coverage, much as Gary had when he was a twenty-something staffer during Bush forty-one's tenure. But he understood the dynamic hadn't changed in thirty years. Sure, now there were hundreds of media outlets and the internet, but writers and opinion mongers were the same graduates of elite universities who were landing staff positions on Capitol Hill and in the West Wing in the late '80s. Now, as then, the young staffers were building social and professional networks to segue into consulting or media gigs. The only difference was today they sought the cherished blue check mark and fished for social media followers with snarky, partisan Twitter posts.

Gary's boss gave the media praetorians ample fodder for self-righteous indignation. The media anointed heroes and villains, and it was clear Senator Sterling was the hero of the current narrative. Gary had thought the senator a conniving political animal but was moved by his display of strength and humanity under such circumstances. Meanwhile, the media's villain was tweeting from the Treaty Room on the second floor of the Executive Mansion.

The dark Suburbans turned off Seventeenth Street and passed through the White House checkpoints, entering West Executive Avenue and stopping alongside the West Wing's white awning. Alex opened Gary's door. Returning the iPad to his satchel, Gary stepped out.

"Al, can you please shoot me in the head?"

The Secret Service agent grinned.

"I think that would be a violation of my oath, sir."

"Today is going to suck."

"We have a saying in the Service, sir. 'Embrace the suck.'"

"I may steal that. Who's working this afternoon?"

"Jason, sir."

Gary winced. Jason Prickman was an assistant detail leader who never stopped talking, incapable of gauging the chief of staff's mood when he wished to be left to his thoughts.

"I'll tell him to shut the fuck up, sir." Alex smiled.

"Just do it nicely."

"I will, sir."

◉ ◉ ◉

Sitting at his desk, Gary sipped his third cup of coffee as he reviewed the president's daily schedule. It was light: executive time until 10:30, an executive order signing in the Oval for first responders, lunch with congressional leaders, a roundtable with energy sector CEOs in the Cabinet Room, to include a press pool spray, and various meetings in the afternoon, along with a visit from the president of Kosovo. The scheduling office informed him of an impromptu morning meeting with Senator Bratton of West Virginia. Gary did not trust Senator Bratton, sensing ulterior motives behind his every action. This wasn't rare in DC but seemed particularly pronounced in Joe Bratton.

Shortly after nine o'clock—*Fox & Friends* having concluded— President Frum made his way back down the colonnade bordering the Rose Garden. His secretary had called him fifteen minutes prior about the arrival of Senator Bratton, but he was preoccupied with a news story regarding a teacher in Nebraska who continued to recite the Pledge of Allegiance in defiance of school policy. President Frum finally meandered back and entered his secretary's office.

"Jennifer, you can have Joe come in now. And hit Gary up as well. I'd like him here." Frum disappeared into the Oval Office.

"Good morning, Joe." The senator's fleshy face—Scots-Irish features reddened from drink—creased with a wide smile. "You look like a man about to be paroled," the president joked, referencing the expiration of Joe's term come fall.

"It's been a good run, Mr. President. But the time has come to move on."

"My offer stands. Take a little vacation over the holidays, and by spring I want you to be my energy secretary." When elected, Frum had wanted to appoint Joe to the seat but was pressured by advisors to select the former governor of Ohio, Steve Terry, who was a strong campaign supporter.

"Thank you for that, Mr. President. Steve's a good man—"

"Steve's a pussy," Frum interrupted. "A goddamn Indian claims some burial ground in the middle of butt-fucking nowhere, and he balks on the pipeline, saying his hands are tied by a fifty-year-old ordinance. Can you believe that? Thousands of potential jobs in swing states, and he's pussy-footing around some obscure law. I know you, Joe. You're a fighter. I know something about fighters. You were with me early on, and I'll never forget that. You're not the type to get pushed around by these left-wing pussies."

"Thank you, sir. You are the right man for these times. The only one who knows the plight of the working man." Joe dutifully stroked Frum's ego, having little choice but to support the president considering West Virginians' approval for him hovered above 70 percent.

The chief of staff entered from the secretary's office.

"Gary, finally, where have you been?" The towering president, rotund senator, and diminutive chief of staff made for an odd-looking threesome.

"The meetings ran long. Good morning, Senator," said Gary as he shook Joe's hand. "How's Gene doing?"

"As good as can be expected."

"Is he staying in?" Frum cut to the chase.

"Yes. He's going to keep running. Of course, it's going to be difficult to campaign with the tumult in his life. The worry and strain must be unbearable. When I speak with him, his distraction is apparent. I certainly couldn't do it."

"He won't need to campaign. He's on TV more than me," noted Frum. "The networks are going to get him elected. What did he tell you?"

"He feels this is what Kat would want," Joe said.

"Boy, that line's going to do him some good. He's going to milk this for all it's worth. It practically writes itself," Frum mused. "If he wins the nomination, we have a big problem." The president's political instincts were always firing—calculating every incident to predict its effect on public sentiment. "Hell, if you watch CNN, you would think I broke into the goddamn house myself and took that lady." All present knew it was true, and Gary suspected that along with his morning presidential tweets, the coverage over the next week would further dampen his numbers. Television screens were already filled with pundits' dour summations of the sitting president's culpability in the kidnapping.

"I would still prefer to run against Gene than Cassandra," Joe asserted.

"How do you figure?" Frum settled behind the Resolute desk.

"Gene is a friend, and I don't wish to speak ill of him. But truth is, he's never really experienced a difficult, bare-knuckled campaign. He's an environmentalist, big-government liberal from California. Hell, he looks like he came out of central casting to play a senator. He's so cemented in California politics the elections are a mere formality. If he's nominated, you can take him. Of that I feel certain."

"Is there something you know that we don't?" asked Gary, sensing once again that Joe was privy to more than he let on.

"I've been in this game a long time. I've seen senators come and go. Gene will get the upper hand now, since the tragedy is fresh in the public's mind. That will fade. Americans have very short memories. Hell, the governor of Virginia was caught wearing blackface, and folks have already forgotten. If we have to run in the general against Cassandra, the press will canonize her. She touches all the intersectional erogenous zones for the Libs. The press won't let a liberal, gay woman of color go unelected. They'll break every rule to get her the White House. They won't do the same for Gene. We need Gene to win this primary, and his tragic loss may be just what he needs to garner the votes to pull it off."

"I think you're right," noted Frum. "Gene has been on the Hill for decades and produced nothing. He enriches himself by peddling influence year after year with nothing to show for it. That's how I'd go after him. We paint him as the poster boy for Washington corruption—something I couldn't do to Cassandra."

Joe nodded his approval.

"Have you met that green-energy kid? Chet Bateman?" asked Frum in an abrupt change of topic, last night's *O'Hanlon Show* still on his mind.

"Um, yeah, I have once," Joe said. "He met Gene and I for dinner at the Monocle after testifying about clean air legislation. Kat was there as well. She and Chet were pretty tight."

"What did you think of him?" asked Frum.

"He's charismatic and passionate, which is how he's generated such a following. At first, he was pretty cold toward me but after a couple glasses of wine opened up a bit. Frankly, he struck me as all hat, no cattle. Just a repeater of talking points and platitudes sermonizing to those already converted."

"He seems like an asshole," President Frum said.

"He is a huge supporter of Gene's—both politically and financially."

"If Gene were to become president, he'd get that kid's green-energy outfit a shit ton of subsidies," noted Frum.

"And they would regulate the hell out of coal," Joe added as Gary stood by, folder in hand.

"We should regulate the fuck out of the green-energy sector," Frum said.

"Sir, deregulation has been a huge win for us. We would be handing them a bat to beat us over the head with if we dive into focused, punitive regulations," Gary observed, hoping to temper his boss's impulses.

"If we show some patience, Mr. President, and if Gene indeed pulls off the nomination, we'll have an opportunity to discredit Bateman and his outfit, Emerald Solaria, which would do great harm to Gene's chances of beating you," stated Joe.

"What makes you so certain?" asked the president.

"Like I said before, I've been at this game a long time. I do what needs to be done. I have inside information on the company that would discredit the whole venture. But it's a card too early to play. We need Gene to win the Democratic nomination. Public sympathy over his wife will help, but you need to bash him as well. They'll pull the lever for him just to spite you."

"I don't think that's appropriate or wise," Gary interjected.

"Hold on, Gary," President Frum began. "From what I'm hearing, Joe, you think I should go after Gene to rally Democrat voters to him and secure him the nomination. And you have dirt on this Bateman kid's company?"

"We can hamstring the Sterling campaign in a way we can't Congresswoman Lightner," Joe confirmed.

"You'd do that to your friend?" asked Frum.

"To win? Yes."

"I'd hate to see how you treat your enemies." The president smiled. "You're a tough son of a bitch; that's why I like you. You're going to make a great energy secretary."

⊙ ⊙ ⊙

"I ordered three hash browns," announced JC after rummaging through the McDonald's sack. The skeletal gal behind the counter stared blankly at him. "Did you hear me? I'm missin' a hash brown."

"It'll be just a minute," relayed the anorexic-thin, sleepy-eyed teen as she turned toward the fryer. Though irritated, JC wished Frank and Jerry a good morning as they joined him. Like clockwork, by seven the friends were in their booth at the Harpersburg McDonald's. Both men retired and grossly overweight, Jerry wore his "Vietnam Veteran" ball cap while Frank sported bib overalls as they drank coffee and shared news.

"How are y'all this morning?" asked JC.

"We's fine." Jerry smiled. "You find any work yet? I remember you sayin' you had a job lined up."

"Did a job the other day. Just somethin' temporary to help earn a few bucks."

"Think it'll lead to somethin' steady?" asked Frank.

"Naw, I doubt it."

"You hear about that Donovan fella?" asked Jerry. "John, I think his name was."

"You mean Squinty? Naw, ain't heard nothing, but I haven't talked to him since last week. Did he get arrested?"

"Naw. Worse. They found him dead."

"Dead? You can't be serious?" said JC in disbelief.

"Sir, your hash brown is ready," droned the teen as she placed a small sack on the counter that JC ignored.

"Afraid so. Last night the Waterman gal went by to check on him, and he was dead. We asked Officer Corbin this morning about it, and he was pretty tight-lipped but mentioned they suspected foul play," Jerry shared. "So, you know him?"

"I knew him. We'd drink beer together and whatnot." A disturbed expression crossed JC's face.

"Well, my condolences. I wasn't aware you was tight."

"I got to go. Thanks for the news," said JC, preoccupied. Grabbing his hash brown sack and making for the door, he heard Jerry console him—"Sorry for your loss, JC"—as he exited. During the short drive home, he mulled the news of Squinty's murder. Was he stabbed, strangled, shot? He held out hope it was simply a heart attack. Squinty drank like a fish and was by no means the picture of health, but the timing made JC uneasy. Even with the windows cracked on this cool morning, he began to sweat. He turned Cornhole's Dodge Dakota into the driveway.

"I've got your breakfast, my love," he greeted Myrtle and placed the sacks and mega-sized Coke cup on the nightstand. "How'd you sleep?"

"Not well," replied Myrtle. "My legs are sore."

"Maybe later I can help you move them a bit. That's worked in the past."

"I'd like that—oh good, you remembered my third hash brown."

"I'll let you eat. I'll be outside, my love, if you need anything." He kissed her forehead.

"Is everything okay, sweetie? You're acting funny."

"Everything's fine, my love."

"Did that job go well for you, dear?" she mumbled as biscuit crumbs cascaded from her mouth.

"Yes, honey." He forced a smile through his scraggly beard. "Got me a hundred bucks; straight cash."

"That's good. Damn, this hash brown is hot."

"Fresh, just for you, my love. I'm gonna go check on Corn." JC grabbed a beer from the fridge and headed out the back door of the trailer. When leaving for McDonald's, he'd noticed Cornhole and Chrissy weren't in the living room. His suspicions were confirmed as he approached the gray Saturn and found both passed out in the front seats, which were reclined as far as possible.

Opening the driver's door, he momentarily feared he'd lost a second friend before detecting Cornhole's shallow breathing. Powdered remnants of crushed Oxy dotted the middle console between them. He pulled Cornhole out of the car, causing the skinny bastard to grab his lower back and shriek in pain, but the commotion didn't disturb Chrissy's slumber in the least.

"Goddammit, what the hell's wrong with you?" yelled Corn as he came to, his eyes adjusting to the morning sunlight.

"Squinty's dead," JC declared. Cornhole's eyes widened beneath his stringy mane.

"What? He can't be. We just saw him last week," slurred Corn, still affected by the previous night's binge.

"I know. But he is. I can assure you that."

Cornhole shook his head. Disbelief morphed into grief as his eyes welled up.

"What are you cryin' for? He was my friend."

"He was my friend too."

"You two bitched at each other constantly."

"They was spirited debates, that's all. I loved Squinty."

"He pulled a knife on you, Corn. What kind of friend does that?"

"It was my fault. We was arguing cars again, and I said Kevin Harvick was an overrated pussy. We was both piss drunk. He was doggin' on Jimmie Johnson, and I just can't stand by idly when someone tarnishes the good name of Jimmie Johnson. It just got out of hand, but we was friends."

"Alright, never mind. Don't matter anyhow," JC conceded.

"Dear God, I can't believe this. Do you know what happened?"

Cornhole leaned against the car, still tearing up and wincing with back pain.

"They think somebody killed him."

"Who would kill Squinty? He didn't have no enemies. And what makes you think he was killed?"

"Those old guys at McDonald's said they heard it from that asshole cop Corbin."

"He's a prick."

"Agreed, but he wouldn't tell those old fellas that if it weren't true. Said Lisa Waterman found him."

"My God, JC, this is just awful."

"You thinkin' what I'm thinkin'?" Judging by Cornhole's empty, drugged stare, it was clear his friend wasn't thinking at all. "Buddy, we got to run. We got to get the fuck out of here," JC hissed.

"Where we goin' to go? I don't want to go nowhere. I want to stay here with Chrissy."

"Corn, do you think it's a coincidence Squinty ended up dead days after we took that gal off the senator's hands? Think about it. Squint refers us to Oscar, we do the job, he pays us, and now Squint is dead."

"But we ain't killed nobody."

"Goddammit, don't you get it? We're in deep shit."

"Well, ain't no need to raise your voice."

"Remember when we took those pictures of Chrissy over there in the grass?"

"Yeah. You know, afterward, I found two ticks on her."

"Focus, Corn. Jesus, you need to get off that Oxy."

"Don't worry about me. I'll be just fine."

"Listen to me; focus for just a minute. The only guys who knew we were in on this was Squinty and Oscar. Ever since those old fellas told me he was dead, I've been thinkin': why would Oscar want him dead?"

"You think Oscar done this?"

"I don't know." JC downed the rest of his beer to ease his nerves. "I'm getting' another beer."

"Get me one too."

Returning with two Natural Lights, JC said, "Oscar knew that gal was the wife of a senator. He never told Squinty or us."

"How come, you think?"

"Don't know. I suppose he thought we'd back out if we knew the gal was married to a big-time senator."

"I wouldn't have done it had I known," Cornhole confirmed. "Wonder how that gal got out of our trunk. Where do you think she went?"

"I don't know where she disappeared to, but the whole damn country is looking for her, and we are the last fellas to see her. Goddammit, if you hadn't dozed off, we wouldn't be in this mess."

"I wish you'd quit rubbin' it in my face."

"Well, it's true."

"How you suppose Squinty knew that foreign fella?" asked Cornhole.

"I don't think he did. It sounded to me like someone introduced him, but he was always tight lipped about it. My point is, if Oscar wants to completely get rid of any connection to that gal's kidnapping, he's got to take us out—just like he did Squinty. I thought he might kill me when I met him to get paid, but the Lord must've protected me."

"Oscar don't know where we live," Cornhole said.

"We don't know what Squinty told him. But that Oscar fella scares the devil out of me. He's smart. I think we got ourselves in a mighty bad pickle, and it's best we make each other scarce."

The gravity of their predicament had their brains churning as they sipped their beers in ponderous silence. JC stared off in thought as Cornhole watched a hawk floating above the wooded hills.

"I have an idea," began Cornhole. "Maybe we could go to the

TV people? Tell them the senator was behind it all and that we never killed his wife. We could tell the authorities about Oscar—the whole kit and caboodle. You know, just come clean."

JC wanted to dismiss Cornhole's idea out of hand, the usual protocol when Corn shared a thought. But for a brief time, he mulled the option of going to the press. Sure, they'd open themselves up to federal charges, but the G-men would want them to turn state's evidence and get a plea deal.

"That's not the worst idea you ever had, but we don't know where the gal is," JC observed.

"We just be honest and tell 'em she got away."

"And what makes you think they'll believe us? We don't even know if she's alive. Hell, Oscar may have found her and done what we was supposed to do. It's too risky. We got to get out of here," JC said.

"You think she's dead?"

"Maybe. I don't know. Nobody seems to know, but everybody's lookin' for her. Alive or dead, she's somewhere, and that's the rub; we don't know where that gal is. We go to the feds, the one thing they'll want from us is where she is, and we can't answer that," reasoned JC. Cornhole slammed the rest of his beer.

"I got kin in Kentucky. You might be right. Maybe best Chrissy and I skedaddle up there for a while, let things blow over. What you goin' to do?"

"Don't right know. I got Myrtle to worry about. Don't want her in the middle of this. Like I said, Corn, we got ourselves in one hell of a pickle."

☉ ☉ ☉

"Not having a phone absolutely sucks," announced Kat from the passenger seat. Such utterances increased in frequency each day she had been sans iPhone. Behind the wheel of his pickup, James found her frustrated expression adorable but subdued his smirk lest he annoy her more. "I can't remember being off Instagram and Twitter for four days."

"We all have our crosses to bear."

"Could you not be a smart-ass today? I'm not in the mood."

"You got a blue check mark," noted James, holding up his phone with her Instagram page on display. "And seventy-five thousand followers? Not bad."

"I'm validated on Twitter as well. I don't think another senator's wife can say that," she stated with pride.

"My guess is the pics from Cabo account for a good portion of your followers," he observed as he tapped a bikini-clad photo of her lounging on a beach.

"That was this past Christmas. Gene took the picture."

"You look happy as hell."

"Looks can be deceiving."

James read the caption posted beneath the picture. "'Find the light inside you and release it to the world. The world, in turn, will reveal its love-light to you and gift you the energy of love eternal, of blissful harmony.' That's some deep shit, Kat."

"Is that what I wrote?" James showed her the screen. "I guess I did. Jesus, so stupid."

"How come hot chicks feel the need to include an inspirational quote when they post bikini shots?"

"I think it's a defense mechanism, so we don't feel like jerk-off material. Anyhow, that whole week was awful. I'd rather not be reminded of it."

"Well, you look lovely. With your smiling faces, you wouldn't know you weren't having a good time," James observed as he viewed a pic of a candlelight dinner. "Nice dress."

"The resort was beautiful. But don't let the pictures fool you.

We bitched at each other the entire trip. I was happiest when he left me alone at the pool. He'd run off to the bar, which suited me fine. To be honest, I think he was texting someone else—he was distant, even by his standards."

"You mean to tell me Instagram isn't an accurate depiction of someone's life?"

"Remember what I said about being a smart-ass?"

"It's too bad you didn't have a good time. What a waste. You look really good in this one."

"Oh, I gave him some obligatory sex. We were on vacation, after all. And yes, Instagram is complete phony bullshit."

"What filter is that?" asked James, still eyeing the bikini pic.

"Looks like Amaro or maybe Reyes—why?"

"Just looks good; when did you get those upgrades?"

"Upgrades?"

"The tit job. You were smart. You didn't go with the bigger-is-better myth. They fit your frame well."

"Thanks. I've had them for, like, eight years," she admitted as James swerved the truck to avoid a passing car. "Jesus, keep your eyes on the road."

"Sorry." James put the phone down. "They just look good as hell."

"Don't start getting creepy on me again. Not in the mood for it," she warned with a playful smile.

"Got it. No smartassery and no creepy."

Retrieving a pen and spiral notebook from the floorboard, Kat began jotting notes, periodically stopping to look out the window in thought.

"What are you writing?" asked James. "Noticed you scribbling something last night. Wondered why you asked me to buy a notebook when I made my Wal-Mart run."

"It's kind of a journal," she revealed.

"Helping sort your thoughts?"

"That and I thought it was a good idea to record this stuff in real time rather than try to recall all this craziness. It's hard for me to wrap my brain around how my face is everywhere, but it is, and that means publishers will want rights to my story. When this all sorts itself out, people are going to want to know what happened."

"Good idea. You seem to dig having your face on tv twenty-four seven."

"I tried to make it in acting, so yeah, the thought of strangers knowing who I am is a good feeling, but I'd like people to admire me for something other than my looks. Back home, I was the pretty girl, and that was about it. I'd like to add 'author' to my bio."

"Where is home again?"

"Lamoni, Iowa. I was Miss Corn Cob for two years. First in history to win back-to-back crowns."

"Impressive. I imagine you were popular with the boys of Lamoni."

"I was, but I came to find out LA was full of prettier girls with the same plan. The whole thing is cliché, I know, but I really wanted it bad. I wanted my name on a movie poster."

"How far did you get with the Hollywood thing?"

"I was an extra in a few films. I finally got a talking part in an indie flick. Their vision was to do a throwback eighties college movie."

"Really? What was it?"

"*Life is Beachy*. It was a kind of zany comedy about teenagers partying, making out and stuff. I was Drunk Girl number two."

"Did they bring Drunk Girl number two back for *Life is Beachy: The Sequel*?"

"You said no more smartassery." She shook her head. "At the time, I thought it was my breakthrough, but looking back, they just wanted a hot girl in a bikini willing to do nude scenes."

"Nude scenes?"

"Yeah, my character is drunk, obviously, and hooks up with Biff Nordlinger. I say, 'Do you like what you see?' as I take off my bikini top. It's stupid, I know. I was young."

"Sounds riveting."

"I don't know why I share things with you. Can't you turn it off? Anyhow, once Gene and I became a thing, I stopped going to auditions. I had pretty much given up on acting already. I was depressed, doing coke, hooking up with strangers, and thinking of going back to Lamoni. Then I meet this ambitious congressman who has his shit together, and suddenly his ambitions became my ambitions. It was wrong, but hell, I was doing everything wrong at the time, so what did it matter? To Gene's credit, he straightened me out. I kicked my bad habits and helped him run for the Senate. I was forced to be a lady and take on the role of a senator's wife."

"Until you found yourself bound and gagged in a car trunk."

"Not really the storybook ending, is it? My life is a mess."

"Well, we have that in common. If you haven't noticed, my life is in a bit of upheaval."

"I noticed."

"Once you land a seven-figure deal, get a ghost writer, and sell your book, you'll be back on track. Just make sure you hold off on your first sit-down interview. Get the networks into a bidding war."

"That's a good idea, Jimmy."

He smirked. "You don't have to sound so surprised."

"That flirty smirk isn't as powerful as you think it is. You go to it a lot."

"It's always worked pretty well for me."

"It's too much and super obvious you're trying to be sexy."

"Or, just maybe, you're too much of a life-worn cynic to enjoy a flirty smirk." He flashed it again.

"You're ridiculous."

"Stop flirting with me, princess."

Continuing on I-66, they turned through the Crystal City section of Arlington. Kat scribbled notes until the pickup pulled into the daily parking garage at the Reagan Airport terminal. She put down the notebook. "Okay, Agent Jimmy, what was your plan again? And explain to me why I'm dressed like this." During his trip to Wal-Mart the previous evening, James had purchased khakis, a pair of Merrell-style hiking shoes, and a small, button-down collared shirt for her to wear. Dressed in much the same manner, James wore an untucked, plaid shirt and Columbia khakis.

"I need you to look like an agent."

"Female agents wear this? Poor ladies."

"It's practical. The shirt covers our duty weapon, and before you say it, I know you're not armed, but these car rental people meet a lot of federal agents, and this is how we dress. You got to look the part. It ain't all fancy suits and colorful ties."

"So, we're impersonating federal agents? What could go wrong?" she quipped.

"Need I remind you, I am an agent. I'm just suspended. It just so happens my superiors failed to confiscate my old badge. Now, I don't need you to say anything. Just look official, and here . . ." He pulled a navy-blue ball cap from behind his seat with a gold Secret Service star adorning the front. "Put this on. We don't need someone ID-ing you."

"This thing's filthy. How long have you had it?" Kat eyed the well-worn lid with disgust.

"Just wear it. When we get there, I'm going to tell them we're doing an identity theft investigation and request the car renter's information."

"Can they give you that?"

"I suppose they could be assholes and ask for a subpoena or something, but I think we'll be fine. It's hardly sensitive inform-ation."

"Okay, let's do this."

Being a Friday, Reagan was busy with the Acela-corridor crowd: affluent lawyers, power brokers, pundits, lobbyists, and lawmakers departing for New York, Boston, or wherever their real home existed. "Why are you walking like that?" asked James.

"What do you mean?"

"You keep looking back and forth like you're scanning for threats, and your arms are bowed out. You trying to walk like a dude?"

"Isn't this what you guys do? You know, look for vulnerabilities and things that are out of place?"

"You're walking like a gym bro. Stop that. And no, we don't scan around like some futuristic, cyborg deathbot."

Kat shrugged and relaxed her gait.

"You could be a little softer with your critique."

"I'm sure you were a great Drunk Girl number two; you're just a crappy Secret Service agent."

"I'm not even going to look at you. I know you have that stupid smirk on your face."

They approached the Luxury Car Rental desk. A not unattractive woman in her mid-twenties who could stand to lose thirty pounds greeted them. Her name tag read, GWYN.

"Good afternoon, Gwyn. I'm Special Agent Ford, and this is Special Agent Moore with the US Secret Service. How are you today?" James asked. To Kat, his tone was pleasant to the point of cheesy. Gwyn asked how she could help him while James flashed his badge. "We are investigating a financial crimes case—identity theft, to be specific."

"You guys investigate stuff? I thought you just protected the president."

"We do a lot of things, Gwyn. Financial crimes are another area we cover, and a BMW registered to Luxury was seen during a surveillance the other day. We believe the person may have used the vehicle in the commission of a crime."

"Really? Must be pretty serious if you guys are on it." It was clear Gwyn enjoyed looking at James.

"It is very serious." James smirked, which nauseated Kat but seemed to work on Gwyn. "A lot of victims of fraud, but if you can share some information with us, it could go a long way to closing this case."

"Sure, I can help you out. Do you have a tag number?" James flashed a side-eye glance to Kat, smirk still on his face; she sighed and shook her head.

"I do. It's Virginia, A-E-R-7-3-1, and I really do appreciate you helping us out with this. This will be a big boost to us. Did you ever think about applying to the Secret Service, Gwyn?"

"Me? Oh, no. I mean, I don't think they would take me." James suspected she was right. "This was Tuesday, right?" she asked. James answered in the affirmative. "It shows an Oscar Reese had it until Wednesday."

"Ah, Oscar. I knew it. The clock is ticking on this bastard—pardon my language. But this is a big break for us. Do you have a copy of Oscar's driver's license?" Gwyn provided a photocopy of the license and appeared very happy to have pleased Agent Ford. "We are going to nab this perp." Kat had been around James enough to know he was hamming it up, though Gwyn seemed unaware of his glibness. "Can you print that information for me please? Thank you." James threw Gwyn another smirk for good measure. "One other thing, Gwyn: are your vehicles equipped with OnStar?"

"They are, Agent Ford. Why?" she asked, her eyes starry with lust.

"That may be of assistance to us. But we'll subpoena those records. You ready to go, Agent Moore? Thank you again, Gwyn." He shook her hand.

"Agent Ford, do you have a business card?"

"You know, sorry, I'm all out. As busy as I've been, I seem to be handing them away at a record pace."

"Would you be interested in meeting me for drinks some-time?" Gwyn was making a ballsy play for the handsome fed.

"Thanks, Gwyn. That would normally be a very tempting offer; however, Agent Moore and I are currently engaged in an extraordinarily passionate love affair. It's difficult to juggle the sexual and the professional, but we manage." An awkward expression of stunned uncertainty crossed the clerk's face. James and Kat turned and walked away.

"You're a terrible human being, Jimmy."

CHAPTER 7

"Senator, what keeps you going? How have you managed to persevere amid this horrific ordeal and continue your pursuit of the Democratic nomination?" asked the reporter. *"What keeps me going is knowing Katherine would not give up this fight, not so long as the threat to our way of life resides in the White House,"* answered Senator Sterling. *"She knew, acutely, the need to bring back integrity to the Oval Office. Like I said, I plan to visit Kansas tomorrow, and truth be told, I don't know how I can do it without her."*

"**Y**OU'VE GOT to be kidding me," Kat snorted at the television coverage of Senator Sterling's announcement before swallowing a dram of her vodka tonic. "I've been dead for a few days and he's already going back out on the campaign trail? How about mourning your wife?"

"You sound hurt," observed James from the other end of the couch.

"Wouldn't you be? And these questions, could they be any more softball?"

"Well, he is a Democrat. And not only a Democrat but one whose wife was kidnapped three days ago."

"He is good at this, isn't he?"

"Politics is a performance."

"I want that bastard to hurt, Jimmy. Can't you just kill him? Aren't you a trained killer?" James sighed and sipped his Sam Adams. The vodka was going to her head. "Seriously, what do we do next?"

"Our main focus is to identify those rednecks your husband hired."

"So, trained investigator, what do we do?"

"I have some ideas, but most are a bit of a reach. I keep going back to that dead guy, Donovan."

"What about him?"

"Just wondering where he fits in all of this. Why was he killed? You know the saying 'Dead men tell no tales?' My hunch is he knew something and was offed for it."

"Could have been a coincidence. We know nothing about the guy," Kat stated.

"It's no coincidence. I checked out the *Harpersburg Gazette* website. If their story is accurate, this guy served time in prison for aggravated burglary, which makes me wonder what kind of company he was keeping. They're reporting it as a homicide, and more noteworthy is that nothing was taken from the house."

"Where are you going with this, Sherlock?"

"His funeral is Tuesday. What if one of your boys showed up to pay their respects? If we sat on it, maybe you could identify them."

"That's your plan? Staking out a funeral?" Kat took another sip.

"I don't know how else we can get info on your boys."

"Could you quit calling them my boys? They were going to kill me, so I really don't wish to take ownership of them."

"Fair enough, but I need information and have little means of obtaining it."

"You sound frustrated, Jimmy." She posed an exaggerated sad face.

"You've had too much to drink. And that face annoys me, stop."

"No need to get snippy."

"Got another thought, but it's also a Hail Mary."

"Fire away."

"Remember last night when we saw your friend Chet on *The O'Hanlon Effect* and you told me about his venture Emerald Solaria?"

"Yeah. So?"

"I remember where I'd heard of that company before. There's a friend of mine who I haven't spoken to for some time who had a pet project she'd been toying with for a while. She's a journalist and was doing some prying into Emerald Solaria and was convinced the company was a front to defraud investors. She thought it could be a career maker for her."

"That sounds implausible, but okay. What does this have to do with my kidnapping?"

"If your husband is willing to stage your kidnapping and have you killed for the nomination, he'd have no qualms taking ill-gotten gains for the same purpose. If Chet is involved in some grand fraud scheme, I'd be curious to know how that fits into Gene's plans."

"You've been so good to me that I want to give you the benefit of the doubt. But this is beyond a Hail Mary; this is wishing-upon-a-star nonsense. Besides, Chet would never defraud anyone. He's a good person."

"You mean he would never *knowingly* defraud anyone," James corrected. "It's just a thought. It can't hurt to see what my friend has. Besides, she also has sources in the intelligence and law enforcement communities. I'd like to run the name Oscar Reese by her to see if there's information on Mr. Donovan's possible murderer."

"It feels like you're reaching."

"Of course I am. What more do I have to go on?"

"You're more fun when you're buzzed. Can you freshen my drink?" she asked. He obliged with a light pour. Returning from the kitchenette, he looked to the ceiling as several squeaks emanated from the century-old floor above.

"Brian must be back," James declared as he handed Kat her weak vodka tonic.

"Who's Brian?"

"The kid who lives in the rowhouse above me. He was a staffer in the last administration. We became friends after working on several POTUS trips together. When my life went to shit, he let me crash down here. He travels a lot, but it sounds like he's back from Europe."

"How does he afford this place?"

"His folks own it. His dad was in Congress awhile. Once they moved back to Michigan, Brian moved in. He's a lobbyist now and the only person who hasn't treated me like I have the plague."

"I see." Kat took a sip. "This drink is terrible. You did this on purpose."

"I did."

"If I want to get drunk, it's my prerogative. I'm supposed to be dead."

"Fair point. Next drink, I'll go heavy and see how far I can lower your inhibitions."

"I'm not going to screw you, Jimmy."

"You've made that clear."

"Though you are cute in your own fucked-up way," she admitted with a drunken smile.

"Charming, but back to the problem at hand. I'll reach out to my reporter friend and see what information she can glean for us."

"Worth a shot, I guess." She shrugged.

"This is all contingent on if she'll even talk to me."

"Why wouldn't she talk to you?"

He gave her a discomfited look.

"You didn't."

"I did."

"You are a complete slut. Did she know you were married?"

"Yeah. She was a young staffer helping out with presidential site advances. Looking back, it's hard to imagine how it happened."

"I can imagine. A young girl smitten with some older Secret Service guy; this isn't complicated. You're not a good person,

Jimmy. Jesus Christ, what else am I going to find out about you? Anything you wish to share?"

"Not presently, no. You don't have to pile on. I'm well aware I'm fucked up."

"What makes you think she wouldn't talk to you now?"

"During our affair I may have insinuated something to the effect that I was separated from my wife or something." He winced. Kat's look of utter disgust exacerbated his guilty unease. "I was a different person then. I was a mess—I get it. I'm sure Carly got a kick out of seeing my name run through the mud on every newscast this week."

"Her name's Carly?"

"Yeah, Greek gal, and pretty damn hot. By the way, need I remind you Senator Sterling was married when you two got together? Little Miss Judgy."

"Okay, enough, I'll lay off. We're both sluts," she slurred. "This drink really sucks." She looked into her glass as if angry at it.

"Fingers crossed she'll meet me. Maybe the news shitting on me this week creates enough schadenfreude within her to rub it in my face. If she'll meet, I can bring her around, I think."

"Sounds like a long shot."

"Princess, this whole damn thing is a long shot." Someone rapped on the door. "That's got to be Brian. Here, put this on and wear it low." He tossed her the Nationals cap as he went to the door.

"I'm back," Brian announced, dressed fashionably in skinny jeans and an expensive sweater matching his salon-styled brown hair. Kat was thrown. Having spent several days with James, she had assumed his circle of male friends consisted of meat-headed gym bros and back-slapping frat-boy types. "Santorini was to die for, and, my God, what has happened back here? Everything's gone crazy?" It was then Brian noticed Kat on the couch. "Oh, I'm sorry. I didn't realize you had company."

"It's not what you think," James clarified. "This is, umm, Moore. Agent Moore, Amy Moore. We work together. She just came over to support me. I'm guessing you saw they released my name to the press this week."

"I did. It's such bullshit. I don't see why it's necessary for the public to know your name. Amy, it's nice to meet you." Brian walked toward her, his hand extended with a welcoming smile. Kat stood and stumbled, using the coffee table for balance. Judging by his expression, Brian detected her boozy breath. "You must be a very good friend," he noted.

"You were saying Santorini was nice," James interjected as he made his way to the kitchenette.

"Easily one of the most glorious places we've ever visited. Dante even said I'd outdone myself with this trip. The weather was splendid, the wine magnificent, and we did an overnight dinner on a yacht I cannot stop thinking about."

Handing Brian a beer, James sat. "Brian's quite the world traveler. He and his boyfriend spend more time out of country than in DC. If you're on Instagram, you should give them a follow. How many followers you got now?"

"Twenty-two thousand, but who's counting? But what the hell happened here? I saw Senator Sterling's wife was kidnapped. The European networks were all over it as well—just awful."

"I haven't been following it that closely," said James.

"I can't imagine what she's going through," Kat chimed in.

"It's sad to say, but I'm not surprised," Brian observed. "It really was just a matter of time before one of those 'Bring Back My America' morons did something like this. When those rednecks elected a Nazi like Frum, you knew they would be emboldened. I'm surprised they haven't rounded up people like me and thrown us into work camps."

"Well, you'll likely be overseas when he signs the order," quipped James.

"That's not funny, but you're probably right. We are thinking of going to Chile in six weeks. We're spending this weekend in New York. So, Amy, how long have you known James?"

"Oh, I don't know. You know Jimmy; whether you've known him four days or four years, he's just good old Jimmy," she slurred, the creased ball cap brim shawling her eyes. Brian nodded, looking confused. "We worked together on the president's squad," she continued. The befuddled look on Brian's face grew more pronounced. Having been a presidential staffer, he knew nobody called the presidential detail a squad.

"Jimmy? I've never heard anyone call you Jimmy."

"Amy is a special case. We were on the detail together," James clarified. "She worked with me in Ops. She's had a few drinks tonight, but that's why we have Uber."

"Well, as I was saying, I could have told you this would happen when Frum was elected—or should I say, when he stole the election," Brian said. "I just hope they locate the senator's wife. My dad said he met her once. I told him how beautiful she was, and he said she was even prettier in person. Such a waste."

A wide smile emerged from beneath Kat's hat brim.

"At least it got my nonsense out of the headlines," James sighed.

"You're such a cynic, but yes, it pushed you to the second page," Brian granted. James smirked.

"There's that smirk again. What the hell is that?" said Kat in a drunken garble. "Brian, does he do that all the time? It's constant."

"He does it a lot. I kind of like it, myself," Brian said. "I find it rather sexy." James leaned back and shot Kat a large, self-satisfied grin.

☉ ☉ ☉

Oleg Yumashev never understood how the United States of America managed to become the supreme world power. America's economy and culture dominated the globe, which was hard to countenance considering it was populated by Americans: a smiling species with childlike naivety, always seeking the approval of strangers. Their popular music spoke of an insatiable need for love and validation. It occurred to him few Americans would survive a year in Russia, and he'd happily disentangle himself from this vapid race, but as the CEO of a multinational energy conglomerate, he wasn't afforded the luxury of disassociating with Americans—worse, he had to play their political games.

Oleg was good at manipulating the game, which was not lost on Moscow. Capital Elements ran several oil, coal, and natural gas companies amounting to assets of over $50 billion. These entities spanned from Russia to South America, including numerous investments in the United States. Over several years—while many Americans, fearing climate change, demonized the fossil fuel industry—Capital Elements took one hit after another; mounting regulations dampened energy sector profits. Now Capital Elements' bottom line and Oleg's bank account were both back in the black as regulations died at the end of Frum's pen. President Frum slapped sanctions on many Russian interests due to political pressure, but through gamesmanship and connections, Oleg's remained untouched.

Oleg had invited Senator Joe Bratton over for drinks and discussion, but Joe was savvier than his fellow citizens and declined. The fifty-six-year-old CEO sensed the longtime Washington mover knew private conversations in a Russian oligarch's home were anything but private. Instead, they met at a bar, the Scotsman, off First Street on Capitol Hill. The owner wasn't Scottish but Belarusian, and Oleg was privy to the fact that the establishment was outfitted with eavesdropping countermeasures, courtesy of the Russian government.

Being a Friday evening, the restaurant was full. Unbeknownst to the patrons, a small room attached to the manager's office contained two well-trained men monitoring clandestine screening devices at the entrances. Surveillance cameras were strategically placed to surveil all occupants, and it was impossible to get a signal on smartphones, inducing patrons to log onto the free Wi-Fi and thereby grant Russian intelligence access to their data.

Furnished to resemble an Edinburgh public house, the Scotsman's dimly lit mahogany bar and brass fixtures on paneled walls allowed clueless clientele to enjoy their cocktails in mirthful ignorance. Oleg waited in his booth near the bar where a half dozen tipsy young men were laughing at unfunny jokes. Judging by their lean frames, unearned air of importance, and European-style skinny trousers, the fresh-faced, callous-free band were young Capitol Hill staffers.

Sipping scotch, Oleg observed their frivolity and wondered how such imbeciles—surely the offspring of elite families—had outlasted the Soviet Union.

Sergei, Oleg's body man, conferred with one of the other bodyguards seated at a small table before coming to his boss's booth. "Mr. Yumashev, the senator is here," the square-jawed henchman announced.

"And he's clean?"

"He is."

Oleg took his last swallow of scotch and moved through the crowd to a rear room. Senator Joe Bratton sat alone at a long table made up for a party of fourteen. It was the first time he'd seen Oleg since the kidnapping. He stood to greet him, but the Russian made clear he was in no mood for pleasantries and motioned the ungainly senator to take his seat. Unlike the West Virginian's poorly fitted, outdated suit, Oleg's stylish, tailored duds hugged his frame.

The Russian sat across from the senator.

"Is something wrong?" asked Joe, looking apprehensive. They were the only ones in the private room save for a waiter in one corner and Sergei in another. Oleg's small, close-set eyes beneath his receding salt-and-pepper hair peered at his decades-long associate.

"I am displeased, senator. The help you provided did not prove up to the task." The Russian's accent heightened the rebuke's menace.

"Displeased? You've been watching the news. Gene's wife is dead. You're not happy with the result?"

"I met with Oscar the other day. He showed me a picture. It was a woman facedown in the grass."

"And? What's the problem?"

Oleg motioned to the waiter, who came over and poured each a scotch. "Perhaps you were not listening closely. She was *facedown*, senator. How the hell do I know if the woman is Gene's wife? It could have been any skinny bitch."

"Who else could it be? And if it wasn't her, where the hell else do you think she is?" Joe asked, incredulous. "There hasn't been a hint of her since Tuesday, even with the entire country looking for her."

"I should have had my men do the job," Oleg insisted, then took a sip.

"We've gone over this. If y'all were connected to the murder of the senator's wife after all that transpired last election, you could kiss Frum's chances at reelection goodbye. And if you were implicated in any way, I don't need to tell you how loud the outcry for sanctions against your interests would be."

"My men would have done it right."

"It was done fine. Relax, she's out of the picture. And, even better, there's no way to connect the hired help to us. Even if the cops track them down, they'll only find two loser ex-cons with zero credibility. We're safe." Joe had acquired the minions through the second cousin of a Charleston lawyer he was acquainted with. They were guided by a man Oleg introduced as Oscar. Every possible scenario had been analyzed. But Oleg was not a man who left matters to chance, and he expected a certain level of professionalism, so Joe's assurances did little to assuage his anxiety. In silence, the Russian stared into his tumbler.

"Senator Sterling," Oleg began, "he will beat this congresswoman? What's her name? Lightner?"

"He will now. The loss of his wife has deeply moved our country. Thus far, he's played his cards beautifully. Matter of fact, tonight he announces he's staying in the race."

Oleg motioned to the waiter to turn on the television mounted in the corner.

"Americans are sentimental people. They show much emotion and make many decisions based on feelings, but your people also wish to appear inclusive and open minded, whether they are or not. What if they decide to nominate Ms. Lightner?"

"That would be a problem," Joe admitted. "My fear if she wins the nomination is how Frum campaigns against her. He's a bully, as you know, and if he comes out attacking a Black, lesbian Air Force veteran, it would be a bad look. Suburban women are already looking for someone, anyone, to vote for besides Frum, and Congresswoman Lightner fits the bill." The muted television displayed Gene behind a podium. "Gene hasn't wavered since Kat was taken out. He's all in."

"I was going to ask you that, Senator. He's not regretting any of this?"

"Not a smidgeon. He wants nothing more than the presidency, and besides, he's got that young sidepiece he's been hitting."

"Oh yes, her." Oleg smiled as he took a sip. "And you feel his infidelity along with René's handiwork will be enough to derail a Sterling candidacy against Frum in the general?" Oleg was referring to René Beauvoir, an international investor and renowned playboy credited with founding the promising green-energy company Emerald Solaria. In reality, René was little more than a sophisticated ass-hound under Russian control as Capital Elements propped up

Emerald Solaria with a complex collection of monies from various overseas companies to appease hopeful investors. The venture was nothing more than a mirage of environmental promises attached to the face of its clueless, charismatic spokesperson, Chet Bateman.

"After his nomination, we give it a few weeks. Then we leak stories about Emerald Solaria's fraud. A month later, we release information on the mass corruption in Gene's foundation with all the foreign—especially Russian—money he's accepted. Granted, the press will mostly give him a pass, being that he's a Democrat, but there's one thing they won't ignore and Americans won't abide by, and that's the news he was cheating on his murdered wife for years. They'll replay footage of him sobbing over her death as they share the lurid details of his affair. We tie it all together with insinuations her murder was somehow connected to his infidelity. With Kat still missing and her abduction unsolved, the public will buy it hook, line, and sinker."

A rare smile crossed Oleg's face.

"And the president has given you assurances you'll get the energy secretary position?"

"He can't stand the weak-kneed guy he's got there now. It's a done deal," Joe guaranteed.

"The president does not know of these events?"

"No clue. And he doesn't need to as it really doesn't affect him. We're the ones who need him in office. To your earlier point, if Gene's president, you can say goodbye to the coal industry and hello to massive restrictions on oil production."

Capital Elements had bought up large swaths of active coal mining operations in West Virginia with one of its subsidiaries and expanded its oil drilling rights off the Gulf Coast with another. Both companies were based out of Colombia and puppets of CE. Not coincidentally, Joe owned numerous shares in these ventures and, minus any government meddling, stood to gain enormous profits.

It was clear Oleg liked what he was hearing. With Joe running interference inside the White House, his corporations could siphon energy from the United States while inflating his bottom line.

"You have known Senator Sterling for many, many years," noted Oleg.

Joe nodded. "He's one of my best friends."

"And yet you double-cross him like this?"

"This is Washington. It produces nothing, but nothing is produced without its blessing. It's the most powerful city on the planet, and if you step in this arena, it's understood, friendships are ancillary."

"You are a cold one, Senator Bratton. You should have been Russian."

CHAPTER 8

Saturday, March 5

THE FBI GUYS were dismissive when an early-morning call came in from a small West Virginia police department regarding a vehicle resembling the vague description released to the public. Two individuals were found deceased inside from apparent drug overdoses. Metro detective sergeant Derek Roland's federal counterparts shrugged it off and happily passed the run-out to him.

The investigation—now four days old—had revealed little about the circumstances surrounding Katherine Sterling's kidnapping. Innumerable interviews revealed a married couple's fraying relationship but no signs of violence. The senator had a penchant for sending suggestive texts to his female staffers, and Katherine was not above flirting with personal trainers, but nothing out of the ordinary for married, middle-aged Washingtonians. Derek knew, statistically, if a wife went missing, the spouse was the likely suspect. Unfortunately, the spouse in this case was vying for the Democratic presidential nomination in a country divided amid the most vitriolic, cutthroat political atmosphere in recent memory.

Derek knew this lead was likely a waste of time, but the drive through the Shenandoah into West Virginia on a cold, overcast morning was worth it. Passing through the hills and over the rivers, he looked at the houses perched on the mountainsides and imagined sitting up there, sipping coffee and taking in the sunrise.

When he retired, he wanted a place with a view—get out of Prince George's County and fill his retinas with nothing but hills, trees, and flowing rivers.

Those same eyes had seen sucking chest wounds, dead children, and women begging him not to arrest their husbands after those very husbands had dotted their eyes during domestic disputes. His eyes had seen enough ugly. They needed more beauty while he was still on this earth. With his child support payments, he could only afford a small cabin, but that would suffice. Driving through the mountains and into Harpersburg, he vowed to make it happen. This would be his final case, whether he found Mrs. Sterling or not; it was time to move on.

Derek pulled into the parking lot of an abandoned concrete plant where two marked squad cars and an unmarked Impala surrounded a gray Saturn, the doors open. He pulled on his overcoat as he stepped into the crisp mountain air. Two young, uniformed officers stood by as a middle-aged man in wrinkled khakis and an all-weather North Face jacket took photos of the Saturn's open trunk.

"Good morning, gentlemen," Derek greeted them, displaying his wallet badge. "What do we have here?"

"Morning, sir. I'm Officer Stanley, and this is Officer McGuiness."

"Nice to meet you both. I'm Sergeant Roland; call me Derek. I'm with the Metro task force. What do you got?" He shook their hands.

"We're Chip and Sean, sir. A couple hours ago I was patrolling the area and saw this car parked by itself with the engine running. I rolled up on it and noticed two occupants. I lit it up, but they didn't move. I kind of figured by then I had a couple of passed-out drunks or another overdose. I opened the passenger door, and it was clear they'd been dead a few hours. All the paraphernalia is there—looks like heroin."

Derek nodded and moved to the passenger door. Leaning into

the car, he saw a thin White female wearing a Redskins hoodie leaned back in the passenger seat next to the driver: a tall, lean White male with long, scraggly hair, wearing woodland camo. The male's arm was still tied off, with spoons, lighters, and syringes littering the middle console.

Chip introduced the older man. "Derek, this is Detective Bob Hume."

"Good morning, Bob." Derek shook the hand of Harpersburg's lone detective. Flushed in the manner of a heavy drinker, Bob's full face was highlighted by good-natured eyes.

"Thanks for coming out. I imagine you guys are gettin' swamped with calls about every gray Sedan in the mid-Atlantic," Bob twanged with a smile. "Frankly, I didn't expect y'all to send anyone our way. The guy I talked to didn't seem much interested."

"The boys are buried with leads," Derek agreed.

"I can't imagine. Like everyone else, I've been following it. Gettin' any traction?"

"It's going to be a tough one. As of now, not much. We're inundated, but most of the tips are dead ends. You know how these things go."

"I hope I ain't wastin' your time."

"Well, tell me what you got, and I'll tell you if you're wasting my time," Derek said with a grin. "Let's start with the deceased. Know them?"

"We do. The female is Christine Updike, thirty-eight. Her license shows she's from up near Morgantown, but we have her on record locally for drug charges and petty theft. In the driver's seat is Dustin De Plours, forty-seven. He's a local. I'm a few years older than him, but we went to high school together. Pretty typical guy. Worked at a warehouse, was injured on the job, well liked by folks. He had his habits, folks knew he was a dopehead, but he was harmless. Don't know nobody who's got a bad thing to say about Cornhole."

"Cornhole?" Derek said, eyebrows raised.

"That's what folks called him. He was a member of a cornhole team for several years, and they was pretty good. Dustin here was the best among 'em. His friends started callin' him Cornhole on account of his ability. It caught on, and pretty soon anyone who knew him called him Cornhole."

"What the hell is cornhole? A game?" asked Derek.

"Yep. You throw bean bags toward a slanted board with a hole in it. The aim is to get it in the hole or land 'em on the board."

"You mean bags. It's called bags."

"Never heard of no game of bags."

"We play bags before 'Skins games. We tailgate and throw bags," said Derek.

"We call it cornhole in West Virginia."

Derek smiled; he liked the name Cornhole better and would try it on his Southeast DC buddies. Bob continued, "We also located nearly seven thousand dollars cash in the glove box. Don't know how Cornhole would have acquired that sum of money, but they must have used some of it to splurge on heroin."

"I see," began Derek. "So we have two dead of apparent overdoses."

"Yes sir, and I wouldn't be surprised if the autopsy revealed fentanyl. We've had a bad spate of fentanyl deaths. Last month, the county had over two dozen."

Derek nodded. Before the Sterling kidnapping, news of rural White folks dying of opioid use was a big story. "But that's not why I called you here," continued Bob as he motioned him to the open trunk. Looking inside, Derek saw a half-empty spool of duct tape tucked in the back next to a tangled mess of thin, white nylon rope—the kind one might use to tie up a small boat.

"Is that hair?" asked Derek as he leaned low, observing the trunk's interior, his nose inches from the lining.

"It is, and the length suggests it likely belongs to a female. Looks like the color could match Mrs. Sterling's," Bob confirmed. Derek's pulse quickened. What he assumed was—other than the pleasant drive—a waste of time was taking on unexpected significance. Bob and the young cops observed Derek silently as he surveyed the trunk and the car's interior. Being gloveless, he was mindful not to touch anything. Derek returned to the trunk and read the vehicle plates: TBIRD.

"T-bird? Know who this returns to?"

"Yes sir, a John Donovan residing on Schafer's Mill Road outside of town."

"Is the car stolen?"

"I doubt it. Squinty and Cornhole were familiar. It wasn't unusual to see Cornhole or JC driving it," answered Bob.

"Squinty?"

"John Donovan went by Squinty. If you knew him, it was an apt moniker."

"And here I thought street names were a hood thing. Who's JC?"

"Cornhole's best friend. An ex-con, but he's been out of trouble for a long time now. He was also friendly with Squinty."

"I see."

"Detective, Squinty was found dead in his home less than two days ago. Looks like a homicide," Bob declared gravely.

Derek raised his eyebrows. "We think this guy"—he pointed to the car—"Cornhole did it?"

"The county's investigating it, but they don't have a suspect. They think Squinty was asphyxiated. He was a big, strong fella, and Cornhole couldn't have taken him out that way, even if he had reason to. Besides being a skinny fella, Cornhole had a bum back. The autopsy is scheduled for this morning."

Putting his hands on his hips, Derek sighed and contemplated how the pieces fit. If the hair proved to be Katherine's, then this was the suspect vehicle. Was one suspect dead in the car and another killed in his house? And why?

"Once the bodies are removed," declared Derek, "we seal the car. I'll order a flatbed to remove it."

"Sir," said young Chip meekly, "we haven't fully processed the vehicle."

"Officer Stanley, you needn't worry. This vehicle will be thoroughly processed, but in a sterile location. The Bureau's going to process it, and I'll be sure you receive their findings," Derek assured him. Looking awestruck, it seemed to dawn on the young officer he may have a hand in solving the most infamous kidnapping since the Lindbergh baby.

"Nice work, Officer." Derek smiled. "You did real good." He shook his hand.

Turning away, Derek called the task force: "Kevin, it's Derek . . . yeah, I've been out here for a while; this thing has promise. Found human hair, duct tape, and rope in the trunk. The car comes back to a guy possibly murdered a couple days back. I've got some names and information and plan to have the vehicle sealed and delivered to a garage before it rains. Can you fire up an evidence response team? Good, I can call you back with more details in a bit . . . What's that? No, I don't think I have enough to call a press conference just yet."

◉ ◉ ◉

Her college friend Emily told her she was a fool to meet him—he was a creepy old dude incapable of keeping his dick in his pants. One couldn't dispute the characterization, being that his proclivities had now led to an international sex scandal currently sending talking heads into saintly, pearl-clutching moralizing. Emily was the only person to whom Carly had confided having slept with a married man. She was not proud of it and vowed never to repeat the mistake. She was better than that.

Carly Mavros had plans for her life, big plans. She prided herself on her hyper-focused, no-nonsense approach. In DC, one was surrounded by prideful millennials certain they'd attained their station through merit as opposed to paternal connections. Not having the luxury of cashing in social favors, Carly was relegated to grinding her way to prominence. In the '80s, her father emigrated from Greece as a young man, settling with his brother in the Squirrel Hill neighborhood of Pittsburgh. After driving delivery trucks for several years, the brothers opened a sandwich shop that fused American favorites with Mediterranean flavors. Thirty years later, Mavros Brothers Sandwich Shops boasted eight locations in the greater Pittsburgh area.

Carly remembered prepping at the original store—cutting tomatoes, cucumbers, and mint—before leaving for school. Though her father lacked influence, he provided her something many of her contemporaries lacked: her colleagues got a trust fund; she got a work ethic. They went to Harvard, Princeton, and Yale. Carly was a Pittsburgh Panther. Interning at CBS, she was recognized as a hard worker with natural communication skills. It was also noted that she could write in a concise manner not typical of her generation. Her potential was apparent, so when one of her superiors left to become communications director at the White House, Carly was asked to accompany him. She did.

While doing advance work for POTUS trips, she got to know James—a witty, ruggedly handsome Secret Service agent who carried himself with an attractive, boyish confidence. On a trip to San Diego, it happened and continued to happen on and off for a few years until she came to her senses and realized her feelings for him were inappropriate and her actions disgraceful. Refocusing, she put the episode behind her and grinded out a career in journalism as she jumped from one small publication to another.

Her biting takes on current events earned her over 300,000 Twitter followers, but she was self-aware enough to know much of her popularity was attributed to her Mediterranean beauty. The *National Standard*, a center-right publication, needed to spice up their lineup of middle-aged males, so they hired the young, talented writer with the growing online following. In the DC journo hierarchy, she was still D- or E-list, making 5 AM hits on cable news where she'd take the conservative position on a split screen next to another twenty-something yelling a left-leaning counterpoint.

At twenty-eight, Carly's potential was limitless, which was why she was second-guessing her decision to meet James at Nick's Riverfront Grill. She knew he'd be early—Secret Service guys were religiously punctual—so she planned to arrive at least ten minutes after their planned 12:15 lunch. Two months ago, when she first learned of agents hiring prostitutes in Brazil, she tweeted, "Headline: 'Secret Serviced' . . . you're welcome NY Post." At the time, she wondered if James was involved. When it was revealed earlier in the week that he was indeed the culprit, it wasn't schadenfreude she experienced but pity. When she received his text, it came as a thunderous shock, causing her to initially decline the invite. He assured her his intentions were pure and he only wanted to pick her brain on a couple of topics of which he was suspiciously vague, but her curiosity was piqued, and despite herself, a part of her wanted to see him.

Entering the busy restaurant, she made her way to James, who was perusing the menu at a window table with a view of the Potomac bending from Georgetown past Theodore Roosevelt Island where the trees still awaited their spring bloom. He stood with a nervous smile when he spotted her. Wearing a green-plaid flannel shirt, sleeves rolled to the elbow, he had three days of whisker growth— no doubt intentional—and looked good enough to cause Carly to third-guess her decision to meet. His anticipatory grin disappeared when she answered his open-armed invitation for a hug with her extended hand.

"Hi, James," she said in monotone. With uncertain awkwardness, he shook her hand gingerly.

"Thanks for meeting me; it's good to see you," he began, eying her body wrapped in form-fitting designer jeans and a sweater.

"I'm not sure what this is about. I never expected to see you again, if I'm being honest," she shared with practiced disinterest as they sat.

"I wasn't sure I'd see you again either, Carly. You look good, by the way."

"Knock that shit off."

"Knock what shit off?"

"I saw the way you looked at me."

"Why are you being so short? I'm not here trying to get with you. It was just a compliment." He forced a grin.

"Stop with the smirk. Why is it you want to see me?"

"I'll get to that," he assured her. Carly ordered a house red from their waiter. "I've had a bad week," James confided.

"Sounds like a bad couple of months. The news said you're suspended. What are you going to do when you're fired?"

"I'm not going to be fired. I'm going to get back in the Service's good graces. I have a plan. Why are you being so cold?"

"How would you have me act?"

The waiter returned with her wine as they declined food.

"I don't really know, I suppose. We used to get along just fine. Is it the, um, the Brazil thing?"

"Well, that's a thing. May not be a big deal to me, though I imagine Audrey feels differently."

"Yeah, she kicked me out. We're separated."

"You want me to feel sorry for you?"

"No. It's all my fault. You know that." He sipped his beer for comfort.

"You got caught and outed. Would you feel the same if you hadn't been caught? Be honest."

"I don't know."

"The answer is no. You would have gone on with your fake-ass life. Lying to yourself and pretending to be something you're not—namely, an honorable man."

"Goddamn, you're harsh."

"And you're a child."

"I'm forty-four."

"Age has nothing to do with adulthood. I was more of an adult at fifteen than you are at forty-four. It's about being responsible and forthright. You were a kid breaking the rules and getting away with it. Then you got caught, and now you want to be an adult."

He stared at her, clearly stung.

"Another beer, sir?" asked the waiter, breaking James's trance.

"Jack and Coke, please. Double."

"Anything else, something to eat?" the server asked.

"No, that's all for now." James stared out toward the Potomac. A row team cruised through the still water in perfect unison. Tourists lined up to board for a cold, overcast boat ride down the river to Mount Vernon. He turned back to Carly.

"Did you come here just to beat me up?"

"No. The thing is, James, everybody likes you, so nobody tells you what you need to hear. You and I were a mistake, and I've been beating myself up about it because I'm a better person than that. When I saw the news about you in South America, I felt sick to my stomach. Because I know you—I loved you—and you're better than that." The sincerity in Carly's voice was moving. The server placed his stiff drink before him.

"I can't dispute what you're saying." He took a sip. "You've always been perceptive. I'm sorry about everything. I shouldn't have, you know, pursued you."

"I'm a big girl and make my own decisions—even my own

mistakes. What happened happened. I don't regret anything. I just learned from it."

"How are things with you? I've seen you on TV in the mornings quite a bit, so I imagine things are going well."

"You must be getting up really early if you're catching my hits. Things are well. I love my job at the *National Standard*. They give me a lot of freedom to pursue the issues I'm interested in, and I've learned so much from the writers there. I sometimes wonder if I'm qualified to be in their company, but they make me feel welcome."

"That's good to hear, not that I'm surprised. Like I used to tell you, you'd have been one hell of a Secret Service agent. But you'd be good at whatever you set your mind to. And you're right about me. I've got to make a lot of changes, and I'm working on that."

"Where are you staying?"

"Brian Lattimer lets me crash in his basement apartment."

"How is Brian?"

"Good. He's into his boyfriend, and they travel abroad about every other month. I don't see him all that much, but he's one of the few friends I have left. It's curious how quickly one goes from 'life of the party' to pariah when the media paints you as the world's number one cad for five days."

"I can't imagine the week you've had," Carly observed. James laughed aloud. "What's so funny?"

"Nothing. You just have no idea how truly strange this week has been. I have a feeling it'll only get weirder."

"You going to try and get Audrey back?"

"Initially I tried, but I think she's moved on."

"You know there'll never be anything between us again."

"I know. Are you seeing anybody?"

"No. Haven't had time, frankly. And the guys I do meet just want someone to screw around with while they build their resumés. I'm not on the market for anything that isn't long-lasting and meaningful."

James nodded, took another sip, and looked out as the tourist boat launched. He turned back to catch Carly looking at him admiringly, causing them both to don smiles of reminiscence. She finished her wine. "So, why did you text me? I haven't heard from you in over a year."

"This is going to sound crazy."

"Coming from you? I don't expect anything but crazy."

"Fair," he acknowledged. "I remember, way back when, you bringing up Emerald Solaria. You were certain you had a big story on them. Remember, we were in bed and—"

"I remember," she interrupted. "It's been a long-term project. What about it?"

"So, you still working on it?"

"In between my writing and TV hits. It's been an elusive story. Every time I seem to make headway, people put up smokescreens, which only heightens my sense that something is there. Why are you bringing this up?"

"I'm looking into a few things. I'm afraid I can't be specific, but that company has popped up on my radar." The waiter served Carly a second glass as she eyed James with stern bewilderment.

"What are you up to? James, are you losing your mind?"

"I have a lot of time on my hands, as you can imagine, and I've come upon some information about some rather high-profile matters," he explained, trying to remain vague without sounding like he'd indeed lost his sanity.

"What matters are you referring to?"

"I can't say. But I have a source who's familiar with the spokesperson of Emerald Solaria, really tight with him, and she may be privy to incriminating information, and this brought to mind our conversation way back when."

"Who is this woman, and how does she know Chet Bateman?"

"I didn't say it was a woman."

"You said 'she.'"

"Did I?"

"Yeah, you did. Who is she?"

"I can't share that. But she knows stuff. My question is: what do you need for your investigation? What kind of information?"

"James, I was just beginning to feel some pity for you, and now you're acting very strange." Carly didn't know what to make of his interest in the matter. If she could prove her suspicions, a powerful senator and his A-list celebrity fundraiser could face a public reckoning. She would be Woodward, and this would be her Watergate.

"Trust me on this. I remember you saying something to the effect that Emerald Solaria was a shell company, like a Ponzi scheme of sorts."

"I have some evidence indicating that, yes. In time, I think I can prove the venture was less about the environment and more about political influence and skirting campaign finance laws. Is this woman another one of Bateman's lovers? If so, you can save your time; they'll be of no use."

"She's not one of his girls, but she may know where to uncover information you need."

Carly was intrigued and a bit mystified. James was smart—ridiculous, but smart. If he recognized this information had merit, there was something to it.

"I need to know who's doing business with Emerald Solaria. They are strangely reticent about who purchases their solar-powered hardware, and from what I can tell, most of their sales are to foreign buyers. Hollywood celebrities and rich virtue-signalers have bought into the hype that the new CIGS solar panels will revolutionize clean energy, so they've invested heavily in the venture. If these new panels work as well as Chet purports, they anticipate heavy profits."

"CIGS solar panels?"

"Copper indium gallium selenide panels—they are cylindrical and don't use the crystalline silicon in traditional panels. They're hailed as a breakthrough in solar technology. René Beauvoir was the founder of the company and brought aboard Chet essentially as the face and spokesperson. It was a savvy hire because Chet's celebrity sparked immediate enthusiasm from some high-profile people."

"You're really smart."

"Don't flirt with me," she kidded and sipped her wine. "Beauvoir was a big donor for the previous administration's super PAC, not to mention a personal friend to the former president, who vacationed at one of Mr. Beauvoir's homes on Maui. Coincidentally, Emerald Solaria received over five hundred million in loan guarantees from the Department of Energy. The company claimed over three hundred million in profits last year, yet not one building in the United States is outfitted with their product. Those profits are questionable at best. I want to know who the buyers are."

"If I'm following you, you believe foreign money is pacifying investors hoping for a potential windfall?"

"Yeah, that's about it, plus they get the added bonus of feeling they're saving the planet. They wield a lot of political influence on Capitol Hill. Those loans are now guaranteed by the federal government; that was the previous administration's way of promoting technological development. Of course, my story has one more issue."

"Like what?"

"The largest political supporter of this new technology is Senator Gene Sterling, who happens to be the world's most notable victim of political violence."

"Is that right?" James acted surprised.

"Don't get me wrong, I don't know if Chet or Senator Sterling are in any way knowledgeable of fraud at Emerald Solaria, but my editors would balk at a piece even nominally smearing a senator whose wife is now missing."

"Maybe there's more to the story," James posited. "Sounds like you're definitely onto something." They sipped their drinks and looked out at the tourists, particularly at a spirited Korean group wielding selfie sticks like rapiers. "One other thing: do you know the name Oscar Reese through any of your intelligence or law enforcement contacts?" he asked.

She shook her head. "No. Why?"

"There was an incident in West Virginia I also have information on."

"Where does that fit in? I don't understand."

"I don't know, just a name I've come across. I was curious if you were familiar with it. Run it by your guys. He may have killed a guy in Harpersburg, West Virginia."

"Murder?" An incredulous look crossed her face. "You are losing your mind. Who are you hanging around with nowadays?"

"I would love to share that with you, but maybe later. I'm not going nuts, I swear. You run that Oscar Reese name by your contacts, and I'll see what I can get you on Emerald Solaria. Deal?"

"This is weird, James. I don't know who this source of yours is, but I didn't expect our meeting to go like this."

"Maybe we should just order lunch. This Jack is going to my head."

"Are you okay? I'm seriously worried about you."

"I'm fine, Carly, or at least as fine as circumstances warrant. I miss Emma and Jimmy. I FaceTime them most every day, but they don't understand what's going on. For so long I was a selfish asshole, and now the bill has come due." It was an unusual moment of sincerity from a man she had only known as childishly unburdened. Besides his good looks, he possessed a whimsical ease women were drawn to—a magnetism against which she was not immune.

"I'm sorry you're going through this," she said consolingly.

"It's my fault."

"I know."

"I'm trying to do better. I truly am."

"What happened between us should never have happened. It was the worst wrong thing I've ever done. But I did love you."

"I shouldn't have dragged you into my nonsense. I'd like to say it was 'the worst wrong thing I've ever done,' but all you have to do is tune to CNN to know better."

"What are we to do with you, Agent Ford?"

"They want to put me out to pasture, but I have a plan."

"Dear God, when have you ever had a plan?"

"Be nice." He finished his drink. "I don't want to be inappropriate, but you look really good."

"Knock it off," she playfully admonished. "You're relegated to looking only."

"I'll take it." He smirked.

"And knock that shit off too. I know what you're doing. No flirting."

"Fair enough."

"Excuse me," interrupted a Midwestern, grandmotherly voice. "I'm sorry to interrupt, but are you Carly Mavros?" The questioner was a sixty-something with the short haircut middle-aged women sport once they'd traded glamour for practicality.

"I am," Carly acknowledged, trying to mask her midday buzz.

"Earl and I are such big fans. We're from Indiana and we catch you on *Fox & Friends First*. We think you are so smart and just a delight. I told Earl, 'I think that's Carly over there' and just had to ask if it was you." Earl, in an Iowa Hawkeyes ball cap, stood behind his wife, clearly embarrassed.

"That's so sweet," said a delighted Carly. "I don't have people recognize me very often. What's your name?"

"I'm Tammy. So nice to meet you. We just love President Frum, and a few mornings back, you argued border policy with some socialist moron and cleaned his clock."

Carly stood, obviously enjoying the accolades from a fan, and hugged Tammy as poor Earl took several minutes to figure out how to take a picture of them with his wife's smartphone.

"I apologize for interrupting your lunch," Tammy said to James. "She is so beautiful. You're a lucky man."

"Oh, no, we are just good friends," Carly corrected.

"You look real familiar as well," Tammy continued, studying James. "Are you a TV person too? I swear I've seen you on TV."

"No, ma'am, I'm not a TV guy. Just a good friend of Carly's. She is the best, isn't she?" James tried to dodge the issue.

"No, I've seen you. Just the other day I saw you. Bill Hemmer's show, I think it was. What was that about? Oh, I remember." A disturbed expression crossed Tammy's face. Her eyes showed recognition, then darted to Carly. With stunned revulsion, she covered her mouth in disbelief. "My God, Carly. Do you know you're dining with a sodomite?"

"I do," Carly answered with an easeful smile. "Welcome to Washington, DC. I hope you both have a great time."

◉ ◉ ◉

After the Mickey D's breakfast run, JC spent all morning making arrangements. Squinty's murder sealed the deal; he and Corn had to skedaddle. As Myrtle stuffed her face, he lied about seasonal work he'd secured outside Hickory, North Carolina, saying he wasn't sure how long he'd be gone but it was good money. JC hired Carol Higginbotham to care for Myrtle, ensure she got her meds, and to make her food runs, the menu of which JC wrote down with careful specificity.

Myrtle's disappointment was mitigated by her third hash brown, but she was not pleased; Carol was a retired nurse with a four-pack-a-day smoking habit and the bedside manner of a water moccasin. JC fronted her $1,000 dollars and promised to cover food expenses. He then bought a small, brown, 1996 Toyota

Tacoma beater with only two remaining letters on the tailgate, spelling *YO*, for $300 cash.

After a few more errands, he stopped by Clive's for an afternoon beer. There were few patrons, it being only three in the afternoon, but one was Judd Kenner, who worked the morning shift at the Wal-Mart distribution center north of town. JC was confused when Judd offered condolences.

"You hadn't heard?" continued Judd. "They found Cornhole dead along with that Chrissy gal. Found 'em in their car. Sorry, I assumed you knew."

JC quelled his emotions—shock, grief, terror—with monumental effort. Judd offered a Jager shot in Corn's memory. His mind swimming, JC downed it, thanked Judd for his kindness, and made for the door.

Driving back to his trailer, JC processed the news as he wiped his eyes. One by one, Oscar was taking them out; first Squints, now Corn. Cornhole had been his closest friend. He couldn't help but think this was a sign from God to straighten his ways. He suspected his ma in heaven had asked Jesus to send her boy a sign. JC's ma loved Jesus, and he imagined she and the Messiah hit it off.

Once home, he shaved his unkempt chin whiskers so as not to mirror the description put out across the media. Myrtle asked a shitload of questions while he hurriedly packed. It killed him to leave her, but he was determined to get on the road as soon as possible. He could only hope, for his wife's sake, Oscar didn't know the location of his trailer. Finally packed, JC knelt next to Myrtle's bed and told her he loved her, leaning into her gelatinous frame. As he embraced her cold, squishy shoulders, tears streamed down his face, mingling with the crumbs on Myrtle's skin.

"I'll be fine, honey bun," she assured him. "I'm proud of you."

"You are the love of my life," JC declared, looking into her rotund face.

"Is everything fine, sugar?"

"Everything is just fine." He forced a smile. He had been happy here with Myrtle, the first such happiness he'd ever known. But just as he had done his entire life, JC had screwed it all up.

⊙ ⊙ ⊙

The cool, invigorating air gradually cured Kat's hangover as she walked along the sidewalk off M Street in what had become her uniform: Mountaineer hoodie and Nationals ball cap. James was insistent she remain at his place so she wouldn't be recognized, and she initially tried to stay put. She spent the morning hydrating and watching coverage of the Democratic primaries. Every cable news network was gushing about the courage of Senator Sterling, who was at a Louisiana rally with a scheduled campaign stop in Kansas that evening. The fawning praise of her husband's heroic fortitude aggravated her alcohol-induced nausea. Despite James's insistence, she decided a stroll on the overcast, fall-like day would be a welcome respite from the political news.

As she window-shopped through Georgetown, James continued to pop into her head; having not expected him to be gone more than a couple hours, a sense of jealousy rose within her. It wasn't like her to be covetous of a guy she'd known four days, but she reasoned she could be forgiven her schoolgirl emotions after spending every waking hour with him. Maybe she was suffering from some variation of Stockholm syndrome?

By four o'clock, she returned to James's place to discover him still gone.

I'm sure he's fucking that pretty young journalist, she thought. *Good for him. I sure as hell wasn't giving it up to that libidinous cad; she can have him. Why should it bother me?*

But it did bother her.

She turned on the news. Gene was leading in all four states. Kat tallied the score: her Jimmy was balls-deep in a millennial while her husband was cruising to the Democratic nomination; perfect. She poured a vodka tonic: strong.

James eventually walked into the basement apartment carrying a small shopping bag. Kat was still on the couch, taking in the election predictions, her short, dark hair mussed.

"Welcome home, flannel boy. Kind of a long lunch. Must've learned a lot."

James scanned the room and noticed the CNN chyron—SENATOR STERLING CLEAN SWEEP IN SATURDAY PRIMARIES—before eyeing her vodka tonic.

"Things not going well, I see," he quipped.

"Not for me, but apparently you're just fine."

"What's that supposed to mean?"

"That was quite a lengthy lunch with your old fuck buddy."

With an eye roll and sigh, James shook his head.

"What are you smiling about?"

"You're jealous, aren't you?"

"Jealous? Why would I be jealous of some broad nailing a washed-up, alcoholic man-slut? You do you, Jimmy, while I sit here all day watching the world wonder if I'm dead or alive."

"Jesus, Kat, that's pretty harsh considering I saved your life."

"You were about to drive home drunk—save it." She folded her arms in a full-body pout and stared ahead at the panel of pundits lauding her husband.

"Well, if it makes you feel any better, I wasn't nailing Carly all afternoon, as appealing as the thought is. I did get you this." James placed a white, plastic shopping bag adorned with the Apple logo beside her. "I knew you were missing your social media, so I got you a phone. Figured you could make some bogus Twitter and Instagram accounts; just don't post anything."

She looked at the bag, then up at James. Wiping her eyes, she stood, stepped forward, and pulled him close in an emphatic embrace. Kat felt unloved and alone. James's small gesture was a reminder that at least one person was on her side. She looked up at him, her eyes still moistened with emotion. Sensing his desire to kiss her, she shook her head.

"I can't. Not yet. But thank you. I'm sorry for what I said."

"It's okay, princess. You're not wrong." She pressed her head on his chest and tightened the embrace. His warm flannel shirt was soothing. For a few minutes, they remained interlocked in silence with a CNN panel verbally fellating Senator Sterling in the background. With a sniffle, she let him go and returned to the couch. He grabbed a beer and a Kleenex before sitting beside her. Thanking him, she wiped her eyes and blew her nose at a surprisingly high volume. James took out his phone and looked at his notes app before jotting something down in her notebook.

"What are you doing?" asked Kat.

"Something I should have done earlier," he admitted, putting the phone to his ear. "Hello, is this the TIPS hotline? Very good, I have information on a car I saw in the driveway of John Donovan's house in Harpersburg, West Virginia, the day he was murdered. It was a silver BMW with Virginia tags A-E-R, 7-3-1. I was driving by the residence and thought it was odd. That's all I have. No, I don't wish to share my name. Thank you." James hung up with a smile.

"You called in an anonymous tip?"

"I assume they're anonymous, but that's why I got off the line so fast. Anyhow, as I was driving back, I thought it best to give investigators this tidbit to look into. We need to put Oscar on their radar. I know it's a shot in the dark, but it can't hurt. Speaking of Oscar, Carly wasn't familiar with him but promised to run it by her FBI sources. As far as Emerald Solaria is concerned, said she needs information on who's purchasing their solar panels; she suspects they're mostly foreign companies."

"And what does that have to do with us?"

"Not sure, but Emerald Solaria is the most prominent donor

to Gene's foundation, and its spokesman, your boy Chet, brings in a lot of campaign donors and young voters. If the company turns out to be a Ponzi scheme, that would be a pretty damn big bombshell." Kat looked at him, not following. "Think about it. If Gene secures the nomination—which, after today, appears likely— and goes head-to-head against Frum, news that his chief supporter was defrauding investors and this green-energy marvel was all a bullshit maneuver for power would severely cripple his campaign. Frum would have a field day with it."

"Chet would never be part of a fraud scheme."

"You may be right. Who knows? He could be getting played. Like you said, he's just a spokesman. But if my friend is correct, he's inadvertently in on a big lie." Troubled, Kat stared at the television and sipped her vodka. "You really like Chet."

"I do. He's a good person, and his passion for the environment is admirable. Of Gene's friends, he's the only one I trusted. The only one whose motives I felt pure. The tabloids paint him as the idealistic playboy. He's certainly idealistic, but he is a caring person."

"Very well. When I solve this thing, I'll be sure the prosecutor grants him leniency."

"Do you really think we can find something definitive to put Gene away?"

"I'm certainly going to try. Question: if you had to find dirt on your husband, where in your house would you look?"

"The study," she answered without hesitation. "He keeps it locked at all times. Always claimed to be doing campaign business or managing the foundation. I assumed he was talking to some other woman or watching porn."

"There you go. The study it is."

"If you were listening, I said it is always locked."

"With you gone, why would he need to lock it?"

"I'm not liking where you're going with this."

"Look, while planning your kidnapping, he was keeping you out of one particular room in the house; something's in there."

"How can you be so certain?"

"I'm not always right, princess, but I'm always certain."

"That doesn't instill me with a lot of confidence."

"If someone wanted to get into your house, but they didn't have a key, what would be the best way in?"

"Are you serious?"

"You don't have a key, do you?"

"You know, I must have forgotten it while being tied up. What's going on in your head, Jimmy?"

"Gene is scheduled to have a rally this evening in Kansas. That means he won't get back until after midnight. The Capitol Police have a temporary detail on him, but they won't have security at the residence while he's gone. That gives us several hours to search for something—anything—that could help pin him to your kidnapping or tie him in with the fraud scheme. You said it yourself: if we went to the feds now, it would be his word against yours, and we have no evidence to validate your story."

"What the hell would we be looking for?"

"Not sure. Documents, communications, anything that might help. I mean, he's got to be in with some shady characters. He's tied to two redneck kidnappers who were driving a car registered to a guy found dead; there has to be something there. Did you ever hear him making odd phone calls?"

"He was secretive. I suspected he was seeing someone else. Frankly, I'd gotten to the point where I didn't care all that much." As Kat's attention was drawn to the television, her expression became pained. She turned up the volume:

"I had nothing to do with it. I loved Miss Katherine very much," cried an older Hispanic woman mobbed by reporters

shouting questions. *"I do not remember leaving the door unlocked. I always lock the door,"* the woman insisted as she ducked into a car.

"I saw this earlier," Kat said. "That's Rosa, our housekeeper. The cops questioned her, and people are speculating she left the back door unlocked, allowing the kidnappers to get in. She's such a sweetheart. I love her so much."

"Another one of Gene's victims," declared James. "She looks like a sweet lady."

"She is. She's from Guatemala. I loved to talk to her about her grandchildren. And now she's been roped into this charade. She did absolutely nothing wrong. She doesn't deserve this."

"And neither do you." With one hand, he massaged the back of her neck. "How do we get in there, Kat?"

"Are you sure it's a good idea? A neighbor could see us. The cops could be called. It sounds risky."

"It is risky. I'm not going to lie. But I say we go for it. It's time to go on offense. We can't just sit here and hope for the best." James's voice had a calm resolve. She felt safe with him.

"The door from our kitchen to the garage is always unlocked. If he hasn't changed the code, I can use the garage door opener to get in the house. I'm scared, Jimmy."

"Don't be. You're still alive, and you're a strong woman." He stood and grabbed the tuck-away holster containing his 9mm and secured it in his waistband beneath an untucked shirt.

"Won't this be a burglary or something?" asked Kat.

"You're a resident of the house, so no." From his bedroom, James retrieved a small Surefire flashlight. "We can grab a bite and figure out how best to get into your house. Think of it as a search warrant." Kat found his certitude both appealing and frightening. "Do you like Shake Shack? A burger sounds good to me. Don't forget your ball cap."

Kat grabbed her cap as she followed her energized friend toward the door. In their rush, they forgot to turn off the television; a chyron ran along the bottom of the screen: SENATOR STERLING CANCELS KANSAS RALLY, RETURNING TO WASHINGTON AFTER EMOTIONAL VICTORY.

CHAPTER 9

JUST BLOCKS from American University, Hillbrook Lane extended from Forty-Ninth Street down a slight grade into a circular cul-de-sac. The brick-and-stone mansions of the Spring Valley section of Northwest DC were surrounded by centuries-old trees and exquisite landscaping and were home to a former attorney general, several ambassadors, congressmen turned lobbyists, and other power brokers, including the senior senator from California.

The Sterling residence was five houses down from the Forty-Ninth Street intersection. A majestic structure with peaked gables and dark, brownish stone and a long walkway extending from the sidewalk to the ornate front door, the 4,700-square-foot residence sat on nearly four-tenths of an acre of well-manicured, tree-shaded lawn.

James crouched in the cold undergrowth of Spring Valley Park, which bordered the Sterlings' backyard. The temperature had dropped below forty degrees, prompting him to drape his brown Carhartt work coat over Kat as she knelt beside him. The park was a small arboretum, though the unleafed trees provided little in the way of concealment. Fortunately, the darkness, accompanied by a cloudy evening, made up for the lack of foliage.

The garage was attached to the rear of the house at the end of a long driveway.

"What time is it?" Kat shivered.

"Ten."

"I'm freezing."

"Should be warm inside. I just want to be certain no one's in there." For the past twenty minutes, he'd forced her to remain still as they surveilled the residence.

"Can we go in?" Kat's fear had succumbed to the cold.

"Yeah, we can go. Follow me." He reached out his hand. She clasped it. In the still night, the crunch of every fallen leaf seemed loud as a rifle shot. Realizing the neighbors were likely on edge from the shocking events earlier this week, James took special care to remain silent. He scanned the driveway from the corner of the garage—it was clear. A nod to Kat prompted her to open the keypad beside the garage door. She punched in the code, and the door rattled and hummed. Once it was a yard off the ground, she hit the button to freeze it in place. Her heart was beating through her chest with a mix of fear and exhilaration.

Dropping to his belly, James slid beneath the door, and Kat followed. He clicked on his compact flashlight and made his way between an Audi and Tesla toward the interior door while she pressed behind him. Saying a silent prayer, he grabbed the doorknob, turned it, and pushed. It clicked open.

"Nice place," observed James as they entered the spacious kitchen. Stainless-steel appliances surrounded an expansive island countertop. He switched off his flashlight, and they made their way across the hardwood floors into the vault-ceilinged living room bordered by large windows and a staircase curving to the second floor.

"Mortimer," cooed Kat as the fluffy white kitty lounging atop the couch replied with a high-pitched meow. She sat and cuddled Mortimer. "I'm going to cry," she whispered while relishing the embrace. Allowing his new friend time to bask in furry affection,

James went upstairs to scan the rooms before returning to the living room where Kat was still scratching behind Mortimer's ears.

"Well, the place is empty," he reported. "And I found his study." Kat looked up expectantly. "It's unlocked."

Kat shook her head. "You love being right."

"You'd think I'd get tired of it, but yeah."

Prying herself from the feline's warmth, Kat followed James upstairs. Halfway down the hall, she stopped in front of the open doorway to her capacious bedroom. Images of when she and Gene first moved in raced through her mind. She remembered making love on the canopied bed and feeling—despite all the obstacles— like she had finally made it and her life was settling into something stable. She recalled hosting dinner parties for her political husband. Then memories of Tuesday evening flashed in her head: of calling for help as she struggled with two assailants, then realizing they were there at her husband's behest.

"Kat?" whispered James as he placed his hand on her shoulder. "You alright?"

Nodding, she forced a smile.

"This room saw my best and worst days." She stared as the memories played out before her. "I remember the terror I felt when I was tackled to the floor, certain it was my last day on earth. When I realized Gene was in on it, I'd never felt more helpless and alone."

"But you weren't helpless. You escaped. By yourself, you managed to escape. You didn't allow yourself to be a victim. I admire that about you."

Turning from the bedroom, she looked up at James.

"And you're no longer alone," he promised. She embraced him and exhaled, releasing the pent-up emotion.

"Thanks, Jimmy."

"No need to thank me."

"I'm lucky it was you in that parking lot."

"I'm glad I was there as well, otherwise I'd never have the experience of holding a beautiful woman in a Carhart jacket while committing a B and E."

"You ruined a really nice moment, Jimmy," she whispered, still holding him tight.

"Ruining stuff is kind of my thing."

She gazed up at him, tipping back the bill of her Nationals cap. "Remind me we aren't out of our minds."

"I can only speak for myself, and I am completely out of my mind. But we are going to make this bastard pay. And we have the upper hand."

"We do?"

"He thinks you're dead. He thinks the game is over. But it's still on, and by the time he realizes it, he'll be done." He smirked.

"That smirk's growing on me a little—but just a little."

"Let's see what we can find, princess," he declared and pecked her lips with a lightning-fast kiss before turning to enter the study across the hall. Taking off the Carhart coat, she felt a flutter in her chest. She was beginning to take a shine to this cocky, impetuous cowboy.

The study's décor was a throwback with dark wood paneling surrounding an ornate, oak desk. Behind the desk, a large window provided a view of the mature trees adorning the front yard. One wall was lined with books, the other with photos of the senator accompanied by various politicians and celebrities, notably Bono, Leo DiCaprio, Bob De Niro, Bill Clinton, Alyssa Milano, and Chet Bateman. Using his flashlight to examine the desk, careful not to flash the beam toward the window, James opened a four-foot-high filing cabinet situated along the wall. Several tabs separated reams of papers into categories: finance, insurance, speaking engagements. He pulled the file sleeve labeled THE FOUNDATION, which held a stack of papers several inches thick.

"Let's see who your hubby's been dealing with," said James as he set files on the desk. Beside him, Kat pecked away at the senator's computer keyboard. "Looks like a list of companies paying into the foundation," James observed as he thumbed through the papers. "This might be worth keeping." He noted Kat appeared stumped. "Do you know the password?"

"I told you, he never let me in here."

James opened the desk's top drawer. Scanning it with his flashlight, he located a post-it note with *PW-Senatedog6882* scrawled across it.

"Try this." James placed the note on the desk.

Typing it in, Kat unlocked the computer.

"I've done a lot of search warrants. You'd be surprised how common that is," James shared and returned to the papers. "Looks like most of these are for speaking appearances. He's pulling in five to six figures a pop; what a selfless public servant."

James leafed through more papers.

"Kat, try this: go to his Google tab and check his history. Let's see what's been on Gene's mind."

Kat read the senator's most recent searches: KATHERINE STERLING, BABYSITTER PORN, LATEST PRIMARY POLLS, GANGBANG, GENE STERLING. Peering over her shoulder, James quipped, "Looks like he wants the latest news on his missing wife, how the elections are shaping up, and giving it to young ladies good and hard."

"How did I marry such a perv? I don't really think I should be touching this keyboard. God knows what he does in here."

"Yeah, and I don't see any tissues."

"Ewww." She punched his shoulder playfully.

At the bottom of the screen, Kat noticed a minimized tab and clicked it, revealing an email chain. It was an AOL account she'd never seen under the name doggystyle6969, communicating with another AOL user: mountainman21673. Scrolling through the running conversation, she zeroed in on a portion of recent correspondence:

February 24:

> **Mountainman:** What did you think of Oscar?
>
> **Doggystyle:** He is a cool customer. Sounds like he does this all the time, which gives me a lot of confidence. Didn't realize he was Russian.
>
> **Mountainman:** Well, if you want this sort of thing done right, you gotta get a Russian. I like his idea of using the two convicts. They're complete strangers to us. Even if they get nabbed, your denials will be waterproof.
>
> **Doggystyle:** This is a big gamble
>
> **Mountainman:** If you want it all, you gotta swing for the fences. If it all goes according to plan, you'll get the nomination. Once you have that, Frum will be easy

February 28:

> **Mountainman:** Don't forget. $70k for Wells of Hope for the Congo
>
> **Doggystyle:** The foundation made their contribution yesterday

March 1:

> **Mountainman:** You good for tonight?
>
> **Doggystyle:** A little nervous, but I'm ready.

March 2:

> **Mountainman**: You alright?
>
> **Doggystyle:** I didn't realize they were going to go so hard on me. My head is pounding.
>
> **Mountainman:** It will be more than worth it. Even Fox News is singing your praises. That broad on there is hot as fuck. This is gonna work out for you.
>
> **Doggystyle:** Never met her, but you can tell she's got a nice rack.
>
> **Mountainman:** Oscar will take care of everything from here on. You just win the primary.

"Jimmy, check this out," said Kat, pointing at the computer screen. "This seems like a big deal." Leaning over, he read through the emails.

"They're talking about our murder-boy, Oscar. He's Russian?"

"Doggystyle has got to be Gene. I don't know who Mountainman is, but it's obvious he was aware of the kidnapping. Look at the inbox. It's literally just these two going back and forth."

"What makes you think Doggystyle is your husband?" asked James with a devilish grin.

"Never mind." Kat rolled her eyes. James took out his phone and began snapping screenshots.

"Look at these from yesterday and this morning." He pointed to the screen.

March 4:

> **Mountainman:** Great speech tonight. Your poll numbers look strong. I think you could sweep this Saturday.

> **Doggystyle:** I really need to thank you, without your
> referral I'd still be stuck with that complaining bitch. I agree,
> I think we are going to wipe the floor with that carpet-
> muncher.
>
> **Mountainman:** LOL!!!

"Gene is such an ass," Kat scoffed.

March 5:

> **Doggystyle:** Heading to Louisiana. Feeling good about
> today. The cops spoke to me again yesterday. They still got
> nothing but a gray car. They started asking me some prying
> questions about Monday, but they seem desperate.
>
> **Mountainman:** I think you're good. I expect good news
> today. Louisiana may be close, but I like your numbers in the
> Midwest and it tightened up in Maine a lot since Thursday.
> Once again, your speech last night was golden. You staying
> in Kansas tonight?
>
> **Doggystyle:** No, we plan to cancel the rally citing my
> emotional state . . . it's just so painful not having Katherine
> around.
>
> **Mountainman:** LOL!

James took a snapshot of the final email.

"Did you read that last one?" Kat demanded. "He canceled his Kansas rally." An alarmed expression crossed her face as vehicle headlights streaked through the window. Peering outside, James saw two dark Suburbans pulling into the driveway.

"Dammit, let's put this shit away." He shoved papers from the file into his pants before jamming the rest back into the drawer.

Kat minimized the email, then slipped on James's Carhart coat. Glancing through the window again, James saw an unmarked Crown Vic parked at the curb. Two men walked toward the house and greeted Gene near the front door. A young, attractive woman was with the senator, along with plainclothes Capitol Police officers. Looking sternly at Kat, James put his finger to his mouth and carefully snuck to the top of the stairs.

"What are you doing? We've got to hide," Kat whispered in vain as James lay prostrate at the edge of the landing overlooking the living room. Every fiber in Kat's body wanted some nook to hide in, but, crouching, she snuck alongside her maniacal new friend as the front door opened below.

⊙ ⊙ ⊙

It had been a very long day for Detective Sergeant Derek Roland. His federal task force counterparts, having dismissed his run-out to West Virginia this morning, ate crow when it turned out the hair fibers in the trunk of the suspicious vehicle matched the victim, Katherine Sterling. After several days of dead ends, the evidence was a welcome break. The task force contacted Senator Sterling and requested a meeting upon his return from the campaign trail.

Close to midnight on a cold evening in front of 4949 Hillbrook Lane, Derek and FBI assistant special agent in charge Kevin McClennan were parked in the Metro cop's Crown Victoria. Most of the guys drove Dodge Chargers or Ford Explorers, but Derek couldn't shake his love of the old Crown Vic.

As feds went, Kevin wasn't a bad guy. Typical of FBI types, he was clean cut, well trained, and boasted a master's degree in accounting that gave him license to think he knew more than he did. In his late thirties, the agent hadn't grown comfortable with silence the way Derek had over his quarter-century career. Trying to stir a conversation with the veteran detective, the talkative agent gave up after twenty minutes of terse responses and "I don't knows" until Derek leaned his head back and fell asleep.

"They're here." Kevin nudged the older detective as headlights spun into the driveway. Derek shook the sleep from his brain, sipped cold coffee, grimaced, and wiped droplets from his thick mustache.

"You got the file?" he asked. Kevin held up the manila folder in response. "Okay, let's get this over with."

"This is pretty important, Sarge."

"I know it is. That's why I said, 'Let's get this over with.'" They exited and made their way to the front stoop. Capitol Police dressed in suits and earpieces opened the Suburban limo, allowing Senator Sterling and a young blonde sporting a short, tight dress to exit.

"Senator Sterling, good evening; it's Agent McClennan again," Kevin greeted him. "Sorry our meeting comes at such a late hour, but if we could take just a moment of your time, the task force has some information we wish to share about Katherine."

The senator, his perfectly styled silver mane gleaming in the moonlight, acknowledged Agent McClennan with a concerned look and a nod, then invited them into his residence. Turning on a lamp and taking off his coat, Gene took a seat in the living room, his face still showing signs of the beating.

"Please have a seat, gentlemen," he offered. "Kevin and Derek, right?" The senator appeared exhausted and—to Derek's mind—nervous.

"That's right, sir. I'm with the FBI, and Derek is with Metro PD," Kevin confirmed as the two lawmen sat on the couch across from the senator.

"I'm sorry, ma'am, I didn't catch your name," Derek directed to the blonde.

"My apologies, it's been a long, trying day. This is my chief of staff, Tanya Smith," Gene introduced as all three men stood. The cops shook her hand politely. "Tanya, if you could be so kind as to wait for me in the kitchen, I need to speak with these gentlemen in private." She smiled and retreated. Derek looked on, trying to mask his suspicion.

"Tanya has been wonderful to me during this difficult time," Gene stated. "Today was very hard. I'm accustomed to having Kat by my side during election stops, which is why I cut my trip short. It was too much. The emotions are still so raw."

Derek wondered if the comely lady sauntering to the kitchen mitigated the senator's grief.

"We understand, sir," said Kevin "I can't imagine what you're going through. And I want you to know we are throwing the full weight of our resources into resolving this. But the FBI"—he glanced over to see Derek's wearied expression— "and Metro have located the vehicle used during your wife's kidnapping."

Gene leaned forward. Derek continued to study him.

"Sir, we located this vehicle in West Virginia." Kevin placed several photos on the coffee table. "It appears to match the video footage we obtained from your neighbor's surveillance feed in that it is a gray sedan."

Studying the photos with bloodshot eyes, Gene's forehead crinkled.

"More importantly," continued Kevin, "we recovered hair from inside the car trunk that matches Katherine's." Gene sat back and rubbed his forehead. "Nylon rope and duct tape were also located in the vehicle, but there was no sign of Katherine. I cannot emphasize enough, sir, we did not recover any blood or indications of foul play. We need to remain hopeful."

"How did they find the car?" asked Gene. "You did say West Virginia?"

"Yes sir, West Virginia," answered Kevin. "The vehicle was located during a routine police action."

"Police action?" Gene wondered aloud.

"Sir," interjected Derek, "the vehicle was associated with this individual." He pulled a mug shot of Dustin "Cornhole" De Plours from the file. "Do you recognize this man?"

Once again, Gene examined the photo as a jeweler would a precious stone.

"That's one of them," he declared. "That's the skinny one with the limp from Monday night. So, you arrested him?"

"No sir," answered Kevin. "That's an old mug shot. He's deceased. Believed to be an overdose."

"An overdose?"

"Yes sir, it looks like a heroin overdose, but it'll be a few weeks for the toxicology report," Kevin clarified. Taking it all in, the senator rubbed his mouth, looking circumspect.

"What happened to my wife?"

"We don't know," Derek said before Kevin could answer. "I wish we had a better gauge on her status, but we don't. What we do know is this car was used by the suspects that night. I know this has been a long, trying day, Senator, but we're going to ask one more thing of you."

The Metro detective pulled out a sheet with a grid of six mug shots, all of fleshy, White males in their late forties or early fifties.

"Do any of these men look like the other assailant that night?"

Gene lifted the paper and examined the pics. Reaching to his right, he pulled his reading glasses from the coat he'd draped across the couch and returned to scrutinizing the photos. Derek noticed a slight increase in Gene's breath rate, punctuated by a couple deep sighs. The detective glanced over at Kevin, who continued to look on with sympathy.

"I think that's him," Gene said, pointing to the bottom middle photo.

"Are you certain, sir?" Derek asked.

"Yes, he was the other one. He had a cap on—which he obviously doesn't here—but that's him." Derek's suspicions subsided somewhat as the senator identified JC Klingerman, a good friend of the Cornhole character the detective had seen lifeless about seventeen hours ago; the Harpersburg cops had shared that the two men were tight. When the guys at the task force pulled up JC's criminal history and photo, they thought he matched the description of the other suspect, and the senator's confirmation validated their suspicions.

"We're having a press conference in the morning," Kevin shared, eliciting a sigh from Derek. "The person you identified is JC Klingerman. His house is currently under surveillance. Now that you've identified him, we can obtain a search warrant for his residence. We'll keep you informed."

"Thank you, gentlemen." Gene stood along with the investigators. "I appreciate your efforts. I hope you find Katherine." Shaking their hands, the senator showed both men to the door.

⊙ ⊙ ⊙

The acoustics of the vaulted ceiling allowed Kat and James to hear the conversation between Gene and the investigators with remarkable clarity. Once the cops left, Tanya returned to the living room and hugged Gene. Her tight-fitting dress highlighted a curvy rear atop well-defined legs. Noticing James's approving glare, Kat issued him a sharp jab with her bony elbow.

"Are you okay, love?" asked the voluptuous blonde as she caressed Gene's face.

"I'm worried," he confided.

"Don't be. You swept all four primaries today." Tanya smiled as they cuddled on the couch, their legs intertwined.

"They know who took Kat. One of them is dead—the skinny one. Say they found him somewhere in West Virginia in the car they took her in. They showed me a photo lineup, so I picked out the fat one."

"You told them the truth?"

"That's the idea, isn't it?" Gene retorted. "Oscar said this could happen, and if it did, I was to cooperate and identify them. He said misleading the cops would arouse their suspicions and possibly derail the plan. Seems counterintuitive, but the way he explained it made sense. I had no dealings with them, so there's no way I could be implicated. Oscar's the pro, so I did as I was told."

"Then you did the right thing. I didn't mean to sound alarmed," Tanya comforted him. "We were told Oscar was the best. If we follow his lead, we have no need to worry ourselves with being caught."

"I just wish they hadn't discovered the identity of the kidnappers. Kat's out of the picture, but I don't need this to drag on. And, of course, now I'm wondering what else the cops know," Gene admitted.

"I can help rid you of your worries," Tanya cooed, kissing his neck until their mouths locked in a full-on make-out session. James grimaced at the sight of the old guy pawing at a stunner nearly forty years his junior. Kat turned away just as Tanya reached down Gene's pants.

"Let's go upstairs. I've been very bad," said Gene, slapping his lover's firm backside.

"Oh no, you've been a bad boy again? We'll have to fix that," Tanya replied seductively as the lustful pair stood eyeing each other.

"They're coming up here," James warned. He and Kat began shimmying backward from the edge. James's typically cool demeanor gave way to something closer to panic as his hand went to his pistol's grip.

"What are you doing?" whispered Kat. "We're not going to kill them. Follow me." She guided him into a guest bedroom adjacent to the master, motioning him into a spacious closet before gingerly shutting the door. In the darkness they heard the footsteps of the lovers in the hallway, followed by the click of lamps, opening and closing of closets, and faucets streaming in the master bath.

"You need to learn your lesson. What you did to that bitch wife of yours was very bad, you naughty boy," they heard Tanya mock scold through the wall, followed by a loud slapping sound.

"Did she spank him?" James whispered. Kat sighed.

"That's a bad, bad boy!" Increasingly loud spanks accompanied each syllable. "Bad dog. You've been a very bad dog."

"Bad dog?" James turned to Kat for clarification. A low whimpering sound emanated through the wall.

"Maybe you should kill them after all," Kat whispered.

"Did you spank him that hard?"

"He always complained about my spanking being subpar."

"Jesus, she's smacking the shit out of him." Several loud barks erupted from the bedroom, emphasized by stinging, staccato slaps as Tanya continued her beratement.

"You want to be a good boy now? Can you be a good boy?" Tanya asked in the exaggerated tone of a disappointed dog owner. Her rhetorical questions were answered by several enthusiastic barks. Kat eyed James holding his mouth as his eyes widened. "Fuck me like a good boy. Fuck me like a good doggie. That a boy. Give me that bad doggie cock," Tanya encouraged the senator as the rhythmic sound of flesh on flesh signaled the foreplay had segued to intercourse.

"I have questions," James stated.

"Let's just go," Kat answered with irritation before creeping out of the closet. James followed to the hallway door. The woofing and carnal sounds from down the hall rose in volume as she opened the door. Skulking out of the guestroom, James's curiosity forced him to stop and stare at a sight he knew would be seared in his mind for eternity. The sixty-something senator was—not surprisingly—nailing the young staffer doggy style. Normally, he would be as mortified by the senator's flabby ass as he was pleased by the perfection of Tanya's derriere. But the stunning contrasts were overshadowed by the large, brown dog mask encompassing the senator's entire head, its ears flapping with each emphatic pelvic thrust. All this while he continued to bay and howl as Tanya exhorted his good-boy-ness.

Taking out his phone, James aimed it at the fornicating Fido and snapped a pic before turning to see Kat at the stairs, wearing a murderous expression.

"I couldn't help myself," whispered James with a shrug. "This had to be documented."

"Let's please just get out of here," Kat pleaded.

"How come you never told me your husband was a furry?" he asked as they descended the stairs.

"It never came up. Do we really need to discuss this right now?" The baying continued to echo from the second floor, punctuated with occasional growls. "Bye, Mortimer." Kat rubbed the fluffy feline's head, then moved to the front door. An orgasmic, prolonged howl shook the house.

"Sounds like Rin-Tin-Tin just got his rocks off; time to go," James noted. He peered out the front window at an SUV parked on the street a good sixty feet away. "It's cold out. Those cops will be in their cars." He turned to look through the large windows at the rear of the living room. "They got another post in the driveway," he said. "If we go right and cut in between the neighbor's house, we can get back to the park."

"I'll follow you."

"You don't think they'll track us, do you?"

"What do you mean?"

"That looked like a hound dog upstairs. I just don't what him to pick up our scent."

"You're an ass."

CHAPTER 10

Sunday, March 6

WASHINGTONIANS aren't—by and large—a religious population; most observed the Sabbath with brunch and political talk shows sermonizing the previous week's performative declarations of virtue or indignation. The sets at *Meet the Press* and *Fox News Sunday* were abuzz as the normal rhythms of democratic discord were usurped by the disappearance of Katherine Sterling. Everyone had a theory as to what happened, but since her disappearance five days prior, even with every conceivable law enforcement tool brought to bear, very little about what occurred that evening was clear. TV producers dedicated entire hours to the case, with former law enforcement types on hand to give their analyses. That was, until the FBI announced there would be a press conference at nine o'clock Sunday morning to update the nation on the latest developments.

Detective Sergeant Derek Roland would have preferred to participate in the warrant service. At seven this morning, a search warrant had been executed at a Harpersburg trailer where neither Mrs. Sterling nor the suspect were found. All they located was a distraught woman bedridden with obesity, insisting they were in the wrong house. She did confirm to officers her husband was JC, who told her he was headed to North Carolina for work. That was all they had gleaned to this point, so the FBI decided to call a presser.

Derek hadn't slept all night and was wearing the same clothes he'd worn twenty hours ago when he located the suspect's vehicle and nine hours ago at his meeting with the senator. Agent Kevin McClennan stood next to him with a catatonic stare identical to Derek's. Derek had to hand it to the kid: he had misread him. The young agent stuck it out and remained focused through the waning hours and proved to be an effective investigative partner. Derek first pegged him as some high-degreed show horse, but over the past twenty-four hours, the young fed displayed real grit.

The special agent in charge of the FBI once again stood before the mic, flanked by uniformed police brass, state troopers, and the two bedraggled investigators.

"Good morning," began the SAIC with practiced gravity. "I'm Special Agent in Charge Keith Coleman of the FBI Washington Field Office. I'm here with my law enforcement partners from MPD, Park Police, Virginia State Police, Maryland State Police, ATF, Capitol Police, and West Virginia State Police. I want to update the public on the latest information we have regarding the disappearance of Katherine Sterling, wife of Senator Gene Sterling.

"Yesterday morning, the Harpersburg, West Virginia, police department located a gray Dodge Saturn sedan with two deceased occupants—a male and a female. The deceased male matches the description of one of the suspects described by Senator Sterling. There is no evidence of foul play, and it is believed both fatalities are the result of opioid overdoses, but we will await toxicology reports before issuing a final conclusion. We are not releasing the names of the deceased at this time.

"In the trunk of the vehicle, investigators located duct tape and nylon rope. Among these items we located long, human hairs similar in color to Mrs. Sterling's. Tests of these fibers confirmed they were strands of Mrs. Sterling's hair. In short, this vehicle was used to transport Mrs. Sterling the night of her kidnapping. This morning, at approximately 0700 hours, members of the FBI task force in conjunction with the Harpersburg Police and West Virginia State Police served a search warrant at 1010 Buck's Ferry Lane in Harpersburg. This is the residence of John Charles Klingerman and his wife, Myrtle Klingerman. John—who goes by JC—was not located at the residence, but agents made contact with his wife, Myrtle. Myrtle is not under investigation, and we do not believe she had any involvement in the disappearance of Mrs. Sterling. However, JC Klingerman is believed to be the second suspect involved in Mrs. Sterling's kidnapping.

"Here is a photo of Mr. Klingerman." A screen behind the SAIC displayed a mug shot. "We are looking for this man, JC Klingerman. Mr. Klingerman served eight years at the Mount Olive correctional facility for manslaughter. It is our belief that if we locate Mr. Klingerman, we will locate Mrs. Sterling. Mr. Klingerman was last seen in Harpersburg, West Virginia, yesterday, but we have information he may be traveling to North Carolina.

"We do not have a description of his vehicle. He was last seen with a beard, wearing woodland-camo coveralls and work boots. Anyone with information regarding the whereabouts of JC Klingerman is asked to contact the number on your screen. Do not approach Mr. Klingerman as he is presumed armed and dangerous. Mr. Klingerman, if you are watching, I urge you not to harm Mrs. Sterling and to turn yourself in peacefully. With that, I'll take a few questions."

The room exploded with gesticulating hands as frenzied reporters responded to the bombshell news. The feds simply wanted to get the name and image of their suspect to the public, but the SAIC respectfully fielded questions as the press fruitlessly pressed for speculation on Mrs. Sterling's fate. Derek patted Kevin on the back and slipped out of the room. He needed a nap. There was still a lot of work to be done.

◉ ◉ ◉

The grinding moan of the Keurig woke James from his couch slumber. Trying to focus, he saw Kat in the kitchenette, making no attempt to avoid disrupting his sleep.

It was after two in the morning when they made it back to his Georgetown dwelling. After a long day—coupled with the stressful events at the Sterling residence—they both crashed, zombie-like. James invited her to sleep in his bed, promising no coital provocations, but a disbelieving Kat offered to take the couch. After his insistence she take the bedroom, she acquiesced, and he crashed on the sofa.

"I'll take some coffee while you're up," he yawned, stretching his arms.

"Did I wake you? I'm sorry." She was wearing his T-shirt and gym shorts, a cup of coffee in each hand. "Scooch over." Placing the cups on the table, she sat and took out the notepad tucked beneath her arm.

"After last night, you've quite a lot to take down," James noted before sipping his Colombian blend.

"I've been at it all morning. I don't want to forget anything. Can you imagine what kind of book deal I'll land? I mean, I'd need help with the writing, but like you said, the material is pretty damn compelling. Maybe I could option it for a movie or Netflix series."

"Are you going to include the fact your husband's a furry?" He side-eyed her with a shit-eating grin.

"I don't want to talk about it."

"I got to know, did you do the whole dog routine with him? Was he a 'bad dog'? And what if was a good dog? Does he get spanked? What are the rules? I have several questions."

"Jimmy, that's enough." On the verge of bursting into laughter, the look on his face forced her to give in as they both convulsed in uncontainable guffaws at the previous evening's absurdity. "To be honest, periodically, he'd bring up this fantasy of being on a leash and ask me to scold him. I never gave in. Don't look at me like that. I swear I never played dog owner. I mean, I'm no prude. I'd watch porn and let him pull my hair—you know, slap my ass and stuff. But he never—and I mean never—wore a goddamn dog mask."

"She doth protest too much."

"Don't be a dick. And stop quoting Shakespeare; it's off-brand."

"I'm messing with you. Last night was wild. Maybe if you had let him wear the dog mask, he wouldn't have had you kidnapped."

"Not funny. And too soon. My life is not for your amusement, Jimmy."

"I got a picture of him doing that little gal," he said, staring down at his phone. "His body is a mess. Jesus, he could use some time on the elliptical. How did you let that climb on top of you?"

Taken aback by his boldness, her mouth froze agape in silent shock.

"Just wondering," he added.

"It's none of your business, and I don't want to see the picture. I'm well aware of how his body looks. I've never met anyone like you. You're a very strange person."

"You're the one married to a furry," he deadpanned, then clicked on the television. Kat sighed, shook her head, and returned to jotting down her thoughts.

Sipping his coffee, James contemplated the facts as he knew them: Kat kidnapped by suspects in league with Gene; the suspects' car tags returned to some Donovan guy, who ended up murdered; a rental car leased by a guy named Oscar was observed leaving the murder scene; suspicious emails between Gene and an unknown subject; and Gene was a furry nailing a hot piece of ass who happened to be his chief of staff. All this, and the Democratic primary frontrunner was being funded by a popular eco-celeb fronting a company of dubious legitimacy. It was a lot to take in, and none of it seemed to fit together in any logical fashion. Taking another sip, he saw a ubiquitous Fox News Alert.

"Um, princess."

"Stop calling me that. You're irritating me this morning," she answered, still eyeing her notes.

"This might interest you," he said and increased the television volume until she looked up at an ongoing press conference. A chisel-jawed FBI agent was displaying the picture of a John Charles Klingerman. "That's him," she declared. "That's JC."

"So that's the photo the cops showed your husband last night. And he told them the truth because this Oscar guy told him it would throw the cops off his trail."

"But that doesn't make sense. If the cops get this JC guy and he says Gene paid him to do this, that could put Gene in a really bad spot. Am I missing something?" she asked.

"Don't know. But, like you said, he must have an angle, something we don't know—maybe an alibi that clears him." The news indicated the gray Saturn was located with two deceased occupants, one believed to be a suspect in the kidnapping. "This is big."

"So, JC is on the loose?" asked Kat.

"Looks that way. But he's now the most wanted man in America."

"I wasn't ready for them to find these guys. I don't know how to feel. I need a drink." Her face was taut with stress.

"You okay?"

"Not really. I was thinking about last night. You obviously think it's a big joke, but a week ago, that was my house, and Mortimer was my cat. Now he's got my house, my cat, a young mistress, not to mention probably the Democratic nomination. This JC guy is going to take the fall for Gene. He's winning, Jimmy."

Seeing her despondent expression, James patted her knee softly, got up, and went to the kitchenette. Followed by the sound of clinking ice, he returned with a vodka tonic for her and his own Jack and Coke. Both sipped in silence for several minutes as the newscast continued its gaudy, eye-catching animation announcing BREAKING NEWS.

"You want to go on offense?" he asked.

"More than last night? You want to go to the cops?"

"I doubt they'd buy your story, and the only person who can corroborate it is a suspended Secret Service sexpot."

"Don't be so hard on yourself."

"I say we make him feel the heat. He thinks he's flying high, coming up roses. Let's remind him he's not in the clear after all."

"I like where your head's at, but where's this going?"

"We have his email, right? He thinks you're dead and this JC fellow is going to take the fall."

"Yes, and?"

"What if he gets an email from our boy JC claiming he still has you alive?"

Kat sat back and sipped her drink.

"That email was a correspondence between Gene and some other guy helping him get rid of you. What if he gets an email from JC demanding money? It would mess with his head."

"That's a crazy idea, which isn't surprising coming from you."

"He can't go to the cops, being that he was behind the whole thing," James added. "For all he knows, the guy sending the email has the goods on him." A thousand thoughts spun through Kat's brain. She relished the idea of Gene suffering from the dread of being outed.

"What do you have in mind?"

"We start subtle, then amp it up. Depends on how he reacts, of course," he said. Emboldened by vodka, she wasn't opposed to the notion. "We up the game, princess. We go on offense."

"Okay, let's do it," she declared.

James looked at his phone. "Oh shit."

"What is it?"

"Got a text from my wife. Is today Sunday? I forgot I have Emma and Jimmy today."

"How did you forget that?"

"Oh, I don't know. Maybe something to do with a kidnap victim, murder, Washington intrigue. It was an atypical week."

"I'm sorry, Jimmy," she said, realizing her impulsive rebuke stung. She pulled him into her and caressed his head affectionately. She felt the tension in his body ease. "Go be with your kids. I could use a day down, and you've got to be sick of me by now."

"You have outworn your welcome." Playfully, she punched his shoulder in response, his head still buried against her neck. "Before I go," he continued, "let's send old Gene a Sunday greeting."

"Sounds like a lovely idea. What did you have in mind?"

"Something to let him know someone out there isn't fooled by his play. Someone knows the score, and his world is about to fall apart."

"I like it."

"But there's something even more important he needs to know," added James.

"What's that?"

"He's been a bad dog. A very, very bad dog." She answered with a second punch to the shoulder, eliciting a warm chuckle against her neck.

◉ ◉ ◉

JC sat on a park bench, staring at grazing deer barely larger than hunting dogs. They crunched quietly through the fallen leaves, the trees showing early signs that spring was a month away. He was wearing the woodland-camo coveralls he'd slept in. The overnight temperatures dropped just shy of forty degrees, and he figured if the coveralls kept him warm in a deer stand, they would suffice in his pickup truck at a rest stop off Interstate 81. He didn't manage much sleep.

At sunrise, he'd started south with no destination in mind, but when he realized he hadn't eaten in sixteen hours, he pulled into the quaint river town of Lynchburg, Virginia. Next to a statue honoring Confederate war veterans, he located a quiet diner situated in the historic downtown. The biscuits and gravy did honor to the Confederacy and much to alleviate his doomful feelings—at least until he saw his picture on the television. The few patrons dining early on a lazy Sunday morning paid no heed to the image, but JC's heart pounded like the hydraulic stampers at his former job.

After breakfast, he drove down the hill to the river. He walked across a footbridge to a park on Percival's Island, trying to clear his head. The island sat in the middle of the James River near where a man named Lynch ran a ferry back when this land was an English colony. The river was full and swift from the recent Blue Ridge thaw. The water's rhythmic babbling relaxed his tense mind.

The FBI guy on TV had urged JC to turn himself in. Maybe that was the answer: go to the feds and spill his guts. Tell them about Oscar and the senator who hired him. Tell them the pretty gal had escaped. Recalling the previous week's events, it dawned on him how preposterous he would sound to investigators.

Nothing had turned out as planned, but this wasn't new for JC. Seemed his entire existence was one unforeseen happenstance after another. When he married Myrtle, he thought his fortunes had changed and his life was steering toward a happier direction. Then he was laid off. Options for meaningful, life-supporting work were nowhere to be found in Harpersburg. When Squinty floated the idea of turning a job for easy cash, he knew it was wrong. He had enough Christianity in him to know better. But it gave him meaning, even if for just a few weeks.

Sitting on a park bench on this cool March morning, he saw his foolishness with a clarity he hadn't before. For the first time in a year, he wasn't hungover. His decisions stood before him in judgment, and he declared them all guilty. He had agreed to take the life of a pretty gal. Instead, the pretty gal was—presumably—alive somewhere, while Cornhole and Squinty were ushered to eternity. He figured such an outcome had the hands of Jesus on it. He thought of Corn and Squints standing before an angel, trying to explain why their last act on earth was attempting to kill a lady who'd done them no wrong. In his mind, the angel looked at his deceased friends with the disapproving glare of a schoolmarm.

Jesus had spared him. Watching the gently passing stream beyond the munching deer, JC was certain the Lord was giving him one last chance to make things right. But it was his decision to make. He would not get this chance again. The feds wouldn't buy his story, and they would exhaust every contrivance to elicit a confession and the whereabouts of the pretty lady who'd gone missing; but he would have the truth on his side, and that was enough for JC. It was his time to get right with Jesus, the feds be damned.

He thought of his mother. She had been a good woman left heartbroken by his sinful ways. She married a sinner and gave birth to a sinner, but she always invoked Jesus and believed that one day JC would be delivered.

"Today is the day, Momma," he whispered to himself. Today, amid the flowing river, chirping songbirds, and grazing deer, was the day JC was saved. He felt Jesus in his heart. He smiled to himself. He'd never felt so good sober. Right now, the entire country was looking for John Charles Klingerman. Jesus found him first.

JC decided he would drive to DC. The FBI building was on Pennsylvania Avenue, not far from the White House. He would turn himself in and tell them everything he knew—about the senator's complicity in the scheme, about Oscar's guidance, about the pretty gal escaping; he'd spill it all. JC knew this would likely be his last occasion to quietly enjoy God's creation on a peaceful Sunday morning. So, he sat there at peace on Percival's Island, the breeze baptizing him with serenity.

◎ ◎ ◎

James always felt strange driving into his old Chantilly neighborhood. This Sunday was particularly odd due to this week's revelation that he was the Secret Service agent who'd refused to compensate a Brazilian hooker's carnal services. The unseasonably warm, sunny afternoon motivated residents to begin yardwork or wash their cars, so many a curious gaze slanted James's way as he pulled his F-150 in front of 3535 Evergreen Terrace. In the driveway sat an unfamiliar, red Toyota Tundra pickup.

Exiting his truck, James waved at Tyler across the street, whose expression was a mix of awkward discomfort and dread. The red truck had a license plate frame declaring that the owner's other car was a firetruck. If this wasn't enough to convince anyone of the occupant's valor, a firefighter decal and IFAA sticker adorned the rear windshield. Stopping at the end of the driveway, he took a deep breath as he processed matters. This was no accident. Audrey knew he was picking up the kids today.

Exiting the house wearing an OBX tank top and short athletic shorts, Audrey stormed his way, her blond ponytail swinging. She had lost at least fifteen pounds and looked good as hell, but she didn't appear happy.

"You're late," she accused.

"Good to see you too. Have a visitor?"

"Yes. A friend of mine is here."

"A friend?"

"Don't get accusatory. He planned to stop by well after you got the kids. But like I said, you're late."

"Sorry, I've been busy."

"Busy? Doing what? You're suspended."

"Hard to explain. I suppose we aren't getting back together."

Audrey scoffed, rolled her eyes, and placed her hands on her hips. He figured it was her way to bide time lest she say how she honestly felt.

"What's his name?"

"Matt," she answered flatly. Matt immediately became James's least favorite name.

"What does he do for a living?" he asked, eyeing the truck.

"Can you go one day without being a smart-ass?"

"Rather be a smart-ass than a dumbass."

"I knew you were going to say that. Pardon me if I don't laugh; it's not quite as funny when reporters are ringing your doorbell and shooting live shots with your house as a backdrop. You know, it's hard enough on Emma and Jimmy having their daddy gone. And now there are strangers showing up for no reason. Try explaining that."

"I'm sorry."

"Not good enough, James," she snapped, her arms folded. "You only give a shit about yourself. It's all about your needs, your job; it's all about you. That's the one good thing that's come from all this: I know exactly who you are." Her words stung. They stung all the more because of the sincerity. There was a time he couldn't imagine his sweet Audrey speaking with such venom, but he'd changed that. He changed her.

"Didn't take you long to start dating," he noted.

"Well, at least I waited until I was no longer married."

"Touché. But did it have to be a firefighter?" She was keenly aware of his animosity for firefighters, thinking them self-aggrandizing glory hounds.

"It's not serious, but he's a nice guy, and he's around. More than I could say about you."

"I was protecting the president. That's not insignificant."

"We don't need to rehash this. You were evidently doing more than that. You made the decisions you made. I can't change you. Nobody can change you but you." He remained silent. She was right. There was a time when such admonishment would generate a defense on his part. But there was no defense to be made. He had fucked everything up.

"Daddy!" exclaimed eight-year-old Emma as she came barreling out the front door, followed by six-year-old Jimmy dressed as Batman. Kneeling, James relished the flurry of hugs and kisses. "Where are we going, Daddy?" Emma asked gleefully.

"I think Chuck E. Cheese's sounds fun. How about you?" Both children cheered his idea as Matt emerged from the house. Tall and potbellied, it appeared Matt should think about laying off the pasta dishes at the firehouse. Predictably, he wore a dark-blue T-shirt declaring he was a member of Fairfax Fire and Rescue.

"Matt, this is James," Audrey said, clearly uncomfortable. James stood and shook his hand, both men clasping a bit harder than necessary. Hose-boy was balding with bags under his eyes and appeared to be in his fifties. *Audrey could do much better than this*, James thought. Judging by her expression, she knew exactly what he was thinking.

"I've heard a lot about you," Matt said, continuing the prolonged handshake grip battle, his breath smelling of beer.

"That's nice. Don't believe everything you hear. Fake news and all that," James returned, relinquishing his hand. Turning, he saw the neighbors in every lawn taking in the scene. When they realized he'd noticed, they returned to their leaf raking, car rinsing, or whatever excuse they used to take in the domestic drama across the street.

"You guys ready to go?" James asked the kids, eager to get

the hell out of there. "I'll have them back by seven," he promised Audrey, who nodded as Matt put his arm around her in what seemed a territorial display of affection. She looked mildly put out, perhaps recognizing what Matt was doing.

After strapping the kids in, James waved once more at Tyler across the street and climbed into the driver's seat. He looked through the passenger window at Audrey holding Matt's hand as they strode to the open front door. Just before they entered, she turned back toward his truck. Her gaze caught his. For several seconds, they looked at one another. She gave a mild wave, which he returned, swallowing his emotions. He cranked the ignition and smiled at Emma.

"This is going to be fun," he announced, trying not to imagine what Matt was going to do to Audrey in his old house. That didn't stop his heart from aching. Hiding his longing with a forced smile, he put the truck in drive.

CHAPTER 11

FORTUNATELY for Gene, he had enough foresight to have his friend Chet Bateman cover the Sunday-morning talk show circuit because he was one tired, sore old man. The only downside to a zealous bedroom romp with a fit beauty nearly forty years his junior was the reminder that his lust was more robust than his body. Making matters worse, he'd taken a third blue pill around 5 AM, and here he was at noon still sporting a painful boner.

Sipping his coffee while catching up on the news cycle, he couldn't help but marvel at how well events were playing out. Just a week ago, his poll numbers were trending down, his wife was a pain in his ass, and his lascivious escapades with Tanya were limited to bending her over his desk at his Russell Senate Building office. Now, as his late wife's cat peered at him with disapproval, he could boast fresh primary victories, the freedom to nail Tanya anytime he desired, and all the chess pieces were in place to take on President Ronald Frum in the fall.

The doorbell rang. It was Chet. Gene smiled and embraced his friend.

"Thank you so much for covering for me this morning. Yesterday was difficult."

They made their way to the living room.

"My pleasure, Gene. You know I'll help any way I can. I'm still trying to process that they've identified Kat's kidnappers. One of them is on the run. It's only a matter of time before they find him." Chet sounded hopeful.

"The police came by the house late last night," Gene said dourly. "They showed me a photo lineup. I picked out one of the men who took my Kat. It's him; I'm sure of it."

"If they get him, they could locate her. I feel in my heart she's alive out there somewhere."

"I wish I shared your optimism. But I'm trying to remain realistic about the odds of her being alive."

"Remain hopeful. You can't let your spirit diminish. That's what they wanted to do, break you. Never give up hope," Chet encouraged him. "Off air, both Chuck Todd and George Stephanopoulos told me they think the nomination is yours. They also send their condolences during this difficult time."

"That's kind of them. It's encouraging they're so certain about my nomination, but, as you know, there are two more contests in Mississippi and Michigan on Tuesday. Congresswoman Lightner is doing well in Mississippi. If we split the two, I'll be pleased, which is why I'm heading to Michigan tomorrow. But our message is resonating." Gene smiled.

"You look tired," Chet noted with his typical concern for others.

"I'm fine. But campaigning has become more difficult—and without Kat, almost unbearable." Gene closed his eyes as if trying to maintain his composure. Chet put a hand on his shoulder while Mortimer leered with feline skepticism. "Anyhow, Tanya should be here before long to go over my Grand Rapids and Dearborn trips. We'll stop in Jackson, Mississippi, in the evening. We can't completely give up on the South."

"I don't know how you're able to keep going, but I'm with you all the way, and anything you need—anything—I'm here for you." It was vintage Chet Bateman, sincere and heartfelt. Gene gave his thoughtful young friend an appreciative smile.

"I do it for our country. And to honor Kat," he said. The

conversation was interrupted when Tanya Smith entered the front door, appearing surprised to see Chet. She was wearing impossibly tight jeans and a low-cut blouse, a briefcase in hand.

"Chet, I didn't know you were going to drop by," she confessed. Politely standing, Chet felt a discomfort he only felt around Tanya. He normally brimmed with confidence around the fairer sex, but unlike the warm, flirtatious smiles he was accustomed to, Tanya always greeted him with a cold terseness. A year prior, Gene had fired his former chief of staff when Senator Joe Bratton recommended Tanya. Always susceptible to Joe's recommendations, Gene gave her an interview; the fit and striking blonde was essentially hired once she walked into his office.

"Nice to see you, Tanya," Chet lied. "I did a few TV hits this morning for the campaign and figured I'd stop by."

"Oh yes, I'd forgotten you covered for us this morning."

"You're welcome," said Chet, expecting a word of thanks. She looked at him emotionlessly. "Anyhow, I should be going."

"Good," began Tanya, "because we're expecting Zach to come by and cover tomorrow's itinerary."

"Congratulations, my good friend." Chet embraced Gene once more. "Good luck tomorrow. You're still my inspiration."

"Thank you for all your support. It means so much to me, and if Kat were here, she'd thank you as well."

"Stay hopeful. They'll find her. She's alive. I feel it in my soul." After receiving another fatherly embrace, Chet departed.

Gene grabbed Tanya and kissed her just as the front door latched.

"You're excited to see me again," Tanya noted, patting the pharmaceutical-induced erection through his khaki shorts. "But we have real work to do." She moved to the dining room, placing binders on the table. Ogling Tanya's backside, Gene wanted to bend her over the table but knew she was right; he'd been neglecting his obligations.

"I'll be right back. Need to check a few emails," he declared as he ascended the staircase.

In his study, Gene unlocked the computer and checked his government email account: nothing but a few congratulatory messages interspersed with inquiries from his campaign manager. He logged onto the AOL account he and Senator Joe Bratton used to communicate privately.

March 6

> **Mountainman:** Congrats on the clean sweep! What did I tell you? Leaving Kansas early to deal with your "grief" was a stroke of genius. Press was eating it up. I know why you really wanted to get back . . . lucky bastard.

> **Mountainman:** Just saw on the news one of those rednecks is dead and they identified the other. Said you identified him. Way to stick to the plan. This was a little unexpected but it's going to work out fine.

Below Joe's message was an unopened email sent this morning. He wasn't familiar with the Yahoo email account princess-backfromthedead@yahoo:

> **Princessbackfromthedead:** Good morning Gene. Congratulations on your big victory yesterday. Seems that all your planning and hard work are paying off. Americans love a good comeback story. A grieving husband who perseveres after the loss of his wife? Oh, and your dear Katherine is happy for your primary wins. How do I know? Why, she's right here. I think she's smiling, but I can't be certain being that there's tape over her mouth. Oh, silly me. I forgot to introduce myself . . . I'm JC. You remember me? Yessir, the

authorities are looking for me now, but I ain't worried much. What do I have to worry about? I got you by the balls. See, how I figure, myself, Kat, Oscar, and (of course) you are the only folks who know you're the piece of shit behind all this. So, if you want to go on and be president, you're gonna have to deal with me. With my name out there now, I'm going to need a little extra cash to get to South America. You get me the money, I kill the bitch, and we're all square. I'll be in touch BIG DAWG. -JC

This couldn't possibly be JC. After Gene reread the message, his disbelief was displaced by enough fear to kill his hard-on. The email came with an attachment. He clicked on it to reveal a photo of Katherine. She was seated on the floor with her mouth duct-taped. Gene's nerves fired with electricity. His hands trembled. He peeked out the window, expecting to see a nondescript van parked outside; was the FBI trying to bait him into a confession? The only visible vehicle was the idling Suburban of his Capitol Police detail.

"Are you coming down? We have a lot to cover," shouted Tanya from the ground floor.

"I think you should come up here. I've got to show you something."

"We don't have time for that now. You can let the dog out later tonight," she shouted back.

"Just come up here, please. It's work related."

When Tanya entered, she saw Gene's screen-illuminated, ashen face.

"What's the matter?"

Silently, he pointed at the screen. She leaned over his shoulder and read the emails. "What the hell is this? Who's this from?"

"I have no idea."

"What email account is this? Who knows about this?"

"I made this account for one purpose only: to privately correspond with Joe."

"Joe? Joe Bratton?" Tanya appeared alarmed.

"Yes. We figured if we set up email accounts using bogus information, we could communicate off the grid. He's the only person I gave it to."

Taking the mouse, she scrolled up to view the entire correspondence. Gene was rubbing his mouth as he was prone to do when stressed.

"Joe is the Mountainman account?"

"Yeah."

"This was a bad idea, Gene. You shouldn't be putting anything online."

"It's anonymous."

"No matter, you've created an unnecessary vulnerability. I told you exactly what to do, and this wasn't in the plan. I can't believe Joe would be so careless. You sure you didn't share this with anyone?"

"I swear to you. It was just Joe and I. It's harmless."

"Joking about offing your wife online isn't harmless. Don't respond to it," she ordered with emotionless determination. "The email address is 'princess back from the dead.' That's curious."

"I saw that," said Gene, still rubbing his mouth. "You don't think the FBI is onto us, do you?" His brow furrowed and perspiring, hives began blotting his neck. "Maybe they discovered my email, and this is a ruse to have me respond. Or, my God, maybe they'll wait to see if I report this to them." His whole body shook in full freak-out mode, his eyes fastened pleadingly on his mistress.

"Settle down," said Tanya coolly. "There's no need to panic." She gave Gene a maternal kiss on the forehead. "Go to the bathroom and splash water on your face. We've got to get ready for tomorrow." Staring at him earnestly, her resolve comforted her lover, who nodded, stood, and exited the study. Taking out her phone, she took a pic of the screen. Then, taking a post-it note from the drawer, she wrote down the email addresses. She stared intently at the last message; she knew the task before her: determine who the hell Princessbackfromthedead was, then find them and kill them.

⊙ ⊙ ⊙

James was driving home drunk. He hadn't planned to, but after returning his children, a storm of regret tightened his chest like a vise. Fortunately, the douchebag, ladder-climbing glory hound wasn't there when he dropped them off.

Deep down, he knew the firefighter his wife had been fellating all afternoon wasn't to blame, but James was tired of beating himself up and needed to aim his derision externally. When he stopped at Champs Sports Bar for the second time this week, the bartender recognized him and continued his generous pours. The Jack Daniels didn't erase the thought of the potbellied fire-boy plowing his wife but did mitigate the heartache.

James stayed later than expected and stumbled to his truck. The night was pitch black as he scanned the dimly lit parking lot, praying not to see another kidnap victim hop her way into his life. The thought of Kat brought a smile to his face.

As he headed toward the I-66 ramp, his iPhone chirped an incoming text. It was Kat, inquiring as to his whereabouts and asking if everything was okay; she hadn't expected him to be so late. Her concern was touching. It dawned on James that she was the one person who still gave a damn about him. Looking up, he saw a small pickup truck braking.

"Shit!"

He jammed his brakes, but the F-150 couldn't avoid rear-ending the tailgate as James jerked forward against his seat belt. The pickup pulled to the shoulder, so he followed suit and got out to inspect the damage. The clunker Toyota took the worst of it, the bumper now tucked beneath the tailgate. The other driver remained in his truck a good while.

"You alright?" asked James as the driver finally came to the rear of his vehicle.

"I'm fine. Neck hurts a bit," answered the short, beer-gutted fellow in woodland-camo coveralls. James rolled his eyes, thinking, *Of course it does.*

"Why were you driving so slow?" James wondered.

"I didn't want to get pulled over. Just stopped for gas," he answered with a twang, still rubbing his neck. "You're the one who hit me."

"Doesn't look too bad. What do you say we just exchange information?"

"You've been drinking," the driver accused him. This shook James. The last thing he needed in his life was a DUI. Maybe his best option was to jump in his truck and speed away.

"I've had a couple," confessed James, using the standard drunkard's admission. "But we don't need the cops, do we?"

"Naw, I don't want no cops either."

"I'm James." He extended his hand.

"John," the driver said as their hands clasped. James looked intently at John. Like all cops, he couldn't remember a name ten seconds after hearing it, but a face he could recall for eternity, and John looked familiar.

"You from West Virginia?" he asked, looking at the truck's tag. John had about a day's growth on his double-chinned face. His hair was oily and thinning in front.

"Yes sir, just in town for work."

"Heard on the news the guy who took that senator's wife last week is from West Virginia. Can you believe that?" James eyed John closely, wondering if his drunken intuition was correct.

"I did hear that on the radio. It's a sick world," the stranger opined with a shake of his head.

"I'll get my driver's license and insurance so you can get on your way. I'll just need your info as well," said James as he moved to his truck, thinking, *How does this shit happen to me every time I drink at Champs?* He opened his passenger door and rummaged through the glove compartment.

"Know what, mister? That's alright. Ain't no need to bother with that. It was a simple mistake. Besides, this beater ain't worth a nickel anyhow," said John.

"Really? You sure? It'll only take a second."

"Yes sir. You be careful, now. I gotta go." John turned with a wave. The Toyota Tacoma shook as he plopped his hefty form in the driver's seat. John began pulling the door shut when James's strong hand intercepted the doorframe; his other trained a 9mm semiautomatic Walther at him.

"Where are you going, JC?" asked James.

"Who's JC?"

"If you're not John Charles Klingerman, then show me your ID."

"You a cop?"

"That question's more complicated than you think. But one thing's certain: I'm the guy pointing a pistol at you." John's eyes darted back and forth. James had seen this before, back in his police days. The pudgy driver was weighing his options. "Don't do it, JC," he advised.

"I was going to turn myself in to the FBI. I didn't kill that lady."

"I know you didn't. Now put these on." James pulled cuffs from his waistband and flipped them on JC's lap.

"You always have handcuffs?"

"In the glove box with this guy." James nodded at the handgun. JC cuffed one hand and fumbled vainly in trying to cuff the other.

James reached in and clicked it to his second wrist. Escorting JC to the passenger seat of his F-150, James climbed in the driver's side, placing the handgun under his seat. "Did you need anything out of your truck?" he asked.

JC shook his head. "What are you going to do with me, mister? I was serious when I said I was going to turn myself in."

"You're all over the news."

"I know. Are you hoping to get an award or something?"

"No. It's not like you killed anybody," James slurred.

"That's the second time you said that. Everybody else believes that lady's dead and that I killed her."

"Don't worry about it." James cranked on the engine.

"You're pretty drunk. Maybe I should drive."

"Can you drive with cuffs on?"

"Don't know, never tried. As long as you put it in drive and park, I think I could do it." Thinking on it for several seconds, James got out and helped JC into the driver's seat, fastened his seatbelt, then retrieved his pistol and sat on the passenger side.

"You're not going to try some crazy shit, are you, JC?"

"No sir, I've done sworn off crazy. I swore to my momma, God rest her soul. I've done lost everything. My friends are dead, and I'm no longer there to help my dear Myrtle." JC's voice broke as his lips quivered with emotion.

"Myrtle's your wife?" James asked. JC nodded and began openly weeping, his head bent low as his body heaved in remorse. He wiped his eyes with his cuffed hands.

"I've got nobody to blame but myself," JC shared between sobs. James consoled him with a pat on the back.

"I know how you feel, buddy."

"My life is completely screwed up. I always make the wrong choice. I always fuck it up."

"JC, I think you're my spirit animal. But we better get out of here before a cop stops to check on us."

"You're turnin' me in anyhow, so why does it matter?"

"I think I have a better idea," James said and placed the truck in drive.

⊙ ⊙ ⊙

The Scotsman was closed on Sunday evenings, but it was never closed for Oleg Yumashev. Late that afternoon, the Belarusian owner was informed Mr. Yumashev would be meeting a couple guests around nine. When news broke that the FBI had identified Katherine Sterling's kidnappers, the Russian oligarch was troubled. This disquietude stemmed from the photo Oscar had provided purporting to be proof of her demise. It was sloppy work and had been gnawing at him for days.

Sergei recognized Senator Joe Bratton's lumpy silhouette approaching the entrance in his typical disheveled, wrinkled suit and open collar. When notified Oleg wished to meet him, the senator knew it was tied to the outing of the West Virginia suspects.

"Good evening, Oleg." Joe extended his hand but was answered by a cold side-eye. The owner poured him a bourbon as he nestled next to Oleg at the bar. "Is something wrong?" Joe queried, sipping his Woodford Reserve. The Russian turned his gaunt face toward the senator in silent, menacing Russian reticence. Unable to stand the weighty silence, Joe pressed, "Everything is going fine, right?"

"Why do you say that?" asked Oleg.

Joe was confused. They'd gone over this ad nauseum.

"I'm assuming you called me here because the feds identified those dolts who did Kat in. We knew this was a possibility," Joe reasoned. "Why the concern?" For nearly two years, Joe had sensed Oleg knew more than he let on. Russians were notoriously accomplished chess players, and to Joe's mind, Oleg always seemed a move or two ahead of him.

"You say 'did Kat in.' I suppose this is an American euphemism for they killed her?"

"Of course that's what I meant. You aren't still worried about that photo, are you?"

"I am. I deal in certainties; you know this," Oleg lectured in his thick accent. "That is why Gene's wife was to be done in by Frum supporters. It distanced us from the deed while creating a narrative for the campaign. Tell me, how does one create certainty?"

Joe looked around and shrugged.

"Redundancy. That is how you create certainty. With redundancy, an overlooked concern may be remedied by overlapping systems to diagnose and correct the problem. That is why air travel is so safe: the aircraft have redundant functions. For every system, there are backup systems."

Oleg paused to sip his sixteen-year single malt scotch. Trying to look at ease, Joe did the same, wondering where Oleg was going with this. Oleg motioned to Sergei near the door. For a moment, Joe feared the Russians were going to off him, until Taya Sokolov walked in wearing a low-cut blouse and skin-tight jeans.

A year ago, Joe had introduced Taya to Gene as Tanya Smith at Oleg's behest. Both men knew Gene would prove incapable of resisting the allure of the sexy young woman, who—once she served up orgasms and established trust—could promote Joe's plan for winning the nomination. Now Gene's chief of staff, the Russian mole was securely implanted in the office of the likely Democratic nominee for president.

Taya placed three sheets of paper on the bar between the gentlemen, then kissed each of Oleg's cheeks before shooting Joe his second disapproving Russian stare.

"See, Joe, Taya here is just one of my redundant systems, and she has diagnosed a problem. She has discovered an uncertainty, and Taya detests uncertainty as much as I."

Joe sifted through the papers and realized they showed the email correspondence between Gene and himself. "This is just Gene and I bullshitting."

"You were told only to speak of our endeavor in person—no phone, no texts, no emails, nothing," Oleg reprimanded him.

"These emails are bogus, nothing to tie them to us. We've been communicating like this for years. Just a way to speak our minds without the press or some watchdog using them against us," Joe protested.

"If there's a cell number associated with those email accounts, the feds can easily ascertain to whom they belong," Oleg said, looking grave.

"They were set up with burner phones. There is literally no information they could obtain about us. Zero."

"No matter, you both all but admit to being complicit in Mrs. Sterling's murder," Taya castigated him in her native accent instead of the neutral, Midwest voice she faked as Tanya. "And while you insist this is just innocent locker room talk, take a look at the last email."

She took the bottom page, slapped it on the bar, and pointed at the final email message. "So, do you wish to explain to us, once again, how this email is private and safe? That nobody else was aware of it?" Taya demanded with sarcasm.

Joe reread the final email several times in stunned silence. He downed what remained of his bourbon.

"This has to be a bluff," he concluded. "There's simply no way anyone could have traced this. Seriously, there is no possible way. And this I can say for certain: JC did not write this. He could barely spell his own name."

"You are right. It is unlikely JC wrote this," Oleg conceded. "Maybe the FBI did. Think about it: they pose as the kidnapper to see if Gene will incriminate himself, see if he tacitly admits to the deed. And if he doesn't disclose this demand to investigators, he has inadvertently incriminated himself." Fear flashed in Joe's eyes. "There is one thing that gives me pause. The flippant sarcasm doesn't fit the FBI mold; it's possible it's not the feds, but an outside actor."

"It's possibly a sick joke then? Like I said, a bluff," Joe said hopefully. Taya placed a printed photo of Kat, her mouth duct-taped, on the bar.

"This was attached to the email. This was no bluff," she announced.

"Jesus Christ. This can't be real. Is Gene going to respond?" Joe asked Taya, shell shocked and motioning for another pour.

"I told him not to. My thoughts were the same as Mr. Yumashev—best not to respond for fear he implicates himself."

"How's Gene?" Joe wondered.

"Panicked," Taya said with disgust. "I had to calm him down and refocus on tomorrow's campaign stops."

"So, so what do we do?" Joe was ashen.

"We determine who this emailing jokester is. I know people who can easily determine sources of digital communications," Oleg said. "Once we know who this Princessbackfromthedead is, we kill them."

"Let me do it," Taya said.

"No, we need you with Senator Sterling. I'll give Oscar the opportunity to right his mistake. He should have killed JC when he couldn't prove Mrs. Sterling was dead. If he cannot complete the mission, we go to an alternate plan."

"Alternate plan?" asked Joe.

"We neutralize Oscar," Taya said coldly.

"See, Joe, when someone makes a mistake—like you did with this childish emailing—and creates uncertainty, someone will pay for that mistake," Oleg said. "JC is out there. The feds will find him, or he'll kill himself. We determine if this emailing jokester is an independent actor or the feds. If independent, Oscar neutralizes him. If the US government, we neutralize Oscar."

Joe looked ill. He could kick himself for his carelessness but settled for a swig of warm, amber liquid.

"You Americans talk too much, Joe. Always sharing your feelings and your thoughts. Let this be a lesson." Oleg took his own healthy swallow.

"I must leave. We have a long day tomorrow," Taya announced.

"Did you please the senator after yesterday's victory?" asked Oleg with a subtle grin. Taya sighed.

"Yes. I pleased him very much."

"Did he do that thing where—"

"Yes," she interrupted with annoyance. Oleg appeared amused as Joe looked confused.

"Your friend enjoys rutting like a dog," the Russian revealed.

"Don't all men?" Joe asked rhetorically.

"I will explain some other time."

CHAPTER 12

Monday, March 7

A WEEK AGO, Kat didn't know the guy snoring next to her.

James had teetered into the room after midnight with the exaggerated commotion of a drunk man trying to remain silent. As he flopped onto the bed, part of her hoped for a touch, a gentle hand reaching over to acknowledge her. In the darkness, she peered over her shoulder. James was passed out. She comforted herself that he was back safely. The previous afternoon, she had decided to make love to him, but as she observed him slumber noisily, she figured it could wait a day. She let him sleep.

As morning light pierced the blinds, she marveled at the absurdity of her predicament, wondering why she put so must trust in this guy. It might be the way he looked with those stubble whiskers or the certainty with which he carried himself. Whatever it was, she trusted him. For years, with Gene, she'd had nothing but uncertainty. Like so much of Washington, DC, her husband was an act. Nothing about him was genuine. She never internalized that until the kidnapping.

Meanwhile, her Jimmy was a mess—a drinking, whoring mess. And in his odd, nicknaming way, she could tell he cared for her. She knew who he was, flaws and all, and that's more than she could say about her husband. By her reckoning, life came too easy for James. Handsome, charming, and intelligent, nature made a balancing corrective—as it always does—by making him a self-destructive maniac.

"Why are you staring at me?" he asked, eyes still closed.

"You missed your chance," she countered. He opened one eye.

"My chance?"

"Yep."

"Dammit. I was busy feeling sorry for myself. It's probably for the best. I wouldn't have made a good showing."

"Fair point. And undoubtedly true. You were asleep before your head hit the pillow."

"If we hooked up, you'd still be slapping my pecker, trying to bring it to life," he deadpanned, eyes still closed, causing Kat to cover her face in laughter. "By the way, your short, mussed morning hair? Cute as hell."

"Thanks," she said, teasing her mane self-consciously.

"Yesterday was a rough one, princess. And I handled it with my usual lack of grace."

"I'd expect nothing less." She eased her fingers into his hair to massage his cranium.

"That feels wonderful. My head is pounding."

"I figured as much. Did you have a nice time with your kids?"

Eyes still closed, James sighed to himself. "It's bittersweet. Seeing the kids, I mean. They're nothing but innocent joy. It's adults like me that fuck everything up."

"Can't argue with that."

"Anyhow, Audrey's seeing a new man."

"She is? How do you know?"

"He was there when I picked up the kids."

"That was completely intentional. She wanted to rub your nose in it. That's not right."

"No, she has every right to flaunt it in my face. After all, she's been hearing news flashes about my escapades for months now. But it's even worse than it sounds."

"What do you mean?"

"He's a firefighter."

"What's wrong with firefighters?"

James opened one eye again as she continued massaging his temples.

"Never mind, no need to get into my anti-hose-puller rant. At least he wasn't attractive. Needs to hold off on seconds at the firehouse."

"She aimed down. A lot of women do that when they've been cheated on by a hot guy. It's a subconscious thing, a defense mechanism."

"You think?"

"I read it somewhere; and I have some personal experience with the phenomenon."

"Audrey looked good. She lost weight."

"How ugly was the guy?"

"He's probably a three."

"That's too bad. Going from a nine to a three is no picnic."

"You have me at a nine? Sweet. Gene's about a two or three."

"Yeah, the guy before Gene was easily a nine, maybe even a ten. It's a judgment call."

Eyes still closed, James nodded, then felt her moist lips touch his. Their tongues gently caressed before she pulled back with a grimace.

"What's wrong?" he asked, disappointed.

"Jimmy, your breath is awful. How about I get some coffee, then we discuss the possibility of some revenge sex."

He smiled. "I like where your head's at. I can brush my teeth first."

She kissed his forehead and sprang from the bed to the door. Just as she left the room, James recalled last night's unlawful detention and leapt in a panic but couldn't intercept her before she screeched in fear and scurried back to the bedroom.

"There's a dude on the floor!" she warned, hiding behind James.

"I know. I should have mentioned this earlier: I met someone last night." He put his arm around her trembling shoulders. "Don't be scared, princess, we're safe. Come with me." Taking her hand, he guided her through the kitchenette to the living room where a plump man lay on his side, secured to an eighty-pound kettlebell by handcuffs threaded through the handle. Awkwardly, he began sitting up, sliding the exercise weight toward his front.

"Didn't mean to scare you, ma'am," twanged the unexpected guest in woodland camo. "I preferred to crash on the couch, but your boyfriend wouldn't oblige." In disbelief, Kat stared at the dude hobbled on the floor. Sans her morning coffee, processing what the hell was going on was proving difficult.

"Jimmy, can you explain why there is a man handcuffed to a metal ball?"

"I literally ran into him last night. See, I was leaving Champs— where I met you, if you recall—and rear-ended this guy. You two know each other."

"We do?"

"He's shaved since last time you saw him," James noted. Stepping forward, she peered closely at the prisoner.

"Do I know you?" she asked when the man's eyes widened with recognition.

"Holy shit, you are alive. Why'd you cut your hair?" he asked. Kat's eyes lit up like a flame.

"Why you rat fuck," she cursed and lunged at him, flailing her fists about his face in a flurry of unpenned emotion. Unable to fend for himself, JC fell backward while she meted her whirlwind fit of profanity-laced vengeance. From behind, James pulled her off and penned her arms in an embrace.

"Settle down, princess. I get it." James held on as she struggled fitfully. "But this isn't the way to go."

"What the hell, Jimmy? Where did you find him? What in

God's name is going on?" she asked, her face covered in tears and bewilderment. Holding her tight, he pulled her to the couch as the tension in her body began to subside. JC rolled to the side and fumbled into a seated position, the kettlebell situated between his splayed legs.

"I deserved that, ma'am," he admitted.

"No shit, asshole. Why didn't you tell me, Jimmy?"

"I had every intention to, but then you started talking about sex and I got sidetracked. Now, can I let go of you? I don't want you attacking JC. Let's be adults about this. He drove me home, and we had an interesting conversation. Came to realize we have a lot in common. Mostly our mutual propensity to screw things up."

"He drove you home?" she asked with incredulity as James removed his arms.

"I had a really bad day. Remember, that's why you were going to have sex with me?"

"I was going to sleep with you because, for some reason, I let myself believe you weren't some lowlife loser—not to mention I saw my husband wearing a dog mask while nailing his staffer thirty-six hours ago." She wiped her face.

"I'd leave you two alone, but this thing is really heavy," JC chimed in, eyeing the kettlebell.

"My bad, JC. It's been an eventful week," James said, turning to Kat. "He's really not that bad a guy. He planned to turn himself in, until I hit him, of course."

"Not a bad guy? Do you hear yourself? He kidnapped me six days ago."

"I'm sorry about that, ma'am," JC interjected.

"See, Kat, he's sorry."

Kat looked at James as if a baby arm were growing out of his head.

"And what in your brain thought it was a good idea to handcuff him and bring him here?"

"For one, I needed a driver. And I figured we had a lot of questions for him."

"No kidding. So does the FBI."

"We know more than they do. So, if I may formally introduce you: Kat this is JC. JC, Kat."

"I'm surrounded by crazy people." She buried her face in her hands.

James rubbed her shoulders. "This'll be great material for your book."

"Let's just call the FBI. They're looking for him. He's here. This is exhausting," she retorted.

"We have him now. Don't you have questions? Afterward, if you still want to call the FBI, then go ahead." Numbed with confusion, she remained silent. "I'll start," announced James. "JC, who hired you?"

"A man named Oscar, sir."

"You don't have to call me 'sir.' That's interesting. Was his name Oscar Reese?"

"Don't know his last name, just went by Oscar."

"How do you know Oscar?"

"We didn't know him, sir. Squinty, my friend, told us about a job where some rich fella wanted his wife dead. It was a lot of money for Cornhole and I." JC's lips quivered with emotion as his eyes welled up.

"We heard about your friend on TV. Sorry about your loss," James consoled him. "I'm sure Cornhole was a decent man."

"Um, you do realize Cornhole kidnapped me," noted Kat.

"Have a heart, princess. He was JC's good, best friend."

"Don't call me princess. Pretty sure I don't like you anymore."

"Who's Squinty?" asked James.

"John Donovan," JC answered. "He's dead too." He broke down, his fleshy body heaving as he lowered his head and cried. James retrieved a Kleenex.

"It's hard to lose friends. I've lost close friends before. It's very painful. I hope you find closure."

Being that the big man's hands were restrained, James dabbed JC's fat cheeks with the tissue. Returning to the couch, he received a "What the fuck?" look from Kat.

"Can't you see he's hurting? Show some humanity." James returned to questioning. "So, Squinty introduced you to Oscar?" JC nodded affirmation. "Was Oscar at the house when you kidnapped Kat?"

"Yes, sir, he was. When Corn and I got there, the garage door was open as planned, and we parked in there. He closed the door, and we waited upstairs for the old man to return with his wife. Oscar told us what to do. Just had to tie the lady up, throw her in our trunk, and drive off. He ran the show. Even when Ms. Kat and her husband arrived, Oscar told each of us what to do. Oscar gave me a phone, and I was to reach out to him when the job was finished so we could get the rest of our money."

"And the job was?" James asked. With an uneasy look, JC looked up with tear-stained cheeks.

"Well, you know, sir."

"You were going to kill her?" James asked, to which JC nodded in confirmation.

"Sorry, ma'am. We was poor and couldn't find work. Corn hurt himself at the warehouse and got hooked on the feel-good pills. Don't make it right, but we wasn't making good choices. I'm sure you're a nice lady, and I feel bad for what I done," JC confessed. "I suppose this is Jesus's way to right my soul." Kat took in JC's raw, emotional confession in silence.

"What happened when Kat got away?" asked James.

"Corn was supposed to had filled up the car. I was stupid to trust him with that, but anyhow, when I asked him if he had, he said he didn't remember. I knew of a Shell station nearby, so I pulled off into a parking lot, and that's when the car died. We was out of gas. I go to fill up the jerry can and come back to find Corn passed out and that little lady gone."

"What did you guys do?"

"Next day we find out the old man was a senator and that they couldn't find the lady. Like I said, we was hurtin' for money. Corn's girlfriend was a skinny little filly, so we dressed her like Ms. Kat here and showed Oscar a photo like she was dead. He must of bought it, because he gave me a shitload of cash."

"Pretty ballsy," observed James.

"Thank you, but like I said, we was broke."

"Desperate times call for desperate measures."

"I suppose."

"We know something about that, don't we, princess?" James asked rhetorically. Kat sighed and shook her head. "What does Oscar look like?"

"Lean fella, dark hair all slicked back, with a funny-sounding voice, like a foreigner's voice."

"Oscar killed your friend Squinty," James announced.

"I reckon you're right. Nobody really had a beef with Squints."

"How were you going to kill me?" Kat cut in. JC appeared as discomfited as a schoolboy before a pop quiz. "It's a fair question. After all, you're the asshole who tied me up and put me in a car trunk."

"It is fair, ma'am. I was by the river yesterday in Lynchburg thinkin' about what I'd done. I ain't proud of it. And don't right know what got in my skull to thinkin' that killin' a lady for money was the answer to my problems. The devil knows when a man is desperate, when a man is afraid of appearing a failure to his woman. The devil preys on such men. I didn't want to let my Myrtle down and fell prey to the devil. I prayed to Jesus to rid my soul of the devil's thoughts and decided to turn myself in."

"That's lovely, JC, it really is," Kat snarked, "but you didn't answer my question."

"We was gonna take you to the woods and shoot you with a twelve-gauge, then bury you. If we'd done it early in the morning, folks would of assumed we was hunting small game."

"And how much money did they offer you?" she asked.

"Twenty-five grand for us to split. I'm awful sorry, Ms. Kat, for my evil intentions. Jesus said to love your enemies, and I hope you have it in your heart to find forgiveness just as Jesus forgave."

"I'm an atheist," she revealed flatly.

"Well, I hope you are saved one day."

"You know, I don't really need to be proselytized by my Christian would-be murderer." Seeing her jaw tighten and fists ball up, James intervened.

"Um, this is a good thing. This is a healthy dialogue I think will help us heal our grievances so that we can move forward," James pronounced, summoning his inner Dr. Phil. "JC is clearly sorry for his misdeeds when he was dealing with some personal issues, and, Kat, you're understandably upset he kidnapped you for money and planned to blow your brains out before burying you in a shallow grave. This is very, very healthy."

He beamed a confident smile, pleased with his summation. Both JC and Kat stared in disapproving silence.

"Don't you see? We are giving these problems oxygen. Like they say, sunlight is the best disinfectant."

"Jimmy, can we speak in the kitchen?" Kat asked, though it sounded more like a demand. James complied.

"Jimmy, I can't do this. This is too much."

"Okay? But what else should we do?"

"I told you. Go to the FBI."

"Not a good idea."

"And why is it not a good idea to just report this like normal people do? We have my kidnapper in the living room."

"What do I tell the cops, princess? This is a uniquely fucked-up situation, and I don't know exactly how to make this right for me."

"Make it right for you?"

"Yeah, for me. You're not the only one caught up in this mess. I have a career I'm trying to salvage."

"So, you won't call the cops because you're afraid it'll ruin your chance of getting back into the good graces of the Secret Service? Tell me you're kidding."

"Don't get accusatory; you're taking notes for a tell-all. All I'm saying is I have skin in this too. I have an interview at Inspection Division this afternoon. I meant to tell you before, but we've been preoccupied."

"Inspection?"

"Yeah, it's internal affairs," he sighed. "It won't take long. All I ask is we hold off calling the feds."

"Wait, do you mean you're going to leave me alone with that monster?"

"He's actually kind of a sweet guy when you get to know him."

"I really am, ma'am," JC interjected from the living room. "I won't be no nuisance."

"You can hear us?" asked James.

"Yes sir. Clear as day. And I ain't no monster, Ms. Kat. I'm a reformed man."

Grabbing her by the shoulders, James looked intently into Kat's eyes.

"You've trusted me this far. Just hold off calling the feds until I get back," he pleaded. "I just need to think this through."

She was torn and tired. Just when she'd begun to allow her heart to ponder the possibility of opening up to this rugged, rogue lunatic, he brought home a felonious redneck claiming reformation. Audrey must be one amazing woman; being married to this guy would test the patience of Job.

"I'll hold off. But you come straight back after your interview. I don't want to be alone with him any longer than I have to. You may think he's a sweetheart, but he never locked you in a trunk."

"I said I was sorry, ma'am," JC responded from the living room floor.

"I know you are, JC," Kat acknowledged over James's shoulder before locking her gaze on his eyes. "I'm trusting you, Jimmy."

"I know you are, and you can. This morning didn't really go the way I planned, but I was compromised yesterday. Oh, and one more thing: Brian and his boyfriend, Dante, get back from Napa Valley today. If he knocks, don't answer. It may be hard to explain why you're here with a handcuffed Frum supporter. I'll text him so he knows I'm busy." Kat nodded, still looking into his eyes. He leaned in and kissed her softly.

"Jimmy," she began as he looked at her expectantly. "Please brush your teeth."

CHAPTER 13

Crying Gene is a loser and always has been. He belly-
aches about the climate hoax and offers nothing but big
government and taxes that would kill our economy. An
economy bigger and better than any economy in the history
of our country. If his dear wife were alive, she'd file for
divorce from this loser. #BBMA - @PresidentFrum

CHIEF OF STAFF Gary Boxterman was reviewing today's presidential line-by-line when his phone buzzed. It was a text from the vice president: "Check Twitter."

With understandable hesitation, he did so, resulting in the immediate urge to cut himself. The president's tweet was in response to Sterling's rally where the senator railed against the administration's stance on climate change and warned of the impending cataclysm if government didn't take action. It wasn't lost on Gary that the president not only labeled a senator who'd lost his wife a "loser" but also indicated she was no longer alive, which the police still hadn't determined. Everything about the tweet made Gary ill, and the fact that it already had over 20,000 likes was horrifying.

He popped two Tums. The thought of resigning crossed his mind. He could revert to making hits on the cable shows while media companies lined up, their ghost writers in tow, to sign him to a seven-figure book deal. At 12:30, he was scheduled to have lunch with the president and Senator Bratton in the Oval Office dining room. Walking down the hall, he felt like a convicted man facing lethal injection. He knew what President Frum would ask.

Entering the small dining room, Gary was greeted by Joe Bratton.

Shortly afterward, President Frum entered from the Oval Office. "What did you think of that tweet, Joe?" He appeared very pleased with himself.

"Very clever, Mr. President. Keep pushing the Frum economy. That's all that matters in the end," complimented Joe as they shook hands.

"What about you, Gary?" asked the president.

"Probably could have left out any mention of his wife."

"You're such a pussy. Isn't he, Joe? You'll see; I'm right on this. Trust me. This will do the trick. By attacking Gene, I'm boosting him up to my level. You've said it yourself: you'd rather take on Gene than Cassandra. I'll keep going after him, and the Dems will get pissed and nominate him to spite me so I won't have to take on that colored broad."

Gary winced. Joe did not.

"Come on, let's eat," the president announced as they sat for lunch: burgers and fries. "So, what have you got for me, Joe?"

The senator's thick face was full of burger when he answered.

"Mr. President, Gene's a friend of mine, as you know, and this brings me no pleasure, but he has many political liabilities." Joe finally swallowed his bite. "And politics being what it is, I'm just going to lay it out there. But first, may I say, this needs to remain here between us three, and I'll explain why in a minute. First off, I have reliable sources indicating the company run by Gene's golden boy, Chet Bateman, is a scam."

"Emerald Solaria?" asked Gary.

"Yes," Joe said as he munched on a fistful of fries. "All these Hollywood celebrities and virtue-signaling woksters are investing in a Ponzi scheme."

"How so?" asked an unusually inquisitive President Frum.

"Aren't they building solar panels? How's that a Ponzi scheme?"

"The rumor is their factory in Tennessee is just a front. There's information foreign money is being used to prop up the charade and mollify investors, who believe they're saving the planet while turning a profit—the proverbial win-win. Plus, they know if Gene wins, he'll grant federal subsidies by the truckload, only making the company a more attractive investment." Joe took another healthy bite of burger.

"Where's the foreign money coming from?" asked Gary.

"Don't know," the senator said, mouth full, knowing full well the scheme was propped up by Russian money siphoned through various offshore accounts.

"Shouldn't the FBI be looking into this?" Gary pressed. "Or maybe the trade commission?"

"That's not important now. Stop being such a damn Boy Scout," the president interjected. "This is about politics. How does this help us?"

"First, we get Gene nominated. I think you're right, Mr. President. Your tweet will piss off the Left, and they'll vote for him tomorrow in Michigan and Mississippi. There's a feisty little reporter at the *National Standard* who's been on record about the dubious nature of Emerald Solaria. She's the only one out there banging this drum. Her name is Carly Mavros, and she also happens to be a fine little piece of ass."

This prompted a devilish grin from the president and disgust from Gary.

"In time, we could use her to get this story out. Hell, there's a whistleblower working within the company I could hook her up with right now. Around the time of the Democratic Convention, we leak this to some friendly media outlets to stymie whatever momentum the convention generates."

"I like it, Joe." President Frum nodded. "You know what I also like? We can tie this fake company over Gene's head. Make him look foolish and discredit the whole green-energy movement at the same time. Voters in coal states will love it. My base loves watching the Libtards make excuses for these frauds."

"My thoughts exactly," Joe concurred.

"Can we keep a lid on it for three or four months?" asked the president, his instincts working out the political timing.

"We can," Joe confirmed. "But there's more."

"I'm all ears."

"Gene's been involved in an extramarital affair for about a year," Joe dropped with an air of self-satisfaction.

"How do you know?" asked Gary.

"We're friends. He confided it to me long ago. The woman's in his inner circle."

"Just because he told you doesn't mean it can be proven," Gary noted. "We can't put a camera in front of a Republican senator and expect people to buy his claims that the Democratic nominee is a philanderer."

"Settle down, Gary. Gene is a well-known ass-hound. It's one of his few interesting qualities," the president said. "What do you got, Joe?"

"So far, we have a few photos of them. But we have plenty of time to gather more dirt. I know who she is; it won't be difficult. I envision having her confronted about the affair on camera. Thrust the evidence in front of her and record the reaction."

"Sounds shady," Gary observed.

"I love it," Frum said. "The Emerald Solaria fraud stuff will put a dent in his campaign. Most of the media will bury it, which is to be expected. Fox will dig further into this mess and keep it breathing. In October, we spring the affair on the public. Can you imagine? His wife goes missing and now it's revealed he was cheating on her all along. We'll imply her murder and his infidelity are connected.

It's beautiful." The president was glowing. "You're going to make a great energy secretary, Joe," the president predicted. "Don't you think he'll make a great energy secretary? This is good stuff. You're the best."

"Just doing my part to 'Bring Back My America,'" the GOP senator responded with a smile.

"See, Gary, this is how it's done. You got to go for it." The president slapped the table with emphatic ebullience. "Get in the mud. Nothing gets done without getting dirty."

◉ ◉ ◉

James would just as soon drink bleach as enter Secret Service headquarters. Situated on H Street a few blocks from Chinatown, the nondescript building symbolized all he was trying to avoid when entering law enforcement: boredom and office politics. It seemed everyone was pushing him to retire. Several of the guys implicated in the Sao Paulo incident had already done so; having completed their twenty, they popped smoke to ensure their retirement.

James's diminutive attorney, Larry Dubois, was an appointment sent from the Federal Law Enforcement Officers Association. Had James known FLEOA would send such a spineless little wuss to defend him, he'd had saved his dues money. It seemed Larry's sole mission was to convince him to quit. It would free James to pursue another line of work without the stain of a dismissal on his record. Self-aware enough to know he was hardheaded, James still wouldn't acquiesce. He didn't think his transgression negated twelve years of unblemished work. Punishment was in order for his human fallibility, but he would not relinquish his badge—and all his sacrifice and dedication—without a fight.

Walking through the government halls and riding up the elevator with his lawyer, he felt the curious stares of passing employees.

It wasn't animosity he sensed so much as morbid curiosity, like slowing motorists hoping to get a better glimpse of the car accident.

The special agent in charge greeted James and Larry curtly as they entered the Inspection Division office. Years ago, the SAIC had been James's immediate boss in Chicago where they'd gotten along really well. James's financial crimes investigations inflated the squad's arrest stats, making the boss look like a rock star. After each conviction, they'd grab beers, but today he shook James's hand with all the warmth of a claim's adjuster. James didn't fault the SAIC. He had his part to play in this fiasco and was under no obligation to greet them. Deep down, James suspected the gesture was a subtle way to put him at ease.

They were escorted to a windowless room containing a small, rectangular table and four chairs. The walls were the muted, gray, lifeless variety typical of federal government buildings. As Larry checked his phone messages, a dreadful, sunken feeling weighed on James's chest. He knew what was coming next, these meetings being the bane of his existence.

The door opened, and there he was: Chandler Peele. The impeccably tailored suit couldn't fully disguise a slight paunch to his belly. The salt-and-pepper hair, frozen in place with product, complemented the French collar, half-Windsor knot, and pocket square combination that rounded out the purest image of empty-suit, nonoperational douchebaggery in the Service. James and Larry stood respectfully, but Chandler sat without offering a handshake. Next to him was a heavyset man James didn't know but assumed was formerly Protective Intelligence. The tubby embarrassment of an agent placed several large binders on the table.

"I realize we haven't gotten together like this in a month, Agent Ford," began Assistant Special Agent in Charge Chandler Peele.

"You can call me James," James interrupted. Staring at him, Chandler looked displeased.

"Like I was saying before you interrupted me, it's been a month since we met. I see you have your lawyer present once again." ASAIC Peele had a law degree but never practiced, which didn't stop him from mounting said degree prominently on his office wall. "There have been numerous details regarding the incident in Sao Paulo I think you need to be made aware of. As I said during our previous discussion, though you have been, and currently are, on paid leave, we have continued to investigate the incident and are in the process of terminating your employment with the US Secret Service."

Chandler looked across the table with the self-satisfied demeanor of a chess player declaring checkmate.

"You said this last month. I know you guys want to get rid of me."

"So, you're not going to resign?"

"The answer is still no."

"Is that what your counsel is advising you to do?"

"That's between me and my lawyer, dumbass. You know better. I thought you went to law school."

"You won't be so strident when the details of this incident go public."

"Are you threatening me?"

"It's not a threat," Chandler sniffed. "We have completed our investigation and advised Rafaela Pero she is free to pursue whatever monetary gain she wishes to glean from these events. There are some pretty lurid details she disclosed to us. You are one sick bastard."

Playing it off, James smiled nonchalantly, though he tried to recall what those revelations might be. His memory of the evening was so fuzzy he couldn't honestly dispute anything she revealed.

"What's the point of this?" asked James.

"The point is Ms. Pero wishes to monetize this situation and will likely reveal some of your activities to the media. For instance, your interest in rectal play." A gleeful smile etched Chandler's face.

"I never asked if I could do that to her."

"No, James, not you doing it to her. She mentioned putting a couple digits in your ass while you had intercourse. And she did so at your request." The agent next to Chandler repressed a laugh. Taking a deep breath, James bided time to form a witty comeback that never materialized. He didn't recall asking the hooker to finger-bang him, but it wasn't implausible.

"You can't fire me," he insisted.

"We can and we will."

"For what? She was a willing participant. Everything was consensual."

"Conduct unbecoming of a special agent. Paying for sex while on assignment is about as grossly negligent as it gets."

"It's legal in Brazil. I didn't break any laws."

"You also asked Ms. Pero to call you Papi. That's a Spanish word. She's Brazilian and speaks Portuguese. Pretty insulting, James," Chandler pointed out. "Next time you're overseas fulfilling your sick fantasies with impoverished prostitutes, please get the language right. Maybe peruse a travel guide."

"Next time, I'll come to you, Chandler. The way you suck cock around here, I don't see a need to waste my time with Latinas."

"You're fucked, James. Resign or find yourself terminated."

"You're a staffer with a gun—a nonoperational, boot-licking pussy."

A smug grin flashed across Chandler's face. "This meeting is over. You'll be terminated within a month. Good luck finding more work with your stellar record." Chandler stood and stormed out of the room as his toady gathered up the binders and followed.

"That didn't go very well," Larry observed. James's face was hot with anger. "Are you sure about not resigning? I think it's for the best."

"Not resigning, Larry."

"What are you thinking?"

"I'm trying to decide if I leave in dignity or go kick Chandler's ass."

"As your lawyer, I feel it my duty to advise you against kicking anyone's ass. Though, I concur, Chandler could use a good ass whooping." It was the funniest thing James had ever heard Larry utter, which was admittedly a low bar.

"Sounds like it's about over," James concluded.

"What do you plan to do?"

"Currently looking into something, something pretty important. And when I figure it out, and I will figure it out, all the Chandlers of the world are going to eat shit."

"Is this something you think you should share with your lawyer? To be honest, judging by their tone, you're likely out of a job in a few weeks. You've milked this out long as you can." James nodded silently. "You seem on edge, James. You alright? You're not suicidal, are you?" This elicited a grin and wry chuckle.

"Not suicidal, Larry. Self-destructive? Sure, but not suicidal." As James walked out of headquarters, his iPhone buzzed. It was a text from Carly: "What are you up to?"

James returned:

Not much. My life is a heaping pile of bat guano doused in accelerant and set to flame.

Carly: I knew that.

James: Is this a booty call? If so, your timing is impeccable.

Carly: Those days are over. Meet me at Fiola Mare. I'm at the bar.

James: This is a booty call.

Carly: STFU and just get here. And don't get the wrong idea.

James: En route.

James didn't know what to think, but after dealing with Chandler's gloating, the thought of a drink and gazing at Carly's body was appealing. Stopping briefly to think of somebody other than himself, James remembered he'd left Kat with her hillbilly kidnapper. He began to worry. Hopping in his truck, he shot a text to the phone he bought her:

How are things going, princess?

He waited several minutes for the incoming reply.

Kat returned:
We're good. You were right. JC is a really sweet guy. Told me about his wife. She's lucky to have him. Watching TV now. I really hate the picture they keep using of me on these news shows. How'd it go?

James replied:

Pretty shitty. You okay if I am a little later than expected?

Kat: That's fine. Don't get hammered and drive. 143 ☺

James: 143?

Kat: Means I love you, sorry, drinking wine and got carried away 😆

He received a selfie of her and JC grinning with their heads next to each other. The redneck held a beer can, she a glass of merlot. James could barely process what he was seeing.

James: You sure that's a good idea?

Kat: We're fine 143 🍷

James: Ok. Won't be long. 143.

Shaking his head, shocked by Kat's texts, James smiled to himself and thought, *This is getting really weird.*

CHAPTER 14

DETECTIVE SERGEANT Derek Roland managed to get five hours of sleep. It was heavenly. He would have slept longer, but his mind spun like a dryer through a universe of information, none of which contained the answer he obsessed over: where was Katherine Sterling?

Eighteen years younger and forty pounds heavier than him, his wife, Monique, shook her head in disgust as he ambled into the kitchen in a dreary haze. She thought Derek being assigned a high-profile, complex case on the eve of his retirement nearly as bad a crime as what happened to the rich White lady. While brewing his coffee, she muttered about how he'd done his time and how an old man shouldn't be made to forgo sleep. Wasn't there some young, eager cop in Metro to do this shit?

Derek loved Monique, but it didn't take much to get her bitching. At times, he considered moving on. But this was wife number three, and that was enough; besides, beneath all the griping and chub was a good heart. As he slammed three cups down and showered, she laid out a brown suit with a bright-yellow shirt and swirly-patterned tie. She liked him in bold colors. The looks he got from the FBI guys when he walked into their field office sporting his flashy shirts and audacious ties amused him.

After driving in from Prince George's County, Derek entered

the FBI's war room in his wife-chosen ensemble. Agent Kevin McClennan shook his hand with a bemused look.

"Get some rest?" the young man asked. Derek shrugged. "We'll get you some coffee."

"I'll need it," Derek acknowledged. "Anything new?"

"Yeah, we expedited the phone records for John Klingerman. He was in Harpersburg Sunday morning. Then he began pinging cell towers all the way down to Lynchburg."

"His wife indicated he was heading to North Carolina for work," Derek iterated.

"Did you think that was legit?"

"No, I imagine it was just his excuse to skip town."

"Well, he appears to have remained in Lynchburg for a night, but yesterday he goes up 81 to 66 and heads east toward DC."

"No kidding. Do we have any wireless tracking vehicles?"

"We couldn't get them up in time. The signal dropped in Fairfax. That was last night, and we haven't had a ping since. Either he turned his phone off or it ran out of juice."

"Wonder what would prompt him to come to Washington?"

"I asked myself the same thing. Oh, and we received word on the autopsy results for the Saturn's owner, John Donovan: strangulation."

"Really? Do we think Klingerman or the dead druggie did it?" asked Derek.

"We don't think so. By all accounts, all three were really tight. Besides that, Squinty Donovan was a big, strong guy; hard to imagine those two could overpower him." An agent handed Derek a coffee. Leaning against the cubicle, the Metro detective took a sip and mulled the fresh information.

"What's the Bureau doing?" he wondered.

"We're actively monitoring the cell towers and have those mobile teams up in the event he pings us in Fairfax or DC. And we have agents in West Virginia assisting the locals with the two opioid deaths and monitoring the investigation of the Donovan murder. There have been a few anonymous tips, but little of substance. And, of course, we're flooded with tips concerning Mrs. Sterling. Our task force meeting is in the conference room in an hour. Should flesh out what we got, which is not nearly as much as we'd like."

Derek liked Kevin, a sharp young man and more straightforward than most feds.

"What do you think, Sarge?" Kevin asked.

"We don't have a vehicle description for JC?"

"No sir."

"You know what I really want to do? I want to confront the senator and request he take a polygraph."

"Nothing in his texts, emails, or anything has indicated his involvement—just typical marital spats. Even his work email was clean. What makes you think that'll do any good?"

"We talked about this before: why would 'Bring Back My America' goons take the wife and not the senator? Why the wife? Hell, he got his butt whipped but was out of the hospital in a day. These guys supposedly hate the liberal senator but simply rough him up. It doesn't make sense to me. Plus, the other night when I told him we located the vehicle used in his wife's kidnapping, something about how he reacted didn't sit right. If it were my wife, I'd be relieved they found the vehicle, but he looked downright fearful. It was odd. I've been doing this a long time, and something was definitely off."

"My superiors will never go for a poly," said Kevin flatly. "Certainly not until we get a whole lot more hard evidence of his involvement. He's one of the most powerful senators in DC, and the whole world is pulling for him. I get what you're saying. And who knows, if nothing turns up in the next few weeks, maybe the Bureau's position changes."

"I don't consider politics when I'm working a case," Derek stated.

"You don't work for the Bureau, Sarge."

The detective smiled, shook his head, and sipped his coffee. Another agent handed Kevin several papers.

"Dimitri Romov," said the agent. "The guy who rented the Beamer under the alias Oscar Reese is actually Dimitri Romov. That's all declassified there. Came over as a student, several ties to Russian businessmen."

Kevin nodded as he examined the papers.

"What's this about?" Derek was confused.

"We got a tip about a rented BMW seen at Squinty Donovan's house the day he was murdered," answered Kevin. "Came in on the tip line. It was rented under the name Oscar Reese, but the phony identification used to rent the vehicle, along with information gleaned by the Bureau, has us certain this Romov character rented it. Intelligence has a pretty extensive dossier on him."

"Wait. Are you telling me we're now dealing with Russians? I should have stayed in bed."

◉ ◉ ◉

At this early hour, most of the tables at Fiola Mare were set for patrons to dine on the sea's bounty while viewing moonlit reflections off the Potomac's brackish water. Foreign diplomats, legislators turned lobbyists, and possibly a cabinet member would make up the clientele. As an assistant detail leader, James could recall a half dozen times sitting alone, protecting Gary Boxterman as the president's chief of staff enjoyed a lengthy meal with colleagues.

The L-shaped bar, in contrast to the sparsely populated dining room, was thick with sport coats, coifed hair, and expensive fragrances. Scanning the throng mingling beneath the colorful bottles above the bar, James searched for his Greek ex-lover amid the cocky, fresh-faced trust fund babies and leathery-skinned, Georgetown comb-over crowd.

There are those legs, he thought as his eyes caught her defined, Mediterranean-skinned calves protruding beneath a red, skin-tight dress. She was seated in a swivel barstool with a back, being hawked by an open-collared gray-hair twice her age who made certain his Patek Philippe watch remained visible.

Setting up down the bar, James ordered Buffalo Trace straight up and took in the scene. Carly was the picture of raven-haired beauty and disinterest as turkey-necked old money continued firing on her. James sipped his bourbon, amused by her vain attempts to locate him. When she caught his gaze, he saluted her with a raised tumbler. She glared at him with telepathic disgust, realizing he'd purposefully left her out to dry. It was time to save her. Taking his drink, James sidled up next to her.

"Carly, is that you?" he asked enthusiastically. She turned and smiled in feign surprise. "You look wonderful, it's been a while." He gave her a friendly, one-arm hug. "I'm sorry, I didn't realize you were here with someone. That was rude of me; my name's James." He extended his hand.

"James, this is Glenn."

"Good to meet you, Glenn. I used to sleep with Carly. I'm still trying to, but it's a futile exercise." The old man refused a handshake, eyed James's handsome looks, then muttered to himself before retreating in disgust.

"I see you're still an ass," Carly noted.

"It's in my DNA."

"How long were you over there?"

"Only five minutes. You look cute when you're uncomfortable. But I feel for Glenn. This dress is unfair."

"Knock it off."

"You couldn't get one of these douchey, Capitol Hill staffer boys to hit on you?"

"Apparently not, but I have caught about a hundred glances."

"You do dress to be noticed."

"You know me too well." She smiled and raised her glass. After a silent toast, he noticed her eyeing his suit and tie.

"Are you gut checking me?" he asked, grinning.

"I like your tie. Been a while since I've seen you in a suit."

"Your eyes stayed at belt buckle level for a while. You're gut checking me."

"Gut checking?"

"When a guy's in a suit, it's hard to determine what's underneath, so women eye his gut to see if his stomach extends over the belt. Suits not being particularly revealing, it's the only way to gauge what's going on underneath."

"You're ridiculous."

"You just did it again. You can't help yourself."

"You are an idiot."

"That's not a denial." He took another sip. "Anyhow, you invited me here, and you're in a dress screaming to be crumpled on a bedroom floor, so are we getting together?"

"Seriously, you need to get that notion out of your head. It's never happening again."

"I'm messing with you. Thanks for the memories."

"You can be so aggravating."

"That's the consensus." He smirked and ordered a second drink.

"You're drinking awfully fast."

"Been a rough day. I was called into headquarters for an interview, apparently so some prick could spike the football on me. It appears I'll be Joe Q. Citizen soon. I guess I should have expected this."

"I'm so sorry, James. No chance you can get reinstated?"

"Doesn't appear so. They want me to resign."

"Why don't you?"

"Because I'm a stubborn son of a bitch who won't give in."

"I know how much it meant to you to be a Secret Service agent. You were really good."

"Thanks, but I made my bed and now have to lie in it. I let my priorities get way out of sync. I put the job and myself ahead of the most important things in life, and now I'm paying the price. I'm trying to change." He knew he was repeating himself.

"Don't beat yourself up. We're all flawed. I know I've made mistakes, and you weren't my only one." She grinned warmly. "But people like you. They like you, James, because your goodness comes through despite what a mess you can be. You're not perfect, but you're one of the good guys."

"That's sweet of you. And I know you mean it." For a moment, pheromone-fueled adrenaline rushed through their veins. Carly turned away as an overwhelming urge to kiss him boiled up inside her. Noticing she was fighting the same amorous impulses, James changed the subject. "Why did you want to see me?"

"When we met last week, you mentioned the name Oscar Reese."

"Yeah, did you find anything?"

"I ran it by a source who's an intelligence analyst at the Bureau. He didn't recognize the name initially, but after a few days he hit me up and was very interested in how I obtained it. After some time, I pressed back, and he revealed it's an alias attached for Dimitri Romov, a suspected Russian operative. Don't know what they have on him, but he was pressing me hard. I'll reach out to him later to see if he'll give up more on Dimitri."

"No kidding? You didn't out me to him, did you?"

"Of course not, but his interest piqued my curiosity. How did you come by the name? Why did you ask me about him?" James couldn't hide his amusement as she pled for answers. He grinned and sipped his drink. "You're not going to tell me what you're up to, are you?"

"There's a part of me that wants to share what I know, but I can't. All I'll say for now is I witnessed a rental car leased by Oscar Reese leave a crime scene."

"I hate when you're evasive. You worry me. You're suspended, James. Maybe you should lay low and not play detective; just a suggestion."

"I have a lot of time on my hands." She side-eyed him with suspicion. For an older guy, he had a mischievous quality that was both appealing and infuriating. "Your FBI guy didn't share anything else with you, did he?"

"He may have."

"Don't be cryptic. What did he say?"

"Me? Cryptic? Have you listened to yourself?" She feigned offense. "He's tied to Oleg Yumashev. Oleg is a Russian oligarch whose family's prominence dates back to the Stalinist years. He has holdings all over the globe, but he's primarily invested in energy; runs Capital Elements, a coal and oil conglomerate. He's well known in Washington. Has the ears of his fair share of congressmen. My source was vague as to what role Dimitri played within Oleg's universe but hinted he had some attachment to Russian intelligence. Said Oleg has been on the intelligence community's radar for some time."

"No shit?"

"Something's on your mind."

"I'm pretty sure this Dimitri guy murdered somebody."

"Wait. What?"

"I know it sounds crazy, but a John Donovan was murdered last week in West Virginia. This Dimitri guy did it."

"That's the crime you're investigating as a hobby? A homicide?"

"That and some other things. Look, I saw his rental car leave the Donovan residence. I know you're going to think I'm out of my mind, but I saw it."

"Why were you in West Virginia?"

"Long story that I can't share just yet."

"Did you tell the police?"

"I called the tip line, so yes. That may explain why your contact was so interested in how you obtained his alias. The Bureau could be looking into Dimitri as the likely suspect. And another thing: I believe this murder is tied into the Sterling kidnapping."

"You're out of your mind. You're going through a lot, James. More than most people could handle over such a short period of time. Do you feel like maybe this little investigation of yours is an attempt to rectify your self-worth?" Carly posited in the soft tone of a therapist.

"Even after these past few months, I have a surplus of self-regard. This isn't a vanity project. I've had some weird things hop into my life recently I hadn't expected. Oh, that reminds me. I have something for you." James pulled folded papers out of his coat pocket.

"What's this?"

"Appears to be payments to a senior senator from California for various speaking engagements. The second one lists some seven- and eight-figure donations to his main source of wealth, the Sterling Foundation."

"Where the hell did you get this?"

"That isn't important. Rest assured, no laws were violated."

"I don't believe you."

"I said I'd get you something for your Emerald Solaria investigation. I wouldn't be surprised if the same foreign companies ponying up for Senator Sterling and his foundation aren't also propping up the Emerald Solaria scam." Carly sifted through the papers before looking up at him, dumbfounded.

"No need to thank me."

"You're crazy." She put the papers in her purse. "Don't tell me any more; I need plausible deniability."

"Just trying to help. Look, you're the one who invited me here. Was it simply about the Dimitri Romov guy?"

"That, and I was tired of rich old men hitting on me."

"Cute."

"The real reason I'm here just walked in." She nodded toward the hostess station where a young, dark-haired gentlemen was taking selfies with a few patrons.

"Who's he?" James asked.

"That's Chet Bateman, the chief spokesman for Emerald Solaria. The doorman at his apartment on Wisconsin told me Mr. Bateman comes here most evenings when he's in town."

"I'm familiar with him. You never struck me as a celebrity groupie. Does he know you?"

"I'm sure he knows of me, but we've never met. Since he refuses to let me interview him, I've decided to run into him by accident."

"That explains the tight dress. What do you want to get out of him?"

"Not sure yet. I want him to know his company is a fraud. My theory is he's getting played. He's a pawn."

"Interesting."

"Maybe sometime you can tell me why you think Dimitri has some involvement with the Sterling kidnapping. That's a scoop."

"Maybe someday, but I'm a crazy person, remember? Not sure I can be trusted."

"You are not sane, but I also know you're smart as hell." She pressed a quick kiss to his cheek. "And if you're investigating something, I'm sure it has merit. Just be sure to give dibs to your favorite reporter. By the way, you look really good. Just don't get any ideas. Now, I gotta go butter up Chet."

"I won't get any ideas, but I plan to stare at your ass once you get up from that stool."

She smiled. "I'd expect nothing less."

⊙ ⊙ ⊙

"Do you have room for one more?" asked Carly as Chet pecked away at a text while leaning against a round high-top. Two things were obvious when he looked up: she had worn the right dress, and he was at least a couple drinks in.

"I most certainly do," he answered as his eyes returned to her face. "I'm Chet."

"I know who you are," she simpered, offering a polite handshake. "I'm Carly. Here by yourself?"

"Meeting a friend."

"Oh, I'm sorry. I don't want to interrupt."

"It's a guy friend. What are you drinking?"

"Chianti."

Chet ordered wine and a dirty martini. "Have we met before? You look familiar, and I usually have no difficulty recalling a beautiful woman's name."

With a flirty smile Carly answered, "I've always wanted to meet you, but we've never met."

"Good, because I would have felt foolish." Though she preferred men with more prominent shoulders, Chet was attractive with a self-assurance void of arrogance and eyes that exuded a sweet earnestness. The waitress placed their drinks on the table. "To my newest friend?" He lifted his martini glass. She returned the toast.

"You in DC often?" she asked. "I think of you as an LA guy."

"I have a place here as well. I found myself in Washington so frequently, I decided to go in on an apartment. I've become acquainted with a lot of DC friends in my fight for the environment."

"You also have more than a few enemies here," Carly noted.

"I do. I call them Republicans," Chet countered. Carly smiled at him in the manner of a woman interested in a man. "You live here?" he asked.

"I have a condo near Twenty-Fourth and M. I've been in DC for years now. I know you probably get told this a lot, but I really admire the work you do for the environment. That's why I had to introduce myself."

"That's kind of you. So, you're dressed like you're meeting someone. Whoever it is, he's a lucky guy," Chet flirted. Carly feigned a shy laugh.

"I should confess. I heard you frequented this place. I figured I had better stand out if I was going to get your attention."

"Well, you certainly have my attention. I shouldn't be alarmed, should I?"

"I'm not a stalker, I promise."

"I've had stalkers before. None could hold a candle to you, so stalk away." He was a charmer. Carly began to feel some guilt about her less-than-frank introduction. "So, Carly, what is it you do?"

"I'm in media."

"Social media? You look like you should be on TV."

"I'm a reporter, but I do TV hits from time to time."

A look of recognition morphed onto Chet's face.

"I can't believe this," he said, his stare a mix of disappointment and scorn. "You're that chick from the *National Standard* always criticizing my work. This is unbelievable, that you'd stoop to getting dolled up to hit on me."

"I never misrepresented myself during any point of our conversation," she said.

"Oh, come on, everything you just said and did was disingenuous. You introduce yourself as a fan, I buy you a drink, and all the while you're the columnist writing the most scathing critiques of my life's work."

"I happen to admire your work and passion for the environment."

"You could have fooled me."

"There's more nuance to my writing than you're giving me credit for. Have you ever read any of my pieces? I've been trying to speak to you for over a year."

"I've never read your stuff but seen enough interviews to know your point of view. You crush me every time."

"Look, I'll concede flirting with you was borderline unethical, but I've wanted to talk to you for some time, and it's been an impossibility from the get-go. To be clear, I agree climate change is a real thing. My only issue is Emerald Solaria. It has nothing to do with you, Chet."

"It's unfair, you coming in here looking like that." He sipped his martini, his expression softening.

"You're more charming than I had expected," she admitted.

"I'm still not giving you an interview."

"That's fine, but how about your number?"

"My number?" He was amused.

"One day, you'll learn the truth behind Emerald Solaria, and you'll want to call me."

"And what is the truth?"

"It's being funded by foreign monies with dubious ties. I have reason to believe all the high-profile celebrity investors buying into this promise are being duped. They're being preyed upon. Senator Sterling uses it as a sugar high for potential voters. All the while, we haven't seen one of their solar panels put to use."

"So, you think it's all bullshit? You're pretty, but you're nuts."

"Have you been inside any manufacturing centers? What do you know about the inner workings of the company?"

"I told you, I'm not doing an interview," he reminded her and ordered a second drink. "Want another?"

"No thanks. I plan to leave soon." They both fell silent. Their brief conversation only confirmed what she had suspected: Chet was a genuine advocate for healing the planet but ignorant of the details concerning the venture for which he was the public face. She broke the ponderous hush. "You seem like a really good guy. I apologize for being less than frank."

"No need to apologize; just go easy on me in the future."

"I will." She smiled. "Ask yourself: what do you truly know about Emerald Solaria? Just keep your wits about you. Fair enough?"

"Fair enough."

"One other thing, before I go. I know you're close to Senator Sterling and his wife. I know it must be tough on you, as a close friend. I pray they find her alive."

"Thanks, Carly. It's been difficult. I still can't believe it's real. Everything has gotten so toxic. It was only a matter of time with all the rhetoric and hate spilling out of this administration. Kat is such a good person, and she doesn't deserve this."

"I'm sorry, Chet. Don't lose hope."

"Thanks, I haven't, though it's hard some days."

"I should go."

"Carly," he said before she could turn to leave, "let me give you my number."

CHAPTER 15

BOTH JC AND KAT toasted James as he entered. They were seated on the couch, watching a West Virginia Mountaineers basketball game and looking as comfortable as old college buddies. It was a jarring sight for James, who had left that morning with JC handcuffed to a kettlebell and Kat disquieted with the notion of being alone with her kidnapper. Taking off his coat and loosening his tie, he eyed empty beer cans and an open pizza box littering the coffee table.

"Welcome home, honey," laughed Kat, a glass of wine in hand.

"Honey? That's obviously not your first glass. Leave me any beer?" he quipped, walking to the fridge. "Can't say I expected you two to hit it off."

"JC's a sweetheart. Did you know he was an all-state football player in high school?" Kat slurred. Popping a Budweiser and flopping into his easy chair, James looked at her as if to ask, "How the hell would I know that?" as JC wore a prideful countenance.

"So, I have to ask: how did this come about?" James asked.

"Well, it's kind of funny to think about now," began Kat, who shot JC an elfish grin, causing his substantial belly to bob with a chuckle, "but we got to talking, you know, just sharing things about ourselves. I mean, what the hell else were we going to do, being stuck here by ourselves all day?"

"Let me guess," James interrupted. "You realized that despite your dramatically different backgrounds, you actually have a lot in common."

"No, Jimmy, we don't live in a Disney movie," she quipped, eliciting more laughter from a buzzed JC. "We have almost nothing in common. But he told me about deer hunting, which I used to think was cruel, but to be honest, I found his knowledge of the outdoors really compelling. Plus, he is so sweet when he speaks about his wife, Myrtle. He cares about her so much, which is endearing. I wish I had a husband who cared for me half as much." She patted JC's shoulder. "Anyhow, I tried to convince him climate change is real, and that Democrats aren't all communists, but we ended up agreeing to disagree."

"And the tying you up and car-trunk thing? We're all good?" James appeared skeptical.

"Oh, we made amends for that by lunchtime," Kat assured him.

"I've asked Jesus for forgiveness," JC said. "And I feel in my heart of hearts he has forgiven me."

"Just like that?" James wondered.

"Yes sir; that's how Jesus works."

"I should have married Jesus," James concluded.

"Be nice, Jimmy. Ignore him, JC. He's reflexively sarcastic," Kat chided. "Poor JC couldn't find work. Neither could any of his friends. I had no idea how hard it is to find good employment in West Virginia. And the drugs; his best friend hurt his back, got hooked on drugs, and died. Six of his former classmates were killed by opioids as well. Told me he was broke and desperate, so when a chance to make money came along, he jumped at it for his dear Myrtle."

"That money-making opportunity involved kidnapping and killing a senator's wife."

"I didn't know we was kidnapping the wife of a senator," clarified JC.

"Not entirely mitigating, but noted," said James wryly as he scooped up a cold pizza slice.

"I've forgiven him," Kat declared. "He made a bad decision, but his motives were pure."

"She'd be a good Christian if she believed in God," JC opined.

"We disagree on religion and politics, but I told him about my struggles in LA. He told me about being laid off and what it was like in jail and having nowhere to turn for a better life. Said I was the prettiest lady he'd ever seen other than Myrtle."

"You two are too cute," James deadpanned.

"How did the interview go?" asked Kat.

"Wasn't so much an interview as a pencil-dicked asshole gloating over my misfortune."

"Kat told me you're a Secret Service agent. That's damn cool. Too bad you was caught with that spic hooker."

"That's sweet of you, JC—very poignant."

"I'll pray for you. You seem like a good guy."

"That assertion is in dispute, but I'll take whatever divine intervention I can. It doesn't appear I'll be an agent for much longer. They keep trying to make me quit, but they're going to have to terminate me. Looks like that's where this is headed."

"That's a shame," JC said consolingly. "I saw Fox News interview the little brown filly you nailed in South America. She was hot."

"She was; wish I remembered it."

"Sorry, Jimmy." Kat sensed that beneath his sarcastic veneer was real pain. She stood, leaned over, and kissed his forehead while rubbing his hair.

"I could use something stronger than this," he said, holding up his beer.

"One Jack and Coke coming up." She smiled and pecked his lips before making for the kitchenette. JC wore a quizzical look and began mouthing something that James couldn't make out.

"What are you saying?" asked James.

"Have you tagged that?" JC asked in a beer-enhanced whisper.

"I can hear you, JC," Kat called over her shoulder. "The answer is no. But that'll likely change tonight." Both men nodded with devilish grins.

"So, as a Secret Service agent, you protected the president and flew on Air Force One and all?" JC asked.

"Yeah, I did it all, I suppose. Drove the president, conducted advance work, both domestic and overseas—been to Afghanistan, Ghana, Argentina, China, and a thousand places in between. It was grueling, exhausting, exhilarating, and I sometimes would look in the mirror and wonder why they let some Midwest cop protect the leader of the free world. Most countries protect their heads of state with their military. There's something particularly democratic about America protecting this powerful office with citizen police."

"I never thought of it that way." Kat handed him his drink. For the first time, she looked on him with genuine admiration. "You're looking even more handsome." She sat with JC.

"What's he like? The president, I mean," JC asked.

"President Frum? Behind the scenes, he's a good guy. Nothing like his tweets."

"I love him," JC admitted. "He doesn't give a shit. Just tells it like it is. Looks out for us. Nobody thought he'd get elected, but he beat 'em all anyhow."

"The Secret Service guys knew he was going to get elected. We saw his rallies and the enthusiastic crowds. If you want accurate election predictions, ask a Secret Service agent, not the press."

"Can you kill a man silently with your bare hands?" JC inquired. "I heard somewhere y'all had a technique to kill assassins all quiet like."

"We're cops, not ninjas. Doesn't matter anyhow—appears those days are about over for this old cop. Cheers to a good run." He raised his glass. All three toasted.

"Oh." Kat choked down a sip of wine. "I forgot to tell you your friend upstairs is home."

"Brian? He didn't knock down here, did he?"

"No, but I was worried about him coming down. It was about an hour ago."

"Was he with his boyfriend?" wondered James.

"Yes."

James grinned. "He won't be down here then."

"This fella has a boyfriend?" JC grimaced with disgust.

"Yeah, he's gay," James informed him.

"I've never met a gay guy."

"No, you've never met an *openly* gay guy," corrected James.

"It ain't holy and right to fornicate with a man. Jesus said so," JC pontificated self-righteously.

"You were paid to kill and bury the woman next to you, and you're passing judgment on gay dudes? As a former altar boy, I seem to recall something about casting the first stone and a commandment frowning on killing folks."

"Jesus don't like sodomy," JC pronounced.

"Boys, that's enough," interrupted Kat. "JC, you should be less judgmental."

"I love sodomy," admitted James. "Do you like sodomy, Kat?"

"I do."

"Sodomy's the best." James grinned and took a sip. Kat flashed a wine smile.

"You're the devil, Jimmy," she declared. "What's that?" she asked JC as he fumbled with something.

"Just realized my phone was in my pocket," he replied. "It died on me last night. Y'all got a charger?"

"Don't turn it on," said James sternly. "You're the most wanted man in the United States. You start pinging towers, and I'll need a new door within an hour."

"What do you mean?"

"We should have left that in your truck. Fuck, I can't believe I didn't check you for a phone. Thank God it was dead, or we'd all be in custody by now."

"While we're on the subject," cut in Kat, "what the hell are we going to do? JC and I were talking, and if we went to the FBI, between his story and mine, they'd have Gene dead to rights. Unless we're missing something." James sipped his Jack and Coke as he mulled what he knew of this ordeal. "I've never told you, but I like that thoughtful look you get when you're thinking."

"You're usually pointing out my ridiculousness," he noted.

"You're a crazy idiot, but you're oddly intelligent, and I never called you ugly. Keep in mind, I've had a few glasses of wine."

"Y'all are rather taken with one another," declared JC as he popped open another can.

"This isn't representative of our week, JC," Kat deadpanned. "It's taken awhile for me to shine to this lunatic."

"They always come around. Some just take a little longer." James smirked.

"You're such a slut." Her sparkling eyes softened the insult.

"The thought just came to me," interrupted JC. "You know, y'all would've never met had I not taken Squinty's offer to stage a kidnapping of Ms. Kat. Think about that."

"Not sure I get your point," said James.

"I'm sayin' it's all part of a larger plan. Had He not guided me, you two would never have met or fallen in love."

"It's not love," corrected Kat.

"Whose plan is this, exactly?" James asked.

"Jesus's."

"So, if I'm following your logic," James mused, "Jesus had me fail to pay a foreign hooker while I was blind drunk, which led to my separation so that I'd drink heavily at a mall bar. He then enticed you to take money in order to fake a kidnapping but commit real murder only to have you run out of gas so that princess here could pop the trunk and hop her way into my life? Jesus is pretty gangster."

"The Lord works in mysterious ways." JC looked skyward.

"Color me skeptical," said James.

"Then how do you explain you rear-ending my truck?"

"Bacardi."

"But think of the odds of that. Of all the cars out there, and you get into a fender bender with me? While you got Ms. Kat here at your place?"

"It does seem highly implausible," James concurred.

"See? It's God's plan," JC resolved with a Protestant flourish. Unblinking, leaning forward, JC stared at James in silence, looking for any sign of the Holy Spirit's spark. "We are instruments of God, and he is using us for a righteous cause."

James nodded. The silence and JC's Christian-induced, maniacal stare put him ill at ease. Kat tried not to laugh.

"Going to agree to disagree on this 'God's plan' stuff," James asserted. "I love your spirit, but my stupidity made me bang that hooker, not God. Kat, would you be a dear and pour me another drink?" She took his glass and released a suppressed laugh as she entered the kitchenette. "What were we talking about before we got biblical?"

"I asked if we should go to the FBI," Kat reminded him as she handed him a drink. Wincing from the whiskey burning his throat, James mulled their circumstances. He was bothered by what he didn't know. It was clear the senator set the whole thing up, but there was little else he could be certain of. He wondered what investigators had gleaned from his anonymous tip; maybe they were onto Dimitri Romov. Were they aware the kidnapping was a hoax? If so, they were playing their cards close to the vest as no news outlet dared speculate about the senior senator's possible involvement. Studying JC and Kat, it was clear he'd taken this thing about as far as he could—but what if he could produce one more piece of incriminating evidence? One final evidentiary nugget to hand over to investigators. He pulled out his phone and checked his email.

"I say we take our story to the FBI tomorrow morning," James declared.

"Really?" asked Kat.

"Yes, it's time we give them what we've got, but I have an idea to sweeten the pot."

"What's that?"

"JC, take a look at this. I was pretending to be you a couple days ago." James handed him the phone. For what seemed an unnecessarily long time, JC examined the email exchange. "That email belongs to Senator Sterling," James explained. "Everyone assumes Kat is dead, so we thought we'd mess with him. So far, he hasn't responded."

"Do you think he read it?" JC asked.

"I'm sure he has," concluded Kat. "I hope he's freaked out." She smiled at the notion. "I wonder if he believes it's really JC."

"I've wondered the same thing," James shared, "but we have the real JC now. And a buzzed, happy one at that."

"What do you have in mind?" she asked.

"We send a little reminder to the distinguished senator that JC is still out there, and he has the country's number one witness with him. But this time, we give Gene visual proof. It would be hard to ignore picture proof the wily JC has him by the short hairs. I bet we get a response, which would amount to tacit acknowledgment he's involved. It'd be nice to hand this to the feds when we drop by their headquarters tomorrow."

"Dang, that's pretty smart." JC looked at him in wonderment.

"Don't give him too much credit. He gives himself more than enough," Kat said.

"Cute, princess."

James, acting as JC, composed a message and couldn't help but reference the senator's affair with his staffer. Attached to the email was a smiling selfie JC took as a distressed Kat lay on the floor, mouth duct-taped. As it was JC's first attempt at a selfie, it took almost an hour of taking and retaking the photo to get it right.

"What do you think, JC?" James asked as the West Virginian reviewed the pic.

"Pretty damn good. That dog'll hunt."

⊙ ⊙ ⊙

Dimitri Romov had conducted surveillances from rat-infested buildings, run-down work vans, even lying in damp culverts. So the tinted-out Audi A8 where he encamped in Georgetown was an easy stint. The target location was an O Street rowhouse. This was his one opportunity to clean up his reputation with the boss, whose furious response to the handling of Mrs. Sterling's kidnapping still rang in Dimitri's ears. When Oleg lost faith in you, your life expectancy was considerably diminished.

If he met an untimely end, it could well be the result of Taya Solotov's orders. The professional seductress was sculpting her *David* with this performance as Tanya. She was the lynchpin of the operation.

The goal was to play the bleeding-heart American public with the senator's tale of redemption following the murder of his wife. Americans loved their Rocky-style comeback stories, and their predictable, sappy natures were easily manipulated. His superiors wanted Senator Sterling pitted against Frum so the president—and his pro–fossil fuel administration—could coast to a second term. Once the general election commenced, they had plenty of dirt on the California legislator to thwart his bid and avoid a President Sterling clamping down on oil and natural gas, effectively shutting off the spigot to Russia's primary source of income.

But Sterling winning the Democratic nomination was

contingent on his wife being the victim of partisan murder by two West Virginia Frum supporters, a fact now in dispute. The senator had received an email from one of those Frum fans claiming Mrs. Sterling was still alive.

The Yahoo email account was registered to a phone number returning to a James Ford. Taya's handlers in Moscow fed her this information from long-compromised email service providers. More intel on the address was provided by an informant known as Angry Bird—a DHS employee receiving a generous monthly stipend from the Russkies who'd built a solid reputation of reliability—who obtained records of a Ford F-150 registered to James Ford at a Chantilly address. Angry Bird further advised that Mr. Ford was separated from his wife and now received mail at the O Street residence Dimitri was currently eyeing.

Setting up at ten that morning, the Russian operative had seen little more than normal Georgetown activity: dog walkers, joggers, and cars jammed on the eighteenth-century streets. In the late afternoon, a slender female in a ball cap and hoodie exited from a door below the main stoop. She was Caucasian, but little more about her identity could be ascertained. She walked up the street and disappeared for ten minutes before returning with two bottles of wine. Using a zoom lens, Dimitri took several images of her, noted the time, and forwarded the pics to Taya for analysis. At dusk, a taxi dropped off a slightly built White male and a broad-shouldered Black male curbside. They climbed the elevated front stoop of the target rowhouse and kissed passionately.

Close to ten in the evening, a dark Ford truck parallel-parked along the curb. Using a low-light camera, Dimitri snapped images of the White male wearing a suit, who fumbled with the keys before entering the lower door of the rowhouse. Dimitri called Taya: "The truck has arrived."

"We know," she answered. "He has been in Georgetown for several hours." Dimitri raised his dark eyebrows; he hadn't realized they were tracking the cell towers—Oleg and his redundancies.

"There is a slender woman in the lower apartment where the driver of the truck entered. It could be Mrs. Sterling. She ran an errand earlier, and I was able to get some photos. I sent you the images. There is a main floor to the building where I saw a gay couple enter. I cannot be certain there is no internal connection between the two residences," he relayed.

"Stay on the target until further notice. We received the images and are still enhancing them to identify her," advised Taya, who hung up. Dimitri harbored doubts about the legitimacy of the targets. Any two-bit hacker could have obtained the senator's email and decided to prank him. Rubbing his eyes, Dimitri managed to stay awake another two hours before receiving a follow-up call from Taya: "Facial recognition systems identified the female as Katherine Sterling. Nice work. You have the green light to go. The cell phone associated with the emails is at the location. Remember, this James Ford is a former federal agent. He is trained and likely armed."

"Understood."

"Confirm your target and remedy the situation. We will have disposal teams on standby at the Scotsman. Any evidence, to include bodies, deliver for destruction."

"Understood."

"I do not need to tell you another failure is unacceptable."

"I will not fail."

"If exposed, everything will be denied," she reminded him and hung up. Dimitri rubbed his goatee in contemplation. Pulling out his Sig Sauer P226 pistol, he ensured a 9mm round was chambered before radioing his two counterparts, Vlad and Ivan, to exit their vehicles and meet him.

It was cold and quiet. Little stirred after ten on these narrow, tree-lined streets. Most of the lights in the bottom apartment were out, though the flicker of a television screen provided some illumination. A small window adjacent to the door had a kink in the blinds on the lower corner, giving Dimitri a view inside. There were beer cans on an end table, and someone was lying on the couch. All he could see was a pudgy foot sticking out from under a blanket. The foot moved and body squirmed as the chubby figure sat up, grabbed a beer, and finished it.

"This can't be real," Dimitri whispered to himself. Scruff had grown in where there was once a beard, but there was no doubting who it was: JC.

CHAPTER 16

Tuesday, March 8

JUST PAST MIDNIGHT, Dimitri gingerly worked the simple deadbolt lock. He eased the door open, keeping an eye on JC asleep on the couch as a basketball game flickered from the television. Pulling the Sig Sauer from his coat, suppressor affixed to the muzzle, he moved into the room, careful to avoid the aluminum cans littering the floor. He lowered the silencer inches from JC's snoring face. At the sound of the hammer cocking into single action, the fat man's eyes snapped awake.

"It was a simple task I asked of you. You had to kill one woman," the Russian chided.

"Oscar?" JC's eyes, wide and fearful, stared first into the suppressor, then at the two henchmen behind Dimitri.

"Where is the girl?"

"Girl?"

"Don't play dumb. You don't have long to live."

"She got away from us," JC admitted. "Somehow, she got out of the trunk. I know it sounds crazy. We ran out of gas and she escaped." Dimitri responded with a dismissive sigh.

"There's a door past the kitchen. Go check it," Dimitri ordered Vlad and Ivan.

Looking past the silencer, JC noticed Oscar's attention diverted to his partners moving in on their quarry. The Russian, unaware his pistol was trained on a former West Virginia all-state quarterback, was taken off guard when, like the snap release of a football pass, JC grasped the pistol-toting wrist; the muffled weapon discharged into a throw pillow as both men knocked aside the coffee table and fell to the floor in a struggle for the weapon.

"Kat! James!" was the only shouted warning JC could muster as he wrestled the Russian.

⊙ ⊙ ⊙

Walking into the bedroom, James grinned. "It's late. Are you really filling out your journal now?" he asked as Kat, sitting up in bed, scribbled in her notebook.

"It's not every day you and your kidnapper become BFFs." Still in her hoodie, she hadn't changed clothes before hopping in bed to frantically record the day's events. "We go to the FBI tomorrow, by afternoon the press will catch wind that I'm alive, and by next week, the publishers will get into a bidding war for my book deal."

"You've got this figured out. Well, once you make your millions, I may be looking for a job—if you're hiring."

"I could use a bodyguard." She smiled. "Don't want to be kidnapped again, and Gene has powerful friends. I'm guessing you're wanting me to put this away so you can get some." Looking up from her notepad, her smile was at once playful and seductive.

"You're such a romantic."

"I do like how you look in a white dress shirt. Don't get me wrong, your typical flannel is appealing, but you're quite capable of pulling off a more sophisticated look." James was still wearing his suit pants with his open-collared button-down. Finishing his drink, he crawled up beside her. "Don't distract me," she ordered with mock abruptness as she continued writing.

"I've had this beautiful woman living with me for a week, I finally get her in bed, and she's journaling."

"Has it been a week?"

"Yeah, and you've been wearing that Mountaineer hoodie the entire time."

"It's grown on me. So has the short hair. It's nice not having to get all dolled up to be your husband's eye candy at some snooty embassy soiree."

"Well, no need to put on airs anymore. With me, you're in the light beer, buffalo wings crowd. I'm quite a date."

Kat put down her pen and pad.

"I'm from Iowa. Beer and wings are fine by me."

"Then it's a date. After we go to the feds tomorrow, it's Miller Time."

"Is it bad that I'm about to have sex with you before we've gone on our first date?"

"Under the circumstances, I think you get a pass. We have been living together for a week. It's a miracle we held out this long." He smirked.

"There you go with the smirk." Leaning in, her arm slipped around his back as she snuggled close. "I'm so glad it was you I found in that parking lot, Jimmy. You may be ridiculous with questionable sanity, but you've grown on me."

"I'm an acquired taste, princess," he admitted, leaning down. They kissed softly, their mutual attraction cascading into effortless, passionate carnality, both panting and pawing at one another. With frantic, desirous anticipation, James was lifting up her hoodie when he heard panicked shouts from the living room.

He jerked his lips off of Kat's and got to his feet just as the bedroom door flew open to reveal a lean, long-haired man training a sound-suppressed Sig Sauer at the senator's wife with rigid calmness, firing several rounds as Kat spilled over the side of the bed. With an athlete's agility, James trapped the man's extended arms beneath his own armpit and clasped the weapon's frame with both hands. It was then he spotted a second assailant behind them. Pushing back into the doorway, James used the long-haired henchman's body to check the second thug into the kitchenette.

James's training kicked in. Having removed the gunman's support hand from the pistol grip, and still trapping his arms, James put counterpressure on the trigger arm, then twisted the weapon, forcing it to the weakest part of the grip: the thumb and forefinger. The pistol thudded to the floor; suddenly James felt something tighten around his neck and pull him backward into the kitchenette. Relinquishing the long-haired assailant, he clasped the garrote as the struggle crashed him into the refrigerator with the other man.

In the living room, he glimpsed JC using his considerable girth to his advantage in a wrestling match with a third intruder. As Long-hair ran into the bedroom, James forced a warning from his lungs: "Kat, look out!" He pulled frantically at the cord around his neck.

The report of a single gunshot echoed from the room.

James's heart sank as his adrenaline spiked. With animalistic ferocity, he jerked and manipulated his body, slamming the strangler into the kitchen countertops. Oxygen becoming scarce, he opened a drawer, scrambled its contents, and settled on a steak knife, seized it, then plunged it several times into the side of his attacker. The garrote loosened; James pulled free and ran into the bedroom.

It appeared empty as he scanned the corners. On the far side of the bed, James found the long-haired intruder on his back, a gunshot through his nose. Blood blanketed his face. Shaking on the floor, her back pushed against the nightstand, Kat was holding the Walther 9mm PPS James kept by his bed.

"Princess, are you okay?" he whispered in relief as he knelt before her and examined her for wounds.

"I think he missed me." She trembled, her eyes tearing up, and he kissed her forehead, then caressed her face and kissed her lips gently in reassurance.

"1-4-3?"

"I love you too." She smiled as he wiped her tears.

"I'll take that," he said, retrieving the pistol from her trembling hands just before Kat yawped a terror-filled cry. He whirled and found the second goon bearing down on him with a knife. Dropping the pistol, James parried the attack, falling backward on the floor where the two combatants struggled and slipped in the blood pouring from the attacker's abdomen.

"Run, princess," James grunted. Kat jumped on the bed, then hesitated. "I said run, Kat! Get the fuck out of here."

Kat bolted through the kitchenette into the living room, where JC was pinned on the floor beneath a lean, foreign-looking man. Stopping momentarily, the assailant ceased beating JC's face long enough to catch her gaze.

"Oh my God, it's Oscar," she whispered. A look of recognition crossed the Russian's face.

"Mrs. Sterling?" Dimitri grinned.

She made a dash for the front door, as Dimitri lunged and caught her ankle, tripping her to the floor. The Russian agent scrambled to his feet and pinned her beneath his sinewy body as his hands clasped her neck. With startling immediacy, she was unable to breathe. Staring up at the murderous, veiny face of the man straining to end her life, she had accepted her fate when a pair of Popeye forearms wrapped around him. With a heave, her would-be murderer flew back with JC bear-hugging him from behind.

Taking the exaggerated inhale of a swimmer resurfacing, Kat recovered her wits and saw the West Virginian and the Russian writhing in a struggle just feet away.

"Run, Miss Kat," JC howled. "Don't know how long I can hold this sumbitch."

Conflicted, she hesitated. "Go, Miss Kat. Go! Jesus will save me." She looked back once, then ran into the cold evening.

JC's country strength was waning, and the wiry Dimitri wriggled from his grasp. Beneath the TV stand, he saw his pistol and retrieved the weapon, then got to his feet and ran toward the door, blindly popping off several rounds in JC's direction as he pursued Kat into the street.

⊙ ⊙ ⊙

Slickened with blood, James thrashed on the floor as he held the knife-wielding intruder at bay. He sensed the life oozing out of his opponent's stab wounds and knew that if he could keep this asshole from plunging the Ginsu into him, the fight would soon be over. Their plasma-lubricated hands lost control of the handle, sending the blade into the darkness beneath the bed. James lifted the Russian by his shirt and threw him against the wall. The henchman's legs were noodle limp as he flopped on the floor, propped up in the corner like a rag doll.

Panting, James looked down to see his white shirt reddened from the melee; he checked himself for wounds. Retrieving his pistol near the nightstand, James stood over the assailant, whose eyes wore the dejected acceptance of the inevitable. Though the man was dying, James wasn't taking any chances, so—more as an insurance policy than an act of mercy—he sent a 9mm round into the intruder's head before stepping past the body and placing a fully loaded magazine into his pistol.

From the living room he heard JC implore Kat to run, invoking Jesus. Hastily passing through the kitchen, James saw the final henchman pop off rounds as he darted out the door.

"JC, are you okay? Where's Kat? Are you hit?"

"Don't think so." JC felt his body for wounds. His panting, swollen face was spitting blood. "It was Oscar."

"Who?"

"Oscar. The bastard I was in a scrape with was Oscar; he ran after Kat."

"Shit" was all James managed before taking off in pursuit.

⊙ ⊙ ⊙

Kat raced shoeless into the middle of O Street, uncertain what to do. It was cool, dark, and silent as the Rapture. Taking her phone from her jeans pocket, she unlocked it, intending to call 911 until she turned to see Dimitri silhouetted by the streetlamp. As he raised his arms in a shooter's stance, she ran toward Thirty-Fifth, zigging and zagging for her life. The sound of the airy, crisp report of a muzzle-suppressed pistol followed by the unnerving whizz as rounds passed her ears sent her shrieking in fear behind the engine block of a street-parked Audi. Covering her head, for the first time since childhood, she prayed: "I'm so sorry, dear God. I know I haven't been perfect. Please, forgive me" was all she mustered before a shadow blanketed her from behind.

"It is a week late, Mrs. Sterling," Dimitri stated in his flat, Russian accent. "But it ends here." The extended suppressor was trained at the top of her skull when the air was pierced by explosive gunshots from across the street. Dimitri's left shoulder jerked from impact. Grunting, the Russian operative crouched beside Kat and returned fire over the vehicle's hood. Rounds struck the engine block with metallic pops and pings. In the distance, the sound of approaching police sirens grew. With time running short, Dimitri decided to end the mission. He pointed his sidearm at the quivering mass next to him.

"Goodnight, Mrs. Sterling," he said and depressed the trigger. The hammer clicked on an empty chamber. Reaching for his belt to reload, he realized his extra magazines had been lost during the struggle with JC. So he struck Kat's cranium with the pistol butt.

"You're coming with me," he announced, seized Kat's arm, opened the passenger door, and threw her in the Audi. Slamming it shut, Dimitri rounded the car. Two loud reports and fiery muzzle flashes burst from across the street as the assassin slipped into the driver's seat unharmed. Dazed from her pistol whipping, Kat stared at Dimitri woozily. He responded by striking her face with such verve that her head ricocheted off the passenger door's window. The engine revved as the Audi lurched forward; behind them a man yelled, "I'm coming to get you, Kat. Hold on!"

CHAPTER 17

A STREETLIGHT at Thirty-Third and O Street provided just enough illumination for James to make out Kat's short, dark mane protruding above the hood as she cowered on the opposite side of an Audi. Slicked-back hair glistening, the lean Oscar trained his pistol at her head. Decades of honed muscle memory came into play as James brought his Walther pistol into position, aligning the glowing tritium sights on the bastard about to kill his princess. The first shot appeared to land; Dimitri jerked and disappeared behind the car. James hoped he'd struck center mass as return fire forced him to shelter behind a tree. JC, unarmed, sought refuge behind a parked car, bullets whizzing by. Visibility was terrible as James put rounds downrange to preoccupy Oscar and keep Kat's skull bullet-free.

James fired a few more desperate shots as the Russian made his way around the vehicle; then his pistol slide locked open on a dry magazine. Distant sirens sounded. The good citizens of Georgetown were undoubtedly dialing 911 in record numbers.

"I'm coming to get you, Kat. Hold on," he yelled as the Audi sped off. James darted for his parked truck.

"James, what the hell is happening?" A panicked Brian stood on the stoop of his rowhouse, Dante behind him, both in their pajamas.

"Having a bit of a rough night," James yelled, running past them toward his F-150. "Stay inside. The cops will be here soon." JC hustled to join him as flashing police lights appeared atop the hill.

"I'll stall the cops. They're looking for me anyhow," said JC.

"Thanks. Hope we meet again under better circumstances."

"Go get Kat. I'll pray for you." The West Virginian's eyes teared up.

Cranking the ignition, James responded, "You're a good man, JC."

For nearly two years, James had been assigned to the Transportation Section of the Presidential Protective Division where he conducted motorcade security advances and vehicle operations. He'd driven the presidential limo countless times, with President Frum bitching behind him about some uncooperative senator or biased journalist. But James had also received intense operational training, which—coupled with his years as a cop— gave him an instinctive sense of vehicle operations.

As the V8 revved beneath his truck's hood, he knew his skills would be tested if he wanted to catch an Audi A8.

James accelerated down O Street and made a right onto Thirty-Fourth. The barren streets at this ungodly hour allowed him to track the Audi's taillights. Speeding down the narrow street, zipping by rowhouses and parked cars lining the curbs, he set up another left onto N Street, the tires barely holding their grip as he gunned the accelerator at the turn's apex.

The Audi bounced through several intersections, ignoring stop signs with frightening recklessness. Turning right out of the quiet Georgetown neighborhood, Oscar steered the sportster onto Wisconsin Avenue. James's truck clipped a Nissan Sentra as he made the turn onto the wide, business-lined thoroughfare, scattering remnants of its right headlamp onto the asphalt. James couldn't figure out where the Russian planned to take Kat. The

Audi's erratic driving and last-second turns indicated Oscar might not have a plan at all. Both vehicles rushed downhill toward the Potomac waterfront. James took out his phone.

Head still fuzzy from the blow to her head, Kat felt her phone buzz inside her hoodie's pouch. She leaned near the door to shield the screen from her kidnapper and read, "Put on your seatbelt, princess." Turning, she saw the bright headlights of James's truck pursuing them with manic determination.

"I love that crazy cowboy," she whispered and pulled the seatbelt across her shoulder. At Water Street, Dimitri slammed the brakes to make a right-hand turn beneath the Whitehurst Freeway. James seized the opportunity to ram his fender into the rear quarter panel, sending the Audi into a spin as tires screamed along the pavement before halting in the middle of the T-intersection at Wisconsin and Water Street. The thought of escape flashed through Kat's mind— just as the engine revved again to dispel any notion of a getaway. The A8 hastened down Water Street beneath the freeway.

The businesses to James's right flashing by with increasing speed, he pushed his truck to its limit. To his left, the obsidian Potomac was a silent observer to the chaos.

James knew Water Street dead-ended ahead and concluded this Oscar fellow wasn't familiar with Georgetown. Mashing brakes abruptly, the Audi peeled right onto Thirty-Fourth Street between two converted, brick warehouses. The road dead-ended into a dirt path amid a copse of trees. Slowing considerably, the Audi snaked behind a business, pulled up a short hill, and climbed onto a dirt path paralleling the C & O Canal. The Chesapeake and Ohio Canal once transported coal from the Alleghenies, but the remnant now lay empty, winding through Georgetown, paralleled by dirt towpaths used long ago by horse teams to pull barges.

As the Audi began increasing speed, Kat concluded this was her last chance to break free. She had been lucid since James's truck spun them but put on a show of wooziness to avoid another head blow. Before Oscar could get to full speed, she unlatched her seat belt, popped the door, and rolled out onto the dirt path. James's truck skid to a stop behind her.

The reverse lights of the Audi illuminated, brightening the pitch-dark night. The wheels spun dust as the vehicle backed aggressively toward her. Slipping on loose gravel, Kat couldn't find her footing, finally scrambling away just as the sharp crunch of metal on metal signaled James had intercepted the Audi by slamming his F-150 into its rear. The American V8's RPMs increased to a crescendo as gravel shot from its spinning tires. The Ford's torque pushed the lighter vehicle forward against its will, and James saw Oscar vainly attempt to turn the vehicle as it gained momentum. Two support pillars flanking the path supported the Whitehurst Freeway above. Adjusting the angle of his truck's hood, James maneuvered the Audi toward them, gritted his teeth, and prepared for impact.

The Audi collided into the cement pillar with stunning force. The truck's forward momentum spun it right. With the accelerator floored, James lost control, overcorrected his steering, and plunged into the eight-foot-deep, waterless canal. His face slammed into the safety air bags. Gathering himself, he reached into the glove box and retrieved a pair of hinged handcuffs. Bubbling to the surface was a primordial rage—as if every frustration, every setback, every heartache now sought release.

◉ ◉ ◉

When the pickup's door opened and James emerged unharmed, a wave of relief washed over Kat. Forty yards distant with little light, she strained to take in the scene. He climbed out of the canal and walked purposefully toward the Audi. Bending over, he picked up a large rock.

"Jimmy," she yelled. His head whipped her way. "Are you okay?"

"I'm fine. Are you hurt, princess?"

"I'm okay. Thank you for coming to get me."

"I'm a Secret Service agent. I'll keep you safe. Besides, I wasn't done kissing you."

"I love you."

"Love you too, princess."

"Let's go, Jimmy."

"I've one more thing to do," he answered as the brake lights on the Audi lit up. "No you don't, motherfucker." James yanked open the passenger door and, cocking back his rock-gripping fist, dove into the car and slammed the stone into Dimitri's skull. The entire sedan shook as if holding a panicked animal, curses and exclamations indicative of a struggle. Abruptly, the sounds ceased, and the reverse lights came on as the Audi backed up a short distance.

For a moment, Kat considered seeking refuge in the canal, worried Oscar might make a second effort to run her over. Then the reverse lights clicked off, and the car lurched down the path beyond the overpass before it turned left and stopped. The vehicle sat idle, facing the dark Potomac below the bluff. Kat stood with her hand over her mouth. *What is happening? Are they fighting?* There did not appear to be a struggle. The brake lights went out as the rear tires spun dirt and the engine gunned to full throttle. Kat's heart dropped. The car sped forward.

Nearly two hundred years ago, an aqueduct bridge had traversed the Potomac from Virginia to DC. All that remained was the end point: a stone structure—now covered in graffiti—jutting out toward the water. The Audi bumped over the stones and continued its acceleration until it launched off the stone ramp into the cool, dark morning. Arching downward, engine still whining, it plunged eighty feet before splashing into the Potomac's moon-reflecting waters.

"No, no, no, no," Kat screamed as she rushed down the path. Stopping at the edge of the bridge's remnant, she saw the taillamps short out, leaving the sinking vehicle invisible in the darkness.

"Jimmy," she yelled as tears spilled from her eyes. "Dear God, Jimmy, can you hear me?" The sound of approaching police sirens grew louder. She felt cold and lonely.

Kat wanted to ask James what to do, but he wasn't there.

CHAPTER 18

EREK ROLAND fumbled for his phone on the nightstand, hoping to stop its incessant ringing before it woke Monique. After only a few hours of sleep, he was in no condition to deal with her attitude.

"Yeah, this is Sergeant Roland," he answered as the bed shifted from his wife sitting up. "No kidding? How long ago? I'll be there as soon as possible. Keep him on scene." He hung up and clicked on a lamp before turning to Monique's menacing expression.

"Let me guess: they calling you back in," she spit with disgust.

"They caught him," he stated. Her face morphed from indignation to glowing pride. She leaned over and wrapped him in a fleshy embrace.

"Go get 'em, boo. I'll pick out a tie for you." She beamed.

An hour later, pulling down Thirty-Fifth Street in his Crown Vic, Derek found the corner at O Street littered with police cruisers. Their overhead lights danced off cars and windows in the predawn hours. Most front stoops were filled with residents, coats over their pajamas, taking in a rare scene for this part of town. Kevin McClennan waved him over. Donning a tan trench coat preferred by cops of a certain vintage, Derek moved to him.

"We sure it's JC?"

"It's him," the FBI agent said, his excitement evident. "And this thing is getting weirder by the minute." Derek nodded laconically. The kid's enthusiasm was endearing, but he'd decide for himself if this was indeed the break they'd hoped for.

"Is he talking?"

"Yeah, he's cooperative. Said Katherine Sterling was here."

"He said that?" Derek asked. Kevin nodded. "She's alive?"

"That's what he's claiming."

Derek was skeptical. "Then where is she?"

"He doesn't know."

"Interesting. Well, let's see what we got here." Derek approached the crime scene. Both men passed under the yellow tape—the entire block had been sealed off—and meandered through cops and CSI personnel. Kevin directed him to an open door at the basement level of a rowhouse.

"Who are they?" asked Derek, nodding to a small White guy and an African American male being questioned on the main stoop.

"A gay couple living upstairs. Just returned last night from vacation," Kevin replied. "The White guy owns the place. Says the basement level is a finished apartment he rents out. They seem credible."

"I'll need to talk to them." Stepping into the ground floor, Sergeant Roland observed a living room in chaotic disarray: an overturned coffee table, with throw pillows, beer cans, and pizza boxes strewn haphazardly about. Plastic yellow markers flagged the locations of several shell casings on the floor. With deliberate steps, Derek walked through the living room, examining the scene with experienced eyes. He saw a significant amount of blood streaked on the walls and counters of the kitchenette, the obvious result of a struggle. On the floor tile rested a two-and-a-half-foot cord.

A streak of blood led to the bedroom, where several federal agents and Metro detectives were eyeing the macabre scene while a technician snapped photos. On the floor at the foot of the bed lay the remains of a long-haired male with a gunshot through his nose. On the opposite side of the bed, propped against the wall in a seated position, was a lean male shot through the cranium. Examining the scene, Derek noted the amount of blood smeared on the walls.

"Jesus. What do we got, Tom?"

Tom Gorman, jowly and beer-gutted, breathed heavily through his tar-filled lungs as he shared his deductions. "The long-haired guy here on the floor died with a shot to the snot-box. The fella over there"—he pointed to the blood-blanketed corpse leaning against the wall—"may have been in some kind of struggle." Tom pointed to the various smears on the rug and along the far end of the room. "He was stabbed a couple times in the abdomen and finished off with a headshot."

"There's a pistol with a sound suppressor," Derek pointed out next to the long-haired one on the floor.

"I was about to mention that; it's a Sig," Tom said. "So far, it's the only firearm we've found. Looks like the deceased dropped it when a slug went through his nasal cavity." Carefully, Derek stepped past the body and examined the bloody area with the dead man against the wall.

"Do we know who these guys are?" he asked.

"No idea."

"Who's our suspect? Has JC given us any indication?" asked Derek.

"Says he was sleeping on the couch when a guy he knows as Oscar broke in. JC claims he and Oscar were in a struggle when these two"—Tom pointed at the deceased—"went after Mrs. Sterling and a man he says is a former Secret Service agent."

"So, we think this former agent took these guys out?"

"That's our best guess," continued Tom. "JC doesn't know what happened in the bedroom, but at some point, Mrs. Sterling runs out of here while he was still wrestling that Oscar fella. Oscar goes after her, a shootout occurs in the street, Oscar somehow manages to get Mrs. Sterling in his car and takes off. According to JC, the former agent hopped in a truck and gave chase."

"And are we certain the guy we have in custody is John Charles Klingerman? Katherine Sterling's kidnapper?" asked Derek.

"It's him. He has ID, waived his rights, and admits to being involved in the plot to kidnap the senator's wife. Says the gal who was taken by the intruder was Mrs. Sterling."

"Do we believe him?"

"Sarge, I don't know what to believe anymore," said an exasperated Tom as he wiped his forehead. "The owner of the property is the kid that lives upstairs. He said the guy he lets crash down here is the one who went after Mrs. Sterling. Said his name is James Ford."

"James Ford? Where have I heard that name?"

"The owner says it's the Secret Service agent caught getting his dick wet down in South America. The one that's been all over the news. His old lady kicked him out for nailing the señoritas, and he's been crashing here ever since."

"You mean the agent that refused to pay the hooker?"

"That's the one."

"Kevin, you're right: this is getting weirder by the minute," Derek conceded. "First order of business is finding this woman and determining if it is indeed Mrs. Sterling."

"Well, we may be closer to that than you think," Tom relayed. "We believe we have located Agent Ford's truck. A call came in about a disturbance off Water Street. Found a truck in the canal with a 9mm in it; no subjects located. We have men on scene." Derek nodded as his brain mulled the new data. Something on the nightstand caught his eye: an open notebook. Picking it up, he thumbed through a few pages and realized the loopy, feminine penmanship was a recording of the past week's events.

"Take a look at this, Kev," said Derek as he handed the notebook to his FBI counterpart.

"What is it?"

"Mrs. Sterling telling us everything we don't know."

Kevin flipped through the pages. "Holy shit."

"My thoughts exactly. Let's talk to the owner."

The slightly-built property owner, Brian Keaton, sat in his dining room, face red with anguish. Derek introduced himself. "I know this has been a traumatic evening for you, Mr. Keaton, but there are a lot of things we are sorting through. Did you at any time see this woman in the downstairs apartment?" He held up an image of Kat Sterling.

"I know who she is," Brian stated, "but I've never seen her."

"Did you ever see a woman with your friend Mr. Ford?"

"About a week or so ago, I returned from a trip and stopped downstairs to catch up. There was a woman there James said he had worked with. I think I remember him introducing her as Amy."

"What did she look like?"

"She had a ball cap on, short hair, tall and lean. She didn't say much of anything. It was a little surprising to see a woman there with James. Wait, are you insinuating that was Katherine Sterling?"

"Maybe. We don't know. It's very early. So, what happened last night?" asked Derek. Brian relayed what he'd seen and heard. When the shooting stopped, he stepped outside to see James running to his truck and then speeding away in pursuit. Derek believed the kid.

"Sarge," a uniformed Metro cop greeted him. "They're calling in the Park Police and Coast Guard to the Water Street location. They believe there's a submerged vehicle in the river near the old aqueduct."

"Copy that," Derek acknowledged. "Still no one found?"

"No sir."

"Sir, did they find James?" asked Brian meekly.

"No. We found his truck. His whereabouts are still unknown."

"And did that officer say there's a car in the river?"

"He did," Derek said. Brian's face twisted with grief as he buried his head in his hands.

⊙ ⊙ ⊙

Fear, confusion, and uncertainty enveloped Kat as she vainly attempted to calm her brain after Jimmy plummeted into the brackish obsidian of the Potomac. The cold, dark, early morn added to her sense of living in a nightmare.

Finally, a solid thought appeared, and she grasped onto it, using the phone James had gifted her to text her trustworthy friend.

> **Kat:** Chet, I know you won't recognize this number, but this is Kat. I'm alive. Please tell me you're in DC. I'm free and need HELP.
>
> **Chet:** Whoever this is, I want you to know this is sick and I have your number and will report you to the police.
>
> **Kat:** I got away from the kidnappers, but I'm all alone. I need you to pick me up. I just need to gather myself. Don't get the police involved, not yet. And do not call Gene, he is the one who did this."

She attached a selfie of her face to the text.

> **Kat:** I know I look different. I cut my hair. I will explain when you get me. I'm really freaked out right now.
>
> **Chet:** OMG Kat, is this really you?

Kat: Yes. I need help but you can't call Gene.

Chet: Where are you? I should call the cops.
Kat: DON'T . . . not yet. Tonight has been the worst of my life. Please God just come get me at 35th and Q in George-town. I had to kill a man. Please Chet, if you ever cared about me like I know you do please come get me. I'm cold.

Chet: On my way.

Kat dared not step out under the streetlamps as she waited. As she huddled in the shadows adjacent to a prep school soccer field, not knowing if her hunters were still in pursuit, the reality that she had taken a man's life set in. Her heart felt as if it were being squeezed in a vise. She longed for her Jimmy—to hold her drunken, ridiculous friend. The friend who risked everything to free her. In the cold shadow of an oak tree, she realized no one had ever displayed such selfless devotion to her.

Headlights beaming down Q Street interrupted her meandering thoughts as a car slowed. When the Tesla S Model turned right and stopped, Kat jumped from her hiding spot. A silhouette emerged from the driver's door.

"Kat?" She pulled back her hood. "Oh my God, Kat," Chet exclaimed as they embraced, his small frame squeezing her with pent-up affection. "I can't believe it's you." His eyes welled up in disbelief. "Are you hurt?"

"Chet, I just need to rest. Please, let's go back to your apartment. I need time to internalize all that's happened. If you can just give me that." With a frenetic nod, he guided her to the passenger door and, in short order, was off to his luxury Wisconsin Avenue apartment.

It wasn't until they entered his place that Chet noticed the blood on her hoodie and bruises forming on her face. As she plopped in a chair, exhausted, she saw Chet staring at her in disbelief as if she were some apparition. Realizing what a jolting sight she must be to her old friend, literally returning from the dead, she gave him a faint smile of reassurance.

"I killed someone tonight," she monotoned. He knelt before her and grabbed her hands.

"Was it the guy who kidnapped you?" She shook her head. "I don't know what to do, Kat. I can't believe this is real. That you're alive. I really don't know what I'm supposed to do." A sardonic laugh escaped her. "What's so funny?" Chet asked.

"Nothing, it's just that I've spent a week with a guy who always knew what to do. Maybe not always the right thing to do. But he always had an answer." She stared through him until tears formed. Chet hugged her. She took a deep breath. "Gene did this," she revealed. "He hired some thugs to take me away and staged the kidnapping." Relinquishing the embrace, still kneeling, he gazed at her.

"Gene couldn't have done this to you."

"He did, Chet. When we returned from Topeka, there were three men in our house. Some guy known as Oscar and two West Virginia men." Shaking his head, dumbfounded, Chet tried to process the revelation.

"Where have you been for a week?"

"A guy found me and took me in. I've stayed with him." Her lips quivered as tears streaked her face. "He saved my life tonight." She pulled her phone from the pouch of her hoodie; she had texted James six times since witnessing the Audi dive into the river, but still no response. "I don't think he survived."

"Tell me what's going on," pleaded Chet.

"I'd love to tell you all I've been through this past week. But you'll think I've lost my mind."

"You can tell me. I won't think you're crazy."

"Gene staged my kidnapping. I think the Russians were involved. I escaped from my kidnappers and ran into a former Secret Service agent, who is the sexiest, most ridiculous person I've ever met. We began running down leads to my case and found a dead body. Tonight, three Russians tried to kill me. Oh, I left out the part where I became friends with one of my kidnappers." Chet stared at her. "I told you that you'd think I'm crazy."

"I never gave up on you," Chet shared. "I always felt you were alive."

"And that's why I turned to you. You've always been a true friend." She sipped her cocktail. "Gene is having an affair with Tanya."

Chet nodded but didn't appear surprised. "How do you know?"

"I just know. That's one reason he wanted me gone."

"Why not just divorce you?"

"The election. He always wants everything his way—the hot, young lover and the presidency." Stiffly, she eased back to lie on the couch.

"You okay?"

"Just sore and needing time to get my head straight."

Chet placed a blanket over her. "Just tell me when, and I'll take you to the authorities," he promised. Kat pulled the blanket over her face, not wanting him to see her cry.

⊙ ⊙ ⊙

Non-defensive and matter-of-fact, JC was the picture of sincerity when he waived his Miranda rights in a J. Edgar Hoover Building interview room. The interrogation was unlike any the two seasoned law enforcement professionals had experienced. Sipping his Coca Cola, the suspect recounted how Squinty had introduced him and Cornhole to the kidnapping plot. He soberly relayed the events of the night in question when a man named Oscar, in cahoots with Senator Sterling, directed the West Virginians to tie up the senator's wife, kill her, and dispose of the body. JC told of her escape and his religious epiphany after Cornhole's overdose that prompted his decision to turn himself in.

What floored the lawmen was the revelation that—little more than twenty-four hours ago—JC had been rear-ended by a former Secret Service agent who was harboring Kat Sterling. JC insisted he and Mrs. Sterling made amends and a decision was made to go to the feds the next morning, but their plans were disrupted by Oscar and his henchmen's home invasion. When Oscar managed to get away with Mrs. Sterling and the former special agent gave chase, JC insisted it was the last he'd seen of them.

Detective Sergeant Derek Roland looked at Assistant Special Agent in Charge Kevin McClennan as if to say, "Do you believe this shit?" The sergeant had interviewed thousands of suspects in his career; he knew a liar, and nothing in JC's body language indicated untruthfulness. The doubt in Derek's mind stemmed from the outlandish improbability of the story itself. The cop and the fed tried to pry holes in the suspect's recounting, but JC never wavered from his assertions.

"Is there anything else you feel we should know?" asked Derek.

"No sir." JC shook his head as he thought. "Only that I'm very sorry for what I done. I feel Jesus Christ is givin' me a cross to bear, a cross I done made myself. I feel I am an instrument of the Lord. I'll do whatever you need to make sure Miss Kat and Mr. James are safe. Y'all still haven't found 'em?"

"Last I heard, they were still missing," answered Derek. "Need another Coke?"

JC nodded. Derek and Kevin exited the interview room and made their way down the hall to the command post where, for a week, the FBI had been piecing together information on large, white dry-erase boards. Kevin and the FBI special agent in charge exchanged updates before Kevin poured Derek another coffee.

"That Audi we found in the river? There was a body in it," Kevin advised Derek. "It was the driver, who was severely beaten, handcuffed to the steering wheel, and driven off of the old aqueduct; a large rock was holding down the accelerator."

"Do we know who he is?"

"Dimitri Romov."

"You mean Oscar? The guy we think offed Donovan?"

"That's the guy."

"This is a big deal."

"For sure, and get this," Kevin continued, "the call to the tip line was made by the phone we recovered from the residence tonight. We believe it belongs to Agent James Ford. Our Operational Technology Division has a digital access evidence team working to extract more from it."

"And the journal I found?" asked Derek.

"It's Katherine Sterling's. The handwriting matches samples we've obtained. She was chronicling this past week's adventures."

"So, our boy JC is telling us the truth."

"Appears that way, Sarge. Kat was in that apartment. She's out there somewhere. Don't know if the Russians got her, but she was alive and well mere hours ago."

Derek responded with a deep sigh and furrowed brow.

"And this James Ford guy is still out there," Kevin added.

"Do we think he sent Dimitri into the Potomac?"

"It was his pickup left in the C&O where Dimitri took his plunge."

"JC said Senator Sterling was complicit in Mrs. Sterling's abduction," noted Derek. "I believe him. How else would Dimitri and his friends locate her at some random Georgetown residence? A government has to be behind it."

"You're onto something, Sarge."

"I know you spooks know more than you're letting on. You have him wiretapped? Hack his email? What do you all know?"

"I know we have to find Katherine Sterling."

Derek smiled. "Nice dodge."

CHAPTER 19

"We are on location near the 3300 block of O Street in Georgetown where police have cordoned off the entire block as an active crime scene. Police are being tight lipped about the details but have confirmed that John Charles Klingerman is in custody. As you know, Klingerman has been wanted for the past several days in connection with the disappearance of Senator Gene Sterling's wife, Katherine Sterling, who was reported missing a week ago following a home invasion.

"Sometime after midnight, neighbors reported gunfire breaking the silence of this normally tranquil neighborhood. According to police, there are two deceased males inside the residence. They are not releasing their names or cause of death at this time. Police have advised Katherine Sterling's location is still unknown. When asked if they believe she had been at the residence, police advised there is evidence supporting she was indeed once at this location. What's more, we at Fox 5 have confirmed the residence was being rented by former Secret Service agent James Ford.

"Agent Ford was the member of the elite Presidential Protective Detail in Brazil who set off an international scandal when he was caught with a prostitute in his hotel room. When pressed on Ford's involvement, police declined to provide a statement but confirmed Ford's whereabouts are also unknown at this time. And as if this incident wasn't strange enough, a vehicle has been pulled from the Potomac near the old aqueduct. We are told one body has been located inside, and police believe it is related to the incident here on O Street. This is breaking news, and we will provide more information as it becomes available. Back to you in the studio."

Carly Mavros stopped peddling halfway through the news flash and stared into the screen attached to her elliptical machine. The other morning regulars at her trendy Twenty-Third-Street gym were likewise transfixed to their screens. Hand over her mouth, Carly thought, *What has James gotten himself into now?* A melancholic dread came over her, fearing what fate had befallen her former lover.

Driving back to her apartment in early-morning gloom, she texted James's phone: "I saw the news. Are you ok? Where are you?" She still hadn't received a reply when she reached her parking garage. Her head swimming, she crossed I Street and was fumbling for her apartment building's front-door key fob when a figure emerged from the shadows, nearly sending her into cardiac arrest.

"Carly, it's me. I've had a really bad night. I need your help."

"James! Are you okay? Why are you soaking wet?"

"It's a long story."

Relieved he was alive, she was about to embrace him when he rebuked her and looked down at his shirt. The once white button-down was stained red as a butcher's apron.

"Oh my God. Oh my God." Carly was on the verge of losing it. Grabbing her trembling hands, James looked around, hoping nobody would exit the apartment building.

"I need to go upstairs," he said in a calm, forceful voice. "I can explain it all to you, but I've got to get off the streets. I didn't know who to turn to, but I trust you, Carly."

"You, you're, um, you're on TV," she mustered.

"I am? Again? Dammit, that's the last thing I need."

"Come with me," she said, managing to find the fob. In her apartment, Carly had him take off the bloody shirt and soaked pants as she beelined it to her bedroom. Removing his shirt, he slid off his slacks, feeling odd about being in her living room in his skivvies. She returned.

"No need to look so uncomfortable. I've seen you wearing less. Try these," she said, tossing him an OBX souvenir T-shirt and a pair of athletic shorts. "Shirt belonged to an old boyfriend."

"Thanks."

She sat on the sofa, trying to collect her thoughts. James sat at the other end, closed his eyes, and leaned his head back. For a minute, the room was silent as each processed the insanity of their circumstances. Carly piped up, "The news said there were two dead guys at your place and another in a car found in the Potomac." James stared straight ahead in silent reflection. "What the hell happened? You look like you've been through a war." Carly eyed his scuffed face and bruised neck.

"Three guys busted into my place last night. Not amateurs, mind you, but trained men. It was a scrum."

"The news said they arrested Katherine Sterling's kidnapper."

"They did?" James raised an eyebrow.

"Was he at your place?"

"He may have been."

"Goddammit, James, this is no time for your glib nonanswers.

Just what in the fuck is going on? I deserve to know at this point. The cops want to question you. Did you kill those guys?"

"Two of them. I took out two of them. Okay, Carly? That's why I came here."

"How the hell was the kidnapping suspect at your place? Did you . . . ? Please tell me you didn't kidnap the senator's wife."

"Wait, what? Are you serious? You think I'd kidnap someone? I have my flaws, but come on, Carly. You know me better than that."

"You've been under tremendous stress."

"Which is why I drink too much. I don't kidnap women for stress relief. Look, want to know what happened? I was heading home Sunday night when I got into a fender bender with that John Klingerman guy."

"Hold on, the whole country is looking for the Sterling kidnapper, and you just run into him? You expect me to buy this?"

"I know it sounds crazy, but yeah, I quite literally ran into him. JC thinks it's the work of Jesus Christ. I don't know if it was Jesus, but it happened."

"So, you arrested the kidnapper?"

"I did—good guy, by the way. Fell on some hard times of his own making, which I can relate to."

Carly rubbed her temples, looking overwhelmed. "Are you going to tell me Katherine Sterling was also at your place?"

"She was there."

"How's that possible? She's been missing for a week."

"She wasn't missing. I knew where she was."

"So, you had the victim and the suspect at your place?" Manic incredulity shot from her eyes.

"They're friends now."

"James, why is it always this way with you? Why always with this crazy bullshit? What in the holy fuck is going on?" Her

Greek ire up, Carly's arms emphasized each syllable with frantic gesticulations.

"I found Kat Sterling the night she went missing. I was drunk and upset, and she came hopping into my life."

"Hopping?"

"Long story, but yes. She managed to escape from the car trunk, and I found her."

"So, when you met me for lunch, she was at your place?"

"That's right."

"This whole time, you had the world's most sought-after kidnap victim, and you sat on it? Why didn't you tell me? Why didn't you go to the authorities?"

"For one, I didn't know what kind of reception I'd get from you. Last time I'd seen you, you threw a plate at me. Second, I knew you had contacts in the intelligence community and hoped you could shed some light on Oscar, which you were able to do. Kat didn't want to go to the cops; she didn't think they'd buy her version of events." Arms folded, Carly eyed him with an odd mix of bewilderment and disapproval. "Are you mad at me?" he asked.

"I don't know what I am. I didn't know you could be more messed up, and then you show up at my place covered in bloodstains, admitting you've been rooming with a kidnapped senator's wife."

"It's been an eventful week."

"I hate your understatements. So, we've established you sheltered Mrs. Sterling and located her kidnapper. The one thing that's unclear is how you managed to come by the name Oscar Reese."

"Kat memorized the license tag of her kidnappers. It returned to an address in West Virginia. We took a trip out there to see what information we could uncover on the suspects. Long story short, we saw a rental car leave the address before we find a murdered guy inside who, according to JC, recruited him to kidnap Kat. Anyhow, the car that left the scene was rented by Oscar Reese, who, with your help, we know is actually Dimitri Romov."

"Another dead body?" Carly's mouth was agape in disbelief.

"Maybe this was a mistake," James concluded. "I'm sorry to involve you in this. I don't know, a part of me thought I could get back in the good graces of the Service if I pulled off the impossible and uncovered evidence to support Kat's story."

"It wasn't a mistake. I'm glad you trusted me," Carly said before taking several deep breaths to regain her composure. With a thoughtful expression, she said, "I have more on Dimitri Romov. My source wouldn't share much but said he's a low-level player with Russian intel. More a lacky and not a chief player, but definitely connected. The interesting thing is—and this stays here—the feds are looking into ties Senator Joe Bratton has to a Russian oligarch named Oleg Yumashev. Yumashev runs an energy conglomerate with major investments in traditional fossil fuels. Dimitri is closely tied to Mr. Yumashev. The feds have been eyeing Senator Bratton's dealings over the past year and are particularly concerned about his cozy relationship with the Russians."

"Hold on, think about this: Joe Bratton and Gene Sterling are tight," began James. "If Dimitri is this Oleg guy's lackey, then—"

"Then Senator Sterling could be tied to Kat's kidnapper via Joe," interrupted Carly, "giving credence to his involvement."

"JC insists Oscar was the fixer who colluded with Senator Sterling."

"What makes this JC so credible?" she asked with a reporter's skepticism. "He was given money to kill Kat Sterling. He's probably covering his own ass. We still can't be one-hundred-percent certain Oscar is Dimitri Romov."

"I believe JC, no matter how implausible his story may seem."

"If it is true, this is the biggest lead of my career."

"It gets better. Kat and I snuck into her house last week and got some dirt on the senator. Those documents I got you, I took them from Senator Sterling's office. Even better, I managed to get a picture of him fucking his mistress. He's a furry."

"A furry?"

"Dresses like an animal to get his rocks off. He's a dog, so you can imagine his favorite position."

"Ewww."

"It was horrifying."

"Is the pic on your phone?" she asked, still disgusted.

"Yeah, but it's at my place."

"And what's the story with the guy they found at the bottom of the Potomac?"

"A rage came over me like never before in my life. I struck him several times with a rock, handcuffed him to the steering wheel, and placed the rock on the accelerator. Problem was, the car door locked when I put it in drive, so I went with him."

"Thank God you didn't drown."

"Thank my training."

"Do you think it was Dimitri?"

"I do."

"I still have my doubts. Where did you go last night?"

"There's a homeless veteran near Rock Creek and Virginia named Stan. Used to give him cash every week on my way home. He remembered me and let me crash at his shanty."

"You bunked with a homeless guy?"

"The thing about homeless guys is they don't ask why you're covered in blood."

"You're not a sane person."

"I'm well aware."

"This is too much. I can't think." She took a deep breath. "I'm going to take a shower and gather my thoughts." Standing, she looked at his bruised, pitiable face. "James, you're a good guy, but you always find yourself in these storms of your own making. I'm your friend, and there was a time I really loved you. But the chaos, I don't know how you survive it. I'm happy you're okay. And I'm glad you turned to me for help."

She leaned down, kissed his forehead, and with a contemplative smile turned for the bedroom. James sat motionless, wearing a distant stare.

Closing her bedroom door, Carly leaned her head against the wall. Was he crazy? Maybe the stress of his broken marriage and the wall-to-wall coverage of his South American tryst had broken him. Could any of this be true?

She turned on the TV before starting the shower. Pulling her sports bra over her head, she heard the news anchor: *"We are now reporting that the deceased individual located in the vehicle discovered early this morning in the Potomac was Dimitri Romov. Officials have confirmed Romov is a Russian national and released his identity after informing the embassy. Police cannot, at this time, rule out foul play but refused to provide further details."*

"Oh my God, JC is telling the truth," she said to herself. Throwing a sweatshirt over her exposed torso, she returned to the living room to inform James, only to find him slumped in the corner of the couch, his battered, listless face snoring peacefully in deep, much-needed sleep.

CHAPTER 20

MOUTH DRY with anxiety, Senator Gene Sterling sat on the edge of his enormous bed, staring at the wall-mounted television airing nonstop coverage of the Georgetown crime scene. The burning, itchy feeling on his neck signaled his hives were reemerging. What was his next move? To him the answer was clear: deny any allegations as the preposterous rantings of a racist xenophobe, then allow the press to carry his water. Looking over his shoulder, he eyed his sleeping lover and took a moment to admire Tanya's bare, squats-enhanced derrière. With her help and a little political jiu-jitsu, he could remain the innocent victim warranting the public's sympathy.

The question he could not answer was why JC was in Georgetown. There was no way that fat bastard could kill two men and send a third to a watery doom. Gene sensed there were latent elements to this scheme of which he was unaware—levers being pulled for his White House bid more sinister than he appreciated. He turned to the one man he trusted most in such crises: Joe Bratton. Grabbing his cell phone, he went across the hall to his study, nearly tripping over the furry dog head on the floor.

Once Joe answered, Gene asked, "Are you seeing this?"

"Of course I am. I figured you'd call once you were up, but I know yesterday was a long day. I can come by so we can talk. You signed off on the Capitol Police, I heard."

"I didn't need them around any longer. Just wasn't necessary," answered Gene, not mentioning that he'd discontinued protection so the cops wouldn't uncover his affair.

"Remember, you're the victim in this," Joe reminded him. "I'll be by later." The West Virginia senator hung up abruptly, which struck Gene as strange. A malaise enveloped him, an overall feeling events were souring. It was unlike Joe to be so terse. Nothing in modern America had more political currency than victimhood. Every accusation must be spun to bludgeon the accuser with self-righteous indignation.

Peering through the blinds, he saw media trucks parking along Hillbrook Lane. He took a long, meditative breath.

Remain cool, Gene, his inner voice said. *The cops have JC, but there's no sign of Kat. She's rotting in some backwoods grave, never to be found. Just deny any knowledge of it and appear stung at the implication you are capable of colluding in such a despicable act.*

He logged onto his computer. The first thing he noticed was that the mail icon for his AOL account indicated an unread message. He'd promised Tanya to refrain from checking this account, but in light of the morning's news, his curiosity was too strong to resist. He clicked it.

A selfie of JC's fat, smiling face in the foreground with Kat duct-taped on the floor beneath him came with a message sent last night:

> I never heard back from you, Gene. I'll forgive you this one
> time, considering you're out campaigning with that tight
> little piece of ass you're nailing. Oh, you didn't know I was
> privy to that? There's so much you don't know. Anyhow,
> I never named my price—perhaps you were waiting for
> that. I want twenty grand. (That's $20,000. Wasn't sure

how hip you elitists were to the commoners' lingo.) In case you thought I was bluffing, here's a little pic of your dearly departed wife (oh, she's not departed, not yet, that'll cost you that $20k). Kisses, JC.

Gene's heart raced with panic until it burst forth and he began wailing like a grieving mother. *My God, she's there with JC. She's alive and in Georgetown!* Bursting from the bed, Tanya tripped over the furry dog head, climbed to her feet, and crossed the hall to find Gene writhing on the floor, his desk chair overturned, yowling as if doused with acid. In nothing but an oversized T-shirt, she knelt and pulled him into an embrace before looking up at the computer to see the source of his anguish.

"I'm fucked. I'm so fucked. It's fucking over," he cried. "The cops got JC. Kat's alive. The primaries are today. Oh my God, Tanya, what do I do?"

The squishy, wet-noodle sniveling was the least attractive, most emasculating display Tanya had ever witnessed. Soothing him like she might a whimpering child, she watched the hives forming on his neck as she asked how he knew JC had been arrested.

"The news," he said with a quiver. "It's all over the news."

Releasing him, she returned to the bedroom and stared at the sensationalized reporting of JC's arrest and the unknown whereabouts of Katherine Sterling. Her mind pieced together what she knew with what was being reported; it was clear Dimitri had failed once again. Bowed and defeated, his face glistening with tears, Gene entered the bedroom and sat next to her.

"Pull your shit together," she ordered. "They haven't located Kat."

"How can you be so sure?"

"If they had located her, the FBI would already have held a press conference to pat themselves on the back. She's out there somewhere." The fact that Kat's location was still unknown seemed implausible. The television displayed a picture of Dimitri Romov, identifying him as the victim found in the submerged car.

"Holy shit, they killed Oscar," cried Gene. "Why was Oscar there with JC?" Ignoring him, Tanya pulled on her clothes left on the floor from last night's role-playing coitus. "Where are you going?"

"To meet Joe."

"The press is outside."

"I'll go out back. Don't talk to them. Not until I get a better sense of where we stand. Besides, we don't need shots of you hysterical and covered in hives." Her demeanor was professional and direct. "I will have our office put out a press release before noon saying we are not commenting at this time and are monitoring the news and praying for Kat's safety. Got it?" Gene nodded and sniffed like a reprimanded schoolboy.

⊙   ⊙   ⊙

The amazing men and women of the FBI have caught the suspect who kidnapped Mrs. Sterling. By throwing all the resources of the federal government into finding this dirtbag we were able to serve justice, this in spite of Senator Sterling's very unfair treatment of me. I won't get so much as a THANK YOU. But that's ok, because we are BRINGING BACK MY AMERICA! #BBMA @PresidentFrum

Chief of Staff Gary Boxterman sighed and put down his phone. Having woken farmer early, he'd anticipated the day would be ruled by the Democratic primaries. That was before hearing the extraordinary news that the suspect in the Sterling kidnapping case had been apprehended. Most jarring was the revelation that he was located at the residence of James Ford. Ford had been Gary's assistant detail leader for the first year of the Frum administration and became one of his favorite agents. James was always prepared and thorough but personable, which wasn't always the case with the stereotypically stoic Secret Service guys. When James's escapades in South America came to light, Gary had been shocked by the news.

The Suburban pulled up to the West Wing entrance.

"Looks to be another quiet day in DC," quipped his Secret Service detail leader.

"Funny, Alex. That's why I got these." Gary shook his bottle of Tums. Grabbing his briefcase, he entered the West Wing and immediately headed to the Oval Office where President Ronald Frum had just finished his phone call with the FBI director.

"Do you believe this shit, Gary? The FBI is looking for Katherine Sterling and that Secret Service horndog. The director told me there's a seventy percent chance she's alive."

"How do they come up with that number?"

"Hell, I don't know. They're the FBI; they're smart. All those dead guys they found are Russians. I bet the media cocksuckers will find a way to blame this on me." The president was almost giddy with the morning's drama. "I'd love to know how that Secret Service agent is involved. I bet he lost his marbles after getting canned, then decided to kidnap her." Though he thought the theory absurd, Gary remained silent. "I wonder how this affects Gene going forward. You know, in the primary races."

Gary shrugged, having not given the political ramifications much thought. "I'm curious when he'll make a statement. With so many unanswered questions, we could be getting breaking news all day. I don't see how this will affect voters in Michigan and Mississippi today or, depending on the outcome of this morning's events, what effect it'll have on the rest of the primary season."

"If they find that broad alive, I think it hurts Gene's chances.

He's a far more sympathetic figure as a widower," the president opined. "If they find her alive, she'll soak up all the attention with interviews and such. If he wants to win, he's better off without her."

Gary had grown so accustomed to the president's matter-of-fact, sociopathic analyses that he didn't flinch at the appraisal.

"We will see how it plays out, Mr. President. I, for one, pray for her welfare."

"Anyhow, I've ordered the FBI director to keep me briefed. This afternoon we've added a meeting in the Situation Room to my schedule. The director will bring me the latest on the investigation." The president appeared eager to hear the details.

"I get the feeling this whole tragic episode has far more to it than a simple kidnapping," shared Gary. "This morning's events are just too odd. And the fact the assailants were Russian."

"You're right. There is more to it. The director told me the Russkie found in the river is tied to Russian intelligence."

Gary's eyebrows rose. "Do we think the Russians kidnapped Mrs. Sterling?" he asked.

"Don't know, but I bet we find out this afternoon." The president's eyes glimmered with youthful anticipation as if eyeing an unopened present.

◉ ◉ ◉

At only a quarter past ten in the morning, the Scotsman was closed. Sunlight pierced the shut blinds, providing the only illumination in the room as Oleg Yumashev smoked a cigar at the empty bar. He was not pleased. Four days ago, he had been concerned about the scheme unraveling when he saw shoddy proof of Mrs. Sterling's demise. Now he was certain she was alive somewhere in Washington. The once propitious plan was a bold endeavor. But all the painstaking planning was for naught. Dimitri, while attempting to redeem his previous sloppiness, only produced a sanguinary night in Georgetown, ending with him as fish food in the dark waters of the Potomac.

After Sergei conducted a cursory patdown, Senator Joe Bratton left his cell phone at the door and walked to the bar, a look of trepidation on his face. Finishing a long drag of his Arturo Fuente, Oleg leveled a cold, Russian stare through the billowing smoke.

"Have a seat, Senator," he ordered with his thick accent. As Joe uneasily mounted the stool, Oleg took another drag. "She is alive."

"You know this?" whispered Joe.

Oleg nodded coolly. "And I assume you are aware your cunning kidnapper, JC, is now in the custody of the authorities."

"I saw the news." Joe's forehead sprouted beads of sweat. "Is it true, you think?"

"Yes, it's true! We have no reason to believe otherwise. Why wouldn't it be true? We have pictures of him with the woman just before we tried to clean up this mess. Now Dimitri is dead."

"Who's Dimitri?"

"Oscar, you idiot. He was the fixer, and about as useless as your kidnappers. Now he's dead and his identity revealed. The woman is God only knows where."

"Maybe she's dead too. Maybe she went into the river with Oscar and is floating toward the Chesapeake as we speak," posited Joe. Oleg puffed and pondered a moment. Wishful thinking not being a dominant Russian trait, he dismissed the thought. "What do we do now?" asked Joe. "There has to be a way to clean this up."

"If Mrs. Sterling is found alive and discloses the senator's involvement, he can deny it and pin this on JC in the hope it sticks. To be frank, I never imagined her being found alive as a real possibility. If she was killed last night and a dead body surfaces, the senator simply plays the aggrieved spouse and continues the campaign. The issue is we do not know. Is she dead? Is she alive?

Will a body surface? We do not know, and you're aware of my distaste for uncertainty." Oleg placed his cigar in an ashtray.

"That doesn't answer my question. What do we do now?" asked Joe.

"I have already answered your question: we hope she's dead." The sound of the front door opening disrupted the conversation. Both men leaned over to see Taya—wearing a blue, puffy jacket and yoga pants, her blond ponytail protruding from a Nike running cap—enter with her typical stoic professionalism.

"Mr. Yumashev. Senator," she greeted.

"How is Senator Sterling holding up?" asked Oleg.

"About as poorly as you'd expect. He saw the email with the picture, then broke out into hives and fell to pieces, crying hysterically. These American men can be such groveling creatures." It was always disorienting to hear Taya's natural Russian accent, Joe having become accustomed to her accentless alter ego. "I ordered him and his staff not to speak publicly until we have a better idea of what transpired last night."

"And what, may I ask, did transpire last night?" Joe asked.

"We identified the target at the location. I gave Dimitri the green light to eliminate the problem."

"Is it true she was with that Secret Service guy?" Joe interrupted.

"It appears to be so," replied Taya. "What we do know is there was great resistance to our efforts to eliminate the problem."

"Well, that's just fucking wonderful," the senator drawled. "I thought you Russkies knew how to kill folks. You kill your own folks all the time."

"You are in no position to gloat, Senator." Taya stared through him. "If your men had done their part, we would not have to deal with this mess. And as for Russia's aptitude for killing, I'd gladly give you a demonstration of our effectiveness." She pulled a pistol from beneath her jacket. Joe leaned away, his sweaty forehead glistening. "No one knows you're here, Senator, and no one will know where to find your body. Unlike your hillbilly friends, we will finish the job."

"Put the weapon away," ordered Oleg. "We cannot change what has transpired. What options do we have now?" Still wanting to send a slug into Joe's distended belly, Taya tucked the weapon away.

"We have an idea where she might be," she disclosed, piquing the men's interest. "There is a particular subject whose online activities and cell phone use we've been monitoring. While eavesdropping, we believe we picked up her voice on his phone's mic. We have eyes on the building."

"The building?" asked Joe.

"Yes. Here in Washington."

Oleg demanded, "And this subject is?"

"Chet Bateman. Last night, he was speaking to a woman we believe is Katherine Sterling."

"And what do we plan to do this time? This is our third chance to rid ourselves of her. We won't get another," Oleg observed.

"It will be done today, Mr. Yumashev. I will see to it myself."

Oleg nodded approvingly and allowed a subtle smile. "Very well." He checked his watch. "I must be going. I've arranged a flight to the Seychelles. I could use some sunshine and the Indian Ocean."

"You're leaving. Don't you think you're needed here?" asked a concerned Joe.

"You have Taya, and she can do more than I can under the circumstances. Just do as she says, and we can make this go away. As for me? I have been in your country and attended to my business interests, but I have interests around the globe which I can no longer ignore. Besides, the FBI just found three of my countrymen dead, and I do not intend to stay long enough for them to ask my thoughts on the matter. Goodbye, Senator Bratton. I wish you well."

With a befuddled, uncertain look, Joe shook the Russian's hand.

As Oleg made his way to the door, Joe heard Taya behind him: "Senator Bratton, I have an idea, and I think you can help us." Nonplussed, he turned, pointing his finger at himself.

"Me? Sure, tell me what you need."

CHAPTER 21

LEANING HER HEAD against the shower wall, Kat's body quaked with sobbing convulsions as tears mixed with the warm water cascading through her hair and off her chin. When her husband betrayed her a week ago, she could not have imagined a more spirit-destroying pain. Now the thought of never seeing Jimmy's smirk again was doubly heartbreaking. Guilt panged her chest as she obsessed over her complicity in his demise. She'd give anything to hear him call her "princess" again in his cocky, ironic, smiling manner. She shut off the water.

Chet awaited with two cups of coffee and ibuprofen. Wearing jeans from the night before, her bloodied West Virginia hoodie replaced with Chet's American University sweatshirt, Kat entered the living room and delicately nestled into the sofa. Her body was stiff and sore, but at least she was clean. She absently tousled her damp hair.

"How are you?" he asked.

"Okay, I suppose."

"I'm still in disbelief. I never lost hope, but I didn't know if I'd ever see you again." She gave him a grateful smile. "Did you get enough rest?"

"No. But I'm fine. Have you watched the news? Did they find Jimmy?"

"I had it on earlier. Still nothing."

"He went into the river. I was there." She shook her head as her eyes welled up. "He asked if I was okay. When I told him I was, he picked up a rock. He looked like a man possessed. I don't know what happened in that car, but he gave everything he had to avenge me."

"He sounds like a badass," observed Chet. Kat responded with a plaintive grin.

"You'd think so, being he was a Secret Service agent. But Jimmy was so certain of himself and felt no need to exude bravado. I remember attending events with Gene and seeing the Secret Service agents. They were always sexy with their stoic, silent stares. Jimmy undoubtedly looked the part, but he was nothing like what I would have expected. He was smart, yet unpretentious—a kind of flawed, handsome goof; like a thirteen-year-old boy trapped in a forty-something's body."

She smiled in reflection, then lowered her head, set her coffee down, and wept. Chet gently rubbed her back. For several minutes she sobbed lightly, sinking into the misery of how much she missed James's carefree ease, his calm certainty. She hadn't noticed it during her week with him, but those traits kept her sane. She missed him terribly.

Chet's iPhone interrupted her lamentations. He fumbled with it before showing her the caller ID: it was Senator Joe Bratton.

"Senator?" answered Chet as he placed the phone on speaker so Kat could listen.

"Chet, I'm glad I could get hold of you. I'm sure you've seen the news this morning."

"I have. I'm in shock. Have you spoken to Gene?"

"I did briefly. As you can imagine, it's an emotional roller coaster for him. Did you speak with him?"

"No, I figured things were chaotic enough. When I saw the

breaking news this morning, it made my stomach turn. I'm worried sick about him." Chet shrugged at Kat.

"He's stronger than you know."

"This incident in Georgetown—I can't figure out what it means." Chet feigned ignorance. "I mean, they have the kidnapper in custody and there are a bunch of dead guys. What do you think is going on? You think Kat is still alive?"

"Well, that brings me to the reason for my call." Joe's voice took on a grave tone. "I sat in on a classified FBI briefing this morning. Not only do I believe Kat is alive, but—and I know this will be hard for you to fathom—I think she may have staged the whole thing." Looking up from his phone, Chet saw Kat's red eyes widen.

"I—I don't know what to say," stammered Chet.

"I'm only telling you this because the FBI indicated she may have gotten in over her head with some foreign group and faked her own kidnapping. We don't yet know the motive, but it's possible she was having an affair with this Secret Service agent, who, by the way, is believed to have been sharing secrets with the Russians."

"My God."

"I know. It's hard to believe Kat could involve herself in something like this. I'm telling you this because if she somehow reaches out to you or contacts you in any way, you need to let me know ASAP. I know you two were close."

"I don't know what to say. This morning's news was overwhelming, and now this. There's no way Kat could have done what they're alleging. Why the hell would she do that?"

"The speculation is she wanted to be famous. Look, I'm just relaying to you what I was told. I'm with you: there is simply no way she could have done this, but they feel they have a case against her, and I don't want you getting caught up in this mess. Aiding a known suspect in an FBI case is not a predicament you want to get yourself into. That said, if she does reach out to you, let me know first. I can arrange to have her brought in peacefully, plus I know a lot of good lawyers if she needs representation."

"This is heavy."

"I know it is. There's more I'd like to share with you, but I don't wish to do so by phone. Frankly, I've already disclosed more than is prudent. Can you come by my office this afternoon to speak privately?"

"Sure I can."

"Chet, she hasn't reach out to you, has she?"

"Um, no. I'd tell you if she had."

"I'm sure you would. My secretary will get back to you with a time. This is going to be a hectic day to say the least. I'll see you this afternoon." With that, Senator Bratton hung up. Chet looked puzzled.

"You know that's bullshit, right?" asked Kat. "You don't believe them, do you?"

"Of course not. I believe you. I know you better than that. But why would Joe say this? I can't remember the last time he even called me. I just don't know what makes the FBI think you would attempt something like this."

"Like I said all along: it's Gene. No one can pull the levers in this town like he can. This is why I didn't go to the feds in the first place."

"Kat, you can't hide forever. At some point, you've got to come forward."

"And be a suspect in my own kidnapping? I killed a man last night, Chet. Who's going to believe me? You heard Joe; the FBI is buying Gene's story."

Rubbing his temples, Chet pondered what to do. "Joe seems to believe in your innocence. Maybe he can help us."

◎ ◎ ◎

The worst part of an investigation was when blurred evidentiary lines came into focus yet eluded a conclusion. Dull hours filled with caffeine and fidgeting passed while investigators sat at the mercy of forensic labs and uncontrollable events. Following the harrowing events of the predawn hours, Detective Sergeant Derek Roland and ASAIC Kevin McClennan spent the remainder of their morning in this anxious purgatory as they hoped for word that James Ford or Kat Sterling had been located. They also prayed the lab would extract some revelatory evidence from the smartphone located in the Georgetown rowhouse.

Wearing rubber gloves, Derek thumbed through Kat's notebook journal for the umpteenth time. Mrs. Sterling had recorded a story too absurd to be believed. Looking up from the notebook, he saw Kevin staring at the dry-erase boards covered with scrawls and lines connecting elements of the investigation.

"Is staring at that thing helping to make any sense of this?" asked Derek with an exhausted yawn.

"Don't know, Sarge. Is staring at that notebook wringing out any new leads?" Kevin replied without turning. Derek smiled; the young fed was pretty cool. "Need any more coffee?"

"Another cup and my heart will explode," Derek sighed before downing the last sip from a Washington Capitals mug. "You know, if what Mrs. Sterling wrote here is in any way accurate, you guys are going to be busy."

"We're investigating the kidnapping of a senior senator's wife while he's running for the presidential nomination. It was never going to be easy."

"I'm just saying, if this notebook is accurate and she isn't just cuckoo for Cocoa-Puffs, not only do you have a senator plotting a murder, but you have international espionage."

"We're way ahead of you, Sarge."

"I figured. So, if the senator did it, what do you guys do?"

"Above my pay grade."

"Do you think he did it?"

"Ask me that after we find Mrs. Sterling. What I can't square is how this Secret Service guy fits into this."

"According to her journal, he found her."

"I'm not so sure I buy what's in that journal," Kevin cautioned.

"JC's story backs it up awfully well." Kevin finally turned around. "You can't refute that," noted Derek. Several agents from the digital access evidence team stormed into the command center with enough urgency to bring Derek to his feet.

"What do you got, Nick?" asked Kevin.

"We've got you an early Christmas present," responded Nick, his button-down shirt tucked tightly into pleated khakis. Kevin and Derek glanced at each other and nodded as if to say, "Game on." Nick spread several papers on the table in front of the whiteboards. "First off, we confirmed the telephone you located at the residence belongs to James Ford. What's interesting are the incoming phone calls to this device from 12:46 until 1:27 in the morning. Sixteen unanswered calls to this phone were received within that timeframe." Nick pointed at the repeated number highlighted on the call log.

"And who does that phone number belong to?" asked Derek.

Looking up with a clever, nerdy grin, Nick replied, "That's what's so interesting. The number sending the calls belongs to a phone Mr. Ford purchased several days ago. And get this, there were also texts." Pulling a sheet from beneath the phone log, Nick pointed to a series of texts during the same timeframe:

"Jimmy, are you okay? Where are you?"

"It's cold out here. Please let me know you're okay."

"If you get this . . . I hope you know I love you."

Kevin and Derek leaned over the documentation. The phone calls and texts fit the timeline of events from the night before. Someone was worried about James Ford and reaching out to him around the time Dimitri Romov went off the high dive with his right wrist handcuffed to an Audi's steering wheel.

"According to JC, the only people at the residence prior to the home invasion were Mr. Ford, Mrs. Sterling, and himself," observed Kevin. "So, this phone can only be in the possession of one person. Am I missing something?"

"No, you're spot on." Nick grinned.

"So, Mrs. Sterling is alive and was trying to get hold of Agent Ford," Derek concluded.

"Looks that way," Nick said. Derek nodded as a giddy smile crossed his face.

"We've got to find that phone," Kevin announced.

"You're right there," said Nick, "but there's more. There were some photos saved on the device that piqued our interest. Take a look at these."

"What the hell is this?" Kevin examined a photo with a mix of marvel and bemusement. "Am I actually seeing this?"

"Looks like a minotaur screwing a Hooters girl," Derek snorted. The photo was taken from down a hallway. A muscle-toned blonde was on all fours while a flat-assed, flabby old man laid his pipe to her. The picture would not be particularly remarkable in Washington, DC, had the seasoned deep driller not been wearing an oversized, floppy-eared dog mask.

"We zoomed in and enhanced the image," Nick added.

"Of course you did," said Derek. The enhanced photo clearly

identified the woman getting filled up by Fido: Tanya Smith, her disinterested, "get this over with" expression indicating the pipe layer's lack of stroking prowess. Derek examined the photo. "Damn, that's his chief of staff. Is the senator in the dog mask?"

"That's her alright," Kevin verified.

"So, hold on a moment. Agent Ford was in their house and took this?" wondered Derek.

"Appears likely," said Nick. "They were taken late this past Saturday night. But there's more."

"Two days ago? There's more?"

"Here are some photos, screenshots actually, of a computer. It's an email exchange between the handle 'doggystyle6969' and 'mountainman21673.' Seems Mountainman is congratulating Doggystyle."

"I'll give you three guesses who Doggystyle is," Kevin quipped.

"Can we get the IPs on these?" asked Derek.

"Working on it," Nick said.

"I'd like to know who Mountainman is," Derek mused.

"Checking the email account on the phone," continued Nick, "we found these emails sent to the doggystyle6969 address." Pulling out two printed emails, the latter with attached photo, Nick laid them proudly before both investigators. The sender claimed to be JC and taunted Doggystyle mercilessly. The final email sent last night had a pic of JC and Mrs. Sterling.

"JC was telling the truth," concluded Derek.

"I think you're right, Sarge. Let's find that phone. Let's go find Kat Sterling."

"Nice work, Nick," Derek congratulated the agent. "Merry Christmas indeed."

CHAPTER 22

"ARE YOU OKAY, Senator?" asked Zach Tyler, eyeing Gene with studied concern. At Tanya's request, the campaign manager had dropped by the senator's house. He was told to keep Gene away from the gaggle of press parked near the front yard. It became clear why she'd emphasized the need to keep him off camera: Gene's neck and chin were blotched with hives below a face of fearful dread.

"I'm going to be fine," Gene assured him, still in pajamas and sipping coffee in the kitchen. "Has Tanya reached out to you recently?"

"No, Senator, which is why I think we should just sit tight and gather ourselves. In light of all that's going on, she wanted you to take it easy."

"I'm a big boy. I can handle myself."

"I realize that, sir."

"One thing I cannot do is hole myself up here all day. With these events unfolding, I have to say something."

"In due time, sir. There are just too many unanswered questions."

"You got that right—a lot of unknowns." The senator's face grew taut, veins protruding from his forehead. Zach gazed at him with genuine concern. "I can't dodge the press for long," Gene reasoned. His cell phone buzzed on the countertop.

"I can take that," offered Zach.

"No, I got it." Gene answered the phone.

"Senator Sterling, this is the office of the president of the United States. President Frum wishes to speak with you," announced the president's secretary. "Please remain on the line for the president."

"Um, okay." Gene's stressed expression took on a stunned uncertainty.

"Gene, it's Ronald. I'm calling to see how you are doing." Thrown by the president's unexpected empathy, Gene hesitated. "Gene? You there? I just wanted to ask if you were alright." The abrupt, staccato delivery was vintage President Frum.

"Yes, Mr. President, it's me, Gene. Thank you for the sentiment. As you can imagine, it's been a shocking morning."

"Well, events are moving fast, and I wanted to be sure you were up to date on the latest developments, including the more sensitive, classified information. The FBI is briefing me in the Situation Room at three this afternoon. I've been told much of what they're sharing cannot be conveyed outside a SCIF. I'd like to invite you to the White House to attend the briefing. I think it's only right you are there. The fake news will fuck up the coverage of this thing, and you should get, firsthand, all of the facts."

"That is thoughtful of you, Mr. President. This is rather surprising. I'd like to attend, of course, but currently my front yard is filled with reporters." Gene spoke hesitatingly, the president's gesture still mystifying.

"Not a problem, Gene. I'll send a driver from the White House Military Office. Be ready by 2:30, and we'll be sure to get you here. You in?"

"Yes, Mr. President. Um, thank you," Gene signed off as the president hung up.

"What did the president want?" asked Zach.

"I'm going to the White House this afternoon for a briefing on the investigation."

"Senator, I was specifically told to keep you here. Tanya was adamant on this front." Zach's urgent plea aside, Gene mulled the unexpected invite. If he could glean how the Bureau was tracking the investigation, it could prove helpful in countering whatever leads pointed his direction.

"No, Zach. I'm going to the White House. I deserve to know what happened to my wife."

⊙ ⊙ ⊙

Having determined Katherine Sterling's phone number, Kevin activated the FBI's wireless tracking vehicle. The hope was to intercept the phone's signal and pinpoint her location. Both Derek and Kevin were electrified with anticipation as the tracking unit went hot, but their collective hopes were dashed when no signal was located. Sitting in Derek's Crown Victoria outside the Willard Hotel, they ate fish tacos from Surfside and watched tourists on the sunny, unseasonably warm day. Across the street, the sidewalk along Sherman Park was lined with sightseers queued for a White House tour.

"I bet she's charging the phone. It's probably turned off, that's all," offered Kevin after swallowing a bite. Derek looked over and motioned to bits of cabbage slaw on his partner's mouth. Kevin wiped his lips. "This happens all the time. She probably couldn't get near a charger and drained the battery."

Leaning his head back in exhausted frustration, Derek let out a sigh. "Or it's in the Potomac," he posited.

"If that phone's in the District and working, we'll find it. Let's try and stay positive, Sarge."

"I've been a Metro cop for twenty-six years, Kev. I lost my optimism about ten years in."

"You going to finish that last taco?"

"Naw, you can have it. Where do all those calories go? Damn, what I'd give to have a metabolism again."

Laughing, Kevin tore into Derek's surrendered taco. "So, how much longer you got? You know, before you retire?" he asked, his mouth full.

"I think this is it. I just want to find Mrs. Sterling alive. I'm too old for this shit."

"Come on, you're being too hard on yourself."

"There comes a time when you're just tired of being lied to. That's most of police work, really, just people lying to you—most intentionally, and some just skewing the facts subconsciously. But you find yourself not believing anybody, even your loved ones. You feel everybody's working an angle. That's where I'm at, so it's about time to pop smoke. Besides, my old lady's about had it with the job, and I can't afford any more divorces."

"What are you going to do when it's over?"

"Damn, you finished that taco already?" Derek shook his head, grinning. "Going to take my old lady on a cruise. Maybe catch one out of Miami, one of them Carnival cruises that stops in Jamaica or Mexico. She likes to eat, so I bet she'd like them buffets and laying about on the deck."

"Sounds like a good plan," Kevin noted as a high school tour group passed by.

"Of course, I got to do it soon. Cops don't tend to live long after retirement."

"Really? Is that true?"

"It's true. I think the crazy hours, all the caffeine to stay awake, then the alcohol to come back down—not to mention the dead kids. You see too many dead kids with small entry wounds and big exit wounds. Then you interview another kid who tells you how he put them there. A few decades of that wears a man down, and what's strange is you're not even aware of it. The toll it all takes." A thick silence filled the car as the sun-drenched parade of tourists continued their marches. "Sorry, Kev, didn't mean to get so heavy."

"No worries. Let's just find Mrs. Sterling and get you home."

"How do you think this thing turns out?"

"Senator Sterling did it."

"I think you're right."

"Titan to Lead, we have a signal. Target appears to be southbound on Mass past Thomas Circle. Judging by speed, target is vehicle borne. Copy?" radioed the wireless tracking vehicle. Throwing fast-food wrappers aside, Kevin buckled up as Derek returned the radio traffic.

"Lead copies, en route." He popped the vehicle into drive and turned up Fifteenth Street where he slammed his breaks to avoid a group of jaywalking tourists. A quick whoop of his siren urged them along before his tires squealed forward in pursuit.

"Titan to Lead, target in the area of Vernon Square, still tracking eastbound."

"Lead copies," Derek replied into his radio mic. "Any units in the area have eyes on a possible target?" With no response, his urgency increased, and he turned sharply onto K Street, violating several department policies as he operated his vehicle in the manner of a code one response.

"Titan to Lead, target continuing on Mass towards the area of Union Station." Red lights and tour buses were frustrating Derek's efforts to reach Massachusetts Avenue. Holding the dashboard as Derek weaved erratically through traffic, Kevin was clearly regretting that last fish taco. "Don't puke on me, Kev."

"Damn, Sarge, even if we catch up to her, we don't know what the hell she's in."

"We'll worry about that once we get there."

"Target is southbound on New Jersey."

"She's down near the Capitol. Why the hell would she be heading there?" Derek wondered aloud. Turning right onto Massachusetts, he continued to drive as if trying to get a pregnant woman to the ER.

"Target appears to be on foot; D Street near First Avenue." Derek turned onto New Jersey Avenue, then D Street. *"Lead from Titan, we've lost the signal. Continuing to monitor. Last located near First and Constitution."*

"Lead copies. Notify Capitol Police and get more units in the area," radioed Derek as he slapped the car in park. "Dammit."

◉ ◉ ◉

The intel was accurate, and just as Taya Sokolov had anticipated, Katherine Sterling was indeed at Chet Bateman's apartment. She witnessed the tall, slim female wearing an American University sweatshirt and LA Dodgers cap emerge from the apartment building with the dark-haired idealist just before the couple slid into their Uber ride. Taya knew Chet was meeting Senator Bratton; what had been uncertain was whether Mrs. Sterling would accompany him.

Unlike Dimitri, Taya surrounded herself with the best talent by requesting Anton to assist in eliminating their elusive prey. The black, heavily tinted Cadillac Escalade blended well in DC traffic's overabundance of dark SUVs. Anton parked along Constitution Avenue within eyeshot of the Capitol Police checkpoint outside the Dirksen Senate Office Building. Just a block away, the Capitol Dome gleamed heavenly on this sunny, springlike afternoon. Capitol Hill was a flurry of interns, lobbyists, and sightseers on a day when everyone in DC was making excuses to enjoy the weather. It wasn't an ideal location to complete a hit, but Taya did not have the luxury to wait for more preferable circumstances.

The vehicle had been modified with armor and a nearly soundproof seal. The senator would facilitate a ride for Mrs.

Sterling and Chet from the Senate Office Building to the FBI. Once Kat was in the car, Taya would use her suppressed Sig Sauer P226 to lodge a 9mm slug in her brain. From there, Anton would drive to the loading dock behind the Scotsman where a disposal team would do their part. Once Kat was out of the picture, Taya could concentrate her efforts on getting Senator Sterling the nomination, even though it meant the sickening prospect of continuing to cater to his bizarre fetishes.

How they would handle Chet Bateman's disappearance was an issue she hadn't fully worked through. But they would in due time; eliminating Katherine was the primary concern.

"So, we just wait until they come down?" asked Anton.

"That's right. We get them in the car, I finish them both, and you get us to the Scotsman," Taya summarized.

Anton nodded. "And if they don't play along?"

"If I must go off-script, then I go off-script. Only one outcome is acceptable: Mrs. Sterling cannot survive the afternoon."

CHAPTER 23

ENTERING the Dirksen Senate Office Building, Kat pulled Chet's Dodgers cap low. The Capitol Police officers screening them were familiar with the eco-celeb and chatted him up while ignoring the woman accompanying him. Once inside, the friends made their way to the third floor and Senator Joe Bratton's office.

The office walls were covered with picturesque photos of West Virginia's beautifully forested mountains. Especially prominent was a Mountaineers football helmet and an old picture of the senator with John Denver.

"There's no phone service in here," announced Kat.

"I'm not surprised; this place is built like a castle," Chet observed.

"Hello, Mr. Bateman, it's been a while," a smiling blonde with adorable dimples greeted him. "Senator Bratton mentioned you were coming to visit, and it just made my day." The slightly built twenty-four-year-old came out from behind her desk to embrace him for several excessive seconds.

"Good to see you too, Maddie. My schedule has been rather full, you know, with the primary elections and all," explained Chet, looking uneasy. "How are you?"

"Good, really good. I'm not going to be with the senator much longer. I got a job at CNN. Going to be a producer." A prideful, dimpled smile crossed Maddie's face.

"A producer? That's amazing! Congratulations. I'm really happy for you."

"Oh, I'm sorry, who's with you?" she asked, peering at Kat huddled behind Chet for fear of being recognized.

"Maddie, um, this is, well, this is—"

"Amy," interrupted Kat, holding her hand out while keeping the cap's bill over her face.

"She's a friend of mine," Chet explained.

"A friend?" Maddie appeared put out by Kat's presence. "I see. Well, it's nice to meet you, Amy."

"You don't have Wi-Fi here by chance, do you, Maddie?" inquired Kat.

"Yeah, the guest Wi-Fi is clearly posted on the sign." The secretary motioned dismissively. "I'll let Senator Bratton know y'all are here," she finished before giving Chet one more unexpected hug.

"What was that all about?" Kat whispered as Maddie entered the senator's office.

"Senator Bratton had a Fourth of July picnic a couple years ago, and that's when I met Maddie. Nice girl."

"She doesn't seem to like me."

"Don't take it personal. We got together a few times, and ever since, she's had it in her mind that I'd come around to wanting something serious."

"The senator can see y'all now," announced Maddie. As Chet headed to the office, Kat heard Maddie whisper, "It was good to see you again. Text me sometime. Maybe we could grab a drink, you know, to celebrate my new job." Chet nodded and smiled.

"Chet, my God, what a day," Joe Bratton welcomed as he stood. "Gene holding up?"

"I suppose. It's been hours since I've spoken to him. He was understandably exhausted. It's a lot to process."

"Who, um, do you have accompanying you?" asked Joe, taking several deep breaths before licking his dry lips.

"Can we sit first?" Chet requested.

"Of course, please, over here." Joe motioned to four chairs around an oak table in the corner. "Ma'am, I'm Senator Joe Bratton." He shook Kat's hand, eyeing her in an attempt to see the face beneath the cap's bill.

"Joe," began Chet, "I really don't know what to do. The past twenty-four hours have been unlike anything I've ever experienced. I feel like I'm underwater. I'm not prepared to handle all of this."

"I know it's a lot. What do you need help with? How can I help you?" asked the senator.

"Men were killed last night, Kat's kidnapper was arrested, and now there's speculation she's alive. Last night's events floored me, but when you told me the FBI thinks she staged her own abduction, that's simply not possible. You knew Kat. There is no plausible way she was involved," Chet retorted.

"Chet, I realize last night's events, hell, this entire past week has been enough to crush the souls of everyone that knew Kat. Like I mentioned on the phone, I don't believe she did it either. I told the FBI briefer just that. Truth be told, I could see Gene being behind this entire scheme." Kat looked up at Joe, encouraged by his prescience. Tired of running and wanting it all to be over, she took off her ball cap and set it on the table.

"It's me, Joe. It's Kat," she stated, expressionless. The senator examined the woman with dark, short hair, her face partially bruised. A disbelieving expression and a hand to his mouth signaled his epiphany. He stood and lifted her from the chair in an embrace.

"My God, Kat, I cannot believe you're alive." All the senator's strength constricted her.

"Joe, I'm very sore. I appreciate the sentiment, but last night I went through hell." Kat wriggled out of his grasp.

"Sorry, are you okay? I'm beside myself. This is unbelievable. It's as if you've risen like Lazarus. What happened last night?"

"We were attacked. I took a man's life; it was self-defense. But there are forces behind this whole plot I cannot begin to fathom—foreign elements. You're right: Gene was behind the whole thing. He had me tied up and taken from our home to have me killed."

"Gene did do this? I knew it couldn't be you," feigned Joe.

"The whole kidnapping was a sham. Gene had a pro come in and stage it all to make him out as a victim. But I have to know, Joe, what has the FBI told you? I am innocent. I've been through hell, and I've lost everything I ever had, including a dear friend last night. A friend who gave his life for mine. What did they tell you?" Her eyes blazed with a decisive intensity the senator had never associated with his friend's socialite wife.

"Kat, they're saying you were in on it with that JC fella they nabbed last night. Said you were likely involved in an extramarital affair with the Secret Service agent and wanted out of the marriage. They had some behavioral psychologist work up a profile on you and theorized you were sociopathic or something. I never believed them, mind you, but that's how we were briefed."

"They did this to me, Joe. I did nothing wrong. They did this to me."

"I believe you, Katherine. I do. Which is why we need you to speak with the FBI. Share your story with them so they can verify your innocence."

She looked over at Chet, who nodded in agreement.

"And if they don't believe me? If they think I colluded with JC?" countered Kat.

"The truth is on your side. Don't you want the truth to come out? To expose Gene for what he is?" asked Chet rhetorically.

She knew she couldn't run any longer. It was time to share her story.

"Can you get us there? To FBI headquarters?" she asked Joe.

"I can. I know the director well. I'll have them come get you. It's our safest bet."

"Don't tell them it's me they're picking up," directed Kat. "Just tell them you have a credible witness, and leave it at that."

"Understood. I have the investigator's number. I assure you that your identity will remain anonymous," pledged Joe. "I still cannot believe you're alive. It's truly a miracle."

"You do believe me, don't you?" she asked.

"Of course I do. I'm going to step out a moment. Need water? No? Okay, I'll be back momentarily." Joe exited the office, leaving Kat and Chet alone.

"This is the right thing to do. Joe has a lot of pull in this town. He can vouch for you," reasoned Chet. "You okay?"

A feeling of disquietude enveloped her. "Something just doesn't feel right. Something about Joe seems off." She pulled out her phone and saw a red *1* on the text icon: "Kat, this is James. Are you okay? This phone number belongs to Carly, I'm with her," read the message from an unknown number.

"What the hell is this?" she said to herself. She texted back, "Who is Carly? Don't mess with me. What have you done with James?"

"What's wrong, Kat?" asked Chet.

"Look at this. Someone claiming to be Jimmy. I don't know the number," she responded, showing him the phone's screen.

"I do," Chet claimed. "Carly Mavros. Ran into her last night at Fiola Mare. Look." He pulled out his phone and showed her the contact. "She's a reporter."

"That's right, Jimmy told me about her."

A text dinged: "Carly is the friend I had lunch with, remember? You were all jelly about it. I'm at her place resting. Thank God you're alive, princess!! Where are you?!"

"Dear God, it is him. It's Jimmy," Kat remarked as her eyes moistened with relief.

"Are you sure?" asked Chet.

"Positive. He's the only forty-something that calls me 'princess' and would use the term 'jelly,'" she confirmed while typing a reply: "I'm with Chet. We are at Senator Bratton's office. We decided to go to the FBI."

"Senator Bratton? Are you serious?" replied James.

"Yes. Why? He's going to help us. He's going to make sure we get to the feds. They think I did this and I'm gonna clear my name."

"You need to get the fuck out of there, princess!"

"You're freaking me out. Why?"

"Bratton is tied to the Russians and possibly our boy Oscar. I don't know what his involvement is, but he can't be trusted. What building are you in?" texted James.

"The Dirksen."

"We're headed your way. Keep your phone handy. 143."

"143," texted Kat in reply before looking up at Chet.

"Why are you looking like that? What's wrong?" he asked.

"I knew something was odd about the way Joe was acting." She looked back at the door. "He and Gene have known each other for decades. Did you notice how quickly he was willing to believe his longtime friend was behind the kidnapping? Why would he so readily suspect Gene?"

A confused, frightened look crossed Chet's face when the office door opened.

"They're on their way," declared Joe. "I'm so glad we found you. You made the right decision. This is about to be over." Kat forced a smile.

☉ ☉ ☉

"Damn, that's cold," complained James as Carly applied an ice-filled baggie beneath his bruised eye. His body ached as if he'd gone over Niagara Falls in a barrel.

"Well, it is ice," she answered sarcastically. Moaning in pain, he flashed her a look of mixed anguish and mild amusement. "The jeans I got you seem to fit." While he slumbered, she had bought him a pair of jeans to replace his bloodstained attire.

"I caught you looking at my ass, so they must," quipped James.

"I didn't look at your ass." She rolled her eyes. "Your shoulders maybe, but not your ass."

"We had some good times," he noted as he closed his eyes and reminisced.

"We did. Now get that shit out of your head. It's never happening again."

He opened his eyes wide before flashing his smirk. "Fair enough." He winced. "Forgive me. Violent, murderous evenings make me horny."

"You're fucked up."

"That's the consensus. Seriously, though, thank you. Thanks for the jeans and your ex-boyfriend's shirt. When I had no one to turn to, I knew I could count on you to not freak out."

"You're the only person I've ever known who could show up in bloodstained clothes, claiming to have killed a Russian hitman in an attempt to rescue a senator's wife, and have it not surprise me. And you're welcome. I know you're telling me the truth. When you passed out, the news identified the guy you sent into the Potomac—none other than our boy, Dimitri Romov."

"No kidding? Well, then we've confirmed Oscar's identity beyond a doubt. What else is the news saying?"

"They haven't found Kat. But you two are the most sought-after targets in the District. We've got to figure out what we're going to do. I'm a reporter, James. I can't sit on this forever."

"Turn on the TV. What time is it?"

"It's almost two," sighed Carly as she clicked on the tube.

"Let me gather my thoughts for a second." He held his head and tried to shake out the cobwebs.

"I'll get us some coffee." Carly got up, kissed his forehead, and went to the kitchen as James watched her saunter away. "Stop staring at me."

"Stop wearing yoga pants." He smiled and turned to the news. As the aroma of Colombian blend wafted in the air, James took in the latest press releases, which consisted of blind speculation and "expert" theories. Carly set a coffee in front of him.

"So, what do we do, Secret Service man?"

Contemplatively, he sipped his coffee.

"Let me see your phone," he requested.

"Why?"

"I bought Kat a smartphone several days ago. Unfortunately, my phone is probably state's evidence now." Carly handed over her phone, and his thumbs fired away. "My God, I've got her." His thumbs went into action, then paused. His eyes glistened with emotion as he eyed the phone's screen.

"Are you okay?" asked Carly.

"I'm good. I was just worried about her." He wiped his eyes.

"Oh my God, you love her."

"Don't get carried away. I've known her a week. But she is special. And I'm glad she's okay."

"Well, where is she?"

"She's not sure it's me." He typed with ferocity as if his passion would convince Kat it was indeed her Jimmy. Carly watched him alternate between texting, sipping, waiting, and sighing in despair. "We've got a problem," he declared.

"You mean a new one or the same big one?"

"Same big one with added complications. You still have that Prius? Because we've got to roll—like, now."

"What complications?"

"She's at Senator Joe Bratton's office."

"Oh shit."

"Exactly, let's get them out of there." They both stood and made their way to the door.

"Them?"

"She's with Chet Bateman."

Carly stopped and eyed him.

"What?"

"Nothing," she said, shaking her head in amusement. "Never a dull moment."

◉ ◉ ◉

"Are we screwed?" whispered Chet, shielding Kat as they walked ahead of Senator Bratton through the Dirksen Building's immense hallways. The marble floors were filled with journalists ambushing senators for remarks on the morning's harrowing events. Kat could hear Senator Bratton behind her, opining to the remora-like reporters.

"Let's just get outside for now. Do as I do," she advised Chet. "I don't know what Joe has in mind, but I've got a sick feeling. James said he's tied to the Russians."

"Tied to the Russians? What does that even mean? Can you be certain? When did the Russians get involved in this?"

"We think Gene received help from the Russians. Look, I know this is crazy, but I trust Jimmy more than anyone alive." Descending the staircase, they made their way through the foyer and past the Capitol Police checkpoint. Senator Bratton wrapped up his impromptu interview and followed Kat outside, acting as though he didn't know the Dodgers fan.

Kat turned to Joe as he approached her. "There it is. Over there, that's the ride sent by the FBI. They don't know who you are—just as you requested—but the agents will take y'all to headquarters," explained Joe, squinting in the sunlight. Kat looked where he motioned to see a black, tinted-out Cadillac Escalade parked along Constitution Avenue, facing west atop Capitol Hill.

"The Cadillac?"

"Yep, that's it," the senator confirmed as he meandered through a student tour group toward the vehicle. "I'll get the door for you."

"Thank you for your help," said Kat as they neared the rear passenger door. From beneath her Dodgers cap, she peered at Joe's expression, hoping to catch some tell—any sign he could be trusted. Looking back at her was an anxious, pudgy face shining with perspiration he wiped with a handkerchief.

"Anything I can do to help, you know I'm willing to do," he assured her. Joe flashed an insincere smile as he opened the door. Kat hugged his neck and peered into the car to see a thick-necked driver seated next to a blonde with a ponytail in the passenger seat. As she climbed in, Chet opened the door across from her.

"Hello, I'm Kat. I appreciate you picking us up. I want to turn myself in." As the blonde turned, Kat's chest tightened from recognition. "Chet, run!" A long suppressor peeked around the front seat, and airy reports burst from the weapon's muzzle. Kat disrupted the weapon's accuracy with a kick to the back of Tanya's seat, then slammed up against the door and scrambled for the release while upholstery stuffing exploded from her seat back. Finding the handle, she bolted out the door.

"What the hell is happening?" Chet cried as he came around the vehicle. Kat was already sprinting down the hill.

"Just follow me and don't slow down," she yelled. She paused once and looked back to see the blond assassin outside the Escalade, staring after them with menacing expressionlessness. The driver—broad shouldered with an expansive forehead—stepped out. Behind him, the sweaty, fat senator looked on with an ashen gaze.

"Why do I keep trusting senators?" Kat panted as she continued her flight downhill through tour groups and staffers.

"Did what I think happen really just happen? Was that Tanya?" Chet gasped, running alongside her.

"Yes, it was, and she tried to kill me."

"She tried to kill you? I can't believe this is happening."

"Sorry I dragged into this, Chet, but you get used to it."

CHAPTER 24

"WOAH, careful, easy." James braced his hand on the dashboard as the tiny Prius weaved around tour buses, taxis, and foreign drivers unacclimated to aggressive, American traffic.

"Relax, I got this," Carly assured him. "My pops was a car guy." Looking over, James watched her coolly manipulate the steering wheel around Constitution Avenue traffic, her raven hair framing a perfectly calm, Mediterranean face. Passing the south grounds of the White House to their left, she slammed to a halt when a taxi cut in front of them.

"Jesus," blurted James.

"Quit being a little bitch. I thought you were a tough guy."

"It's a control issue. I'm not in control, and it's an issue. You're doing great, kiddo. I'll try to keep it together."

"Then leave me alone and check out the joggers," she ordered. James shrugged. It was a good day for people watching. Sunshine gleamed off the Washington Monument as throngs of tourists— usually not seen in such numbers till later in the month—swarmed the National Mall. Since his last text, he had been unable to reach Kat.

"Do you think they're still in the senator's office?" asked Carly.

"No idea. I'm trying not to worry, but between my concern for Kat and your driving, I could use a Xanax."

"You really like her."

"I do. She's a hot mess, but a cool hot mess."

"Sounds like someone I know."

"Cute. Watch out! Jesus!" He braced himself again as she jacked the horn and cursed an out-of-state driver before flashing James a disapproving glare. "Okay, I'll settle down," he said. "I'll try reaching her again." Using Carly's phone, he shot Kat a call: "Princess? You okay? You're breaking up. Where are you?"

"Jimmy, they tried to kill us. We are—" Kat was panting heavily. *"Chet, do you know where we're at? We're near the Capitol grounds with a group of tourists; I think they're from Peru."*

"Who? Who tried to kill you?"

"Gene's sidepiece, Tanya, along with some other guy. You were right. Joe's in on this."

"Okay, where are you specifically. We're almost there."

"Um, the Peruvians are looking at a statue of a soldier, looks like from the Civil War. It's really big and he's on a horse."

"Princess, sweetie, there's a statue with a dude on a horse on every corner in DC. Look on the portal."

"Ulysses S. Grant."

"Okay, perfect. Get to Third Street. Just walk toward the Washington Monument. Do you see Tanya anywhere?" Over Spanish voices in the background, he heard Kat's stressed breathing.

"I don't see her."

"That doesn't mean she's not around. Get to Third and keep a lookout for her." Traffic was deadlocked on Constitution Avenue as a motorcade blocked the right lane in front of the National Gallery of Art. James turned to Carly. "I'm going on foot to find her. Tanya and some guy tried to kill them. If last night proved anything, it's that they won't stop until Kat's dead."

"Who's Tanya again?" Carly asked.

"Senator Sterling's chief of staff and mistress; apparently she's also an assassin."

"A woman with many hats. This is insane. What can I do?"

"When I find them, I'll have Chet hit you up so we can rendezvous."

"Be careful, James."

"Always." He smirked before bursting from the Prius into a sprint down Fourth Street toward the Mall.

⊙ ⊙ ⊙

"Titan to Lead, we've picked up the signal again," radioed the wireless surveillance team. *"Appears to be moving along the west portion of the Capitol grounds. Tracking speed indicates the target likely on foot."*

"Lead copies," Derek acknowledged as he turned onto Louisiana Avenue. "She must have turned her phone back on," he surmised. Putting the mic to his face he radioed, "Do we have any units in the area?" Derek was pushing his old Crown Vic hard, the frame of the car swaying side to side as the detective slalomed through traffic.

"Target still moving westbound on foot," Titan informed him. *"In the vicinity of the Capitol Reflecting Pool."*

"I don't get it. Why the hell is she over here?" asked Kevin.

"Beats me."

"You think someone else has her phone?"

"Possible, but God I hope not." Derek hit his siren several times as he made an illegal left onto Third Street.

"Lead from Titan, target located at the Mall adjacent to Third Street."

"Goddamn, she's right around here." Kevin scanned the landscape, wide eyed. A large mob of tourists were trying to organize themselves on the Mall's edge. Nearby, a tour guide with a couple dozen upright, two-wheeled Segway vehicles assisted the less athletic tourists aboard them. As Derek slowed the car to a crawl, Kevin continued to survey the crowd for Mrs. Sterling.

"Is that . . . ?" Kevin leaned close to the windshield. "Doesn't that look like the Secret Service guy?"

"It does," said Derek, who engaged his radio mic again. "Be advised Lead will be on foot on Third Street at the Mall entrance. Got a possible target location." As they pulled over, each cop undid their seatbelts before coming to a stop.

Stepping out, Kevin's eyes widened. "Holy shit, that chick just kicked him in the face!"

⊙ ⊙ ⊙

Entering the Mall on Fourth Street, James continued toward the Capitol in an urgent jog, his eyes probing the horizon for any sign of Kat. The warm weather had emptied the Capitol Hill offices as joggers and government workers mingled with the ubiquitous sightseers to complicate his efforts. A blonde caught his eye— initially because she was exceptionally attractive in her dark, tight suit, and golden mane pulled back in a ponytail, but something about her was off. Unlike the lost tourists and government-office slackers, she wasn't cheery on this springlike day but instead sternly eyed the crowds in search of something. Then, as she turned, he got a better look: it was Tanya.

"Shit," he muttered, wishing he had his phone. Weaving through a sea of Segways mounted by vacationers uttering excited accolades about the city's grandeur, he heard an emphatic "Jimmy." A slender woman in a Dodgers cap and American University sweatshirt nearly tackled him to the ground with her embrace. Pulling her cap up, he saw her short, dark hair and hazel eyes.

"Princess." He beamed and kissed her like a soldier returned from war. He caressed her bruised face. "You okay? You're hurt."

"Never better." She smiled breathlessly. "You may find this hard to believe, but I missed that smirk. Looks like you caught at least one right hook yourself."

"You think that's bad, you should see the other guy," he quipped before kissing her again, their tongues synchronizing in perfect rhythm. Not wanting the reunion to end, he caught himself, pulled his lips away, and looked about.

"What is it?" asked Kat.

"I saw Tanya; she's nearby and almost as anxious to see you as I was."

"Um, Kat?" interrupted Chet.

"Oh, I'm so sorry. Jimmy, this is Chet," she introduced.

"Heard a lot about you," said James as they shook hands.

"Not near as much as I've heard about you."

"Jimmy, that guy over there. He's with her. He was in the driver's seat when she tried to take me out," Kat reported, tugging at his sleeve. Looking over the clamor of red "Bring Back My America" caps and obese, jean-short-wearing brochure collectors, James located the balding Eastern European, who wore a dark, tieless suit, his scowling face set atop kettle-bell-enhanced shoulders.

"Yeah, it's clear he's not in town for Ben's Chili Bowl and a White House snow globe." Scanning about, James caught Tanya's visage opposite her partner. "The dog whisperer's over there. They have us flanked."

"I see her," Kat announced. Then she saw Tanya give her a double take before locking her gaze with determined recognition. "My God, she sees me." Holding her chest, Kat looked up at James. "What do we do?" He exhaled heavily and looked around at the cankle crowd mashing their melons into bike helmets for their Segway tour. Tanya was closing in on one side while the king of shoulder shrugs had caught on and was doing the same from the opposite.

"What's going on? The look on your faces is freaking me out,"

Chet whispered. His diminutive build precluded him from seeing the pincer movement closing in on them. Kat recognized the decisive look on James's face.

"Sir? Do you have room for two more?" he asked the tour guide.

"Why, sir, yes we do," the guide replied with well-practiced, cheesy flair. Handing the kid cash, James thrust helmets into his companions' chests.

"You guys are going on a tour."

"Wait? What?" Kat was incredulous.

"Stay in the middle of the pack as best you can. The Mall is packed, and they're not going to want an incident that draws attention. This tour group is the size of the Cowboys O-line; you should have plenty of cover," reasoned James.

"I'm not leaving you again, Jimmy."

"Princess, do you trust me?"

"Of course, but what about you?"

"Chet, you have Carly's number, right?"

"Yeah," Chet confirmed.

"She's in her car nearby. Call her. She can get you guys out of here."

"Jimmy, you didn't answer my question. What about you?" James pulled her close and pressed his lips against hers, relieving—momentarily—her debilitating anxiety.

"I'm still a Secret Service agent. I'm here to protect you. I'm taking that bitch out." He kissed her again. "Now go. Don't straggle behind."

Kat turned to see the bulbous Segway operators acclimating themselves to the devices' operation. After one final kiss, he secured the bike helmet to her head before she boarded her conveyance. Chet by her side, she turned the machine and began rolling away to catch up with the flock of oglers. She didn't know what Jimmy had in mind, but she had faith in him.

She turned to see him once more as her Segway continued

its thirteen-mile-per-hour pace. James's right hand signaled to her solemnly, "1-4-3: I. Love. You." She signaled back: raising one finger, four fingers, and three fingers in succession. For a moment, her heart was comforted. That was when Tanya landed a textbook roundhouse kick on the unbruised side of Jimmy's face, sending him to the pavement as two plainclothes cops, pistols drawn, began barking orders.

CHAPTER 25

"DON'T MOVE! Metro Police," ordered Derek, his Glock 19 trained on James's prostrate, moaning figure. "Are you James Ford?"

"Yeah, it's me." James rolled up into a seated position, making certain his hands remained visible.

"Are you armed?" asked Derek.

"If I was armed, would I have let that little gal go Chuck Norris on me? Where'd she go, anyway?"

"She ran off," Kevin said, his pistol's muzzle also aimed at James.

"Shouldn't you be arresting her for assault or something?" James asked, gingerly touching the side of his face; a semicircle of bystanders began forming around the curious scene.

"Edith, that's the Secret Service man they's looking for," drawled one Southern onlooker. "I swear that's him. The newsman was talking 'bout him."

"You're wanted for questioning, James," Derek said.

"We really don't have time for that. There's kind of an ongoing situation here."

"A situation?"

"You're looking for Kat Sterling, right?"

"Of course. You know where she is?"

"She's taking a Segway tour of the National Mall with a couple hitmen in tow. Including the comely blonde who just roundhoused me."

"What the hell are you talking about? Kevin, pat him down," Derek commanded. The FBI agent holstered his sidearm and helped James to his feet before searching him for weapons. By now, two Metro squad cars, four Capitol Police bicycle units, and three Park Police cruisers had arrived. "Any phones on him?" asked Derek. Kevin shook his head in the negative and handed over James's driver's license. "Put him in the car before more folks start gathering around."

Handcuffed and belted into the backseat, James's impatience was evident as he glared down the length of the Mall toward the Washington Monument. "Look, Detective, I don't know what you know, but I know a lot of details about Kat's kidnapping, and you may not believe me, but she's not far from here. We're wasting time. We need to find her." After firing the ignition, Derek looked over his right shoulder at James. The detective made a U-turn and grabbed his radio mic.

"Titan from Lead, the Ford subject has been located and is now in custody. Update on the target?"

"Lead, target is westbound on the Mall."

"Vehicle or foot?" radioed Derek.

"Hard to say, sir. Speed in excess of walking speed."

"And what is that?"

"Approximately fifteen miles per hour." Stopping at Pennsylvania and Third, Derek turned again toward James.

"What were you doing on the Mall, Agent Ford? How do you know Mrs. Sterling?"

"Being that I'm handcuffed in your car, I should ask for my Miranda rights, but due to exigent circumstances, I'll just say we got separated last night. I think you're familiar with my Georgetown pad?"

"We are."

"Then you know we had a few uninvited guests try to finish the hit job on Senator Sterling's wife. The senator used Russians to hire JC and his friend to off Kat." Kevin and Derek looked at each other knowingly. "You guys do know about the Russians? I can testify to all of this. Squinty was offed by Dimitri Romov, who goes by the moniker Oscar." Pulling out a notepad, Kevin began scribbling down James's revelations.

"You know about Dimitri Romov?" asked Kevin.

"Kat and I did some prying. We have testimony and evidence to fill any gap in your case," James assured him.

"Lead from Titan, target still westbound on the Mall past Seventh; speed unchanged."

"Copy, let's ensure Park Police are tracking and are able to make contact," radioed Derek. "You said she's on a Segway?"

"Yes," James confirmed.

"And why is that? Why is she even down here?" Derek could not make heads or tails of what the hell was going on.

"She was going to Senator Bratton's office. She knows him and wanted to turn herself in. She trusted him, but he's clearly embroiled in this shit because the hot blonde who Bruce Lee'd me tried to kill her. Look, I know it sounds crazy. I realize I've probably handled the past week about as poorly as a person can—if you knew me, you'd understand this isn't atypical—but I'll tell you everything. We've just got to get her out of this jam."

The longtime cop sensed this wasn't the normal bullshit spewed from cuffed perps. He looked at Kevin, who pointed to his notes and nodded; he bought the agent's story as well. Derek hit the accelerator, then turned onto Constitution and sped past the National Gallery of Art.

"Titan from Lead, do we have an updated location?" asked Derek into his mic.

"Target stationary at Fourteenth in the vicinity of the African American Museum. Park Police nearly on scene."

"So, you believe me?" asked James.

"I believe her phone is near Fourteenth Street," conceded Derek. "I'm not sure what to make of you." He blared his siren twice, startling a family of tourists crossing the street as he pushed his Crown Vic's speed to unsafe levels, cutting through traffic like a tailback.

"Target remaining stationary at Fourteenth. Park Police almost on scene. Stand by," transmitted the mobile tracking vehicle. *"Radio reports of subjects struck by gunfire—repeat, reports of gunfire in the area of Fourteenth Street across from the Washington Monument."*

Derek activated his vehicle's strobes and flipped the siren, which wailed as he gassed it while turning into oncoming traffic to circumvent the deadlock. Turning onto Twelfth, then making a right on Madison Drive, Derek accelerated past the Museum of Natural History before jumping the curb and maneuvering the Crown Vic onto the Mall grass. James leaned forward and peered through the windshield, seeing a throng of panicked tourists on the Mall lawn. Derek stopped the car, and he and Kevin exited in a rush.

"Guys, what about me? Get me out of here," yelled James as they slammed their doors. Taking in the chaotic scene, it was clear to James that at least two in the crowd of the sightseers had been wounded. He monitored the radio traffic: *"Lead from Titan, signal still showing target on the Mall near Fourteenth."* Frustrated with his restraints, he tried to track Derek and Kevin as they plunged into the pack of frightened bystanders. Metro and Park Police squad cars littered Fourteenth Street, and crowds of onlookers gathered near the museum.

"Please, God. Kat, don't be hurt," James whispered to himself. Emerging from the milieu, Derek and Kevin mall-walked toward the car. Once back inside, Derek showed James a phone with a lock-screen selfie pic of Kat and JC wearing drunken grins.

"That's her phone. Did you find her?" asked James.

"No, just the phone," responded Derek, "but two tourists were hit with gunfire. My guess accidentally. Sounds like a general shootout took place."

"All units be advised, a vehicle accident just occurred at Seventeenth and Con involving a Toyota Prius and pedestrian. Vehicle and driver on scene; medical en route," said dispatch via radio.

"Did they say a Prius?" asked James.

"Yeah, why?"

"Sarge, we need to check that out." Turning around, Derek saw James staring forward with an expression of both concern and determination.

"It's just an accident."

"I don't think it is. I've got a strange feeling."

"Strange feeling?"

"You're a cop. You know what I mean. That sense that this isn't a coincidence. Kat's there, and she's in trouble." Derek nodded and jacked the handle on the steering column to drive.

◉ ◉ ◉

"Holy shit," Kat exclaimed while motoring forward on her Segway.

"What happened?" asked Chet, who, not being particularly athletic, was struggling to stay atop his two-wheeler.

"Jimmy just got arrested."

"Oh my God," Chet despaired, realizing they'd lost their one formidable ally. The tour motored along the wide pedestrian walkway lining the north side of the National Mall. Ahead, the Washington Monument loomed as the tour guide droned on to his company of helmeted tourists: "To our left, across the

Mall, you'll see the red-brick building which is the Smithsonian Institute. Founded in 1846, the legislation created a national museum housing artifacts and specimens from the United States' exploratory expeditions. To our right is the National Museum of Natural History built in 1910 to display more artifacts as the Smithsonian ran short of floor space for the remarkable number of items collected."

"Do you have your phone?" asked Kat. "Jimmy told me to call Carly." The tour stopped while the guide extolled the Smithsonian's cultural significance. Chet fumbled for his phone, and Kat scanned the sea of pedestrians for their pursuers.

"Carly, it's me, Chet," he said into his phone. "Where are you? No, I'm with Kat. We're in a tour group, just trying to lay low. Apparently, James was nabbed by the cops."

"Oh shit," said a deflated Kat.

"What's wrong?"

"They're onto us," she revealed. Following her gaze, Chet spotted the blond femme fatale riding a motorized Lyft scooter rental—ubiquitous on DC streets—toward them along a pedestrian path. Her unnerving, expressionless stare bore through Kat. It appeared the predator stalking them was biding time for the best opportunity to strike. "Wonder where her partner is."

"We see one of them. The woman is on a scooter and trailing us," Chet relayed through his phone to Carly. "Yeah, one of those things you see everywhere. Like a motorized skateboard with a handle. I hate them too."

"Have her meet us at Seventeenth and Constitution," ordered Kat.

"Ma'am, can you please keep it down back there; people are trying to enjoy the tour," reprimanded the overly bubbly tour guide, smiling throughout his rebuke. "Okay, please follow me as we continue." As the platoon of Segways continued down the Mall, Kat and Chet stayed in the middle of the pack, keenly aware that Tanya was trailing them. Suddenly a high-pitched, supersonic whizzing sound cut through the atmosphere. The tourists, enthralled by the guide's fact nuggets, paid no heed. Kat looked across the lawn to see Tanya's burly partner, also aboard a motorized scooter, returning a smoking suppressed pistol to a shoulder rig beneath his suit coat.

"He just shot at us," whispered Kat. "He's over there."

"What do we do, Kat?"

"We've got to get out of here. We're putting these people in danger. Let's get to Carly. We can lose these two." The tour was approaching Fourteenth Street across from the Smithsonian National Museum of African American History, which was surrounded by more out-of-towners. Kat turned to glance behind them. Tanya, stoic as ever, continued trailing by thirty yards. Kat wished James were with her. Chet was a kind, sensitive soul, but she needed her brawny, decisive man-child. But James wasn't there—it was up to her. It was her time to act.

"We're going to make a break for Seventeenth Street," she told Chet. "We can't stay here. Will Carly be there?"

"I don't know her very well. Actually, we met for the first time last night."

"We're trusting a stranger?"

"She promised she'd be there," Chet assured her just as Kat noticed Tanya's scooter accelerate while the blonde reached beneath her coat.

"Look out, Chet," Kat shouted. She turned her Segway to face the aggressor and hastened forward. Holding the silenced firearm near her side, Tanya fired a projectile that struck the front of Kat's vehicle. Kat dove off the Segway and fell on her backside, then stripped off her bike helmet as her Segway knocked Tanya of her scooter.

"Let's get out of here." Kat regained her feet and bolted toward the African American History Museum. Stunned, it took Chet a moment to register what had transpired before he jumped off his conveyance and ran in his awkward manner toward Constitution Avenue.

Hearing several wispy reports from the silenced Sig Sauer, Kat began to weave back and forth. She heard high-pitched screams and whirled to see a flurry of panicked tourists. Through the pandemonium, Tanya, weapon holstered, continued her pursuit on foot. Kat focused on her goal as she passed through the crowds gathered outside the museum: Seventeenth and Constitution. A marathon runner, she trusted her lungs, slowly increasing her pace until she was at a full run. She looked back to see the uber-fit Tanya matching the speed of her quarry. Chet was nowhere to be seen. Pedestrians gave Kat quizzical looks as she passed at a full sprint. The Washington Monument looming, she turned toward the White House South Lawn.

As she arrived at the corner of Seventeenth, it dawned on her that she had no idea what Carly was driving. Looking to her right, she saw the relentless blonde streaming through foot traffic. Kat couldn't wait. She made her way across the unprotected intersection and, with alacrity and luck, avoided being killed by several honking automobiles before reaching the north side of Constitution where bystanders frowned at her recklessness. Panting, she surveyed the cars.

The crosswalk light changed, opening the intersection to pedestrians. She finally spied Chet on the other side of Constitution, bent over and winded. He waved her on just before a bull of a man shouldered him from behind, sending the diminutive environmentalist to the avenue's asphalt. Horrified, Kat watched the Russian pull his sidearm with Chet splayed before him.

"Oh my God, no," she screeched, certain she was about to witness the execution of her friend by a round to the skull. Onlookers bleated out shrieks as they shielded themselves. The would-be assassin was depressing the trigger when the murder was interrupted by a Toyota Prius slamming into the assassin's side, sending the Russian operative careening through the intersection; his face struck Constitution Avenue with mortal force. The pistol slid from his grasp, a round still in the chamber.

CHAPTER 26

WIG-WAG lights alternating and siren wailing, Derek drove counterflow down the left-hand lanes of Constitution Avenue to avoid the westbound standstill. He pulled behind the blue Prius surrounded by one Metro and two Secret Service Uniformed Division squad cars. Adjacent to the Prius, a man was laid out on the street with a raven-haired woman kneeling beside him.

"That's Carly," declared James as Derek put the Crown Vic in park.

"Who's she?"

"Friend of mine. I think that's Chet on the ground," James shared, looking about for Kat. "Guys, you can't leave me in here. Kat has to be nearby." Derek looked back at James's pleading face, then over to Kevin, whose shrug indicated, "Your call."

Derek nodded. "Let him out." He exited and moved toward Carly and Chet. Bicycle cops kept the crowd at bay as other uniformed police diverted traffic from the crime scene. "You Carly, miss?" Derek asked as he approached.

"Yeah, how did you know?" She was holding Chet's hand.

"You guys okay?" James asked, jogging toward them, hands cuffed behind his back, as Kevin followed. Though she had just deliberately slammed her car into another human, Carly remained composed; meanwhile, Chet had clearly not come to terms with his near-death experience.

"We're fine. A bit shaken, but good," she said.

"She saved me." Chet smiled, pleased his demise had been thwarted by eco-friendly technology.

"Do you need an ambulance, any of you?" Derek asked; both declined. "Miss, did you strike that man with your vehicle?"

"I did. He was trying to kill my new friend," Carly answered before redirecting her attention. "James, Kat ran up Seventeenth toward the White House."

"She did? Was Tanya after her?"

"She was," said Chet. "She's relentless."

"Kevin, take these off me," James ordered. Once again, the FBI agent was at a loss. Nothing that had transpired in the past twenty minutes was covered by the manual. "Look, the senator's kidnapped wife is on the loose and being chased by a trained killer. I know I can find her, but you've got to take these goddamn cuffs off me."

Carly had never seen her ex-lover so frantic.

"Kat's on the run and in danger. James can find her," she said.

"They shot at us over by the museum. A blond lady in a dark suit with a ponytail. Carly's right: she's in trouble," Chet added.

"Take them off," ordered Derek.

"You sure?" asked Kevin.

"Take them off," Derek confirmed. Dutifully, Kevin retrieved his keys and spun the cuffs away from James's wrists. With a short, appreciative nod, James turned northward and raced up Seventeenth.

The detective sergeant had seen countless suspects run from him. The figure he saw fleeing wasn't a man running away from something; it was a man running to someone. "Kevin, get in the car."

⊙ ⊙ ⊙

When Senator Gene Sterling arrived at the West Wing, he was greeted by President Ronald Frum, White House Chief of staff Gary Boxterman, the attorney general, and the director of the FBI. With solemnity, they escorted him to the Situation Room to reveal the latest information regarding his wife's disappearance. Emotionless and matter-of-fact, Director McMann detailed the recruitment of JC Klingerman and Dustin "Cornhole" De Plours by ex-con John "Squinty" Donovan. He also indicated evidence of foreign influence, namely Russia, providing money to both Donovan and the kidnappers. Investigators believed the two West Virginians were used to mask Russian involvement and Mr. Donovan was murdered as an added measure of operational security.

"It is our belief," continued the director, "that Mrs. Sterling escaped her kidnappers before they could commit the murder and dispose of her body. We have solid evidence she was staying in a Georgetown rowhouse with former Secret Service agent James Ford and that, last night, Russian agents attempted to finish the task Mr. Klingerman and De Plours could not."

Senator Sterling rubbed his mouth, processing the revelations.

"If you believe she is alive, do you know where she could be?" he asked.

"We're throwing every resource we have to determine that, Senator. But, for now, we do not know her whereabouts. As you know, we have Mr. Klingerman in custody, and he has been very cooperative."

"I can't believe the Russians would want to kidnap my wife. It doesn't make any sense. Why? Why would they take her?" posed Gene.

"We wondered the same thing," the director said, "and we have some ideas why." He placed a photo before Gene. "Do you know this woman?"

"Of course I do. That's my chief of staff, Tanya Smith."

"Sir, her name is Taya Sokolov. She was, at one time, a foreign exchange student with known ties to the Russian government. She has infiltrated your office, and evidence indicates she is heavily involved in the plot to kidnap your wife."

"That's preposterous," Gene insisted. "Tanya has worked for me for a year now. It's simply not possible she's a Russian spy."

"You know her well, really well," President Frum drawled. "You were banging that piece of ass. You're not fooling anyone, Gene. Your time is up." Pained expressions crossed the faces of the director, Gary, and the AG; prior to the meeting, they had pleaded with the president to refrain from making any accusations.

"What the hell are you talking about? I've done all I can to find my wife."

"The hell you have. You're a fraud. But worse than that, you're a sicko and an unwell person." The president pointed at the senator from across the conference table. "You have this young hot chick in your bed, and you put on a dog mask? Who pretends to be a dog when you're banging a ten? What is that? Am I right?" The president looked about the room for affirmation, only to be met with uneasy silence.

"Senator Sterling, what do you know about Senator Joe Bratton?" asked McMann, trying to remain on topic. Gene's façade was cracking. A fearful, uncertain look crossed his face, and he hesitated, trying to formulate an effective answer. "Let me be clear: do you know of Senator Bratton's ties to Oleg Yumashev?" the director pressed.

"I mean, Mr. Yumashev knows a lot of people in Washington, but I'm not aware of any special relationship with Joe."

"Joe was trying to wag the dog, you dumbass," yelled President Frum. "Don't you get it, Gene? Joe was playing you. Emerald Solaria was a bullshit company; it only existed on paper. Joe's tied in with the Russians and helped stage Kat's kidnapping so you could keep tapping that blonde while scoring sympathy points to win the nomination."

The president conveniently abstained from sharing that Joe had secured a promise to become Frum's energy secretary should the president win a second term. Gary Boxterman stared at the ceiling in frustration, the attorney general appeared bewildered, and the FBI director, hands folded on the table, never flinched.

"Senator Sterling, our meeting here is adjourned as far as I am concerned. However, we wish to speak to you further at FBI headquarters," McMann said stoically. Frozen, Gene remained silent in thought.

"May I have my lawyer present?" he asked.

"That's your right, sir."

The door opened abruptly as three Secret Service agents rushed into the room. "Tycoon is secured," one agent radioed, using his wrist mic and President Frum's code name.

"What the hell's going on, guys?" asked the president.

"Sir, we have shots fired and a possible breach of the North Lawn."

◉ ◉ ◉

Passing the Eisenhower Executive Office Building, James avoided the gazes of the Secret Service Uniformed Division officers posted there with their rifles slung in a heightened state of readiness. By the time he reached Pennsylvania Avenue, he still hadn't located Kat. He passed through the bollards portioning off Pennsylvania Avenue from vehicular traffic and made for the north fence line of the White House where throngs of people had ventured on the sunny, Chamber of Commerce afternoon.

It was good protesting weather, and much of the gaggle were enjoying their dopamine-inducing, performative virtue-signaling by chanting the unoriginal, "Hey, hey, ho, ho, Ronald Frum has got to go!" DC tourists were fascinated by protestors, who in turn relished the attention of onlookers. This feedback loop played out in front of the Executive Mansion as James waded into the herd, assuming Kat had learned her lesson about the safety of crowds. That's when he spotted Tanya scanning the throng from beneath the statue of the Comte de Rochambeau in the southwest corner of Lafayette Park.

He thought to notify one of the Uniformed Division officers of the armed subject, but just as this occurred to him, the blonde began moving with alarming deliberation toward the crowd. Keeping his head down, not wanting to be recognized, James nudged past the selfie-takers and drum-banging inciters, hoping to intercept the assassin before she located her prey. He spotted Kat mingling in a group of animated agitators, trying to remain inconspicuous.

To his left, Tanya weaved through the pack like a stalking lion. James continued to elbow his way into the crowd, hoping to intercept her. After he pushed aside one protestor, then another, a third shoved him back, asking derisively, "What are you, a pig?" James plunged his shoulder into him, then barreled over a selfie-taking couple. The commotion drew the desired effect as Tanya turned toward him.

With his loudest voice, James hollered, "Gun! She has a gun!"

Amid the gaggle, Tanya drew her Sig Sauer, trained it at Kat, and began depressing the trigger, drawing the hammer back in double action. James closed in and came over the top of the firearm with his right hand, jamming the webspace of his thumb and forefinger between the falling hammer and the firing pin to prevent the weapon's discharge. He and Tanya were struggling for the pistol when the Russian headbutted his nose, kicked his shin, and jerked her hand from his grasp, causing both to lose their balance and fall to the ground. The pistol clanked on the cement several feet away. Bystanders scrambled and shrieked in panicked confusion as James looked up to see three Secret Service Uniformed Division officers moving their direction.

The pistol lay opposite Tanya. The small, surprisingly strong and athletic spy went for the weapon, determined to end her mission regardless of the consequences. James scrambled toward Kat with equal determination. Grabbing her hand, he pulled her along.

"Where do we go?" she asked.

"Where it's safe. Stay with me, princess." His hand clasped to Kat's, he made his way to the White House with her in tow, hearing gunshots to his rear.

CHAPTER 27

THE WHITE HOUSE was a magnet for crazy people: the type of people who believed the CIA had a direct com link to their brain or were certain they possessed information vital to national security and therefore must speak to the president immediately. For the Secret Service, it wasn't unusual to have a gate-knocker approach an officer or agent to inform them they'd traveled from Ohio or Jersey or Colorado to see POTUS about some urgent matter. It was often a sad reflection of mental illness but, not infrequently, also an amusing sidebar to break up the tedium of shift work. They were a harmless bunch—typically—and some would even return after dismissal from their mental evaluation to continue their chat with the Service guys.

Fence jumpers were another matter. Occasionally, some tinfoil-hat-wearing nutcase possessed enough athleticism to leap to the top portion of the wrought iron fence and maneuver their body weight to the other side. Almost always, this ended with a swift bite from a K-9 or a muzzle tap from the emergency response team's Stoner rifles. In 2014, a Mr. Gonzalez not only scaled the fence but also managed to give himself a free tour of the East Room before a counter assault team member who'd already completed his shift gently showed him the error of his ways. This was enough for the federal government to decide a taller fence was preferable.

Of course, advanced government projects—such as fences—took time, the National Park Service had strong opinions on the matter, and senior members of Congress argued over funding—some legislators none too keen on securing the home of Ronald Frum without attaching funds for their home districts to the bill; so other than lining up a bike rack as a deterrence twenty feet in front of the old fence, no improvements to the complex had been made.

Kat and James ran toward the White House, spurred by the sound of gunshots to their rear. Leaping the bike rack, they galloped toward the fence. James bounded up and secured the top of the vertical iron bars as, beside him, Kat made an impressive leap to latch on just below. Making use of decades of pull-ups, James heaved himself to the top, getting his first leg over the pointed crowns of the vertical poles and managing to grab Kat's American University sweatshirt to pull her to the summit. Simultaneously, they spilled over the top and flopped prostrate side by side onto the cool grass of the North Lawn.

"What do we do now?" asked Kat.

"Get away from the gunfire." James pulled her to her feet, and they ran hand in hand toward the north entrance of the White House. As if morphing out of thin air, two emergency response teams appeared, their members decked out in black tactical gear and moving in trained unison. They aimed their SR-15 rifles and barked urgent demands for James and Kat to get on the ground.

"Jimmy, I love you, but this is really stupid."

"Yeah, I think this is as far as it goes. Get down, princess." Pulling her arm forward, each did their best Pete Rose impersonation, sliding headfirst to the turf. "Keep your arms out like Superman." Two German shepherds joined the Secret Service welcoming committee and bayed out their pleas for a nibble of the intruders.

As James pressed his head to the ground, he felt the warm breath of the German shepherd barking inches from his head. Several hands began patting them down.

"Are you armed? Do you have a bomb? Sir, answer me," ordered the officer whose knee was planted on James's back.

"Freddie, it's me." Tilting his head up, James forced a sheepish smile.

"James?" Freddie asked in bug-eyed disbelief. "Please tell me you didn't come to blow up the White House."

"No, not at all. Can someone shut that fucking dog up?" Freddie motioned the K-9 officer to back off. "I'm not armed. I don't have a bomb, and I have not lost my mind. My job, yes, but my mind is just fine."

"Put your hands behind your back," ordered Freddie. "Jesus, man, what in God's name are you doing?"

"I'm still in a bit of a transition phase," James quipped. Freddie handcuffed him before noticing four television cameras aimed toward them from Pebble Beach, the portion of the north grounds where the press conducted their live shots.

"Well, looks like you're going to make the six o'clock news again," shared Freddie, who rolled James into a seated position. "You know, this isn't normal behavior, even for someone going through a transition phase. Goddamn, James, I never thought you'd be a fucking fence jumper." Freddie wore his evident disappointment. "Is this in any way connected to the tag you had me run last week? Because I was grilled about it before being told to stay mum on the subject. Now Inspection's on my ass."

"Sorry about that. As usual, I did it for a woman." Officers helped James's cuffed accomplice to her feet as Freddie lifted James to his. "Freddie, meet Katherine Sterling." Freddie side-eyed the short-haired brunette. "I gave her a haircut," admitted James, "but it's her."

"Nice to meet you, Freddie." She smiled. "I'd shake your hand but, unfortunately, I'm handcuffed." Freddie stared at her intently, his face holding the frozen expression of a man uncertain whether he was living in reality or some dreamlike, alternate dimension.

⊙ ⊙ ⊙

Exiting his Crown Victoria, Detective Sergeant Derek Roland looked for James amid the horde gathered along the north fence line. He finally spotted him pushing through the throng, and the detective urgently picked up his pace to something resembling a run. In his head, Derek heard Monique warning him about his blood pressure.

The heterogeneous mass of protestors, sightseers, and homeless muddled his view as he reached the crowd's edge. Derek heard someone yell, "Gun," followed by shrill cries and curses as the swarm dispersed in frantic fear. He drew his service weapon. James scampered to his feet just as a small, blond woman got to hers with feline prowess. It was then Derek saw the profile of the meaty Sig Sauer extend toward James's fleeing figure. Reflexively, he raised his Glock and placed the front sight on his target, then squeezed off four rounds in rapid succession. The blonde got off two rounds before falling to the ground. Keeping his pistol trained on her, Derek ensured the threat was neutralized before sensing several figures closing on him.

"Metro Police, Metro Police, I'm a cop. Blue, blue, blue!" yelled Derek, raising his badge for the Secret Service Uniformed Division officers approaching with drawn weapons. He advanced toward the supine woman. Her Sig Sauer lying nearby, the wounded Russian agent eyed him with the pained look of failure. Derek knelt beside her and located several entry wounds on her torso.

"Don't touch me," she admonished, struggling for breath.

"Why were you trying to kill that woman?" asked Derek. She responded with a defiant stare. "Who do you work for?" he pressed. Taya silently cursed Oscar's sloppiness. Looking over the shoulder of the lawman at a cloudless sky, she saw the lustrous sun shining upon the American flag that waved gently above the Executive Mansion. Taya Sokolov closed her eyes and drew her life's final breath.

"Sarge, are you alright?" Kevin ran up with his FBI shield held aloft. Stopping beside Derek, he looked down at the would-be killer. "Isn't that . . . ?"

"Yeah, the senator's chief of staff," the detective sergeant acknowledged. Hearing a commotion, he turned toward the White House to see two figures inside the fence line, prone on the ground and surrounded by the Secret Service ERT.

"What the hell is happening over there?" Kevin wondered.

"We found Mrs. Sterling, Kev. I think our case is closed."

"Are you sure?"

"I am. And I'm certain about one other thing: Monique's right; I'm too old for this shit."

"So, this is it? You done?"

"I am. Somewhere on the Blue Ridge, there's a mountain cabin with my name on it."

"It's been an honor, Sarge."

Derek smiled at his FBI counterpart, his first real smile of the past week. They gave each other a congratulatory handshake.

"Thanks, Kev. You're a good man, and I couldn't ask for a better partner. You should've been a cop."

◉ ◉ ◉

The news footage was not encouraging. There was Katherine Sterling, on a live feed, holding hands with some philandering federal agent as they dove to the turf of the White House lawn. Joe Bratton knew things had gone to shit when she bolted from the Cadillac Escalade. His only recourse was to cling religiously to the hope that Taya and her goon would off the resilient bitch. Now, in his office, he watched a Fox News Alert stream a live shot of Katherine Sterling prone on the White House North Lawn, surrounded by tactical officers and police dogs. The energetic anchor also reported a shooting on Pennsylvania but could not confirm if the incidents were related. Joe's receptionist, Maddie, stood next to him, also transfixed by the television.

"Oh my God, that's the lady that was here earlier," she realized, looking up at Joe's face. "Are you okay, Senator? You don't look well." Speechless, Joe turned to his tiny receptionist, then back to the screen. None of this was according to plan. Kat should have been dead a week ago and rotting somewhere in West Virginia. Gene should be trampling Cassandra Lightner in the primary race and set up for his coordinated downfall. Joe was supposed to be energy secretary by the new year. He was supposed to get rich.

"Senator? Do you need water?"

Sweet-faced Maddie broke through his haze.

"That would be good. Thank you." It was time to get out of Dodge. His brain rifled through one outlandish escape plan after another. *Maybe just drive to Mexico? Isn't that what criminals do when they're on the lam? Jesus, am I on the lam?* Being that he'd given full-throated support to caging Mexican kids, Mexico was not likely a good option. He wished he'd flown to Seychelles with Oleg, but that was all he could do: wish. Going to his desk, he opened the top drawer as Maddie returned with a water bottle and two figures behind her.

"Senator," began the troubled angel-face, "these gentlemen are here to see you." Stepping around her, two stern, square-jawed men appeared in neatly tailored suits.

"Senator Bratton, I'm Agent Tyler. This is Agent Jackson," the White one formally announced as he displayed his credentials. "We're with the FBI and would like to discuss some matters with you."

"Okay, sure," Joe responded with a preoccupied air. "Maddie, dear, would you kindly wait in the lobby and shut the door so that I may have a private conversation with the agents?" The dimple-faced girl nodded and turned. "Maddie, thank you. Take the rest of the day, okay? Goodbye."

She felt uneasy as she nodded and left, closing the office door behind her.

"This news is remarkable, isn't it?" Joe nodded to the television. The agents didn't seem to care. "Please, have a seat so we can chat." As the men moved toward the chairs facing his desk, Joe removed the Smith & Wesson Model 60 revolver from his drawer. Before the lawmen could draw their weapons, Senator Joseph Bratton sang to himself, "Take me home, country road," placed the muzzle in his mouth, and sent a .38-caliber slug into his brain.

CHAPTER 28

*"Can you hear me? Studio, can you hear me? Okay, we're
live? Ted, Melissa, this is John Baker on the North Lawn
of the White House with breaking news. Panic erupted on
Pennsylvania Avenue just moments ago as my cameraman,
Nick, and I heard several loud pops amid a crowd gathered
on Pennsylvania Avenue in front of the White House. Police
and Uniformed Secret Service officers intervened, and
there appears to be one person down on Penn. Since that
initial smattering of gunfire, we haven't heard any further
indications of a gun battle.*

*"During the confusion, two people, a man and a woman,
jumped the White House fence and ran toward the
mansion. It was about this time Nick and I got our bearings
and captured the footage you now see on your screen.
The United States Secret Service responded to the fence
jumpers, who complied and are now handcuffed and
lying on the ground. No official word yet from the Secret
Service on this situation. President Frum is believed to be
in the West Wing, and, as we reported earlier, FBI director
McMann and Senator Gene Sterling are at the White House
for a briefing on Senator Sterling's missing wife, Katherine*

Sterling. The situation here is very fluid, but it's clear there was a shootout and breech of the White House grounds. Melissa, Ted, back to you."

"John," began Ted, Melissa beside him with an astonished stare, *"we are looking at the monitor, and as Nick's camera zoomed in and came into focus, it appears to us in studio—"*

"Oh my God," interrupted Melissa, her hand over her mouth.

"It appears to us," Ted continued, *"that the woman on the ground resembles Katherine Sterling. Her hair is shorter and darker than when she was last seen, but Melissa and I have both been to fundraisers with Mrs. Sterling, and I'm ninety percent sure that is indeed her. Can you confirm?"*

"Yes, Ted, I'm looking at the monitor here, and my goodness. Oh my God, you're correct. We don't have confirmation, but it does appear to be Katherine Sterling. The person apprehended with her looks familiar as well."

"John, it's Melissa. We in studio believe the male in custody is James Ford, who we know from the South American Secret Service sex scandal that occurred a few months ago."

"Thank you, Melissa," continued John from the North Lawn. *"I'm speechless. As you both know, I'm not one to be at a loss for words, but this is a stunning development. On the North Lawn of the White House, the Secret Service appears to have apprehended both Katherine Sterling, the missing wife of Senator Gene Sterling, and the embattled Secret Service agent James Ford. Of course, the identities have not been*

independently confirmed, but like all of America, we have
seen Mrs. Sterling's face on our television screens nonstop
for a week, and I can say definitively that is her. Why she is
with the discredited Secret Service agent is a mystery and a
question that begs to be answered."

The Situation Room was silent as a funeral home. One could almost hear the heartbeats of its occupants as they viewed the stunning live images shot just outside from where they stood. Even the Secret Service agents could not mask their shock. Director McMann examined Senator Sterling, who continually rubbed his mouth.

"Would you believe that? She's alive and on my front lawn!" said President Frum, breaking the thick silence. "Gene, she's alive, can you believe it? It's a miracle. You should go see her. She appears in good health. It'll be good television." The president wore a devilish grin. "Aren't you happy? What do you say?"

◉ ◉ ◉

"You know, Freddie, you don't have to perp-walk us," chided James. Still cuffed, he and Kat were paraded past the cameras live-feeding the unfolding scene to televisions around the world.

"Where else are we supposed to go? You're the one who jumped the fence," noted Freddie. James conceded with a shrug. The officers guided them near the West Wing lobby entrance as press lenses hawked them from their perch.

"You okay, princess?"

She smiled. "I've been worse."

"That's telling."

"Are they taking us to jail? That doesn't seem right."

"It's unlawful to jump the White House fence. I used to be a Secret Service agent. They taught us that."

"You're the smartest dumb person I've ever known," replied Kat, eyes glowing with affection. "I don't see why I should go to jail. I was just following you."

"Didn't take you long to turn state's witness."

"You know, you two do have the right to remain silent," Freddie reminded them.

"Are we getting on your nerves? Princess, we're getting on Freddie's nerves." Descending a short flight of stairs, the officers guided their prisoners to West Executive Avenue just as a group of men exited the West Wing.

"There she is." President Frum clapped with exaggerated glee. Surrounded by his Secret Service detail, he moved toward Kat and began glad-handing the officers. "Good job, boys. You guys did it. Great work." Hamming it up for the cameras, President Frum opened his arms with an over-the-top sigh of relief. "Mrs. Sterling, it's so good to see you alive. You look healthy and well. Our prayers are answered." His considerable frame enveloped her in an embrace. "But this isn't about me. I have a surprise for you. The love of your life is here. Gene, come forward."

President Frum waved up a hesitant Senator Gene Sterling, who, upon seeing the TV cameras peering down from Pebble Beach, feigned excitement.

"Oh my God. My dear Katherine. Is it really you? My sweet, sweet wife is alive." The silver-headed statesman gently touched her face and stared in disbelief before embracing her. "It's a miracle, but I'm back with my love," gushed Gene as camera shudders clicked. "Together, we can heal each other, make each other whole again. Then we heal our country and our planet."

James silently admired Gene's ability to stay on message. The senator leaned in to kiss Kat, who turned her head so that his lips mashed into her cheek.

"You should take off her cuffs so she can hug her husband," James said while Gene's lips were still pressed awkwardly against her face. Kat shot a knowing look toward the smirking James.

"Yes, of course; come on, guys. After all she's been through, she must be dying to show Gene how she feels about him," the president concurred, relishing every cringe-worthy moment. As soon as Freddie undid her cuffs, Kat forced Gene off her with an impassioned shove.

"You did this. You did all of this," she sneered, icy venom in her eyes. "You wanted me killed, but that wasn't enough. No, the headline couldn't simply be, 'Senator's Wife Goes Missing'; that wouldn't suffice. It wasn't enough for you to be the victim. You had to be a partisan, political victim. And it worked, didn't it, Gene? You figured it out. Hell, you practically have the nomination. But there's one small glitch in your plan: I'm alive."

Gene felt the hives burning on his neck. Scanning, he saw the horde of press, the president's mischievous smile, and the murderous rage on Kat's face.

"You've clearly been traumatized, sweetie." He spoke up for the mics. "She doesn't know what she's saying. She has undergone a thoroughly traumatic ordeal. We will get her the help she needs and, together, we will overcome this. We kindly ask for privacy as we heal."

Gene turned to James accusingly. "What in God's name did you do to my wife?"

That was enough for Kat.

"Don't you talk to my Jimmy that way," she admonished, jabbing her forefinger into his sternum. "I'll tell you what this man did to your wife. He gave her life back to her, nearly killing himself in the process. He showed me you don't have to be perfect to be good. Unlike these phony DC grifters, he's an authentic, decent man who wears his flaws but tries to be better. He reminded me that there are good men and that good men may not be perfect, but they don't pretend to be, either, which is more than you can say for the sanctimonious, condescending pieces of shit in this town." With a disbelieving expression, Gene stared at James, who responded with a sheepish grin.

"It's been a full week, Senator," began James. "Your wife and I kept ourselves busy by unraveling what exactly you and your cronies have been up to. You may be thinking, 'What do they have on me?' Well, I have photos of you dressed as Snoopy, nailing your chief of staff. Not passing judgment; her ass was phenomenal. I'd likely have done her as well—minus the dog mask, of course. Unfortunately, she's a Russian agent. If you'd like to pay your respects, she's on Pennsylvania Avenue. Let's see, oh yeah, Kat and I became BFFs with your would-be assassin—sweet guy; thanks for introducing us. And those pesky emails? That was us. Admittedly, they were a bit sophomoric, but I get that way after a few drinks."

Seething, Gene no longer cared about the cameras.

"You smart-ass piece of shit" was all he mustered before, with all the might Kat's 125-pound frame could pack, she laid her fist into Gene's left eye, sending him stumbling backward as he held his pulsating oculus.

"He's my smart-ass piece of shit," she announced.

Eyeing his wife, then the cameras, all at once Gene realized his campaign was over; he turned and ran for the north gate in an awkward, heavy manner, as if his feet were outfitted with invisible cinder blocks. Everyone—the president, the FBI director, the chief of staff, the uniformed officers, even Kat and James—looked on in silence at the oddity. When he reached the gate along the north fence line, Gene attempted to scale the structure in desperation, managing to get only three feet off the pavement.

"Mr. Director, can my guys take the senator into custody?" asked Freddie.

"I think we have probable cause." FBI director McMann smiled. "Arrest the California senator, and I'll have my agents here in a few minutes."

"North Park One," relayed Freddie into his radio, "take the

senator into custody." Senator Sterling put up a struggle as several Uniformed Division officers subdued the wriggling, resistive legislator.

"I didn't see that coming, princess," James marveled. "You've got a pretty strong right. You telegraphed the shit out of it, but still."

"You're a strange man, Jimmy." She put her arms around his waist. "Thank you."

"Officer, remove his handcuffs. She obviously wants to kiss him," President Frum ordered.

Freddie dutifully began uncuffing James. "Now, remember, buddy, the cameras are on you. Keep it PG." Once released, James kissed Kat with the verve of a drowning man finally surfacing. The two lovers kissed for what seemed several minutes before relinquishing and smiling at one another, their arms around each other's waists.

"So, princess, what are you going to title your book?"

Leaning her head back in an extravagant, thoughtful pose, she answered, "*A Princess in Primary Season.*"

James gave a playful grimace. "Well, we can work on a title."

"You little bastard, I spent a long time on that."

"Spend more time." He smiled.

"Whatever the title, I'll need a bodyguard on my book tour. My Q rating has to be nearing Jennifer Aniston levels."

"I know a guy looking for work."

"What do we do now?" she asked, eyes gleaming.

He smirked. "Let's get a drink."

ACKNOWLEDGMENTS

I was a suburban cop when I met a gal named Melissa at a Super Bowl party hosted by a fellow cop and his wife. I drove her home, and she knew the lyrics to every Waylon Jennings song I played on my Dodge Dakota's CD player. Her father was a Waylon fan. We married in May 2001. Two months later I landed a coveted gig with the federal government; and a month after that, 9/11 occurred. Since then, I have protected presidents and vice presidents, traveled the world, and far exceeded the expectations of my high school guidance counselors. Melissa is my rock. While teaching countless kindergarteners (who affectionately refer to her as Mrs. B), she raised our son and kept everything together while allowing her maniacal husband to live his dream. She is the love of my life and the primary reason I have such a happy one.

Will, our son and only child, is attending Virginia Tech and a member of the Corps of Cadets. He has an inner strength he's not fully aware of. He kicks my butt at golf every time we play, but I always finish the round a winner because I've had one more round with my son; you never know when you will play that last round with your son or father, so enjoy every chunked pitch or shanked drive.

Melissa and Will both patiently listened to my posit ideas for this story's direction throughout the process. Sometimes the best encouragement is to listen and let the person you love figure it out. My family did that for me.

My father, Fred Brandenburg, is the primary reason I read as extensively as I do and have such an attachment to American history. A pilot in the US Air Force and eventually for American Airlines, he is a self-made man. He is also a largely self-educated man. Growing up, I always saw him reading. American history is a favorite subject, but he also reads Clancy and Ludlum novels extensively. He's almost ninety and still reading. Love you, Pops.

My mother, Patricia Brandenburg, is the selfless caretaker of our family. Born to a large, Irish-Catholic family, Mom has always been an outgoing person with a big personality, and she gifted me the dreamlike, imaginative side of my brain. Love you, Mom.

I love Kansas and Kansans so much that I married one. Melissa's parents, William and Louann Maley, were an example of love that changed my life. I witness their goodness every day in my wife and son. My son is named after his grandfather— a grandfather he never met but whom he honors with every hour of his life.

My twin brother, Fred Brandenburg, has been a latent, constant source of support. He was always Batman and I Robin, a dynamic that worked during our childhood and still holds to this day. My sisters, Linda Dipasquale and Susan Pearson, are loving, passionate people who will drop what they're doing at a moment's notice to help family. I love them both.

As a new novelist pecking away at the keyboard, I'd ask myself, Is this working? I have several friends to thank for taking the time to read the early drafts and provide feedback. I am fortunate to have a diverse group of friends from varying backgrounds and sensibilities.

Desmond O'Neill is a friend and former colleague who read my manuscript and provided a sound critique. I thank him for the time and energy he put into reading and evaluating this story. I respect Desmond a great deal, and he will never know how much his honesty and encouragement improved my confidence in my writing. He is married to another former colleague, Evy Pompouras, who is a remarkable person and best-selling author of *Becoming Bulletproof*. I worked with Evy on the Presidential Protective Division, and she has since moved on to a very successful media career. Their support is cherished, and I am grateful for it.

Sarah Lueders is an intelligent, motivated law enforcement professional who also took the time to read the manuscript. Her feedback regarding Kat as a strong female character was important because Sarah is a strong woman. I have a great deal of respect for her and appreciate the time she spent supporting this endeavor.

Amy Joyce, a Midwestern teacher and friend, focused on the relationship dynamic between James and Kat, providing invaluable insight. Her perspective was very helpful in developing Kat Sterling's character.

Jonathan Wackrow is a former Secret Service agent who I served with on the Presidential Protective Division. Since leaving the Service, Jon has built an accomplished media career as a law enforcement analyst on CNN. As a former colleague, and current friend, he reviewed the manuscript and pledged his support for the project. Jon and I share a similar sense of humor, and his positive reaction to this work meant a great deal to me and I appreciate the time he has spent to support this

My cousin Travis Tohill is someone whose perspective I respect a great deal. He's also a storyteller by trade, so his experience in crafting a tale was important to me. After reading the manuscript, he and I drank good bourbon together and talked about *Fence Jumper*. It was invaluable, and I thank him for it.

I also wish to thank my nephew Philip Pearson and my former colleague Ronne Malham for reviewing the manuscript.

Like all writers, I have innumerable artistic and cultural influences. I like a little American swagger in my male protagonists. Whether it's Bruce Willis's John McClane, Harrison Ford's Indiana Jones, or one of John Wayne's sauntering cowboys, I dig the self-assured American character, and bits of that ethos will always be injected in my writing. We cannot lose that. American masculinity is imperfect, but when you're in fear, there are worse things to see than a cowboy hat or an American flag shoulder patch.

Please indulge me as I acknowledge some of my favorite writers: Carl Hiaasen, Jack Carr, Larry McMurtry, Stephen Ambrose, David McCullough, Ron Chernow, Vince Flynn, Ernest Hemingway, Mark Twain, and J. R. R. Tolkien.

Love and appreciation to my alma maters, Mansfield High School in Mansfield, Texas, and in particular Benedictine College in Atchison, Kansas. A writer's output is only as good as their input, and the scholars of the Benedictine College community have greatly shaped my life.

Thank you to John Koehler and Koehler Books for their help and insight. Most first-time authors tend to be about twenty years younger, but I was preoccupied for a while. Creating a published work and beginning a writing career has been a longtime desire. I am thankful to have been published by Koehler Books and truly appreciate their efforts to make *Fence Jumper* a reality.

I have spent twenty-five years of my life as a law enforcement officer. The US Secret Service is my life's work, and the men and women who comprise its workforce are some of the most dedicated, professional, loyal, and determined people I have ever met or will ever meet. Many of them are lifelong friends. Likewise, the FBI and DC Metro Police are professionals that Americans should be proud to have protecting them on the front lines. I have nothing but love and respect for my colleagues.

I appreciate all the readers and wish you well as you live your story. God bless.